Bound By Mystery

Celebrating 20 Years of Poisoned Pen Press

Bound By Mystery

Celebrating 20 Years of Poisoned Pen Press

Original Short Fiction by

Steven Axelrod, Zoe Burke, Donis Casey,
Mark deCastrique, Vicki Delany, M. Evonne Dobson,
J.M. Donellan, Warren C. Easley, Jane Finnis,
Kelly Garrett, Sulari Gentill, Kerry Greenwood,
Charlotte Hinger, Janet Hubbard, Laurie R. King,
J.C. Lane, Ann Littlewood, Tim Maleeny, David Moss,
Vasudev Murthy, Dennis Palumbo, Ann Parker,
Frederick Ramsay, Mary Reed & Eric Mayer,
Priscilla Royal, James Sallis, Jeffrey Siger, Triss Stein,
David P. Wagner, Carolyn Wall, Tina Whittle,
Catherine A. Winn, Reavis Z. Wortham,
and Melissa T. Zobel

Edited by Diane D. DiBiase

Poisoned Pen Press
6962 E. First Ave., Ste. 103
Scottsdale, AZ 85251
www.poisonedpenpress.com
info@poisonedpenpress.com

Printed in the United States of America

To Our Readers, Old Friends and New—
We look forward to another twenty years
Bound By Mystery

"Storytelling awakens us to that which is real. Honest…it transcends the individual…Those things that are most personal are most general, and are, in turn, most trusted. Stories bind…"
—*Terry Tempest Williams*

"To be a person is to have a story to tell."
—*Isak Dinesen*

Contents

Foreword

We have published a diverse group of authors over our twenty-year history. While a few have been fortunate enough to focus all of their time and attention on their craft, most do not make their living as writers; they have day jobs, and write in their spare time—because writers gotta write. They work as insurance agents and pastors and psychologists and medicine women and housepainters and art book publishers. Most reside here in the U.S., but we also have authors from Canada, Mexico, India, Australia, and the United Kingdom; one who splits his time between the U.S. and Greece, when not circling the globe for author conventions and book signings; one who spent many years living in Italy in the U.S. Foreign Service, but now makes his home in Colorado. Their ages span six decades; they are Democrats and Republicans; they are Christian and Hindu and Jewish and Wiccan and Agnostic. Yet as different as they may seem, they all share a predilection for detection and a taste for red herring; they are connoisseurs of crime, bound together by their passion for mystery.

When we first began tossing around ideas on how to commemorate twenty years of publishing as a small press, I immediately lit upon the notion of a short story anthology. What better way to celebrate our little-press-that-could success than by showcasing the talented writers responsible for it? Several authors had expressed interest over the years in publishing short stories with us, but would there be enough interest to justify the project? I wrote a quick e-mail to the authors, asking for a show of hands. I mentioned that I would need at least a dozen participants to make it worthwhile. *Oh, and by the way…the only payment would be author copies.* Our intent was to use the book primarily as a promotional item, to get our authors and their excellent writing out in front of as many new readers as possible. To be honest, I didn't expect an overwhelming response.

The replies came thick and fast, and they formed an exuberant, unanimous "YES!" It seemed the authors were as excited as I at the prospect of an anthology dedicated to their original short fiction. Our only criteria were that the story be original and no longer than 5,000 words (initially we had intended to stick to "mystery only," but quickly abandoned that notion after receiving a few outstanding stories which fell outside the mystery genre). Most of the authors who pledged their interest followed through with a story—and on deadline! Some were current writers, while others had not written for us in many years, whether having retired, taken a hiatus, or moved on to larger houses.

It was especially touching for our publisher, Robert Rosenwald, and our editor-in-chief, Barbara Peters, that so many of the PPP authors, past and present, were eager to be a part of this project—including several who have gone on to great successes with lucrative contracts, film deals, and the like. As you will read in the authors' introductions, our Press has lodged fondly in their hearts, either as the place they got their start or the place they continue to regard as home.

As the editor of this anthology, it was my great pleasure to have so many of our authors as required reading. As I made my way through the submissions, I was impressed by how *good* they were. Not that I was expecting them to be bad, but to have so little work to do as the editor was almost a disappointment for me. A few tweaks here, some changed titles there, and basically all that was left to me was the sequencing of the stories within the volume. Though I confess I was tempted at various points to throw them up in the air and order them as they landed, or to take the simple "alphabetically-by-author" route, I think I managed to arrange them to showcase their marvelous diversity of genre, setting, subject, and style. There is a lot of time-hopping and globe-trotting between these stories, dear readers, lest you fear becoming bored or complacent. Length of story was also a consideration. If, like me, you're chronically time-challenged, and reading for pleasure is a luxury afforded only in small snippets, it's nice after reading a lengthier story to have one follow it that you can easily finish in a few extra minutes.

I am a great fan of short stories. Short fiction is not a novel that ran out of time; it is its own art form. Brevity is at its core, but there is still room for characters to have aspirations and acne, to evolve—or to solve a murder. The challenge for the writer is to accomplish all of this within the confines of the form. For anyone who's tried, it ain't as easy as a good writer makes it look. As Faulkner said, "Maybe every novelist wants to write poetry first, finds he can't and then tries the short story which is the most demanding form after poetry. And failing at that, only then does he take up novel writing."

Short fiction is an excellent way to become acquainted with an author, without a large time commitment. It's like speed-dating; if you like what you see, you can arrange another meeting, and if not—no harm done, just walk away. You may even find yourself playing matchmaker, recommending prospects to friends and family, even if they weren't quite right for you. Whatever the case, we are proud to present our authors to you here via their original short stories. At the very least, you're certain to make a few new friends. If you're lucky, you just might fall in love.

—*Diane D. DiBiase, Editor*

Gold Digger

Reavis Z. Wortham

I was green as grass when Poisoned Pen Press saw the original manuscript for my first novel, The Rock Hole, in 2011. I didn't know a thing about the writing business, other than the art of creating a cohesive story. My editor, Annette Rogers, met with me at the Sleuthfest Writers Conference in Florida that year and made several shocking suggestions to a manuscript that dripped red from her pen.

"Rev, you need to rewrite the ending."

"Why?"

"Because you killed everyone off and we want to make this a series."

I'd never considered the manuscript to be anything more than a stand-alone. She followed that statement with another stunner. "You need to cut out fifty-thousand words. It's a little long."

I followed her directions, cut it down to ninety-thousand words and, when The Rock Hole came out, Kirkus Reviews gave it a Starred Review and listed it as one of its Top 12 mysteries of 2011.

What Annette didn't tell me is that PPP is where I wanted to be, too. They took a rank beginner and gave me the opportunity to grow and shine. Today, the Red River series of six historical mystery thrillers continues to grow in popularity, and has led to this writer's success. I wouldn't have been this far along if not for this outstanding publishing house, and the exemplary staff that is a family to its employees—and to its writers.

—R.Z.W.

● ● ● ● ●

I remember that night's date, May 23, 1934, because it was the day Bonnie and Clyde soaked up about five pounds of lead on a lonely country road in Louisiana, about two hours east of us. We were between dust storms, those big black devils that sweep in from the northwest and dump a good part of the Oklahoma and Texas panhandles onto our little East Texas town of Coffeeville.

The barn dance was already planned, but it turned out to be a kind of celebration of sorts because those two murderers were gone, even though a lot of folks in our part of the country thought they were just trying to make a living in hard times.

For a little while, though, you couldn't tell we were smack in the middle of the Great Depression. Bob Wills and his Texas Playboys were already picking out the "Spanish Two-Step" by the time we got to Old Man Devlin's hundred-year-old barn full of hard-working folks there to have some fun.

The doors were open on both ends to pull in whatever breeze there was, and the stall doors on the sides were propped open for the same reason. My running buddy, Milburn, was sittin' in the hayloft with his legs dangling over the side. I climbed up there to join him and he gave me a good elbow in the ribs when I plopped down on the loose alfalfa on the floor.

He pointed down. "Look over there. Leon Clayton's got Red Devlin's new wife hemmed up against the wall."

"How come?"

Milburn cut me a look and rolled his eyes. A fresh boy's-regular haircut left those big old ears sticking out like handles. "Looky here." He pulled a crushed pack of Chesterfields from the front pocket of his bib overalls.

"Where'd you get those?"

"There's only one. Snitched it from a truck out there."

"You just stole 'em?" I'd never stolen a thing in my ten years on Earth.

"There's only *one*, and I doubt Mack Platt'll miss it. He chain-smokes so much he probably has these coffin-nails squirreled away everywhere."

The song ended and the dancers drifted back to the edges of the barn. Mama and Daddy passed under our feet and stopped in the middle of the crowd of farm folks. She turned in a full circle and finally looked up and found me. She raised her eyebrows and it was a whole conversation.

I mouthed, *I will.*

Miss Driscoll took Mama's arm and they hugged one another. Daddy frowned at me from under his hat like he always did. It meant the same thing.

The band was dressed in flashy cream-colored suits and they looked as cool as spring water at the north end of the barn. Some of the women in their print dresses beat at the stifling air with Jesus-and-the-Lambs paper fans from the local funeral home. Most of the men wore overalls, but a few, like Daddy, were in their Sunday khakis.

"I sure hope ol' Bob hollers while they're making music." I'd been looking forward to the dance for a whole month. Bob Wills tilted his hat back and worked that fiddle over some more.

"Somebody'll tell him to." Milburn stuck the wooden end of a kitchen match between his lips and flipped it up and down.

"Hope they don't."

Him having that match worried me because the loft was full of dry alfalfa and everyone down below was as scared of fire as of a bear. I was afraid he was gonna try and light that Chesterfield up there and I'd already been warned by *both* of my parents to behave myself.

"Why not?"

"Daddy says it makes Bob mad if folks tell him to holler. If he gets aggravated, they say he won't holler for the rest of the night, and that's one of the best parts of his music—him hollerin' stuff."

Bob sawed into his fiddle and they took off with "Shucking the Corn."

"Come on." Milburn jumped up.

"But I want…"

He flipped the crushed pack back and forth between two fingers. "Come on, titty-baby! Let's fire this butt up."

We shinnied down the ladder and into the dark outside. I trailed along behind like always and we circled around behind a truck. I expected to see lightning bugs flickering in the trees on the fencerow down by the slough, but it had been so dry they were all gone that year.

We zigzagged between the cars and trucks scattered around the pasture. We circled a Tin Lizzie and Milburn came up short when he almost walked into some of the local farmers passing around a quart fruit jar in the shadows.

"You boys get on outta here. Scat!"

I didn't even try to see who said it, but we scatted outta there like he said and found another place to share Milburn's snitched toonie. We sat down with our backs to a big red oak tree, with a pickup between us and the barn. He scratched the strike-anywhere with his thumbnail and I saw he already had the butt between his lips.

It wasn't my first cigarette. I'd tried chewing, too, but didn't like it. Both of my grandmothers dipped Garrett's snuff, but I couldn't stand that nasty stuff that smelled up the whole house so bad I couldn't breathe. I was already good at smokin', though. We passed it back and forth, listening to the music while the band played song after song. There was a steady stream of men circling around those trucks and then back inside.

Every now and then some young couple slipped outside to giggle together for a minute. Joe Bill Pines was the constable back then and he pulled up in his sedan and prowled around, talking to one person, then another. He did the same when he came to church, just stayed outside and visited with the men waiting on their wives to leave the service.

Daddy said there wasn't any use in him going inside; if there was gonna be any trouble, it'd be around the cars. I guess he figured the same was true at a barn dance.

Two men stopped on the other side of the T-Model we were hiding behind. Their voices came to us clear as a bell.

"Did you see Red's face just a minute ago?"

"Sure 'nough. Looks like he's mad enough to spit nails and I can't figure out why. They say it was *his* idea to have the dance here. Now he looks like he's mad at everybody who showed up."

"He's nervous as a cat in a doghouse, all right." The car door on the opposite side opened and closed and I heard the ring unscrewing off a fruit jar. "We're lucky he gave in, though." Somebody swallowed like a horse at a water trough. "This is the only barn in the county big enough to handle this crowd."

"I hear it was that little tramp he's married to's idea." The other guy took a long, loud sup, reminding me of Grandpa sipping coffee out of a saucer. "They say she talked him into havin' everybody over here because she's trying to be somethin' she ain't. It was even her idea to hire Bob Wills. But Red ain't said two words to anybody since we showed up."

"Opal May? What's she think she's gonna get out of it? Red's so tight he squeaks."

I knew who they were talking about. The Spit and Whittle Club up at the store talked about her a lot after she showed up with Old Man Devlin. Her bleached hair and tight clothes made her stand out like a sore thumb in our little rural community, but all that makeup she wore made her look like a movie star to me.

"Hell, he has the first dollar he ever earned. I can't believe he paid for the band by hisself. I swear, he don't even *like* most people."

There was a big slurp. "Ahhh. It's a fact. Willie Connors makes the best whiskey I ever tasted. Anyway, back to what we was talkin' about. Leon spun that little gal around on the floor and his hand was a sight lower on her back than it should have been."

Milburn put his hand over his mouth to stifle a giggle.

"Well, it's Red's fault he married somebody thirty years younger'n him."

The ring screwed back on the jar and they walked away. "Yeah, but you know why."

"Poontang!"

I could see Milburn's white grin in the dark and felt my ears burn. I knew what the word meant, but Mama and Daddy never used that kind of language around me.

Milburn took one last drag off the butt and flicked it away. "That sounds like fun. Come on. Let's go see what them two are doin'."

We slipped in one of the side stall doors and worked our way through them that wasn't dancin' until I saw Red's peroxide blond wife sitting on a tack box against the wall with Leon. I nudged Milburn and we found a place so we could watch. He pointed at Red Devlin standing not far away, all swole up like a mad coon and looking like he was about to explode.

Miss Opal May and Red had only been married about a year and they were the talk of our little community, which liked a good gossip. She was pretty as a picture, her hair cut short and parted in the middle. I overheard Mama and Daddy through the screen door one day when they didn't know I was on the porch and listening, and he called her a gold digger, whatever that was.

Miss Opal May and Leon were close to the same age and they were acting like kids, laughing and nudging one another. Leon had on a pair of new Buster Brown shoes and he kept moving them around on the hard dirt floor beside their feed box seat like he was nervous. He probably was, if he'd gotten a good look at Red.

I wondered why he didn't just skedaddle out of there, but I guess the way Opal May was cuttin' her eyes at him held Leon like a fly in a web. She reached up and smoothed a wavy strand that had slipped free of Leon's hair oil.

At the same time, Bob Wills finally hollered in the middle of the song. "*Aw*, shoot low, Sheriff, I think she's ridin' a Shetland, aw *yes!*"

Everyone clapped and whooped except for Red Devlin who stomped past, stiff and mad. His eyes were hard like glass. He had a big chew tucked in one cheek and brown juice leaked from the corner of his mouth. The leak wasn't because he was mad. Red always was a nasty chewer. "Leon!"

The folks around them watched and I could tell they expected something.

"What's up, Red?"

Devlin crossed his arms and spat a long brown stream onto the ground. "I don't want you sitting there." His voice was juicy.

Leon rubbed his feet back and forth, gouging two small trenches. "We're just talkin', Red."

"And dancin'. I saw you. You get on somewheres else."

"I didn't do nothin'." Leon kept moving his legs all nervous an' all, and I glanced down at my bare feet, thinkin' that if I had a shiny pair of brand new shoes I sure wouldn't be rubbin' them in dirt full of dried cow shit and piss.

Bob Wills hollered again and the folks that weren't close by laughed and clapped.

Red licked his lips and waved his hand upward. "Quit diggin' holes in my barn floor with them fancy shoes of your'n. Get up f'm 'ere!"

Opal May gave Leon's arm a pat and batted her eyes. "Red, it's all right for him to sit with me."

Leon cocked his head and didn't look up at Red like I would have if he'd been mad at me. "I ain't hurt'n nothin' here."

"Get up, I said!" Red spit again, then used one finger to dig out his chew. He flipped it away, sucked through his nose and spit between them.

I heard Milburn draw in his breath. It was the same thing boys did in the school yard when they were fixin' to fight.

The gob barely missed Leon's shoe. He glanced up and winked. "Make me."

The couples standing around us backed up when Red reached up and snatched a hay hook from where it was hanging on a support post. "By God, I will!"

You wouldn't believe how fast things happened after that. Red charged in at the same time Leon stood up. Red swung hard with that heavy metal hook and caught him a lick on the cheek with the curved side. It knocked Leon back against the plank wall. That aged oak was like steel and his head thudded against it. Red was on him after that, slamming him in the face and head so fast, it looked like he was beating a tom-tom.

I couldn't believe how quickly he moved for a guy his age, but he was hard and strong from working dawn to dark every day. He'd hit Leon half a dozen times and made a backswing that buried the sharp tip of the hay hook in Leon's skull before some of the men pulled him off. By that time blood was everywhere and Leon's face had already turned black. His eyes rolled up in his head and his arms and legs were twitching like he was having a fit.

Constable Pines came in from outside and slapped a pair of cuffs on Red and threw him into the backseat of his Chevrolet. By the time he got back inside, Leon was dead and folks was cryin' and carrying on.

Bob Wills and his Playboys packed it up and left at the same time Mama grabbed me and we headed for our truck. Daddy, who'd helped some of the men put Leon in the back of a pickup to take him to town, had blood on his starched khakis when he got in the car. Neither one of them said a word all the way home.

Once we got in the house, he stopped to wash his hands in the dishpan. Mama latched the screen and locked the wooden door for the first time since I could remember. "Go to bed, son."

I knew better than to argue. It was so warm I just slid under the sheet and laid still so the springs under my cotton mattress wouldn't squeak. The house was completely silent.

They finally started talking and I heard Mama's voice loud and clear, even though they were talking soft. "I swear, I don't know how Red got so mad over his wife shinin' up to Leon. Him and everybody else in Coffeeville knows she only married him for his money."

"Jealousy turned bloody pretty fast, that's for sure," Daddy said. "It's a mystery to me why he didn't just run her off, instead of killing that boy. He just lost his *mind*."

Mama's voice caught. "Did you see the look on her face?"

"Sure did. Her eyes were lit up like a kid at Christmas. Red'll get the chair for murder and with him gone, she has the whole farm. She'll be set for life, because he runs half the land in these bottoms."

"You really believe that's what she wants?"

The kitchen went dark when Daddy blew out the coal oil lamp. "Yep, and she's got it now."

They were right, Red went to the chair a year later and that dirty-leg got the farm. I heard the men talking up at the store not too long after and they said when she went to clean out the bank account, there wasn't one red cent in there.

She didn't know nothing about farming and before long the taxes caught up with her pretty quick. Everything Red owned was about to go into foreclosure in 1938 when she was killed in a car wreck across the Louisiana line.

• • ● • •

I was laying in my rack on a troopship off the coast of Japan the day after they dropped the bomb on Hiroshima. Ernie O'Brian was across the skinny aisle, rubbing his lucky twenty-dollar gold piece like a worry stone. "Do me a favor, J.B."

"It's illegal for you to have gold."

He gave me his crooked grin. "What are they gonna do, send me to fight the Japs?"

We laughed.

"I mean it. Do something for me."

The fun was over and we both knew it. I shook out a Chesterfield. "Sure."

"They say if the Japs don't surrender, we're gonna have to land and kill everything in sight. Man, woman, and child. They say they're all trained to fight us, even the kids."

My stomach flipped for the thousandth time since we'd boarded the ship. "So?"

"Look, my dad told me something I'm not supposed to tell anyone, but I'm going to tell you, just in case I get killed."

Most of the guys on the ship had already made pacts with each other, just in case they didn't make it. In fact, I had three letters in my duffel from other guys for the same reasons. I flicked my Zippo alight by snapping the lid open on my pant leg and dragging the wheel back across, firing it. "Sure. What is it?"

He held up the gold piece. "My dad buried a quart jar full of these in the northwest corner of the toolshed behind the house. Mama don't know about it, because he called it his retirement fund. If I don't make it, tell Mama where it is."

"Sure."

He leaned across with a toonie in his lips. "Light me up?"

I did the Zippo trick again and he drew a lungful and let it out through his nose. "Thanks."

I didn't have to tell her, because they dropped a second atom bomb, named Fat Man, on Nagasaki, and Japan surrendered three days later.

• • ● • •

I made it through the war, and fought again in Korea before deciding come back home to East Texas and farm. I bought the original one-hundred-sixty-acre Devlin Place and married the prettiest little gal you ever saw. It was the same place old Red Devlin started with. It was all in bad shape by then, but the two of us brought it back with hard work and pinching every penny we could dig up.

Times got better and we lived in a way we never expected, with a big house, central air conditioning, and, finally, television. The decades passed, but it seemed like we were always right on the edge of making it without ever getting over the line.

The years finally caught up with me after she died, and I got to where I couldn't work any longer. There was a little frame house on the far end of our land, and I moved in there so my son, Henry, and his growing family could have the big house. I told them they were in charge of things and settled back to enjoy my retirement with the rest of the Spit and Whittle Club up at the store.

Things got tight for them after that, and one day five years later, Henry came by my little place looking like he'd lost his last friend.

We were sitting at my kitchen table. "Dad, I tried."

"I know, son." I took a sip of hot coffee. "I figured things were tight. Saw you'd sold some equipment and one of the trucks. I watch the news. Small farms are going under just like back in the Depression."

"We'll have to sell this place and a few acres to make the taxes this year."

I looked around the neat little house and sighed. "It was only a matter of time. This drought will break soon. It has to."

Henry hung his head over the cup of coffee cooling between his rough hands. "You'll have to come live with us. We'll make it work, but I don't know about next year."

"We'll deal with that one, and the one after that, as they come."

"I was afraid you'd be mad."

"I'd never get mad at you for trying."

"Come eat supper with us tonight."

"I believe I will." I studied his face. "You look as blue as that ocean I crossed on the way to Japan."

"I failed you and Casey and the kids."

I shook a Chesterfield out of the pack on the table, clicked the Zippo alight on my leg, and fired up. "You haven't failed."

He chuckled. "I always did like that trick. You know…"

"Right. Casey won't let me smoke in the house when I move in."

"Supper'll be ready in about an hour. I'll come and get you."

He pulled out and I settled into my La-Z-Boy to think. Mentioning Japan and doing the lighter trick to make him laugh reminded me of O'Brian and his gold piece story. I took a long drag and wondered if that jar full of gold was still buried under his parents' toolshed, and then laughed.

We sure could use it now.

Hell, it's been so long, it's probably under a shopping center by now.

I turned on my new flat-screen HD TV and caught the end of a show on The History Channel about Bonnie and Clyde. The narrator's voice came over a dim black-and-white movie of the death car. "They died on May 23, 1934, on a lonely two-lane road in Louisiana."

The barn dance that night came back sharp and clear as I closed my eyes and listened to the narrator.

"Some historians say they were the product of the Great Depression, a time when those few banks that remained solvent were foreclosing on farms and houses across a struggling country that eventually began to distrust banks."

I recalled that night so long ago when Bob Wills played to a barn full of neighbors who were struggling to survive on scratch farms that barely provided enough food for their tables each night.

My little frame house wasn't much bigger than the one we came home to that night when Bonnie and Clyde were lying on a slab, and Mama and Daddy wondered how a man could go crazy and kill someone because the guy was talking to his cheap wife and scuffing his new shoes out of nervousness….

"I'll be damned." I took another drag on the cigarette and dug the cell phone from my pocket. "Son, come and get me."

● ● **●** ● ●

I pointed at a shovel hanging on the plank wall. "Take and bring that with us."

"What are we doing, Dad?"

We walked the length of the old barn where Bob Wills made music the night a jealous old man killed a feller who was paying too much attention to his young bride who thought their empty bank account was full of money.

Only that wasn't what happened.

"You remember me telling you about a man who was killed in here when I was a kid?"

"Yeah, you said it was over Red Devlin's wife, but I don't remember much more about it."

"That's what everyone said, all right."

"So?"

I pointed at the timeworn tack box Opal May and Leon had been setting on. "Pull that box out of the way."

"Okie doke." Jeff tugged and grunted it across the packed floor. "Now what?"

"Dig right there where Leon was scuffing his feet."

"What? Who?"

I kicked a dried cow chip. "Right there. Dig."

Jeff planted the shovel's blade and pushed with his foot. "Damn. This ground's hard as a rock."

"Give it to me, then."

"No, Dad. I'll do it."

He made two jabs before the blade bit with the sound of crunching glass. "Something's buried here."

I snapped the Zippo alive on my leg and lit the last Chesterfield in the pack. "There sure is."

Gone Phishing

Tim Maleeny

All authors start off as voracious readers, so once they sit behind a keyboard, they try to write stories that they would want to read. I grew up reading crime fiction, so those were the stories I wanted to write. After my short stories started getting some attention, I found the confidence to finish my first novel, Stealing the Dragon. *I put everything I love about the genre into that novel, then twisted things around to make it unlike anything I'd ever read before.*

Once I started to meet other writers, attend conferences, and visit independent booksellers, I had the good fortune to meet Barbara Peters and Robert Rosenwald at their legendary bookstore, The Poisoned Pen. All the writers I knew told me Barbara is one of the smartest editors in the business, and Poisoned Pen Press is known for publishing consistently great novels, so I would've killed to write for the Press. And that's exactly what I did—I killed someone in the first chapter of my next novel, and Barbara and Rob seemed to like it. I've lost track of how many bodies have piled up since, but I've loved every minute of writing mysteries for PPP.

—T.M.

• • ● •• •

The body bobbed to the surface like a fishing float—one of those white-and-red plastic balls designed to suspend bait at a specific depth, so the fish will stay curious and the fisherman can stay lazy.

The body was also white and red, exsanguinated flesh criss-crossed with pale crimson lines. You didn't have to be a medical examiner to know the poor slob had been tortured before he was killed. The expression on his face removed any doubt that he'd died in agony.

My Uncle Ben used to take me fishing when I was a kid, and then when I got older, he taught me how to phish.

phish-ing
/ˈfiSHiNG/
noun:

1. the activity of defrauding a person of private financial information such as security codes, passwords, and account numbers, either by calling the person under false pretenses or tricking them into clicking on a malicious link that directs them to a bogus replica of a legitimate website
2. a homophone of *fishing*

Ben was small-time, running enough scams on the side to pay off his own credit card debt. But at heart he was a working man. Bartender by night and plumber by day. Had a grip like a vise. I remember him sitting at my mom's kitchen table cracking walnuts with one hand, and I once saw him shape a pipe with his bare hands because he was too hungover to find the right wrench. Anytime my grades slipped, he wouldn't say a word, just look me in the eye and squeeze my shoulder hard enough to make me feel like one of those walnuts.

I loved my uncle, so after my dad took off, Ben was who I wanted to be when I grew up.

But then I grew up. Unlike my uncle, I wasn't a hard-working guy with a blue collar and calloused hands. I had a knack for computers, could make anything connected to the Internet give up its secrets like a lonely drunk. I may speak English with a Long Island accent and know just enough Italian to order off the menu, but expose me to any programming language in the morning and I'll be fluent by the end of the day. I could hack my way into the Pentagon and make it look like the Secretary of State had pulled the job.

And it turns out I'm a charming bastard. I can sweet-talk a mother's maiden name from even the most skeptical person, especially if their caller ID identifies me as their credit card company.

"…calling about a data breach, wanted to alert all our customers. No, your account wasn't compromised, but others were; we're just taking precautions. Yes, we will need to send you a new card. It should arrive in a few days, but you can keep using your existing card until it does. No, thank you for being a cardholder…"

By the time they realize their new card never arrived, I've gone online and skimmed hundreds or even thousands of dollars from their account. And when they get their statement and refuse to the pay the charges, the credit card company eats the loss.

Nobody gets hurt.

Except for the dead guy in the river. He got hurt, and then he got killed. And I was pretty sure it was my fault.

Even from the bank of the river I recognized him. We'd never met, but I'd seen his face daily for weeks, every time I sent out an e-mail using his name. I'd stolen his identity over a month ago.

Anyone looking for me would have found their way to him.

The thought made my stomach cramp, and I felt a trickle of sweat running down the back of my shirt, but I didn't drop to my knees and vomit my guilt into the long grass. Though I hadn't ever talked to him, I still knew the dead guy better than his neighbors ever did.

The world was a better place without him in it. That's why I chose him.

I prefer victimless crimes, so I don't normally steal identities. I just borrow them from time to time. Most credit card companies don't even bother chasing down the loss of a few grand—they just chalk it up to the cost of doing business—but when you jump from credit card to credit card as much as I do, the odds are against you. Eventually there will be a trail and, unless it leads to somebody else, before you can say the last four digits of your Social Security number, you're the schmuck doing time alongside *real* criminals.

The buoyant body belonged to Manny Nolan, and he was a pedophile.

They're easy to find online, so after a simple hack into his e-mail account and a hop, skip, and a click across the seedier side of the Web, I knew more than I wanted to about Manny's site travels and extracurricular activities. The cache of child porn on his hard drive could earn him a felony, and although he hadn't acted on his impulses yet, it was just a matter of time. He'd started posting on craigslist and lesser-known sites with just the right slang, doing some fishing of his own.

I may not be one of the good guys, but if someone hadn't caught up with Manny before I shed his slimy skin for a new identity, I was going to leave a trail that even a federal agent with a seeing-eye dog could follow.

But I wasn't planning to torture him and dump him in a river. Maybe his sins warranted this kind of personal attention, but somehow this didn't feel personal. The setup felt professional.

A simple algorithm sent me copies of any messages sent to Manny, so I could monitor his activity to make sure my cover wasn't blown. So a week prior I saw the Facebook message inviting him to the party at the warehouse, and then I saw the photo posted to his Instagram account the next day, the warehouse burned to the ground.

And then I saw the e-mail with a simple attachment, a *jpeg* of a car trunk. Inside the trunk was an extra car battery, jumper cables, duct tape, and a serrated hunting knife. In the text of the e-mail were GPS coordinates to this spot on the river.

The subject line simply said: *Looking for Manny's Black Hat.*

A hacker like me is a *black hat*, Internet slang drawn from the analog world of Westerns, when the bad guy wore a black Stetson as he rode into town to rob the bank. Like I said, I never claimed to be one of the good guys. The messages were sent to Manny's account but were meant for me.

Manny wasn't a victim, he was a warning.

I did the only sensible thing a person confronted with their own mortality can do. I drove into town and found the nearest bar.

• ● ● ● •

It wasn't hard to find because my uncle owned it, and I'd sat on the stool at the far end of the bar a thousand times. After Mom passed on, Ben retired as a plumber, took the money she left him, and bought the bar where he worked. His old fishing rods adorned the walls, and a pair of oars made a giant X over the door to the bathroom. A wide-mouthed bass hung over the door, but fortunately it wasn't the kind that sang or talked. It just gaped in disbelief over dying so young despite swimming every day.

Ben saw the look on my face and poured a Macallan on the rocks without my having to ask, or pay. Neither of us said anything at first. I worked my whisky as Ben worked the bar.

A lone customer halfway down the bar ordered a beer, and I watched as Ben popped the top with his thumb, even though it was an import without a twist-off cap. I loved my uncle. And like any sane person, I really didn't want to piss him off.

After my second whisky was nothing more than a liquid memory, my tongue was loose and the bar was empty. It was the dead time between lunch and dinner. My uncle locked the door and returned to his spot near the well.

I told Ben everything. He listened patiently, face expressionless as he wiped down the bar and polished the taps. After I'd finished spilling my guts and he'd finished drying the glasses, Ben came around the bar and sat on the stool next to me.

He put his right hand on my shoulder and gave me a squeeze that would make a lump of coal piss diamonds.

"You're an idiot," he said.

But he said it with a smile. Almost.

"Ever see a pilot fish?" he asked.

"The little fish that swims with the sharks."

He nodded. "You know why the sharks leave them alone?"

I shook my head.

"They eat parasites off the shark's body, go around snacking all day on tiny critters that attach to a shark's skin." My uncle paused to make sure I was paying attention. "And in return, the sharks don't eat them. When the sharks eat somebody else—usually a much bigger fish—the pilot fish get to eat any scraps the sharks leave behind."

"Not a bad deal."

"You're too smart to act so lazy."

"Thanks, sort of."

"We spent all that time on your education, what's the return on that investment?" Ben ran his hand through his hair, graying at the temples. "A short ride in somebody's trunk?"

I shrugged. "You're saying these guys are sharks."

"Great whites." Ben brought his hands together and cracked his knuckles. It sounded like the Fourth of July. "You've been to the gas station near the bridge, right?"

I nodded.

"Every credit card reader on the pumps is a skimmer," he replied. "Captures the card number and PIN, feeds it into a database. The Russians have been running it for a year."

"So you think it's the Russians."

"At the train station," Ben continued, ignoring me, "near the ticket kiosks. Look for a couple of kids with a mobile scanner, moving through the crowd. Same kind of operation, only the kids are stringers working for the Azerbaijani mob."

"Okay."

"It's not okay." Ben shifted on his stool. "The guys from the old neighborhood, my former classmates…" My uncle drew a breath. He never said the word *mafia* when I was growing up, but he once admitted he was the only one of his childhood friends who hadn't left town or done time behind bars. "I hear identity theft brings in a third of what they make these days. Instead of extorting a store owner for protection, why not press them to install a custom card reader at the register?"

My bar stool suddenly felt like it was sinking. "You're kidding."

"Welcome to the big-time," said Ben.

"But a pilot fish—"

"—is useful for a while. Then it gets annoying." Ben flexed his fingers in a graceful wave—*Swan Lake*, as performed by sausages. "You kept the banks distracted, splashed around enough to distract the fraud investigators or Feds from seeing the apex predators lurking just below the surface."

"But now…"

"Who knows?" Ben shrugged. "Maybe one of the gangs is getting greedy. The reasons things go sideways usually aren't that complicated. Maybe somebody's making a move and you're caught in their wake."

"Can we stop with the fish metaphors?"

"It's *my* bar," replied Ben. "When you own the bar you can use whatever analogies or similes you want."

"A simile is when you say *like* or *as*—"

"—stop interrupting." He scowled. "They say sharks never eat the pilot fish, because the relationship is mutually beneficial, but fishermen mostly see them near the coast. You know what I think?"

I knew a rhetorical question when I heard one.

"I think in the deep ocean, even your best friend starts to look like lunch. And when you're a shark, you don't have any friends." Ben spread his hands and gestured at the empty bar. "You're in deep water now, kid."

I was feeling seasick, so he must have had a point. "So what should I do?"

"You want a job?"

"You mean working here?"

"No moron, I mean a real job."

"Like a taxpayer?"

"Exactly. You want to be a citizen?"

"Hell, no," I said. "I'm an outlaw."

"An *outlaw*." Ben snorted derisively. "Robin Hood was an outlaw, you're just a tapeworm until you decide to do something with your life." He sighed. "You any good at what you do?"

"Very."

Ben smiled. "You don't have a confidence problem, do you?"

"That's how you raised me."

Ben nodded. "Well, then, there's really only one question, isn't there?"

I waited.

"You want to keep swimming in the deep, dark ocean, or *do you want to fish?*"

• • ● • •

It took me two weeks.

Their guys were good. I traced the original Facebook post to an IP address in Kazakhstan, but that was only a misdirect from a server in Estonia. I crawled through a rabbit hole across three continents before ending up in the Bahamas, trapped on the wrong side of a firewall. Not impassable or impenetrable, but it would slow me down.

But then I remembered the car trunk and got lucky. The thug who took the photo didn't realize every image captured by a phone is encoded with metadata that contains your exact location, your digital profile, and everything else a hacker could ever want.

Find one shark and you're bound to find more. All it takes is a little blood in the water.

By the end of the first week I knew who they were, when they went online, and where they were accessing Wi-Fi in the real world.

The trick was getting them to take the bait.

Gangsters are just gangs with a suffix. Territorial by nature, paranoid by profession. All I had to do was plant a seed of doubt.

Three afternoons at the train station with a scanner of my own cut into the Azerbaijani haul just enough to raise a few bushy eyebrows. Then a well-timed e-mail sent from a hacked account made it appear as if one of them was moonlighting for the Russians.

A morning at the gas station to fill up my tank gave me plenty of opportunity to jam the skimmers the Russians had installed on all the pumps. I made sure my digital signature was faint but still visible enough to trace, then made sure the trail led straight back to their rivals.

The first body was found in a Dumpster behind the gas station. The local news avoided the grisly details, but apparently the dead man had been soaked in gasoline and set ablaze before his demise. The Russians weren't subtle, but they were thorough.

In a freak accident, the suspected Azerbaijani turncoat allegedly fell down a flight of stairs in his apartment building, landing on an ice pick that someone had carelessly left on the floor. The ice pick had miraculously been balancing on its handle, so the sharp end pierced his left eye, entering his brain and killing him instantly.

A few days later, a guy my uncle knew from the old neighborhood met with an unfortunate end, though my uncle only smiled when he heard the news. The gentleman in question was best known for breaking the fingers of bartenders who forgot to pay the insurance that covered them in case anyone broke their fingers. He died of a sudden heart attack, because someone attacked his heart with a shotgun.

I was left alone. Nobody sent me another message on TOR or anywhere else on the Darknet, and my alternate identities were clean. There was so much chum in the water, I think the sharks were too busy eating each other to notice a little fish like me.

• ● ● ● •

Two months to the day after finding the body in the river, I was sitting at the bar watching ice melt into whisky when a cop came in and grabbed the stool next to mine.

The detective's name was Sam and he'd just gone off duty, wanted to grab a beer before heading home. We got to talking, as two guys in a half-empty bar will. When I asked him about work, he ordered a second beer and talked some more.

"Work was out of control a few weeks back," he said. "Haven't seen anything like that since the nineties."

I watched my ice melt and just listened.

"You might've seen some of it in the papers," he added. "But that's only a fraction of what went down." He had another sip of beer. "Dead bodies scattered all over the city."

I held my glass more tightly but didn't say a word.

"I'm just glad it's settled down," he said.

"Settled down?"

He nodded and drained the bottle. "Thirty percent drop in felonies."

"*Thirty percent?*"

"Just plummeted after a steady climb for years. Fewer criminals, fewer crimes I guess. Drug arrests, assaults, even car thefts. Never seen anything like it. The chief says we should take the summer off."

My uncle stepped up to the bar and cleared the empty glasses. "Thirty percent," he said, looking not at the cop but straight through me. "That's quite a return on investment."

I reached for my wallet. "Let me get this," I said, a little too hastily.

"That's okay," said the cop, reaching for his. He pulled out a credit card and laid it on the bar.

"Sorry," said my uncle. "I don't take credit cards."

I pulled two twenties from my wallet and placed them on the bar.

"Thanks," said the cop, smiling. "I'll get you next time."

My uncle says maybe Robin Hood isn't such a bad role model, after all. He thinks I should change sides and apply for a job with the FBI, but he understands why I'm reluctant to put my work experience on my resume. To be honest, I still don't know what I want to do with my life.

But if anyone asks, just tell them I've gone fishing.

The Bomb Booth

Charlotte Hinger

Thrilled was an understatement. My first trip to the inner sanctum. My first book with Poisoned Pen Press. An interview scheduled with the fabled Barbara Peters at The Poisoned Pen Bookstore. I checked out the store and the location the night before. All I had to do was walk across the street.

Makeup looked decent. Outfit to die for. Nerves sort of under control. I arrived an hour early. It was hot out. Really, really hot. Like 109. I pulled up to the curb, parked, and started off. I walked, and I walked, and I walked. The store had disappeared.

I walked eight blocks before I asked for directions, then walked eight blocks back. Sweat-soaked and miserable I entered the store barely in time, gratefully fell into Barbara's arms and once again pondered ways to compensate for my total lack of a sense of direction.

—C.H.

• • ● • •

He was a cute little devil. A cross between Howdy Doody and the puling little brat who sniveled over Lassie. Dwayne Hitchcock, the community leader, coldly eyed the little red-headed bastard as August Winter wound up his project talk at the monthly meeting of the Seekers Not Slackers 4-H club.

"And this concludes my talk, 'Build a Better Bomb Shelter.' Are there any questions?"

Dwayne had some, but he kept his mouth shut. Why in the hell would a country that had just finished a World War fabricate a Cold War? How many countries would America piss off before she was happy? Now even the kids were all riled up.

Augie's mother, Sharon, beamed, turned to Dwayne, and squeezed his elbow. Her eyes glowed with pride. Because he was the community leader, naturally he was always careful to applaud any member's effort. In Augie's case, however, he made it a point to show overwhelmed admiration for whatever the boy did. Dwayne smiled at Sharon and gave a slight shake of his head as though he could scarcely contain his wonderment at the lad's abilities.

"I mustn't show too much favoritism," he whispered to Sharon. She barely heard his words. Barely took her eyes off her son's face.

A fellow club member, Kenny Tillhook, rose to his feet and waited for Augie to recognize him. He was Augie's best friend and although the question sounded spontaneous, Dwayne suspected the boys had concocted it in advance.

"Wouldn't a bomb booth be a great idea for our fair booth this year? Bomb-shelter booth, I mean," he said after the laughter died down.

Augie seemed taken aback. The dusting of freckles glowed on his face and even his cowlick seemed to stand up a little straighter. But Dwayne saw straight into his devious heart. Looked right through to his double-dealing soul.

"Kenny asks would building a better bomb shelter make a good fair booth?"

Of course Augie clearly repeated Kenny's question in accordance with proper club etiquette. Dwayne thought he would go out of his frigging mind by the time his reign was up in this miserable son-of-a-bitching club.

Sharon's hand strayed to his thigh and she gripped it tensely as though Augie's answer were equivalent to passing a major bill in Congress.

"Yes, I think it can be worked out. Are there any more questions?" There were none. "If not, that concludes my presentation." There was a round of applause.

Kenny stood and waited to be recognized. "I make a motion that 'Building a Better Bomb Shelter' be our booth this year."

Becky Straugh, the president, corrected him immediately. "It's 'I move' Kenny, not 'I make a motion.'" She quivered with righteousness as she restated the motion. "Is there any discussion?"

Ted Barrett glanced at this twin brother and leapt to his feet. "Too many of us have livestock projects. We won't have the time."

There was an immediate spirited exchange, done formally, of course, with little Becky wielding her hammer vigorously when the members ignored protocol. She called for a vote. It was a done deal. Becky appointed a committee consisting of members who were not taking livestock projects. Augie and Kenny were on it, of course, and also Abigail Barrow, a mean-spirited girl who could point out the flaws in anyone. Abigail would see to it that the boys stayed on task.

Sharon clapped wildly when the vote passed. Dwayne groaned inside, but kept his smile. He would be expected to spend hours on this committee. The burden of a successful booth was on his shoulders.

It was a heavy price to pay for having a chance to court this beautiful blond widow. Her husband had been killed during the invasion of Normandy. Every night at dinner, Sharon and Augie quietly said grace, then glanced at Captain Winter's photo on the walnut sideboard and chanted together, "we will never forget."

Sharon was close to forgetting. He could see it in her eyes. So very close. He knew what she wanted, craved. She would hold out for marriage, he knew that. But more than sex, she wanted a good father for Augie. It wasn't hard to figure out what her ideal replacement would be like.

The illustrious Captain Winter had seen to it that his wife and son had insurance. Plenty of insurance. That was reason enough to court the beautiful widow. Then things changed. It had never happened before.

Dwayne fell in love.

He loved her innocent blue eyes, her yellow Tonied hair, her little cotton housedresses, her slim form that floated around her little bungalow house, eager to cook, to clean.

He couldn't recall the time when his intentions changed from wiping out her bank account to wanting to marry her. He wanted to spend his life with this adorable lighthearted woman. Wanted to make love to her, make her happy. Wanted to come home for the rest of his life to the smell of soup and good bread.

He joined the church and attended every Sunday. When she timidly asked how his job search was going, he started looking for real and hired on as a copy editor at the local paper. It was plenty good enough. It gave him some income and gave Sharon something to tell her mother and all the other relations.

Augie hated Dwayne. Oh, he hadn't said so in so many words. At first there was a look of sorrow on Augie's face. Like having to put an old dog to sleep when Sharon removed Captain Winter's photo from the sideboard. A blaze of anger when Sharon suggested Dwayne and Augie spend more time together.

Then disaster struck. Augie visited Dwayne's boardinghouse for the first and only time. While he waited for Dwayne to change clothes for a day of fishing, the boy had riffled through his magazine stash and came across an envelope of photos.

Dwayne came back into the room. He froze when he saw the boy staring at the pictures. Augie's freckles darkened in his bloodless face.

"I've got to go. I just remembered…"

"Those aren't mine," Dwayne said quickly. "I swear they are not."

But they were. Worse, they were the ones he had promised himself never to look at again. Not the luscious beauties in *Playboy* and *Hooker*, but the ones with imaginative use of whips and chains and women who looked like they would rather die sooner than later. Not that they had any chance of breaking free of their shackles. And the dogs. He could never explain the dogs. What the dogs were doing.

Augie's cowlick crackled like a sparkler as he stood in stunned silence.

"Listen, kid—"

But the kid wouldn't listen. He slammed through the door.

"She won't believe you," Dwayne hollered after him. "You know she won't."

"I hate you," Augie called back when he reached the end of the sidewalk. "Dad never, never, never would, never would..." His voice broke off in a torrent of tears.

"I'll tell everyone they belonged to your father. Your sainted father."

Augie froze.

"If you ever mention this to your friends, I'll tell everyone where they really came from. From your own attic. I've never been to Germany, but your dad has."

Sobbing, Augie took off at a run.

Dwayne looked up and down the street. None of the neighbors were out. No one had heard. He closed the door. He'd bought the photos through a Nazi memorabilia sale. They had cost him a pretty penny.

He walked back into the living room. He had a little time to think things out. He was good at thinking. It saved him a lot of trouble. He sat on the couch and rested his head in his hands, then smiled. Boys the kid's age would rather cut off their peckers than talk to their moms about sex. Dwayne was a student of human nature, and right now it served him well. Augie was the only one of his friends whose father had died a hero. His friends had to make do with depressing nondescript shadows of men who shuffled off to their jobs day after day. But Augie was the son of Captain Winter, the noble hero.

Augie strutted. Augie was a leader. Augie stood a little taller and was a little smarter than his classmates.

Dwayne eyed the boy's fishing pole standing alongside his by the door and perfected his story. The poor lad had forgotten it. He had been that excited when he caught all the fish this morning. Dwayne smiled, guessing that Augie wouldn't go home until sundown.

Whistling, Dwayne headed to the grocery store and bought three pounds of catfish. When he got back to his house he rewrapped it in newspaper—the most likely thing he would have used if they had been caught fresh. He picked up Augie's pole and walked over to the Winters' house.

"Dwayne! I was just going to send Augie over to get you and invite you to supper. Come right on in. You're just in time."

"Augie ran off and left this evening when his friends wanted him to play a game of work-up. Guess a baseball trumps having to clean fish any time. But he forgot his pole and his share of the fish." He thrust the bundle at Sharon.

"Augie!" She turned to her son. "I can't believe you would shirk your responsibilities. It's not like you. Apologize right now!"

"Sorry." He mumbled and didn't look at Dwayne.

Sharon frowned then went off to finish making supper.

Augie and Dwayne sat stiffly on the edge of the sofa. Sharon's wood floors shone from a recent coating of Johnson's Wax. A faint odor of lemon oil permeated the air. A mahogany table held a lamp with a fringe shade. Handmade white doilies had been placed on the backs and arms of the matching maroon frieze-covered furniture. Satin and velvet pillows softened the corners. The room was the epitome of propriety.

Sharon called from the kitchen. "Tell Augie all about what you're going to do this year as community leader. Honestly, I think it's just wonderful of you to spend so much of your time helping others."

"It's my pleasure, Sharon."

Augie said nothing and sat staring at the wall with his hands pressed between his knees. During supper he kept his eyes on his plate and spoke only when he had to.

"Deviled eggs," Dwayne said. "I can't remember the last time I had deviled eggs. From your own chickens, I assume."

"Yes." Sharon gamely tried to stimulate a little conversation and frowned at her son who normally had exemplary manners.

"My hens have always been excellent layers. In fact, at one time I had enough left over to sell. But I had a bad fright and stopped doing that. Tell Dwayne about the cellar, Augie." She smiled. "It's always been one of his favorite stories."

"Can't remember it."

Sharon frowned, then told it herself, but her heart was no longer in it. "Well, I always cleaned my eggs in the cellar. It's very cool there. I wiped each egg with a little vinegar water and candled them to make sure I hadn't picked up an old one with a chick already started. My eggs had the reputation for being the cleanest, freshest in town."

"Had the reputation?"

"Yes. Silly me. I kept my canning down there too. Vegetables. Fruits. I loved seeing everything put by for winter. Anyway, one day when I was down there a jar hissed and exploded. It scared me half to death. I thought it was a snake. I fell against the wall and a whole shelf of beans came tumbling down. There was glass all over."

"It's a wonder you didn't cut yourself."

"I know. I won't let anyone go near there now. I keep it padlocked and store my canning in the pantry."

"What if a tornado does come someday?" Augie asked. "What if we need somewhere to go?"

"Well, the key is by the back door where it's always been. The cellar is there if we are ever in any real danger. But in the meantime I don't want you near the place. Just because it wasn't a snake that time doesn't mean it won't be next time."

"Enough about snakes and exploding jars," Dwayne said, smiling at Augie. "What say we have a little game of catch?"

Sharon beamed. "Go on now, honey. You've looked a little peaked lately. I think you need a little more fresh air and exercise."

Augie didn't look either one of them in the eye. He simply rose, shot Dwayne a look of disgust and left to get his glove.

Dwayne insisted they play in the front yard so all the good neighbors could see how Mrs. Sharon Winter's exemplary suitor had thoughtfully entered her son's life. It was an hour before full twilight. The odor of burning leaves scented the evening air. Across the street, Mr. Weidman watched them toss the ball.

Dwayne threw the ball to Augie who caught it easily. But when it was his turn to throw it back, Augie threw it wide and Dwayne had to go into the yard next door to retrieve it. He apologized to the elderly man pushing a reel mower around the yard.

Old Man Snodgrass chuckled and picked up the ball. "Guess he doesn't know his own strength."

"Guess not," Dwayne said gritting his teeth.

"Comes from not having a father around. The Captain would have made him fetch it himself. No coddling of that boy when the Captain was alive. None."

Dwayne went back to the game. When it happened the third time he saw the light. He didn't go after the ball. Not this time. He went after Augie. "All right, so this is how it's going to be, kid. You go after that ball or I'll make you sorry you didn't."

Augie stared at his shoes. His glove pressed firmly against his side. "Can't make me," he said just loud enough for Dwayne to hear and no one else.

"Think I can't, boy? Think I can't?"

• • ● • •

Two days later, Dwayne went over to Sharon's house early in the afternoon. She didn't answer the door so he went around back and hollered. Then he spied her out in the chicken yard gathering eggs. "Here, let me help you. Where's your boy? He should be doing this for you. In fact, there are a lot of chores around here he should be doing."

"I think he's with Kenny and his dad. Or maybe just riding their bikes around town. And I think they were going to the extension office to pick up some material on fair booths."

"He should be doing more to spare you so much work."

"He's been through so much. I think he should be free to play."

"Perhaps you're right. Childhood goes by in a flash." He picked up her bucket and they started toward the house. Their path led them past the storm cellar.

He stared. The pin was away from the hasp on the padlock. Kenny Tillhook's bike lay next to the alley. He and Sharon went through the back door into the mud room. The cellar key was missing from the peg.

No need to guess who had it and where they were. He knew. Augie and Kenny were inseparable. Such good, good friends and he knew how things went between young boys with strong bonds. Augie would soon tell Kenny about the photos. And Kenny, the little prick, would tell his father. Kenny's father had been the community leader for the Seekers Not Slackers before him. For fifteen years, in fact. Three of those years Kenny's father had won the state leadership award.

Up 'til now Dwayne had figured there was a strong chance that no one would believe Augie. Would pass it off as the rant of a child who didn't want to see his mother marry or have any kind of intimate relationship. But with Kenny Tillhook's dad backing up Augie's version? Jesus, his goose was hooked. He mumbled something about a deadline and left to destroy the photos immediately. He hated that. They had given him many hours of pleasure.

• • ● • •

Dwayne's heart nearly stopped as he fumbled through the magazine rack, then looked under the chair and the sofa. He looked all through the house. The photos were gone. Simple as that. No need to wonder who had taken them. Score one for the little shit ass.

Excited, he sat in his high-backed chair. He loved high stakes. He loved to think. It was what had saved him two times before. The planning, the anticipation of complications. It was a chess game. Challenging your opponent—making this or that move. Augie's first move was a real humdinger. Bold and unexpected.

But what could the boy hope to gain? Perhaps he had set fire to them. He had to find out first before he did any more planning.

It was now Augie's word against his.

By the time they finished supper the next evening, with Augie replying to questions with monosyllables, he knew the boy had a weapon of his own. Sharon would never marry a man her son didn't like.

Augie would have to go. The problem was when and how.

Sharon cleared the table and came back with lemon pie with a meringue that must have been three inches high. Augie picked at his pie, eating only the occasional forkful.

Dwayne eyed the silent boy. His first step would be to establish himself as a mature, caring adult and the kid as a spoiled brat.

"I'm surprised you didn't take the photography project," Dwayne said. "Kenny's dad is the leader. You and Kenny could have taken it together. You've shown a definite interest in photography."

Augie turned ghost-white. His mouth trembled and he hunched over his plate.

"Augie, I didn't know that," Sharon said. Delighted, she beamed at Dwayne. "There's an old camera that belonged to his dad in the attic. A German brand. A Leica, I believe. Augie, why don't you use it?"

Augie rose and abruptly pushed away from the table.

"Augie…" Sharon called after him as he rushed out of the room. "Augie, honey, are you sick?"

With an apologetic glance at Dwayne, she rose and ran after her son, who had locked himself into the bathroom.

"Augie, let me in." She listened. "Are you throwing up?"

"Go away."

"There's no shame in being sick, honey. Honey?"

Silence.

"You're ashamed of being sick when Dwayne is here, aren't you? Her voice softened. She walked back into the dining room. "I'm so sorry, but my son is very sick and I'm afraid having you here is just making everything worse." Her lovely face tightened.

"He's so proud of being the man of the house since his dad died. Now he's afraid of showing any signs of weakness. I just have to pry information out of him."

Dwayne leapt to his feet and held out his arms. She came to him at once. He kissed her temple and patted her back. "Poor little birdy. So many burdens. All by yourself." He wanted to say more and then checked himself, warning himself to be careful, careful and not overdo.

"Call me tomorrow if you think he needs to see a doctor. I'll go on home. You know best and if my being here upsets him right now…"

"Oh, darling, you understand everything without my having to look for words. Thank you, thank you."

"You get him on up to bed and we'll talk more later about helping him feel a little more secure in making the transition into puberty and understanding what it means to be a man."

"Oh, would you?"

He squeezed her hand.

• • ● • •

She didn't call until the next afternoon. "No doctor needed but he doesn't even want to get out of bed and that's not like him at all."

"If he isn't up tomorrow, I would put my foot down."

Silence on the line. "Really, I don't think…"

"I do." He tried to keep his voice gentle, understanding. "I don't just think, Sharon, I know. The boy needs a firmer hand."

"No."

"Yes, darling. Even the neighbors are talking about it. They say Captain Winters would never let Augie do some of the things he does. They say he's spoiled. He's gotten out of hand."

"No, they don't say such cruel things. I know they don't. Mr. Snodgrass and Mr. Weidman. They've all had nothing but praise for the way he has carried on since his father died."

"To your face, maybe."

Silence. He couldn't tell what she was thinking. Had he gone too far? "Sweetheart, all he needs is a man in his life. A role model. When he is feeling better, why don't I take him fishing again? Or even camping. That's the kind of thing I have in mind. Just a few more manly activities."

"If he wants to." Her voice was hesitant.

"It will be great for him." *Yes, camping,* he thought as he returned the phone to the cradle. Lots of things happened while camping. He would wait a few days before he called her. Let her make the first move.

It didn't even take a week. On a sunny blue-skied morning two days later, dressed for the great outdoors, he knocked on the door of the Winters' house. He knew this outing had been forced on Augie so he was startled when the beaming boy let him inside.

"He's here," Augie shouted.

Smiling, Sharon stood behind her son. "Augie asked Kenny and his dad to come along. I knew you wouldn't mind." She turned and called to the persons on the couch. Kenny Tillhook bounced over to the door. "Dad used to be an Explorer scout. Didn't you, Dad?" John Tillhook rose and reached for an enormous backpack made for woodland hikes. He was a swarthy man who fairly reeked of fitness.

Dwayne froze. What he knew about hiking could be summed up in three words. He hated it.

It was even worse than he thought it would be. Even though it was an overnight trip, Dwayne hadn't planned on sleeping there. In fact, all he had planned was a hasty descent with Augie's little body over his shoulder. That, he had planned in meticulous detail. Just a slip in the creek. The boy had been that eager to fish. Just a slip. A little crack in his head. Just a little time spent in the swollen stream while Dwayne was off in the woods looking for firewood.

Now he was trapped with these two boys and a goddamn Boy Scout leader who wanted to inspect every bug and leaf.

He watched sullenly from the fire. He knew instinctively that Kenny's dad would disapprove of the appearance of a small flask of scotch. A sudden yelp of pain and the announcement that he had a sprained ankle recused him from climbing. Then there was the regretful discovery that he had left his "good" camping gear at home. It saved him from revealing that he didn't have a clue about coping in the wilderness.

• ● ● ● •

Back home, Augie threw himself at Sharon the moment she opened the door. Kenny was right behind him. "Mom, I had the best time. And guess what? Kenny's dad let us sing "Ninety-nine Bottle of Beer" all the way home and didn't even complain."

"My dad's great that way," Kenny bragged.

"That's wonderful, honey."

"Can we do it again? Please."

"Of course. Just as soon as Dwayne has time."

"Right. But first things first." Exhausted, Dwayne struggled to control his temper. "We've got the fair coming up and I haven't seen a bit of progress on the bomb booth."

"Not true," Kenny said. "We're nearly done."

Dwayne froze. *Nearly done?* "Hey, I'm supposed to be your supervisor, remember?"

"We've been keeping it a secret," Kenny said.

Augie's face whitened as Dwayne swung around to look at him. No mistaking the guilt written there. The thought came to Dwayne as surely as the sun came up in the morning. The little shit planned to hurt him. Kill him, even. And he would think he was doing the right thing. Protecting his mom and all that.

He smiled at the boys' not-so-secret meetings in the cellar. He didn't know exactly what they had planned, but he certainly knew where things were being planned. In a flash he knew where the photos were too.

"I'll be by tomorrow to look at the booth."

Augie held himself very still and his freckles were even darker than before against his eggshell-white skin. He said nothing.

Sharon called the next day. "You have an ally," she said cheer-fully. "I told Mr. Tillhook about your worries over Augie and he agrees with you. He noticed on the camping trip how my son edged away from you. He deliberately ignored you. He's going to have a talk with Augie."

"A talk?"

"About character. About rudeness. About respecting his elders. And most of all about the sinfulness of deceit."

"Deceit?"

"Yes. Turns out the boys were lying about the progress they have made on the booth. I'm embarrassed to tell you this, but Kenny finally fessed up and told his dad he lied and they had barely gotten started on the booth."

Dwayne's mind raced. So that's why the little shit looked he had been caught stealing chickens. Honor, and all that.

"In fact, Mr. Tillhook says the boys have something important to show him. And it's why they couldn't think about anything else. They are going to get whatever it is right away."

Dwayne said nothing. He had to get ahold of the pictures.

The dew hadn't burned off yet. The odor of burning leaves wafted across the yard. There were pumpkins in Sharon's dying vegetable garden. Dwayne glanced up at the flock of geese heading south. He looked around before he opened the door to the cellar, easing it shut as he went down the steps. He turned on his flashlight and scanned the dark interior. There was a nest of old blankets and a pillow. Practically a second home. And *Playboy* magazines and a few more racy ones. The envelope of photos lay on a shelf next to a candle holder and a pack of matches. He grinned. He reached for the pictures.

He would burn them here. But one last time. Just one. He slid down the wall and unbuttoned his pants and pulled them to his ankles.

Too engrossed with the old familiar pleasure, he didn't hear the voices until they were nearly upon him. No time to pull up his pants. Frantic, he hugged the photos to his chest and dove under the disheveled pile of blankets.

"The lock is undone." Sharon's shrill voice was right there by the cellar door. "Boys, how many times have I told you to stay away from here? You know there are snakes. You *know* that. Mr. Tillhook, you're going to think I'm a careless mother, but I had no idea they were coming here."

"It's all right, Mrs. Winter. I'm sure you are doing the best you can." His voice was deep and authoritative. "Kenny, I'll deal with you when we get home."

"But we have something to show you," Augie insisted.

"And we never leave the lock undone. I swear it." Kenny's voice trembled with outrage. "Never, Dad. I swear."

"Look. Just look. Please," Augie begged. "Please!"

Dwayne heard the door slowly creak open.

"You are not going down there, kids." Sharon's voice rose another decibel.

"Give me the flashlight. You've got to look," Augie pleaded. "There's an envelope on a shelf. When you look inside it you'll understand."

Beneath the blankets Dwayne held his breath, imaging the play of light on the empty shelf.

There was dead silence.

"It's gone." Kenny's voice was a soft as a mouse's squeak. "Gone."

Augie didn't say a word.

"I'm going to take care of this problem once and for all. Stay right here with the boys, Mrs. Winter, while I get my toolbox from the car."

"I've tried so hard," Sharon said.

Dwayne heard a car door slam. Kenny's dad returned. A metallic lid clanked. Augie still hadn't spoken.

What was the devious little brat thinking?

Wham. The cellar door vibrated as the hammer struck the first of the nails. Tillhook pounded plenty of nails in the door. Plenty.

Dwayne counted twenty.

Ten would have done it.

"Can we help? Augie asked.

Be My Friend

Donis Casey

Working as a librarian for most of my adult life, I had a strong foundation in academic writing, but I've always written fiction privately for fun. I had only been reading mysteries for four or five years prior to trying my hand at my own, but once I began, I felt as if I'd found my true voice. I decided that, just for once, I was going to write from the heart. I allowed myself to be more authentic and not so intellectual. Like a lot of academics, I had always wanted to write the Great American Novel, be like F. Scott Fitzgerald or James Joyce. Writing from the heart was an infinitely more satisfying experience.

Once I finished the first Alafair Tucker mystery, The Old Buzzard Had It Coming, I began looking for an agent and studying mystery publishers. I must admit that I targeted Poisoned Pen Press from the beginning. I had lived in the Valley twenty-one years by then, and I had been hanging around The Poisoned Pen Bookstore from its inception. I was aware when they started the Press and I began reading the books they published. Then I began to read about the Press in publishers' magazines and newspapers, and I knew they had a good reputation. I studied their submission requirements online and saw that they were willing to accept unagented materials, and I thought that while I was in the midst of the agent search, I might as well take a shot and send them a query letter. Poisoned Pen Press was indeed intrigued. After the manuscript went through about ten readers, it was accepted for publication in 2005, before I even acquired an agent. I was thrilled, to say the least. Since then, Poisoned Pen Press has published nine of my Alafair Tucker Mysteries. And thus began a wonderful working relationship, which I hope to continue for some years to come.

—*D.C.*

• • ● • •

He has been watching me for weeks. When I go to work in the morning, come home at night, if I go outdoors for any reason, the old man is there, sitting at his parlor window and observing my every movement. He smiles and waves whenever he sees me. I scowl at him. I ignore him. Yet he smiles and waves.

When I have my tea in the kitchen or when I'm preparing for bed, I can feel his eyes on me. Our semi-detached houses share a wall. I hear him at night, pacing. I've looked for the peephole into my bedroom, but I have not found it yet. I am sure it is there, nonetheless. Somewhere.

He has begun leaving notes, tacked to my door or propped up against the window. Once a note had been slipped under my entry door. It was in an envelope. The notes are all the same. They say, *Be my friend.*

The notes are not signed. I have not seen him deliver one. I have never seen him move from his parlor window. But I know he is the writer. Who else would be? The notes did not appear until shortly after the old man moved in next door.

I do not want a friend. For thirty years I have lived for chartered accountancy. I have added numbers in long columns. I have my ledgers. The numbers never fail, never change, are never unpredictable. For thirty years I have arisen every morning at six, brewed my tea, toasted my bread, and boiled my egg for three minutes, exactly. I prepare a sandwich for my luncheon. I shave and dress. I don my bowler. If it is cold I wrap a scarf around my neck. If it is raining I unfurl my brolly. I board the Number Six bus at seven-forty and arrive at the offices of Byers and Son Shipping Agency, Ltd., Plymouth, at eight a.m. I go through the back entrance and thus avoid having to exchange pleasantries with Mrs. Flanders at the front desk. I hang my hat/brolly/scarf on the hall tree and seat myself at my work station. I enter numbers and balance books for eight hours with a thirty-minute hiatus for luncheon. At five o'clock I close the ledger, put on my hat, and board the Number Fourteen bus, arriving home at five forty-five.

Four times a year I deliver my ledgers to the auditor, Mr Bakely. Once a year I am called to the office of Mr. Byers, Sr., for a performance evaluation. My work never varies. My book-keeping skills are unparalleled.

I had no regard for Mrs. Kellingham, the woman who had lived in the other half of my semi until she died last year. She was a querulous hag with a detestable, flea-ridden cat that made itself at home in my back garden until I poisoned it. I do not know if she ever realized why the filthy beast disappeared. We never exchanged more than two words in the years we lived next door to one another.

After she died, the semi stood empty for months before the old man moved in. He has a son, or some younger male relative, who stops by at least once a day. The younger man has not introduced himself to me, nor have I spoken to him. The old man does not leave the house.

He spies on me from his window when I am in my garden and I am aware that he watches me through his hidden eye-holes when I am in my house. He waits until I am away from home to creep about and leave his nefarious notes: *Be my friend.*

I will not be his friend. I will never acknowledge him in any way. At first I crumpled the notes and tossed them into the rubbish bin. Then I began ripping them into tiny shreds. Lately I have taken to burning them over the wash basin and burying the ashes in the garden.

Yet he persists. He waves at me every morning and evening. I know he presses his ear to the wall to listen to my movements. He watches me sleep. I can feel it. He leaves notes all about my property. *Be my friend.*

I do not know how much longer I shall be able to endure this.

• • ● • •

The notes are coming faster now. I am being inundated. I find a note on my entry door every morning when I leave for the bus and another every evening when I return home. I fear opening the door to the back garden, for sometimes a note is tacked to the lintel and two or three others are scattered about through the rosebushes. This afternoon I found a crumpled yellow slip in my luncheon box. The message was scrawled across the paper from corner to corner.

Be My Friend.

He has been inside my home. How else could he secret a note between my sandwich and my apple? How else could he have slipped the message into the box after I packed it?

How does he get in? How does he elude detection?

Will the demon never leave me alone?

Is there no one else he can torment?

Shall I lodge a complaint with the police? I have no doubt about the old man's trespass, but other than the notes themselves, he leaves no evidence. The constabulary did nothing when I notified them about the depredations of Mrs. Kellingham's cat. I cannot abide the memory of the desk sergeant's expression of disdain. They will laugh at me again. They will tell me that if I wish for the notes to cease, I should be his friend.

It is clear to me that I shall have to take matters into my own hands.

The old man does not want to be my friend. He wants to unhinge my mind. But there is something he has not reckoned upon. When Mrs. Kellingham died and the emergency personnel came to remove her corpse, I crept into her kitchen unseen, and spirited away the extra house key that she kept on the hook beside the back door.

• • ● • •

I planned my course of action very carefully. On Saturday afternoon, I took the Number Fifty-nine bus to Sparkwell. No one knows me in Sparkwell. I walked to a chemist's shop and purchased foot coverings such as are used for clean rooms and hospitals, along with a packet of latex gloves, and a hair covering. Then I returned home with my purchases in a plain brown-paper wrapping. The old man was at his window and waved at me as I opened the front gate. For the first time, I smiled and returned his greeting. I could not help myself, knowing that I was shortly to be delivered.

I did not vary my routine in the evening, since I knew he was watching and I had no desire to arouse his suspicion. At ten o'clock I changed into my pyjamas, turned off the light and went to bed as I always do. I lay in the dark for an hour to make certain that the old man had given up his spying and retired. Even so, I feared that he would hear the pounding of my heart and be alerted to my scheme. I slipped out of bed in the dark, careful to make no noise, and crept downstairs, where I had cached my coverings in the cupboard by the entryway. After I dressed, I searched my house to make sure that he was not skulking about, leaving his notes in the teapot or the parlor grate.

Thus assured, I retrieved the key from its hiding place and slipped out the back door. I had to climb over the wall between our properties. I had feared that I would leave a sign—a footprint or a stray thread—when I dropped over the wall. But the old man's back garden was dry and overgrown, untended perhaps since he had taken up residence. And Mrs. Kellingham had thoughtfully placed stepping stones throughout the garden. I did not have to step on bare ground before I reached the back door of the house, where I donned my foot coverings and gloves before entering.

The lock turned quietly and I was able to creep through the kitchen, into the foyer, and up the carpeted stairs without making a sound. I eased open the first door at the top of the landing, but the room was unoccupied. This caused me some concern. What if he was watching me?

When I saw his form in the bed behind the second door, my breathing slowed. I felt as though I were floating as I crossed the room. It was the work of but a moment to slide the pillow from beneath his head and cover his face with it.

He did not even struggle much—one or two blind swipes and a muffled moan. I pressed down with all my weight, I do not know for how long. It seemed hours, but I was determined to make sure the deed was properly done.

Long after movement ceased, I gently removed the pillow and placed it back on the bed beside the old man's desiccated carcass. Then I walked downstairs, out the back door, over the wall, and back into my own abode.

I am free now. When I left to catch the Number Six bus the next morning, there was no grinning skull-like visage at the window to wave me on my way. I disposed of the clothing I had worn the night before by wrapping it in a plastic grocery bag and spiriting it out of my house inside my briefcase. When I arrived at the offices of Byers and Son Shipping Agency, Ltd., Plymouth, at precisely eight a.m., I made a casual detour to the toilet, which is located next to the stairs to the basement. It took me five minutes to slip downstairs and toss the clothing into the boiler.

When I arrived home in the evening, the old man's body had already been carted away. His front door was open and the son was puttering around in the foyer. When he saw me open my front gate, he stepped outside to inform me that his father had passed away during the night.

The codger was so old and ill that no one thought to question the method of his demise. There was no post-mortem.

It has been a fortnight since my deliverance. There have been no more notes. A "For Sale" sign has been posted beside the old man's front gate, but if there has been any interest in purchasing the house, I am unaware of it.

My joy is unbounded. The sun shines more brightly and the rain falls more softly. My delicate mind has returned to its proper balance.

• ● ● ● •

Detective Inspector Wells stood in the foyer of the semi-detached and waited for the forensics team to deliver its report. The body had been hanging by the neck from the stairwell for nearly a week and was not in good shape. If the other half of the semi were not for sale and a prospective purchaser had not complained of the smell, the body might have hung there until there was nothing left of it but a skeleton. When the medical examiner stood up from the floor where the body had been laid, Wells took a step toward her. Not too close. He didn't enjoy the odor.

"What's the word, Doc?"

She shrugged. "It's just a preliminary opinion, but it looks like death by asphyxiation to me. No obvious signs of trauma. I'm thinking suicide."

Wells nodded. "I wouldn't be surprised. I've been here before, you know. This fellow was a bit bonkers. A few years ago he was convinced that the neighbor's cat was out to get him. Well, we'll try to scare up some relatives to notify. Okay, Doc, you can remove the body now."

Wells stood aside as the medical team hoisted the remains onto a gurney, covered it with a plastic sheet, and rolled it down to the waiting ambulance. Wells was about to follow when a young patrolman appeared at the top of the stairs.

"I found something, Inspector. Come have a look."

Wells mounted the steps and followed the patrolman into the washroom. The detective pointed to the mirror over the vanity. "What do you suppose this means?"

A three-by-five ruled note card was taped to the mirror. Written in large block letters across the card were the words: *BE MY FRIEND.*

Wells lifted an eyebrow. "Strange. Maybe it meant something to the deceased. He was a bit of an odd duck."

Telling Tales

Ann Parker

I dipped a toe in the mystery-writing community back in 1997, when I first conceived of writing a historical series set in Leadville, Colorado, with a female protagonist working "in a man's world." It was my great good fortune to have a friend in the mystery community point me toward Poisoned Pen Press. I did the submit-and-wait game, and dear Monty Montee, the PPP "gatekeeper" (some may still remember him) helped me tweak my synopsis and the prologue, to make them the best they could be. The manuscript then began the vetting process, and I tried to sit back and be patient. It took over a year, and I'll never forget opening the e-mail from Barbara late one night that said in essence, yes, she wanted Silver Lies, *and was I planning to write more? Would this be a series? The Press would prefer a series.*

Sitting there in my little home office, I hooted and hollered (but quietly, because my kids were quite young at that point and I didn't want to wake them). I was happy, I was excited, I couldn't believe my good fortune in having such a high-quality publishing company not only want my novel, but also in having an editor and publisher who understood it for what it was. That magic feeling continues, even to this day, fifteen years later. Thank you, Barbara, Rob, and all the Press folks present and past who brought the magic to life for me and all the other PPP authors....

—A.P.

• • ● • •

Deputy Kirkwood's hand wavered between the two waistcoats. One vest was tan, functional, everyday. The other black, somber, Sunday-go-to-meeting style.

He cogitated.

Tan might be better. All the dust. Stagecoach'll be kicking it up all the way to Buena Vista, and the window curtains'll be rolled down tight. Here's hopin' the stage gets jumped sooner rather than later. We'll be sweatin' like pigs in there.

But then again, Faraday'll be around. He always is, when the gold's loaded up. Having the bank president on my side's important, with the election for county sheriff just two days away. I'd best look sharp and serious, keep that sheriff badge in my sights.

He hooked the black vest from the peg, shrugged into it, and methodically buttoned the silver buttons. Stooped to peer at his gaunt reflection in his wife's washbasin mirror. Picked up the small comb, neatened his coal-black mustache, careful not to disturb the waxed curl at the ends. Gave his reflection a hard stare. The kind of stare he gave to Leadville's bunko steerers, footpads, and sneak thieves who thought they'd call his bluff.

There was no bluff about Kirkwood. If he couldn't tell the truth about something—like to his wife about today's plans—then he chose silence. His reflection stared back, daring him to face up to his discomfort.

I won't lie. Just won't state the whole truth. It didn't sit right with him, but those were Faraday and the sheriff's conditions. It was an honor to be asked to take part in the operation. It showed they trusted him. So when they said he couldn't speak of it to anyone, even his wife, he didn't argue.

He headed down the short hall to the kitchen, slipping his mustache comb into an inner waistcoat pocket. The sting of outside air—chill as winter, despite it being early May—alerted him that his wife must have the back door open. A murmur of voices told him she wasn't alone, either. As he ducked his considerable height under the lintel, he caught sight of Jane Kirkwood, back to him, broom in hand, as if pausing in the process of sweeping out the spring snow that had slipped under the door during the night.

"Company, Mrs. Kirkwood?"

Jane swung around, hands tightening on the broomstick. He was treated to the sight of two pairs of eyes staring at him. Jane's startled brown ones, big, round, like an angel mourning the world's sorry state. And Pretty Boy Sacks' baby blues, narrowed beneath nearly nonexistent eyebrows.

Jane blocked Pretty Boy from Kirkwood's gaze. "Good morning, Mr. Kirkwood. Mr. Sacks came to settle up for some odd jobs I'd set him to doing yesterday. He fixed the loose boards in the steps out back."

"Warn't no need for hirin' someone." Kirkwood didn't mean to snap at her, but there it was.

He strode forward. "Take your thievin' hide somewhere else, Sacks. I find you near my home again, you'll be the worse for it."

Pretty Boy replaced his wide-brimmed hat on hair bleached white by the intense sunlight of Colorado's high mountain country, and retreated off the porch. "Meant no harm, Deputy. Was down on my luck, lookin' for honest work and Christian charity."

"There's no charity here for the likes of you. Get off my property. Now." Kirkwood's hand balled into a fist. He was aching for a word of disagreement; it'd give him an excuse to smash Pretty Boy's good looks with a well-placed blow.

He watched until Pretty Boy, slouching like a whipped dog, was out the snow-spotted back lot and moving down the alley.

Kirkwood closed the door and sat heavily at the kitchen table. "I don't want him around here." He didn't want to say more. Didn't want her to know the full of it. But the thought of Pretty Boy hanging around his neighborhood—his home! *his wife!*—made him itch to knock Sacks down, put a boot on his neck, and shut the air from his throat. "He's been here afore, I gather. And you've paid him. With my money."

Jane moved to the cast-iron stove, her long skirts swishing over the plank floor. "I can't say no to that, Mr. Kirkwood. I've provided, on occasion, a nickel from the household funds you provide me." There was the slightest hint of resentment there. As light as the covering of snow from the previous night. "Or, if the funds have run dry, I offer supper leftovers in return for the outside chores that require doing."

Kirkwood noted she avoided saying anything direct about the long hours that kept her husband from performing said chores.

Kirkwood chose his words carefully, determined to make her understand without offending her female sensitivities. "Sacks is a bad sort. You wouldn't've known this, but I've run him in plenty of times. He's not averse to takin' advantage of the tenderfoots comin' to town these days."

The newcomers poured in, hundreds a day, drawn by tales of the silver rush. They arrived, starry-eyed and fevering for silver, thinking they'd pick it up off the ground and get rich in the blink of an eye. And when they stepped off the stagecoach, there'd be Pretty Boy and others like him, ready with their three-card monte, shell games, and crooked dice, not to mention the more direct methods of coercion such as pistols, knives, and saps. Some of the greenhorns hardly had time for the street dust to settle on their shoes before their pockets and purses were cleaned out.

Jane dropped her gaze. "It seemed the Christian thing to do, to help someone less fortunate."

Kirkwood sighed. "Sacks' misfortune is his own doing. I don't want him round here."

She set a delicate china cup and saucer before him. "When will you be home tonight, Mr. Kirkwood?"

It'd been a long time since she'd called him by his first name—Eugene—just as long as since she'd last turned to him in their bed, all willing and warm. Now, when he slipped under the covers at night, her back was all he saw. Kirkwood had no hesitations about pistol-whipping a man who was hell-bent on causing a ruckus, but he could not find the tender word or touch that would breach the short—yet infinite—distance in their marriage bed.

"I'll be late," he said. "I'll be collectin' business fees and glad-handin' the merchants for the last time afore the elections."

She nodded, without reply.

He wanted to say more. Say that, once the county sheriff position was his, he fully expected to inherit the city marshal's badge as well. That with the salaries of the two positions—plus all the extras that'd come his way from being in charge of collecting fees, licenses, and so on—he planned to surprise her. Buy her a ticket to visit her family back East.

Her family. They were the cause of it all. The silence. The coldness at night, colder than the snow she'd so efficiently swept out the back door. Her family didn't cotton to him taking their only daughter to the wilds of Colorado and the even wilder silver boomtown of Leadville. Still, she'd managed all right the first year. Then, something had happened once Jane'd realized they weren't going back, as originally planned. That he intended to stay. Stay and be part of those bringing order.

They'd had words.

She'd had enough, couldn't take the nine-month winters, the mud, the lack of women…at least, decent women…to talk with. She'd pleaded with him to let her go back home for the winter, and return in the summer. He'd refused. "Wife's place is by her husband," he'd said. "Those vows you took—to honor and obey. This is your home, Jane. I'm your family now."

When her ma had died, he'd felt bad. Worse than ever. But she wouldn't take his comfort. She took her pain, folded it up, and put it away, like the lock of her mother's hair Kirkwood had seen pressed between the pages of her Bible.

Wish I could tell her about today.

He drained the cup, rose. She was at his side, coffeepot in midair.

"No more," he said. Then added, as he always did, "What are your plans for today?"

Her gaze strayed to his waistcoat, then away. "Mrs. Larkin is doing poorly. Again. I thought to visit her. Perhaps go to church first, for a while."

He nodded. Leaned forward to kiss her. She turned her head so his lips brushed her cheek.

With a lump in his throat, he grabbed his hat from the peg and shrugged into his good frock coat. "'Til tonight, then, Mrs. Kirkwood."

She was moving toward the cast-iron stove, not looking his way. "'Til tonight, Mr. Kirkwood."

Outside, the wind cut him. By noon, the wind would die, the snow would melt, and he'd be scorching in his proper black coat and hat. *Still, folks'll be more inclined to vote for a man for sheriff who means business and looks the part.* He bent his head, holding the hat tight, and headed toward the main street. He'd told Jane the truth about going to collect fees, usually the city marshal's job. The town was so big now that the sheriff, who also acted as city marshal, couldn't do it all. Too, the sheriff was tired. He'd said so. Said he couldn't wait for the elections to be over and the new sheriff to step in so he could leave. "Town's outgrown its britches with the silver strike." He shook his head. "Wearin' both hats has worn me down. It's a plum position, mind you, but a job for a younger man. When my term's up, I'm moving on. A small town's my preference. Somewhere you know everyone you bump into on the street."

Kirkwood didn't mind the bigness. Nor the possibility of double jobs. Meant a bigger salary, for one, and more fees and licenses to collect.

But he had to keep in mind the other reason he was doing rounds today. "Listen up and keep your eyes open," the sheriff had advised him. "If you hear talk of the stage robbers, take note. It'd be a feather in your cap if we could capture the sons of bitches today, before the election and before the gold ships out. Would save us some shooting, and maybe some lives."

Hell. He didn't mind if it came to shooting. The stagecoach bandits'd be out of business, one way or another. Kirkwood was determined he was going to be the one to hang the "permanently closed" sign on them and their activities—whether through a lead on their identities this morning or through firepower later on.

He worked his way down the street greeting merchants, scribbling out receipts for fees collected. Pocketing the extra coin and greenbacks passed to him with a wink—"For you, Deputy. 'Spect you'll be in charge before long, right?"—and finding ways to slide in a casual comment about the robbers—"Yep, that's what I'm plannin' on, if I have your vote. First order of business, catch the bandits makin' off with your hard-earned profits."

They all knew what bandits he referred to, and, as merchants whose gold regularly left on those secret stagecoach runs, they were all too willing to speculate and pontificate on the where-abouts and identities of the two thieves.

Noon was approaching when he arrived outside the Silver Queen Saloon, last of two stops. He had his hopes pinned on the Silver Queen and Mrs. Pearl's bordello as being his best bets for gathering information. And for obtaining a free shot or two of rye. He pulled out his comb, gave his mustache a quick straightening, and pushed open the door to the saloon.

It was cool, dark. Comparatively deserted and quiet enough that Kirkwood could hear the soft murmur of a woman's voice blending with the muffled whir of cards being shuffled. Behind the bar, owner Mark Stannert straightened. Across the bar, Inez Stannert—his wife and co-proprietor—said in a voice as cool, dark, and inviting as the interior of the saloon itself, "Good morning, Deputy Kirkwood. Before long, we'll be calling you Sheriff on some days, and Marshal on others, if the talk around town is any prediction."

"Mr., Mrs. Stannert." Kirkwood removed his hat and set it on the bar along with his receipt book. As if it were a signal, Mark Stannert placed a shot glass next to the hat and poured a generous amount of bourbon, remarking, "Time to support the city government again, is it? Mrs. Stannert, do you have the coinage or should I take it from the till?"

The wife set the deck of cards on the bar and pulled a hand-ful of coins from a pocket in her long skirt. She counted out several ten-dollar gold pieces. "For the license. And—" She lay a half eagle on the bar. "—for you. To help pay for the campaign posters I see all over town."

"Thank you, ma'am." The half eagle disappeared into his own pocket. "Would appreciate your support, Mr. Stannert, when the time arrives. I know you and your business're highly regarded."

"As long as our firewater's strong and Mrs. Stannert keeps to dealin' with an honest deck," said Stannert, with a wink at his wife.

Inez smiled back at her husband, the warmth of her expression like the sun slipping from behind the clouds.

Jane's face—stone-cold and emotionless whenever he caught her looking at him—flitted through Kirkwood's mind. He cleared the vision and the tightness in his throat with a cough. "As I've been tellin' everyone, my highest priority is catchin' the stage robbers. It's your hard-earned gold in those shipments. I'd like to see an end to the robberies as much as you would."

"Any leads, Deputy?" Mrs. Stannert tapped the deck of cards on the bar once, cut to the queen of diamonds.

"We're keepin' our ears to the ground. Thing is, the schedule for those gold shipments is secret, close-held information. What's got us stumped is tryin' to figure out how the bandits know ahead of time. If we knew that, we might be able to rustle up some suspects."

"Hmmm." Inez shuffled again, thoughtful. Tapped the deck on the bar. Cut to the queen of diamonds. She looked at him, her gaze straightwise as a man's. "You've a shipment going out today. Am I right?" She laughed at his expression. "Don't worry, Deputy. I'll not spill your secret. What's more, I'll tell you how I know—each and every time—the day before the shipment's due to go out. But—" She waggled a finger; the diamond ring on it glinted. "You must promise to be our very special friend once you've been elected, and whenever you're asked what's the best place in town for a decent drink and a straight game, put the Silver Queen top of your list."

Kirkwood had frozen, unable to work his jaw around a word, at her telling of the shipment. But she'd given him a chance to recover during her speechifying, so he was now able to croak out, "How, how…?"

"Faraday likes to drop in for an occasional game. When he does, we treat the bank president well, just as we do the current sheriff, and plan to do the new sheriff. Right, Mr. Stannert?"

"Yes, ma'am." This time, the wink was directed at Kirkwood.

She continued, "I usually let Faraday win just enough to keep him coming back for more. That's one of *my* little secrets. The other is this." Inez lowered her voice. "Every couple of weeks or so, Faraday comes in, distracted. Not smiling. Off his game. Eschews his brandy for rye. It takes more work to ensure he departs as a satisfied customer, but after all, that's our business. A couple of days later, more times than not, news comes through that the stagecoach has been hit, yet again. The day of the robbery is always the day after Faraday's poor showing at the table." She shrugged. "My point being, Deputy, that anyone with a sharp eye for reading 'tells'—those little tics and habits that give away whether a player holds a strong or weak hand—could put two and two together. So, you might consider: Who knows the schedule ahead of time? Where do they go and what do they do that might, inadvertently, give that information away? It doesn't have to be through words. And, lest you, heaven forbid, suspect Mr. Stannert or me of perhaps scheming to add to our accounts with stolen gold," she smiled again, sweet and slow as molasses, "just consider. I would not have told you all this if that were the case."

She took a snifter from her husband; the brandy glinted like liquid gold. "Thank you, Mr. Stannert." She turned to Kirkwood and raised her drink. "Happy hunting, Deputy."

Who else knows?

Inez's questions churned in his mind as he exited the saloon into the noonday sun.

Who's there when the shipping schedule's decided? Faraday, of course. His right-hand man, that son of a bitch bank manager, Larkin. The sheriff. Me. He squinted, both in thought and against the sun's glare. *Once the decision's made and the schedule's set, who else? The stagecoach driver, but it's not always the same fella. And the manager of the stagecoach line.*

There was just enough time for one last stop before he had to return for the loading of the gold and what was to follow.

He hurried deeper into the red-light district, his destination the whitewashed two-story house standing like a beacon amidst the tiny cribs of low-class whores and slapped-together gin mills. Once there, a rap at the door brought the doorman who doubled as piano player and butler. A black man near as tall as himself.

Kirkwood stepped over the threshold, making sure his receipt book was clearly visible. *Don't want anyone to get the wrong idea about my being here.* "Mrs. Pearl in? I'd like a private word with her."

The huge Negro led Kirkwood, hat and receipt book in hand, deeper into the house than he was rightly comfortable with, and left him in a parlor room full of china knickknacks and whatnot perched on a flurry of delicate tables. Kirkwood stood just inside, feeling like a giant amidst all the miniature finery, uneasy about moving around lest he knock something over.

"Deputy." A familiar female voice sounded behind him. "A pleasure, always, to have you visit. What can we do you for?" Mrs. Pearl—he didn't know for certain if it was her first name or last, real or made-up—was a woman of bountiful God-given physical attributes, as befitted the madam of the best-run parlor-house in town. Nature, though, in a fit of pique, had thrown smallpox at her and the disease had left its permanent imprint on her skin. Not that she let that stop her. Many a man had lost his heart and the contents of his pockets to the madam's charm.

"Mrs. Pearl." He never knew whether to bow, shake her hand, or what. She ran a whorehouse, which made him want to keep her at arm's length. But she was also a businesswoman and had the pulse—and more—of the town's businessmen. He respected her intelligence, something that, like Mrs. Stannert, she possessed in the first degree. Like the woman saloon owner, Mrs. Pearl seemed to sense the inner workings of folks, more so than he did. He dealt with the surfaces effectively, efficiently, some might say even brutally. But the more subtle things—the "tells," he supposed—were where he floundered.

She solved his etiquette problem for him, waving him to a nearby chair and adding, "Whiskey, isn't it?" The stiff pleats hemming her shiny dress hissed along the floor as she moved. The outfit probably cost more than his yearly salary. *That's something else…once I'm elected and got enough put aside, I'll see that Jane gets all the finery and doodads she wants.*

After the obligatory chitchat and exchanging of cash for receipt of licensing fees, Kirkwood turned talk to the bandits.

"Guess what I'm wonderin' is, you know everything that goes on 'round town." Kirkwood picked a thread of lint off his worsted pants. "You ever heard anything 'bout the identity of the gold thieves? It'd sure be good to put those fellas away. If you've heard any rumors and such, I'd be grateful. If I win the election—"

"All odds I've heard are in your favor, Deputy." Amusement shaded her tones, but proper respect too.

At least, it sounded like respect.

"So you see, I'd be most beholden for any ideas you might have. I'm not askin' you to betray any confidences. More like, I'm interested in your opinion. And if you've heard, seen anything that'd help me do my job." *There. That sounded like a man already in the saddle.*

"I've heard a lot of talk, of course. Most think it's an inside job. The shipments are a secret, right? So how would the bandits know, unless they worked for the bank or the stagecoach?"

"Maybe there's another way." He explained about the "tells," the possibility that someone was giving the shipping schedule away through some detail or mannerism.

Mrs. Pearl studied him, as if plumbing his soul for close-held secret desires never spoken or acted upon. "It would certainly put the election in your pocket if the bandits were caught, wouldn't it, Deputy? I'd like to think that, if I could help in some small way we'd be in accord, you and I." She paused. "There is…something. Would I have your word that, should I share my thoughts, they'd remain between us? And that, perhaps, when my girls get on the wrong side of the law for some little transgression—girls will be girls, you know—that I might be able to count on your personal assistance?"

Kirkwood hesitated. Making deals with the madam wasn't what he'd had in mind. Went against his grain. But…*Maybe that's part of bein' head lawman. Dealing with all kinds. In the end, it's the justice of the situation that counts.* "Depends on the transgression," he hedged.

She waved a hand. "Nothing serious. Charges of public drunkenness and disturbance of the peace. My girls don't get drunk and disorderly, they're just high-spirited. When you add up the fines and bail on top of the usual business expenses, city license fees, and taxes, well, they put quite a dent in my accounts. All I ask is, once you're sheriff—and marshal, of course—if you would use your influence to see that, if my girls get a little out of hand while they're out and about, they're brought back here for me to deal with."

"I'll do what I can," he said.

"Well, then." She leaned forward, giving him an unhampered view of a pockmarked expanse of cleavage. "An esteemed member of the banking community is a regular customer. Someone who would not want his visits known. He's married, you see. And he is someone, who, by virtue of his position, knows the shipment schedules, perhaps even arranges them. Sometimes when he visits he is harder to satisfy. When the girl has to lend a vigorous helping hand." She raised her eyebrows meaningfully. "What, I wonder, could so distract a man, every other week or so, from the charms of those he so willingly, indeed enthusiastically, engages the rest of the time?"

"Every other week," Kirkwood said. "The night afore the shipments. Afore the stage gets hit and the news makes the paper."

He sat back. Stared hard at Mrs. Pearl. She stared blandly back.

"You understand it would be indiscreet for me to say more." Her words said one thing, her eyes something else.

"Who's the banker?" Kirkwood said. "Faraday?" *No, couldn't be. Faraday's a widower.* Then, the light dawned. "Larkin?"

Mrs. Pearl smiled.

• • ● • •

The stagecoach creaked and rattled as it rocked down the old road between town and Buena Vista, thirty miles distance. Inside the dusky interior, dust seeped around the lowered canvas curtains. Kirkwood could taste it, knew it covered his mustache and his best clothes, which irked him something fierce. The deputy sat, long legs scrunched up, next to the sheriff, with the bank manager, Larkin, sitting across from them. Larkin's knees kept bumping into Kirkwood's, no matter how much Kirkwood tried to shift himself sideways. The three were armed to the teeth—rifles, shotguns, pistols. Each held fast to his weapon of choice and tried to keep the other hardware from rattling around.

Larkin—never a favorite of Kirkwood's—had been added to the posse at the last minute, before the gold was loaded onto the stagecoach. Faraday had insisted his right-hand man be part of the operation. "I'm not sending the gold today unless I've got one of my own going along," he'd said.

The sheriff shrugged. "Fair enough. I'll just deputize him for the operation. Four against two makes the odds more comfortable anyhow."

It didn't feel comfortable to Kirkwood.

Every time he looked at Larkin's prissy face he started to boil. Thinking of how Larkin always looked at him, Kirkwood, like he was a half-full pisspot. Thinking of what Mrs. Pearl had said about Larkin being a frequent visitor to her bawdy house. And finally thinking of how Mrs. Larkin always seemed to be so poorly, according to Jane, who was always going off to keep her company.

It wasn't right.

"Hope you know how to shoot that," Kirkwood said, staring pointedly at Larkin's firearm. Some high-falutin English rifle, it hardly seemed fitting for the job.

"Oh, don't worry about me." Larkin caressed the stock. "I've won many a shooting match with this. I won't miss when the bandit shows himself."

"Bandits," corrected the sheriff. "There's two. One does the talkin', another gives the orders, silent-like." He shifted the shotgun he was holding and pulled out his handkerchief to wipe his sweating face. "We've got the element of surprise on our side, boys. They won't be expectin' us. We can only hope they'll show this time."

"They'll show," said Kirkwood. "They know the shipment's coming."

"And how would you know that?" Larkin sounded scornful.

Kirkwood glanced at the sheriff. He'd explained to him earlier what he'd learned that day. The sheriff gave him the nod to continue.

"There's only a handful of folks who know beforehand when the shipment's going to go," said Kirkwood. "And some—includin' you, Larkin—are tellin' tales, without even knowing."

Larkin's face soured. "Oh? And how's that?"

"You do things different the day before. And people notice."

The stage wallowed, throwing the passengers to one side, and stalled. The driver whistled sharp, and the stage jerked forward and began to climb. Kirkwood pictured the area they were approaching. Rocks to either side. Road narrowed down. Perfect place for a holdup.

"Do things different? Well, then, I'm not the only one." Larkin's eyes swept the deputy, boots to hat. "Every time you arrive to discuss the shipment, you come dressed for church. Just like today. Trying to impress Faraday with how good the sheriff's badge will look pinned to that black waistcoat."

Kirkwood glared even as the truth of it settled inside him, hard as a stone in his chest. "And your missus—" he shot back. "Heard tell while she's doin' poorly these days, you spend your time at Mrs. Pearl's."

Larkin's face flushed. "That's none of your business."

"It's my business when my wife's always playin' nursemaid to your wife. Like today."

Larkin's expression shifted into puzzlement. "What are you talking about? My wife left last week to visit relatives in Denver."

The stage slid to a sudden halt, nearly throwing Larkin into Kirkwood's lap.

"God-DAMN!" swore the driver. "Not again!"

The men inside the stagecoach froze—arguments dissolved. Those words were the signal they'd agreed to before the stage had left town.

"No sudden moves!" someone shouted. "You know what to do. Toss down the box and we'll let you go your way, no harm done."

Kirkwood knew that voice. He'd heard it outside his back door that very morning. *Pretty Boy, you're a dead man.*

The sheriff threw open the door, shouting, "Throw down your weapons! You're under arrest!"

Two figures, heads covered with hoods, swiveled toward them. Two pairs of eyes…

Kirkwood's scream to stop was drowned out by the twin blasts of shotgun and rifle.

He was by the bodies, not knowing how he even got there. The first hood he ripped off revealed the face he expected—Pretty Boy Sacks.

The other hood revealed the face he'd feared to find…

"Jane," he whispered. "Jane."

Kirkwood sank to his knees. He heard nothing, not the voices of the men behind him, not the horses, not the sound of the wind.

The fact of his wife lying there—dead, dressed in men's clothes, brown eyes wide but still—filled him to the point that there was nothing left to feel…

"What'll we do with them?" The uncertain voice of the driver brought Kirkwood back.

He stood up shakily. The other men stared at him, as if he were already sheriff. Already the one they looked to for orders. The sheriff included.

Kirkwood removed his hat. Pulled a handkerchief—starched and ironed by Jane all of yesterday—from his waistcoat pocket and wiped his eyes. *The waistcoat. The clothes. I never said a word about the shipments, but I told her anyway.*

"What'll we do with them?" the driver repeated. "Should we load 'em in the stagecoach and head back?"

"We're going to bury her right here, by the side of the road," Kirkwood said. "We got our bandit." He nudged Pretty Boy with his boot. "We'll take him with us. As for her—" He couldn't say her name. Doubted he ever would again. "She went home to her family. It's as true a tale as any other."

• • ● • •

Author's Note: This is my imaginative extrapolation of an old Leadville "legend" dated early 1879, which would be during Inez and Mark Stannert's "salad days" in Leadville, about a Leadville sheriff named Kirkham. For a short version of the legend, see: http://blogs.denverpost.com/library/2012/09/30/colorados-wild-women-left-notsodelicate-brand-wild-wests-outlaw-lore/3960/ and scroll down. True or not? Only Jane's headstone remains, and it's telling no tales.

A Lure for Murder

Mark de Castrique

Detectives Sam Blackman and Nakayla Robertson were not the leading characters of my first series. The small mountain town funeral director Barry Clayton was the protagonist of the first novel I submitted to Poisoned Pen Press. It was rejected—thoughtfully. But I'd been persistent enough to submit a second Barry Clayton mystery. Editor-in-Chief Barbara Peters encouraged me to take elements of both books and rewrite a stronger and more complex story. That was fourteen years and thirteen books ago. For each year and each novel, our writer-publisher relationship has thrived on encouragement and collaboration. Not only have I benefited, but I hope the reader has as well.

—M.deC.

• • ● • •

There is something magical about a river in early morning. Maybe it's the sound of the rippling water joining the chorus of waking birds, or the layer of mist hanging a few feet above the surface like a mirrored ghost coursing its meandering path. Maybe it's because everything smells fresh and even the sun's rays look newly minted.

All of these are true, but for me, early morning on a river provides the illusion that I'm the first to touch the unspoiled splendor of its pristine character. At least that's what I tell myself. Actually, I'm never first. My partner, Nakayla Robertson, is always the first to paddle her kayak into the current, and this Sunday morning in September was no exception.

We'd started at six with the most difficult part being the jockeying of our vehicles for putting in and pulling out of the river. Our goal was to kayak down the French Broad on the section that runs through the enormous Biltmore Estate. Our endpoint was several miles downstream, which meant, unless you wanted to hike back toting a kayak, you needed a second car. But only my Honda CR-V had a rack for the boats, making the drop and retrieval more complicated.

The first maneuver in our challenge was to drop Nakayla's Subaru at the take-out point and have her ride with me to Bent Creek, a spot upstream where a sandy public shoreline granted easy access. We unloaded our kayaks and, with Nakayla standing guard, I drove my SUV back to the take-out area and returned to Bent Creek in her car.

She had assembled the paddles and propped them across the bow of each kayak. A year ago, we bought two yellow nine-footers that were lightweight, nimble, and, according to the salesman, very forgiving. These weren't the sea kayaks where you sat on top, but rather the sit-inside variety where the water flowed at your elbow and if you flipped, you needed to extricate yourself quickly or execute the Eskimo roll with the precise movement that up righted you and the boat. I excelled at doing half an Eskimo roll, which meant I was head-down underwater.

So, I proceeded cautiously by first putting the leg with my prosthesis in the kayak and pushing off with my good right one. The technique was a little shaky, but as long as I wasn't cutting across the current, I succeeded without mishap. Nakayla was paddling in a stationary position downstream, ready to retrieve my boat if I capsized. I would have to fend for myself.

When she saw that I was safely underway, she swung her kayak in a tight turn and began a leisurely stroke that propelled her only slightly faster than the current. With the mist still low to the river, it was wise not to outrun your ability to avoid a jutting rock or downed tree.

We'd traveled about a quarter mile when Nakayla suddenly veered to the left. I followed, thinking she'd spotted some impediment. But she continued her turn until she was paddling upstream and passed within a few feet of me.

"I think I saw something snagged on the shore," she said.

"I didn't see anything. How far back?"

"About twenty yards." She bit her blades deeper into the water and surged against the current.

I took her effort as a challenge and pressed hard to overtake her. I was pulling alongside when I heard her gasp.

"Sam." She maneuvered around a toppled sapling that had snared drifting debris.

As her boat cleared the mound of sticks and leaves, I spotted a rubber boot trapped against the brush. A deep stroke brought me nearer, near enough to see that the boot was at the end of a leg.

• • ● • •

"His name is Aaron Culpepper. His wife said he left early this morning. Maybe four-thirty." Homicide Detective Curt New-land leaned against the fender of my CR-V. Nakayla and I stood facing him. Normally closed-mouthed, Newly, as everyone called him, proved to be in a talkative mood.

Nakayla's cell phone had been tucked away in a waterproof pouch strapped under the bow of her kayak. While I waited with the body, she'd climbed up the bank to Highway 191 that ran parallel to the river. She'd contacted the Asheville Police Department and Newly arrived about fifteen minutes after the first patrol car.

While waiting, I'd been tempted to search the body for an ID, but I knew from my experience as a chief warrant officer that until we determined the cause of death, the scene had to be treated as a potential homicide.

The man appeared to have been in his late fifties. The boot was complemented by waders and a vest that looked top-of-the-line. I didn't think he'd been in the water too long, although the river's chilly temperature would make establishing the time of death difficult.

"Who spoke with his wife?" I asked.

"Tuck did. We got the address off his driver's license."

Tuck Efird was Newly's partner. He was a good investigator, but we didn't have the close relationship I enjoyed with Newly.

"Four-thirty seems early," I said. "It would have been dark."

"Territory," Nakayla said. "Stake your claim to a favorite spot and keep the other anglers away."

"Did Culpepper have a favorite spot?" I asked Newly.

The detective shrugged. "We'll find out. Culpepper's Range Rover was discovered along the road a hundred yards upstream from his body."

"You think the current was strong enough to sweep him that far?" Nakayla asked.

"He might have walked downstream. He could have had a heart attack or slipped on a rock and hit his head only a few yards from where you found him."

"Car keys on his body?" I asked.

"Yes. Expensive waterproof watch on his wrist and a couple hundred dollars in his wallet. Maybe he's the poster child for never fish alone."

"I don't remember seeing his rod," Nakayla said.

Newly looked at me. "We didn't remove it from the river."

"Maybe it floated away," I said. "Or the reel weighed it down enough that it's below the surface."

Newly stepped away from my Honda. "Damn, we didn't bring water-retrieval gear."

I looked at the kayaks yet to be loaded on the roof rack. "We can make a pass for you. Can you run us up to Bent Creek and then bring my CR-V back here?"

"Is the Blackman and Robertson Detective Agency on the clock?"

"For you, a six-pack and updates will be the going rate. We found the guy. We'd like to know anything you're willing to share."

"I believe Nakayla found him, but I won't quibble. I will bet you dinner that if either of you finds the rod, it'll be Nakayla."

• • ● • •

We split the river down the middle, paddling in a serpentine pattern back and forth across the current. The process was like looking for a needle in a haystack, a floating haystack. The rod could be submerged and look like any waterlogged stick, with one exception, and that exception snagged my paddle as I approached the spot where Culpepper's body had been discovered.

"I've found his line." I reached out and grabbed the leader just above the fly. Holding the paddle in my right hand, I tugged on the line, trying to free the rod. It wouldn't budge, and the resistance spun me broadside to the current. The force of the water pushed against the kayak with an impact that meant something had to give. The bottom of my boat rolled and I toppled headfirst into the French Broad.

Nakayla paddled to my rescue. Her first words of comfort: "The only thing that would have been funnier was if a fish had been flapping on the line."

• • ● • •

The next morning Nakayla and I arrived at our office shortly after nine. We got off the elevator to find a young woman leaning against our door. She was well-dressed in a gray pantsuit, and I estimated her age to be mid-twenties. She gave Nakayla a cursory glance and then stepped toward me. Nakayla was often dismissed as my assistant—probably because she was a woman, a black woman. I always made the effort to establish that we were equals, and if a potential client didn't accept that fact, then we didn't take the case.

"Can we help you?" Nakayla asked.

"I'd like to see Mr. Blackman or Mr. Robertson."

"I'm Nakayla Robertson. This is my *partner*, Sam Blackman."

The woman blushed. "My mistake. My name's Ellen Culpepper. I want you to investigate my father's death."

We invited her in. Our suite consists of three rooms. Nakayla and I have offices on either side of the center room which was not only the entry space but also where we held client consultations. The conversation area was a cozy arrangement of a leather sofa and two matching chairs set in front of a large window facing Asheville's historic Pack Square. We didn't choose the office for the view, but rather for the proximity to the lawyers clustered around the Buncombe County Courthouse at the opposite end of the square. Lawyers were the bread-and-butter of our business.

"I'll put on a pot of coffee," I said, and headed into Nakayla's office and the Mr. Coffee machine. After starting the automatic brewing, I returned to find Nakayla and Ellen Culpepper sitting side by side on the sofa. I took a chair opposite them.

"What do you think we can do that the police can't?" Nakayla asked.

"Find out what really happened. My father was in excellent health and has been an avid fisherman since he was a kid."

"But accidents occur," I said. "I think you should at least wait on the medical examiner's report."

She shook her head. "I don't care what that report says. Something's not right. Where he parked meant he had to trespass on the Biltmore Estate. You can wade in the river or fish from a boat, but that shore was off limits. And my dad never would have gone fishing on a Sunday morning. He and my stepmother always go to church."

"What time?" I asked.

"Eleven. All Souls Episcopal in Biltmore Village."

"And how far to his house from where he was fishing?"

"About five miles. He lives in the Buena Vista neighborhood off 191."

Lived, I thought, but didn't correct her. Buena Vista isn't a typical Asheville neighborhood. It's an elite gated community with a golf course, clubhouse, and homes running a million plus.

"Legal or not, it was convenient," Nakayla said. "He could have crossed the property undetected and fished for a few hours before church. That would explain the early start."

Ellen Culpepper frowned. "Why won't you take my case?"

"Because an investigation's expensive," Nakayla said. "We're not taking your money if there isn't a case."

"I appreciate your ethics, but it's my money. I want to know the truth and I don't want to depend on a police department interested in closing an investigation the fastest and easiest way they can."

I knew Newly wouldn't take shortcuts, but it was clear to me the daughter was distraught. I looked at Nakayla and shrugged.

"All right." Nakayla stood. "I'll pull the paperwork for our standard contract. We'll start today."

• • ● • •

We learned that Ellen Culpepper was an only child and worked for her father in his real estate company. She lived in a two-bedroom luxury apartment in Grove Arcade, a historic pricey address in the heart of Asheville. Furthermore, Buena Vista had been her father's project, just one of several successful ventures. In short, Culpepper was a wealthy man, and the daughter and widow stood to split approximately ten million dollars.

The widow was the second Mrs. Culpepper. Ellen's mother had died five years earlier when her car tumbled into a ravine during an ice storm. Aaron Culpepper had been devastated, but not so devastated that he hadn't married a ballroom dance instructor a year later.

Nakayla and I did all this due diligence the rest of Monday, and I notified Newly we were now more than interested by-standers.

Tuesday morning, Nakayla and I drove to meet the waltzing widow, Alexia Culpepper. She agreed to see us at ten, although she said she could only spare a few minutes because of funeral arrangements.

We pulled beside the window of the guardhouse at the security gate. The man on duty asked for our names and whom we were seeing. When we said we were visiting Mrs. Culpepper, he dropped his officious tone.

"Is this about Mr. Culpepper?" he asked.

"Family business."

I studied him more closely. His nosey question told me the events of the past Sunday had been a high point in what must otherwise be a boring job. The nametag on his uniform read "Josh Noonan," and I estimated his age between thirty and thirty-five.

"Sorry," he apologized. "It's just I might be the last person to have seen him alive."

"Really? What time was that?"

"A little before four-thirty Sunday morning. I was on grave-yard shift. I had yesterday off and rotated to eight-to-four dayside this morning."

"Did you speak to Mr. Culpepper?"

"Nah. I gave a wave and he gave a wave." Noonan chuckled. "I was just thankful I was awake. I mean, he's the boss man for this whole place."

"Yeah, I know. I assume you talked to the police."

"Sure thing. A Detective Efird. He gave me his card in case I remember anything. But what's to remember? He waved, I waved. I'm sure it's on the video."

"Video?"

"See that camera back there?" He pointed to the flagpole just before the entrance. The guard's vehicle was parked at its base. "It records both lanes by this guardhouse, coming and going. The police should be able to see Mr. Culpepper just like I said." He paused. "I guess I was the last person he saw while he was alive. Sure makes you think, don't it?"

"Yes, it does. Are we good to go?"

"Yes, sir." He punched a button and the crossbar lifted.

"Chatty guy," Nakayla said, as we drove through the gate.

"If I had to sit in a box for eight hours, I'd be chatty too."

We climbed a ridgeline. I kept my eyes on the road; Nakayla watched the mailboxes for the Culpepper address. The houses we passed had two things in common: they were large and they had magnificent views.

"Here's their driveway," Nakayla said. "I don't see the house."

I turned in and drove a couple hundred yards before catching sight of what looked like a French chateau centered on a level plot of vibrant green lawn. The driveway looped around a fountain spouting water ten feet in the air. A spur on the right ended in front of a detached garage that was more of a carriage house for six carriages.

"Mr. Culpepper didn't have to depend on his fishing skills for food," Nakayla said.

"No, he didn't. Which reminds me, Newly owes me dinner. I'll push him to make good on his bet as soon as the medical examiner's report is released."

I parked near the front door. "I'm surprised there aren't more cars. Usually when there's been a death, neighbors descend with casseroles."

Nakayla unbuckled her seat belt. "Maybe these neighbors only know how to order takeout."

Alexia Culpepper opened the large front door as we approached. She'd either been watching from a front window or the guard had notified her we were on the way.

She wore a sleeveless black dress. Her green eyes were moist and red. I wasn't struck by how young she was, but by how much she looked like Ellen Culpepper. If little girls grow up to marry someone like their fathers, do older men marry their daughters? Alexia Culpepper must have been a good twenty years younger than her husband.

"Please come in," Alexia said. "I hate to rush but the minister from All Souls is coming shortly to plan Aaron's service."

"Have you set a date for his funeral?" Nakayla asked.

"Potential dates. We can't know for sure until the police release his body." A sob caught in her throat. "Sorry. It's all so surreal. Why don't we sit in the sunroom?"

She led us across a marble foyer and through a living room so formally furnished that I felt it should be stanchioned off like the rooms in the Biltmore House. The sunroom was at the rear of the house and caught the morning light. The cool slate floor and white wicker furniture were much less formal. The wall of windows overlooked a patio and large swimming pool. Water to the brim showed it was being used, even though we were two weeks past Labor Day. A heated pool, no doubt.

Alexia took a love seat with red cushions. Nakayla and I sat in matching rockers.

"You told me Ellen hired you," Alexia said. "Why?"

"She just wants to make sure the police don't miss anything," Nakayla said. "We work closely with them and are confident they'll give the investigation their full attention. But, you can consider us a second opinion. I think Ellen wants to know she did everything she could to get to the truth."

"Is there any reason to think this wasn't an accident or a heart attack?"

"We're just starting," I said. "There's no evidence to think one way or the other. Tell me, was it unusual for your husband to go fishing so early?"

"Not really. Going on Sunday was unusual. He told me the night before if he was restless, he might get in a few hours before church. I was getting ready when the police came."

"Did he often fish alone?" I asked.

She shrugged. "Sometimes. Usually he went with some buddies or he'd meet Ellen."

"Ellen's a fly fisher?" Nakayla asked.

"Oh, yes. She's gone with her father ever since she was big enough to hold a rod. Now me, the closest I like to get to a river is a picnic table on the bank."

"You said your husband was restless," I said. "Was he having any health problems?"

"No. He was stressed. Property sales have slowed again, and…" she paused.

"And what?" I prompted.

"Well, he was worried about Ellen. She's dating some painter in the River Arts District. Aaron thought he was after her money. And her work suffered. He didn't think she was doing a good job, but how do you fire your child?"

"Had he spoken to her?" Nakayla asked.

"He said he was going to. Maybe he was planning to this week. It would explain his restlessness Saturday night."

And his desire for the solitude of the river, I thought. And the stress could have led to a heart attack.

"Did your husband wake you when he got up?"

"No. I'm a sound sleeper. Besides, he would have changed in the garage. It's where he keeps all his equipment."

"Can we take a look?"

"Sure."

We followed her onto the patio and along the pool. One of those automatic skimmers floated on the surface, picking up small debris. We entered the garage from the side. A black BMW sedan was parked at the far end. The Range Rover must have still been in police custody. The near section had a long workbench complete with vises, packets of feathers, spools of thread, all the materials necessary for making your own flies. Two lockers stood at the end of the workbench.

Alexia opened them. "He kept clothes here. He could change and hang up the damp gear when he returned."

One held street clothes and the other had empty hangers where the fishing wardrobe must have been.

I walked along the workbench. Everything was well organized. Several small zippered leather cases were stacked at one end. I opened one. It contained flies neatly hooked in a mesh lining.

"Have you touched anything here?" I asked.

"No. Ellen will have to go through all this. I don't know what to save and what to throw out."

"Have the police been here?" I asked.

"Yes. That Detective Efird and his partner came back yesterday." She gestured to the workbench. "They saw what you saw."

• • ● • •

Nakayla and I met Newly that night at Lexington Avenue Brewery, a great place for craft beer and good food. Newly ordered us an appetizer plate of beef sliders to start off dinner; I asked a question to start the conversation.

"Do you know where Ellen Culpepper was Saturday night and Sunday morning?"

Newly arched an eyebrow. "Why? You suspect your own client?"

"She and her father used to meet to fish. Just ruling out all possibilities."

Newly nodded. "I guess hiring detectives would be a good move to deflect suspicion. Well, she said she had a date."

"You check it?"

"Yeah. A painter. Lives above his studio in River Arts. She stayed overnight. She's either in the clear, or the boyfriend's in it with her."

"Five million dollars is at stake," I reminded him.

"You think she and the boyfriend are good for it?"

"No. I want to make sure you've ruled them out before I share further information with her."

Newly looked at Nakayla and then at me. "What am I missing here?"

"You've put your finger on it," I said. "It's what's missing. I'd like to see the security footage from the guardhouse and what you found on Culpepper's body."

Newly's curiosity surged. "Consider this a dinner in progress. You eat these. I'll get the check and we'll go to the station."

"Don't you want one?" I asked.

"Hell, yes, but my wife's put me on a diet."

• • ● • •

The footage was cued to the point where Culpepper's Range Rover drove through the gate. Like the guard, Josh Noonan, had said, Culpepper waved his hand out the open window as he passed. The angle of the shot couldn't show facial features through the tinted glass and it looked like the sun visor might have been down. The front of the guardhouse was constructed of stone with windows on either side where vehicles would stop. The guard was out of camera frame.

"Back it up and freeze it where Culpepper waves," I said.

Newly reversed the footage until the hand was out the window.

"Can you zoom in closer?" I asked.

"Tuck and I did this. You can see the sleeve matches what Culpepper was wearing."

"It's what he's not wearing that interests me."

Newly studied the monitor screen. "You smart bastard. How?"

"Pajamas. What's the preliminary M.E. report?"

"A fall and then drowning. A blow to the head consistent with an impact on a river rock. It would have been over pretty quickly."

"Can we see his personal effects?"

Newly laid out the rod and reel, the clothes, the wristwatch, and a leather case similar to the ones in the workshop.

"You know anybody who's an expert on fly fishing?" I asked.

"I've got a friend at Curtis Wright Outfitters. Richard Witt knows everything there is to know."

"Show him the fly on the rod and this case."

"And?"

"And see what he says. I want his opinion before I talk to Culpepper's daughter."

"You want more from the M.E."

I smiled. "You're with me now, aren't you?"

He nodded. "And I hope to stay that way."

Two days later, Newly, Ellen Culpepper, Nakayla, and I stood at the front door of Alexia Culpepper's home. Newly rang the bell with his left hand and held a canvas satchel in his right. We heard chimes echoing through the house. They were still ringing when Alexia threw open the front door.

"What is it?" Her annoyance changed to surprise when she saw us.

"Sorry for the intrusion," Newly said. "We have some new developments that we want to share in person."

Alexia composed herself and forced a smile. "Well, come in. I guess it's important."

We followed her to the sunroom. Alexia sat on the love seat. Nakayla, Ellen, Newly, and I took chairs. Newly dropped the satchel at his feet.

"What have you discovered?" Alexia asked.

"It's more a question of what we haven't discovered," I said. "Pajamas."

"Pajamas. What pajamas?"

"Your husband's. Either pajamas or a bathrobe. It was chilly at four in the morning. You said he changed in the garage, but changed out of what?"

"Well, he slept in the nude. We both do."

"And went naked outside to the garage?"

"No one would see him."

"Buck naked? Nothing on his feet?"

"I guess so. Otherwise, you would have found them in the garage."

"Yes. Several things seem to have gone missing. He had a waterproof watch he wore while fishing."

"Ellen gave it to him for his fifty-fifth birthday."

"He was wearing it when we found his body. Left wrist."

"Yes."

"But when he waved to the guard a little before four-thirty, it wasn't on his wrist."

A nervous twitch rippled at the corner of her mouth. "I guess he didn't put it on till he got to the river."

"Maybe," I conceded. "But there's another possibility. That your husband was dead before he left this house. And that led me to think about the problem of logistics. How could a dead man drive through the gate, put on his watch, and walk down to the river? You would need at least two other people just to shuttle vehicles."

"This is preposterous. I've lost the man I love and now you're accusing me of murder?"

"You haven't lost the man you love."

Newly reached into his jacket pocket and pulled out his cell phone. "You can come in."

Alexia stood and turned around to stare toward the foyer. We heard the front door lock click. A few seconds later Detective Tuck Efird entered with Josh Noonan a few steps in front of him.

Alexia turned around. Her face paled to bleached bone.

"They're making wild accusations," Noonan shouted. "I haven't said anything."

"Like I was saying," I continued, "two people, you and Mr. Noonan here, for example. He parks his car out of view of the security camera. He can also exit the rear of the guardhouse without being seen. So, theoretically, you could drive down, stop before entering the camera's view and take him back up to your house. If you haven't already done it, he helps you kill your husband, and then loads him in the back of the Range Rover. You crouch down behind the front seats, and he wears your husband's shirt and waves to the empty guardhouse. Then you take Noonan's car for the return vehicle, and go to a more desolate spot to dress your husband including his watch and a box of flies."

Newly pulled the fly box and a photograph from the satchel. He handed them to Ellen. "Your stepmother says you're the fly fishing expert. What can you tell us about these flies and the one in the photograph of your father's rod?"

Ellen Culpepper studied them for less than a minute. "None of these are hatching now. Thunderhead, Mr. Rapidan, Hazel Creek—these flies are all for the spring. The one on the rod is a Yallerhammer, which he'd definitely never use in September."

Newly nodded. "That's what I was told by a fishing guide. You use whatever most resembles the current hatching population." He turned to Alexia. "You and Noonan picked the wrong fly box."

"Who's to say Aaron didn't make the mistake?" she countered.

"You're right." Newly turned to Ellen. "He could have met your stepdaughter and her boyfriend."

Ellen drew back like she'd been slapped.

"Exactly," Alexia said triumphantly.

"Except for the medical examiner," Newly said. "Sam's suspicions prompted me to request he take another look. The water in his body contained traces of chlorine, chlorine consistent with amounts added to a swimming pool." Newly looked over his shoulder. "That swimming pool."

Alexia Culpepper said nothing.

Newly pulled a set of handcuffs from his pocket. "Mrs. Culpepper, I'm arresting you on suspicion of the murder of your husb—"

"I had nothing to do with it," Noonan yelled. "I know all about lures. She could've impersonated her husband and met someone else who helped her."

"Lures?" Newly questioned. "No fly fisherman calls them lures. Tuck, how'd you come in the front door?"

Newly's partner held up a ring of keys. "Courtesy of Mr. Noonan."

• ● ● ● •

Nakayla and I were in the French Broad. Not the river. The French Broad Chocolate Lounge a few blocks from our office. I took the last bite of Mocha Stout Cake, thanks to Detective Newland. He had just a cup of coffee, in adherence to his wife's prescribed diet.

"So, the finger-pointing has begun," Newly said. "Both claiming the other forced their participation."

"A plea deal?" Nakayla asked.

"I don't know what the D.A. will do. The case is solid."

"Were you surprised the M.E. didn't pick up the chlorine the first time?" I asked.

"Not really. We found the body in a river. Evidence suggested he hit his head and was unconscious. He would drown without taking in large quantities of water. The chlorine was more prevalent in the throat and nasal passages."

"Couldn't that have been from swimming in the pool?" Nakayla asked.

"Maybe. A nude four o'clock swim before taking the wrong flies to a fishing stream is a pretty desperate defense, especially since Noonan's been forthcoming. He claims Aaron Culpepper was already dead and floating in the pool when he got to the house."

"And the motive?" I asked.

"Two lures that attract a lot of murders. Sex and money."

"That's what attracted me to Sam," Nakayla said.

Newly pushed his coffee cup away. "Too much information." He stood.

"Where are you going?" I asked.

"Diet be damned. I'm going for the lure of chocolate cake."

Quito

J.M. Donellan

My Australian publisher, Pantera Press, had informed me that they'd had a very successful visit at the Frankfurt Book Fair and they'd had some "very exciting conversations." I assumed this was general industry speak for "we ate a lot of cheese and drank a lot of wine and gesticulated wildly at people." Soon after, I was told that they'd had an offer from an American publisher for my book, Killing Adonis. *I had to reread the e-mail several times to check it wasn't a similar "offer" to the one I'd recently had from a Nigerian prince who needed me to help transfer funds into an offshore bank account. When it turned out to be a legitimate offer from the good folks at Poisoned Pen Press, I said yes and then engaged in the traditional Australian post-contract signing ritual of sacrificing a kangaroo to the moon god at midnight.**

*I'm joking, obviously (we usually sacrifice a koala).

—J.M.D.

• • ● • •

I stared at his serene, icicle-encrusted face. Tiny white stalagmites jutted from eyebrows, ears, and nostrils. His eyes were permanently closed, mouth frozen slightly open. I pressed my hand against the cold glass, breathed mist onto it, and drew a curly moustache superimposed over his face. I'd nicknamed this one The Big Chill; he was a portly Latino with curiously large ears and a bulbous nose. His head hung suspended in both the physical and neurological sense in the liquid nitrogen dewar, along with all the other poor saps who hadn't been either rich or stupid enough to have their whole bodies frozen.

The jokes "keep a cool head" and "this is the reason why we can't have ice things" had been made innumerable times within these walls, not to mention endless references to "Netflix and chill" and every last one of Schwarzenegger's puns from the abominable 1997 film *Batman and Robin*. The official term for the various heads and bodies stored in the dewars was "patients." We were strictly forbidden from referring to them as dead bodies because, according to Cryotech, they weren't dead, just "suspended," as though they were delinquent high school students rather than corpses on ice. When the managers weren't around, we called the patients "popsicles."

It had become a sacred ritual to draw straws to decide who would choose a nickname for each new arrival. Carlita tended to go for hip-hop names (Vanilla Ice, Ice-T, Ice Cube), Zoha favored pop culture references (Cool Hand Luke, Cool Runnings, Jon Snow), and the rest of us mostly went in for puns. I'd come up with Christopher Walken Freezer and Keanu Freeze and was happy with those, but Karen had produced Edward Snowedin, which was unquestionably the pick of the bunch.

Working the graveyard shift had a smorgasbord of drawbacks: severely limiting my social life, messing with my circadian rhythm, fucking with my health, but I didn't have any other options and at least it let me sleep in each morning. Most days I spent the first half of the afternoon procrastinating and the second looking for a new job. I'd originally told myself working at Cryotech would be a "stop-gap" job, but I'd been doing it for five years now. I told Zoha that I felt like one of the popsicles—suspended in a null state. I moaned about my intellect being wasted in such a boring job and all the money I'd spent on my worthless arts degree. He laughed and reminded me he'd spent six years working as a surgeon before he'd emigrated from Pakistan and I shut my mouth and never mentioned it again.

At least you could do the job with headphones on; that was a pretty big perk. Most nights I'd flick between albums and podcasts as I worked, and if I listened intently and let myself fall into the muscle memory of each sweep of the mop, I could almost forget where I was. The main problem was that I carried the constant stench of industrial cleaner. No matter how long I showered and scrubbed I couldn't rid myself of that vile, pungent scent. The label claimed it to be "Summer Lemon," but I think a more accurate description would be "Robot Urine."

I waved good-bye to The Big Chill and finished mopping the floor with the sounds of Sigur Rós swelling and rising in my headphones. Icelandic music seemed appropriate; it was sort of a private musical pun. I walked past the frozen pets section—the saddest thing about this place. Once upon a time, you could conceal mortality from your kid by periodically replacing their mouse or goldfish; now you could have your treasured domestic vertebrate frozen with the perpetual deceit of resurrection.

I slid the viewing window back and looked into the frozen face of White Fang. This was his actual name, not just my nickname for him. I knew this because the old man to whom he belonged used this name when he visited and talked to him. There was a strange and brutal irony to the fact that White Fang's owner was clearly himself not long for this world. I wondered if he'd arranged to have himself suspended next to his beloved pet so the two of them could emerge victoriously into some bright, glorious future where we'd all eat food grown in labs, listen to music composed by algorithms, and wear shiny silver Lycra. Or, conversely, watch in dismay as robots took our jobs and made us all work as slaves. It's probably what we'll deserve.

I shoved the mop back into the bucket, washed my hands, went into the kitchenette and scanned the fridge. There was a half-eaten tub of yogurt with a post-it reading *Do not eat. JAN THIS MEANS YOU!!!!!!!!!* I'd never met Jan or the author of the note, but, man, did I want to get in a room with the two of them. There's always a good story behind that many exclamation marks.

On the bottom shelf sat a promisingly large white cardboard box. "Please please please…" I murmured as I lifted it from the shelf and popped it open, then yelped excitedly as it revealed the most glorious of all foods known to humankind; a chocolate mud cake. The inscription read *Hap__ Birt___ J__*, the second half of each word truncated by consumption. I wondered if the cake belonged to the infamous Jan, and if it had temporarily assuaged her lust for illicit yogurt.

I grabbed a fork from the drawer, sat on the bench, waved at the camera, and greedily tucked in. Cryotech had an elaborate array of cameras installed throughout the facility but the recordings were deleted every week and they were only reviewed if there was any kind of incident, which there never was. We kept no cash on site, our tech was all laser-engraved and catalogued, and even the bodies were too much effort to hold any appeal for your garden-variety necrophiliac.

I hummed happily to myself as I shoveled the calorie-laden taste orgy into my mouth. I'd long thought that cake was the pinnacle of human achievements, something that should be enshrined alongside our greatest paintings, symphonies, and novels. I was halfway through what I'd told myself would be my last mouthful (but historical record indicated would most likely be one of a sequence of between twelve and twenty) when the sensor lights at the front entrance flickered spasmodically to life. I closed the lid, pulled my headphones off and hung them around my neck as I ran to the door.

A young woman stood on the other side, her face and expression indistinguishable behind the frosted glass. She banged the glass door and waved frantically at me. Zoha would still be cleaning the bathrooms with his headphones on, so there was no way he'd hear anything. An avid jazz fan, he'd been using shitty no-name headphones for years until his kids had gifted him a beautiful pair of noise-cancelling Bose Qc25s. He'd demonstrated them to me with a proud grin; when he placed the luscious pads over my ears I felt like I had been transported back to Birdland in the 1930s. He was probably jamming out with

Miles Davis and Charlie Parker right now, blissfully unaware of the world outside his eardrums.

I approached the door and yelled, "We're closed!"

She froze, cupped her hands to her mouth and yelled back, "I know! It is an emergency!"

Her voice was distant and muted on the other side of the glass, but her face spoke volumes of Tolstoy-esque length. She wore a ragged hiking backpack, the slender black auxiliary straps dangling around her like effete tentacles.

"Please open the door! I have not much time!"

I hit the security button, and the doors slid open with a smooth mechanical yawn. She rushed inside and gripped my shoulders with both arms. "I need you to listen to me, this is extremely important I—ah, you have…a little something…" she pointed to my cheek and I wiped my face with the back of my hand, cursing Jan and her goddamn chocolate cake. "I know you don't know me, but I am a client here. My name is Ava Zapata, you have my father Ernesto Zapata. You can check this on your database." She pointed to the computer sitting behind the reception desk and looked at me expectantly.

"I'm just a cleaner. I don't have access to the system."

"Is there a security guard or manager or someone you can contact? It is urgent!"

"Security doesn't arrive onsite until the end of my shift, and my manager won't answer his phone this late."

She grunted in frustration and flung her hands into her hair as she murmured a string of Spanish profanities. I barely passed high school Spanish, but like any teenage student of a foreign language, I'd learned all the curse words proficiently. "Please, there must be something you can do? Have you, aaaah, paper copies of your client list, something like this?"

"Maybe, but they'd be in Brett's filing cabinet and he takes the key home with him so—"

Ava screamed, her voice was high and piercing and had a volume and strength that seemed incompatible with her diminutive size. She slammed her fists against the wall. I stood there awkwardly shuffling and wishing I'd never opened the door. Finally she seemed to calm down. When she turned to face me she had tears in her eyes. "Sorry, sorry. I just...you don't know me. But I need your help. Do you understand?" I nodded. "You are a very calm person."

"Thank you."

"It was not a compliment."

She closed her eyes, took a deep breath, then opened them and said, "Ernesto Zapata, dewar number 173869-DJCN, to his left is Simon Wellington, and to his right Simone Leiter. I remember this, because it is funny, he is between Simon and Simone, you see? So now I have proved to you that I have been here before, I must be a client right?"

"Well, anyone can arrange a public tour, so that doesn't—"

"He was admitted here three weeks ago, January 2nd."

I reached back into the anarchic jambalaya of my memory. I'd been still fighting off my New Year's hangover and had recently received my five-year anniversary gift from Cryotech—a fridge magnet. I'd like to think they chose this piece of memorabilia out of a wicked sense of self-referential humor, but it was probably just general corporate obliviousness. The other cleaners had agreed to grant me Ernesto's naming rights as a special anniversary treat.

"Ah, yeah, I know The Big Ch—ah, Ernesto."

Her eyes illuminated and she grabbed my shoulders again. "Great! Now we are getting to somewhere. Please, I have to see him!"

"I'm sorry, you have to come back during visiting hours. We'll be open at—" she shook her head angrily and blurted,

"I have to be on a plane to Quito in four hours!"

"Why do—?"

"I am being deported." Ava looked intently into my eyes, like she was firing ocular lasers from her pupils into mine. "There was a man from Immigration, he knew I was working illegally. I was bribing him to let me stay just a little longer, but my money and his patience are now all gone." She ran her fingers through her hair and sighed, exasperated. "Listen to me, ah, I don't know what is your name?"

"Leon."

"Leon," she repeated. "Leon, like 'lion.'" My mother had said that when I was a kid. It'd been a long time since I'd heard anyone else make that connection.

"Well, hah, sure. I guess."

"All right. Well, you don't know me. And I have come here in the middle of the night, and I am screaming like I am crazy, and I have told you I am about to be deported, so maybe I do not seem like the most trustworthy person, but I am asking you, I am begging you, to *please trust me*. I have to ask you to do two things. The first is to let me see my father."

"I could lose my job..." even as I said the words I realized that this really wouldn't bother me all that much. I was already dreading a tombstone bearing the epitaph "He Cleaned the Floors of the Frozen Dead, But Couldn't Afford Cryo So Lies Here Instead."

"*Please,*" her voice was quiet but commanding. I bit my lip and nodded. We turned and started to walk toward the storage room. It was only then that I noticed that Sigur Rós was still playing, tiny and tinny in my headphones. I hit "pause" on my phone and the only sound was the echo of our feet against the floor.

"What's the second thing you have to ask me?"

"I cannot tell you until I have done the first thing."

"Why not?"

Ava said nothing for six and a half steps and then finally, "You will see."

We reached Ernesto's dewar, she slid back the viewing window and pressed her hand to the glass. The faint outline of the moustache I'd drawn earlier was still there hovering over his face. I winced with embarrassment. She looked at the glass and then at me, and my face went bright red. My heart raced as I waited for the angry accusation to fly at me, but instead she reached into her backpack and pulled out a pair of gloves and a crowbar.

"WHAT THE HELL ARE YOU DOING?" I screamed.

"Now I have to ask you to do the second thing: stand back."
She placed the gloves over her hands and looked directly at me
as she picked up the crowbar and rested it on her shoulder. I
stood frozen to the floor, ironic given the circumstances. "Please,
Leon, I have to do this. We have come this far. Also, if you say
no, I will have to hit you with this crowbar, and I would like to
not do that. You have a nice face."

She prodded me with the crowbar and I stepped back until
I was pressed against the railing of the stairs. She readied her
swing. "What the hell are you doing?" I repeated, this time it
was a desperate plea rather than a demand.

She sighed, rested the crowbar again and looked straight at
me. "My father has spent all of his money on this ridiculous
piping dream."

"Pipe dream?"

"Yes. Thank you, this is what I meant. All my life he pummels
into me, 'Be a good little Catholic and when you die, Jesus will
take you to heaven.' Meanwhile, he sleeps around, he beats my
mother when he drinks, he gambles all our money. He left us
and moved to America when I was just a teenager." She hung
the crowbar by her feet and tapped her boots with it. "A year
ago he calls me, tells me he has cancer. He needs help. He is an
asshole, but he is still my father, you know? So I left everything
behind for him. I sold my business, quit my band. My boyfriend
didn't want to live in America, so we broke up. I said good-bye
to my friends, my home, everything, you understand?

"I come to this country and I work *three* jobs. This is in
violation of my visa. I am paid beneath the table, and all of my
money, all of it, I give to him for his 'experimental treatments.'
I work until my back aches, my feet swell, my bones feel brittle
and old." She snarled these last few words and began knocking
her fist with quiet rhythmic raps against the side of the dewar,
staring into her father's silent, icy face.

"Then, on his deathbed, with his last breaths, you know
what he says to me? Not 'thank you,' not 'I love you.' He tells
me that he was never really paying for experimental treatments,

but giving money to this fucking joke of a corporation. Every cent he had left—money that I would have inherited—and all of the money I had bled and sweated to make so he could end up a frozen skull in a tank."

Ava wiped an angry tear from her eye. I hesitantly began raising my hand to give her a commiserating pat, but she didn't see the gesture and when she shook angrily and growled in frustration, I snatched my hand away. "And then? Not only this, he tells me I must keep working, keep being a good girl, keep paying for his fucking refrigerator fees. We have no insurance, you know? He tells me that if I do not pay the money, he will die. I say to him, you *are* going to die!' and he smiles and says, 'Oh, *mi corazon*, I'm just going to have a little sleep,' and then he has the nerve to fucking die before I can tell him how stupid he is.

"All his life he tells me be a good Catholic, heaven is waiting, and then he raises his middle finger to heaven, and to me. He went from putting all his faith in a God he ultimately did not believe in, to placing his faith in this bullshit corporate pseudo-science. No offense."

"None taken. I just work here." She nodded, sighed and said, "Well, now I must do this. Please do not try and stop me." She raised the crowbar again but then paused and asked,

"Do you believe in God, Leon the lion?" It was a far more philosophical question than I was used to being asked during work hours, or ever. But spending hundreds of hours staring into icicle-encrusted faces meant I spent a lot of time ruminating on the nature of God and death.

"I think that God is essentially an anthropomorphized meta-phor for the infinitely complex relationship between energy and matter."

She raised an eyebrow, a dark semi-circle ascending the portrait of her face, then pulled the crowbar back behind her shoulder and aimed a stern glance at me. I wasn't sure if this was a warning or a request for encouragement. I nodded at her, hoping this would cover both bases. "You are an interesting guy, Leon. My father would have hated you."

The crowbar made a dull 'thud' against the glass, cracks cob-webbing across the cold surface. Klaxons blared throughout the gigantic room that even Zoha couldn't miss. I yelled out, "Hurry up!" and she shot me a deservedly withering glance. She pulled back and struck again. New cracks emerged and the old ones thickened, vents opened beneath Ernesto's head and the liquid nitrogen drained quickly away. On the third strike, the glass splintered and fell to the floor. She tapped the crowbar around the edges, clearing the jagged fragments, then dropped it and reached in to grab the head.

I picked up the backpack and held it out for her. Ava smiled at me, a beautiful, gracious smile. If not for the blaring sirens and the frozen head in her hands, it could have been quite a romantic moment. She put the head, her gloves, and the crowbar into the bag and slung it over her shoulder. "Thank you, Leon. I am grateful that the last person I will meet in this country has been kind to me. This has not always been the case."

Or something to that effect. It was hard to tell, the alarm was really loud. I was probably farewelling a couple of hertz of my upper-range hearing with each minute I stuck around. Ava ran down the stairs and I followed; it was only when she reached the front door that she realized I was behind her. "What are you doing?"

"I want to come with you!"

I watched her brow furrow and her lips form a tiny o that would've surely developed into a bewildered 'why?' but she was interrupted by Zoha emerging from the bathrooms screaming, "*What the hell is going on?*"

I held my palms up at him and said, "Zoha, I have to help this lady steal her father's head!"

It sounded pretty weird when I said it out loud. He looked at me and then at her and then at the frozen head peeking out of the backpack and then back at me again, like he was a spectator of some bizarre sepulchral sport. His face slowly transitioning from shocked to enthralled, he grinned broadly and said, "Is it for love?"

I flushed bright red and replied, "Well, I mean, we just met and she's about to be deported so…"

Ava looked at me, squeezed my hand and then ran over to Zoha, leaned into his ear and whispered something. He grinned, gave us a thumbs-up and said, "Okay, you'd better take the security footage. I'll call the police, tell them some teenage hooligans broke in. You should have a couple of minutes."

I ran over to the desk and unplugged the external hard drive that stored the footage and stood staring at the security monitor.

"Come on! What are you doing, checking your fucking Facebook?" Ava yelled.

"The security footage auto-syncs to a cloud backup every half-hour."

"So turn it off!"

"I told you I don't have a login for the computers!" I kicked the desk, swore, and looked around the room. My trusty mop bucket sat where I'd left it in the kitchenette. I grabbed it and quickly covered the computer in a thick brown sludge. It made a series of grim thanatotic bleeps and hisses, then issued a cloud of sparks and smoke. I grinned at Ava and she rolled her eyes and said, "Steve Jobs would be very impressed. Come on, let's get out of here."

• • ● • •

Her car was a derelict old Chrysler that started with a cantankerous series of clangs and wheezes. We pulled out onto the street and headed for the highway, wheels screeching at every turn. Somewhere in the distance I could hear a fleet of sirens. I let out an ecstatic whoop and turned to Ava, beaming.

"Thank you for helping," she said somberly. It was something of a buzzkill. That, and the fact that she had a disembodied head in her backpack. "Your car, did you leave it at the facility?"

"No, I carpooled with Zoha."

Ava nodded and then asked, "You will lose your job?"

"Probably."

She said nothing for a few minutes. "You are a good man, Leon the lion."

"Yeah, if I only had a brain." I giggled, but she said nothing. "It's from *The Wizard of Oz*..."

"Yes, I know. We have movies in Ecuador, too, you know. But it's the Scarecrow who wishes for a brain. The lion wishes to have courage."

"Oh."

"Which I think you *do* have," she smiled at me and gripped my hand, then released it to change gears.

"Can I ask you something?"

"Well, I think I owe you at least one little favor. What do you wish to know?"

"Why not just let your father stay in the dewar, let Cryotech deal with the whole mess?"

She looked at me intently, held her gaze for long enough that I was worried she'd crash into something. Finally she looked back at the highway and said, "You know what they do to the bodies of customers who cannot pay?" I shook my head. "They burn them. My father lost his faith at the end, but still, the idea of him being consumed by flames. I could not bear it. It is too... ah, you know..."

"Symbolic?"

"Exactly." She tipped her head toward the woods scrolling alongside us. "I think somewhere out here, it is quiet, no? Lots of trees. My father, he liked the out of doors."

"'Outdoors.'"

"What?"

"It's 'outdoors' not 'out of doors.'"

"Ah, yes. I knew this." The sound of the indicator clicked rhythmically over the engine's clunks and clanks. Its orange light pulsed over the dark highway. We drove onto a firebreak and jolted up and down as the car bounced over the unpaved ground. "From here, we must walk."

She killed the engine and grabbed her backpack. The sound of the door opening and closing was monstrously loud in the early morning silence. She popped the trunk, then swore loudly.

"What's wrong?" I asked, stepping out of the car.

"I remembered a torch but not a shovel. Fucking *idiot*!"

"You could…use the crowbar?" I suggested.

She shook her head, sighed and said, "Sure, why not? The perfect end to a perfect evening."

I held the torch as she plunged the crowbar into the ground and levered up some dirt. I wondered if the gentlemanly thing would be to offer to do the digging. I wasn't sure if chivalry extended to illegal burials of severed heads, so I just stood there awkwardly, watching her breath form clouds of mist in the cold January air.

When she'd cleared about a foot of earth she glanced at her watch and said, "That will have to do. I don't have much time before my flight. Give me the bag." I did as instructed and she tossed the backpack into the hole and covered it in dirt. She stomped the ground down, placed a rock over the top and then wiped her brow and looked at me. "I guess I should say something? He never actually had a funeral, you know. Because he did not think himself dead." She laughed bitterly and shook her head. "What an arrogant delusion, to not even accept your own death."

"A funeral would be a good idea, for closure?"

"Right. I'm going to do it in Spanish, if that is okay. So the words can travel right from my heart to the mouth without having to stop at my brain for translation."

"Of course. I understand."

She closed her eyes, crossed herself, and began murmuring in rapid Spanish that was mostly incomprehensible to me, although I did notice that her eulogy contained more profanity than was traditional. She opened her eyes and said awkwardly, "Do you… ah?" she waved her hand in dizzy circles at the broken earth.

"Um…sure." I stepped forward, stared at the stone and said, "Ernesto, I didn't know you well. Or at all. But you raised a confident, intelligent, beautiful daughter, which I guess means that for all your faults you must have had some good in you. At least enough to bring her into the world. It's a better place for having her in it." I felt her gaze on me, but willed myself not to look. "I hope you find heaven, in spite of this rather unusual detour." I turned the torch back to the car and said, "We should probably go."

Ava nodded and we half-jogged back to the car. She opened the trunk and pulled out a packet of baby wipes, then removed her jacket and said, "I will need you to get in the car and not turn around please. I am going to have a 'camping shower' before I go to the airport." I nodded and got in the car, listening to the sound of zips and buckles and finally the slamming of the trunk.

She sat down next to me in a fresh change of clothes, gunned the engine, and asked, "Were you flirting with me, just then?"

I rubbed the back of my neck and replied, "Well, I don't know if I'd call—"

"I have never had someone use a eulogy to hit on me before. I do not know if I should be flattered or disgusted. Perhaps both?" She drove out onto the highway.

I said nothing for a minute and then asked, "What did you say to Zoha, back at Cryotech?" Her smile was fluorescent in the early morning darkness.

"I told him that ours was the kind of love story that Shakespeare would have killed the Queen to have written, that we were going to run away and start a new life together. The old man is a romantic, I could see it in his eyes."

I laughed and replied, "Well, you're right about that. So, ah, did you really mean...?"

"Leon, we are on our way to the airport. I am leaving the country forever." Silence hung between us. The city glowed in the distance, a dull orange aura obscuring the stars above it. "But now that you have no job, perhaps you have time to travel somewhere? South America...maybe Quito?" I studied the highway lights strobing across her face as we drove.

"What's Quito like this time of year?"

"*Beautiful*, filled with color and music and wonderful people. It is the highest capital city in the world, the closest to the stars. You know, of course, that the word 'Ecuador' comes from 'equator'? It is at the middle of the Earth, never too hot, never too cold."

"Like Goldilocks?"

She laughed and said, "Yes. Exactly."

"That's what they call theoretical planets that can sustain human life—not too hot, not too cold. The Goldilocks principle."

"Ah, I did not know this. Perhaps Ecuador might be this for you, 'just right.' Like in the story."

I stared up at the night sky, filled with the ghosts of stars that stubbornly refused to acknowledge that they'd long ago been extinguished. So many of those pinpoints of celestial light were merely luminous afterimages rippling through the cold vacuum of space. Someday, myself, Ava, and every other living thing on Earth would be reduced to particles hurtling through the infinite void. But for now, we were simply two tiny creatures spinning around the sun at sixty-seven-thousand miles per hour, and there was an infinite array of possibilities and potential futures unfurling in front of us.

Nantucket Plunder

Steven Axelrod

My path to Poisoned Pen Press was halting and circuitous. I wrote some sketches about Nantucket. The only hint of a plot was a side story about a wealthy homeowner who stiffed all the people who worked on his house. When he was killed, every tradesman on Nantucket was a suspect.

I decided to develop that angle and rework the stories into a novel. That was in 2004. A couple of years later I had a book called Owners, *and got an agent for it. He put the book up for auction, but it didn't sell. His parting advice was to write another book with the same setting and characters, but more focus on plot, so I did. The novel* Locals *became my MFA creative thesis.*

The agent had passed along the publishers' e-mails, but there was one missing, from the "small but respected" house that might be a "good fallback choice." I checked the company website, saw that agents were not required, and first-time unpublished writers were preferred. So I sent Locals *to Poisoned Pen Press.*

Eight months later I got an e-mail about Locals *from Annette Rogers, an acquisitions editor. She told me they had never read* Owners *because they only read exclusive submissions. I was thrilled at the e-mail, and annoyed at my ex-agent, who hadn't bothered to research the submission policies of the companies where he submitted my work.*

I called Annette, we talked, I agreed to put "Nantucket" into the titles, and the rest is history—my personal history.

Finishing my fourth book, I still can't believe my luck. I still cringe when I get Annette's editorial letters, I still crow when I see the books on a bookstore shelf. It took a long time to get here, but I'm happy and grateful that I finally arrived.

—*S.A.*

• • ● • •

Mike Henderson was in trouble again.

His brushes with the law had never amounted to much—in fact, they had become a small private joke between us. There was the time he managed to give himself the best possible motive and no alibi for the most notorious murder in the island's history, or the time he was seen walking away from a murder scene with what looked like blood all over his hands. He was cleared both times—coincidence and paint.

But this was different. This was serious.

Five customers had filed theft reports on houses where Mike had been working over the winter. They'd arrived for the summer season, opened their houses, and found things missing. The five lists together made an impressive inventory: Tiffany silver, Reyes lightship baskets, a stash of Kruggerands. And there was a startling amount of original art gone missing: Rauschenberg collages, Jim Dine hearts, Hockney swimming pools, along with several pieces of Stickley furniture, and collections of Stafford-shire dogs and Rookwood pottery.

"This is no smash-and-grab break-in artist," Haden Krakauer said after I finished going through the missing property lists. My assistant chief was shrewd and cynical and he knew the island much better than I. He grew up on Nantucket and knew every-one and their families and their family scandals going back three generations. "This is a connoisseur. These robberies were curated."

"So ignore the usual suspects?"

"Well…"

Neither of us wanted to be accused of profiling but the fact remained that most of the house robberies on the island were committed either by drunk high school kids who had the alarm codes or by desperate immigrants trying to keep up with the rent, the food prices, or a shiny new all-American opioid addiction. It could be a landscaper from Jamaica, a mason's apprentice from Ecuador, a bus boy from Belarus—single or married, with kids or without. But those thefts all had a common accent, a familiar grammar—like English spoken badly. Those thieves stole bling and electronics—Apple watches and Xbox systems, flat screens and costume jewelry. Lots of fake diamond rings and pearl necklaces, along with the occasional valuable item, because they didn't know the difference.

This guy knew the difference. This was an educated, discerning thief who had access to the most well-guarded and expensively alarmed houses on the island. Which narrowed things down drastically—that was what Haden meant.

"I need the next list," I told him. "The list with the names of everyone who worked on those houses over the winter. Put Kyle Donnelly on it."

It took Kyle a few days of leveraging a lifetime of island contacts to pry information out of the close-knit community of builders and contractors. My friend, Pat Folger, had put up a guest cottage for one of the burglary victims; Billy Delavane had built the custom staircase. Kyle got a list of all Folger's subs—from electricians and plumbers to plasterers and painters. The other houses had no large-scale projects going on through the winter months, but Kyle contacted the owners, and through them he found the caretakers, and the caretakers gave him lists. Some owed him favors (a warning instead of a DUI), some had been pals with his grandfather. Some accepted the standard bribe: a Bud Lite eighteen-pack.

When the roll call was complete, Kyle surprised me by taking the next step. I'd been teaching him for five years; he was finally starting to learn something. Baby steps—simple procedure. But I made sure to give him what my old boss in L.A. used to all an "attaboy" when he laid the five long lists—and the one short list—on my desk the next Monday morning.

He had done the cross-referencing. Only three people had worked in all the burglarized houses in the off-season. Arturo Maturo, the plumber, Tom Danziger, the electrician—and Mike Henderson, the painter. They had all worked on the Lomax house a few years back and had all been suspects, briefly. They all had other secrets they were reluctant to share, and by the end of the investigation I felt more like a parish priest than a police officer. I gave them the only absolution I could; I let them go with a thank you and an apology.

But now they were all on the blotter again.

I cleared the first two quickly. Maturo had been draining the pipes after one of the families came up for Christmas and the kids had returned in March to grab some summer clothes. Their selfies showed most of the loot in the background. That let Maturo off the hook.

Danziger had done extensive re-wiring in two of the houses, and the inspector remembered various stolen objects still in place when came over to sign off on the work.

None of that cleared them of every house on the list, but we were assuming one thief and one modus operandi for all the crimes. Beyond that, Danziger and Maturo were unlikely suspects. Plumbers and electricians ruled as blue-collar royalty on Nantucket. They had no need for petty theft to augment their incomes and no reason to jeopardize their standing in the hierarchy of the building trades by stealing from their customers. At around two hundred bucks an hour, most people thought they were stealing anyway.

That left Mike Henderson.

As usual, he had no alibi. All the circumstantial evidence was against him. He had worked in all the houses, mostly alone. He had often remarked that painting was a socially sanctioned form of trespassing, and more than one client had fired him, accusing him of that very crime. He was always broke, scrounging a living from job to job, so he was motivated to pick up a few extra dollars by theft. He charged according to the model of car he found in the garage and felt no compunction about gouging the wealthy. So why not help himself to the odd silver teapot or lightship basket?

But he was angry and baffled when I brought him in for questioning. It's hard to fake that level of outrage.

"Check my bank account! See if you can find all this money I'm supposed to be stealing. I hope you do find it! I could use it. We're a month behind on our mortgage payments right now."

I pushed against the edge of my desk, rolled my chair back a few inches. We were talking in my office, much to Haden Krakauer's dismay. He liked doing things by the book. As far as my assistant chief was concerned, Mike was a suspect in a string of B&E felonies, and ought to be treated that way. I wasn't so sure. I hadn't arrested Mike, and I didn't want to Mirandize him. I wanted to talk, but I wasn't going to shove him into an interrogation room like a common criminal.

At least not yet. "Your bank account is the last place I'd expect you to stash stolen money, Mike. You told me yourself—small-time house-painters are the last stalwarts of the cash economy."

"Thanks a lot."

"You don't work for big contractors. You don't carry worker's comp. Not since the Lomax job. You don't have big crew any-more, either—or a big payroll to meet. When you need a forty-foot ladder, or someone you trust to roll a ceiling, you ask your friends. Right?"

"Right."

"It's a collective. You all fly under the radar and you all prefer cash payments, rolls of hundreds—"

"Nantucket Sawbucks."

"Exactly."

"Some people call them Nantucket Tens, but that sounds like a political movement."

"Maybe you are a political movement. Guerilla painting… steal from the rich and give to the poor. Which would be you, I assume. Unless you're also donating to the food bank."

"I can't afford to donate to anyone! It's like my dad used to say, I have to take out a loan to pay attention."

"And yet your wife is driving a brand new Jeep Grand Cherokee."

"That was a gift. From her father."

"And you can prove that."

"Do I have to?"

"You might."

"So you can just…audit my whole life over some random accusation?"

I shrugged. "It's one way to prove you're innocent."

"When we asked Cindy's dad to help us pay for Montessori school, it was just like this. 'Should you really be going out to dinner in your financial situation?' 'That sounds like quite the expensive vacation for a fellow in your straightened circumstances.'"

"So what did you do?"

"I told him to take his money and go fuck himself, and I put the kids in public school."

"Good for you."

"That wouldn't really work in this case."

"No, but I'll tell you something, Mike. I'm going to stick with the foundational assumption of American jurisprudence—that you're innocent until proven guilty. Still, someone's been stealing stuff out of the houses you work on."

"So…what are you going to do?"

I gave him my best encouraging smile. "Catch them."

Unfortunately, I had another criminal matter to deal with that day, one much closer to home. It had begun the week before, with Jane Stiles' yard sale. Rain had forced the event inside and we spent the morning hastily arranging antique furniture, glassware, rugs and runners, and a rack of vintage women's dresses in the cramped confines of her cottage.

Otherwise, the sale was normal: advertised for ten o'clock, with the first early birds showing up at eight, helping themselves to a Downyflake donut from the traditional box of a dozen Jane always set out for the shoppers.

The usual crowd appeared by the formal start of the sale—long-time customers (Jane's family ran a legendary consignment store back in the day), old friends, and the small tribe of local hoarders and collectors, along with the occasional tourist.

The scroungers were a diverse group—from high school history teacher Roy Danvers to Sam Trikilis, my garbage man; from landscapers and masons to Sheriff Bob Bulmer; and a dot-com millionaire who had just bought the giant house next door. The music from his parties on those early summer nights made Jane feel like Nick Carraway in *The Great Gatsby*.

The kids all pitched in, Caroline talking up the merchandise and horse-trading the prices, Tim manning the cash box. Jane's son, Sam, helped carry the smaller items to the cars. The sale went well and the rain let up in the early afternoon, with a fresh south wind tearing the clouds apart, revealing ragged patches of blue sky. In accordance with another long-standing Stiles family tradition, we skimmed some of the cash proceeds and treated ourselves to dinner for five at the Sconset Café.

That was Sunday night. Tuesday morning Jane noticed that her fore-edge books were missing. She hadn't included them in the sale and never would. They had belonged to her grandfather and she had inherited them after a scuffle with her sister, who had taken the five volumes from the old man's house the day he died, along with a Matisse screen and various other valuables. Fortunately the will specified that Jane got the books, and she managed to recover them. Her sister already had them packaged up and ready to auction off on eBay.

I had never seen a fore-edge book before and neither had my kids. They're the perfect artifact for a detective, because the art they feature—in the case of Jane's books, paintings of various Nantucket landmarks—is hidden. The images only appear on the outside edge of the pages when you fan the book open. With the book closed, there's no way to know the pictures exist.

It's a book! It's a toy! Tim seemed particularly fascinated with the trick, as well as the subject matter. Many of the featured destinations no longer existed—the black Washing Pond water tower, the old Straight Wharf Theater. He even said he'd love to buy one if he only had the money and Jane was willing to part with it. I think she found his enthusiasm touching.

But then, on Tuesday, she saw him riding away from her cottage on his bike with his school backpack bulging.

And the books were gone.

It may seem like an open-and-shut case from this brief description: Tim had motive and opportunity. But Jane was mostly living with me that summer, and only used the cottage for a writing studio. Most of the time the place was deserted and she'd never even owned a key to the front door. Anyone who'd been snooping around at the sale could have come back for what my old boss in L.A., Chuck Obremski, used to call a "five-finger discount." Everyone there had a motive, and anyone who took the time to study Jane's routines had an opportunity.

But Tim was the only one Jane saw at the scene of the crime.

"I hate to even bring this up," she'd said that night after dinner. We had strolled into town and were walking along Easy Street. She sat down on one of the benches facing the harbor.

"Tell me," I said.

So she did.

We sat in silence for a while.

"You know he didn't do it," I said finally.

"I hope he didn't. But he was out there by himself the day after the sale. What was he doing there?"

"I don't know."

"You're going to have to ask him."

"Yeah." Then after a few moments: "How would it work in one of your books?"

She relaxed a little, reached out a hand to let a passing Labradoodle take a sniff. She had time for one quick ruffle behind the ears before the owner, a slim blonde in a yoga outfit, yanked him away. Jane squinted in thought. "You'd need parts of all five books to crack a code. Or maybe they'd be clues to some kind of crazy scavenger hunt."

"How about someone just taking them and selling them to collectors?"

"Naaa. Too boring."

"But this is the real world, and they're worth a lot of money."

"I guess."

"Tim doesn't need money. He's a kid. He gets an allowance."

"Unless he's on drugs. Or something."

"But he's not. I know the signs. And so do you."

She nodded. We sat for a while more. An artist started setting up to paint the view. "You still need to talk to him," she said.

I shrugged. "Interrogations are my specialty."

"Innocent until proven guilty," Mike Henderson said the next day, riding shotgun in my cruiser. "Not too many people really believe that. In America it's more like you're guilty even after you're proven innocent—like O.J. Simpson, or that car guy. DeLorean. He was acquitted, too. But everybody knows he sold coke to finance his car company."

"You're a cynical man, Mike," I said.

"Which makes me normal. And you're not cynical at all— which makes you kind of a freak, to be honest. But in a good way."

"Especially right now."

I was investigating the burglarized jobsites, talking to the families. I had Mike with me because I wanted his painter's eye on the crime scenes, and I was curious to see how he'd react to the victims. More importantly, I wanted them to see Mike on good terms with the chief, and cooperating with law enforcement.

Nothing we had found out so far made his case look any better. Two houses had surveillance cameras working year-round, and both had been crudely disabled. One was covered by a piece of the burlap used by landscapers for wrapping shrubs to block the cold. Hungry deer chewed through the burlap sometimes, and the wind could have blown a scrap against the lens. But this piece of fabric was cut cleanly, with a knife—like the Swiss Army knife that Mike always carried. The other house was even more damning. What looked like bird droppings obscuring the camera lens turned out to be paint—the very paint Mike had been using on the job.

The victims didn't share my quaint beliefs about innocence and guilt any more than Mike did. They weren't pleased to see him, but they had to pretend to welcome me. At least I got detailed inventories of the missing items. "My *belongings*," one of the women moaned to me.

"A Stickley table, two Tiffany lamps, a first edition of the 1930 Random House *Moby Dick* with the Rockwell Kent illustrations. You have quite an eye, buddy," I said to Mike.

"Someone does."

I sighed. "It's hard to hate a criminal who loves Rockwell Kent."

"He doesn't love Rockwell Kent! He knows he can get a couple of grand for the book. He's probably sold it already."

Cynic.

We caught a break on the last house Mike had painted, a hulking pile on Medouie Creek Road in Polpis. Mike still had the keys and the alarm codes. The family wasn't going to arrive for another week. As usual, they had threatened to be on-island by Memorial Day to crack the whip on the tradesmen, but weren't actually due until the Fourth of July. "They think we work because we're afraid of them," Mike said. "Actually we work because we want to get paid. False panic is not required."

It was a perfect late-June day, the island lush and green after a rainy spring, the sky a flawless blue. Even the humidity had broken. We approached the silent house over the perfectly mani-cured lawn and Mike said, "This is what they pay the million dollars for. A day like this. But look—" He pointed to the small squat city of air-conditioning condensers buzzing at the side of the house. "The most delicious sea breeze in America and they never even open their windows. That's the new money around here, in a nutshell."

"An impeccably climate-controlled nutshell," I added.

"Exactly. Well, here we are."

He let us in, and poked the alarm code into the pad by the front door.

"Did you notice anything missing?" I asked as we walked into the hotel lobby-chill of the foyer.

He shrugged. "I really don't pay that much attention."

"Not a great slogan for a house painter."

"Come on, Chief! I notice a bad cut-in, okay? I'm the king of latex touch-up. But I'm not casing the joint when I'm supposed to be stripping the trim."

I looked around the massive "great room" with its thirty-foot ceiling and wall of fifteen-light French doors. "So you're finished here."

"Yeah. We packed up yesterday."

"But the cleaning people haven't started."

"I think they come in tomorrow."

"Well, that's a plus."

I found the stain ten minutes later. I saw it as an irregularity in the pattern of a woven-cotton area rug, sticking out from the hem of the cloth draping an end table. I was on my knees sniffing it when Mike walked up behind me.

"Did you spill coffee here?" I said, moving the table aside. The lamp teetered and Mike reached out to steady it.

"No."

"You're sure?"

"No coffee on the job. That's one of my rules. People leave the cups around, or knock them over. It looks bad, unprofessional. Most of my customers don't even let their kids eat anywhere but the kitchen. They're neat freaks. You have to respect that."

I nodded. "Well someone spilled hazelnut coffee here. Take a sniff."

He got down, put his nose to the rug. Standing, he said, "Yeah. And it's fresh. Maybe a couple of days old, tops."

I pointed down to the wedge of carpet between the couch and the end table.

"Crumbs," he said.

I smiled. "A trail of bread crumbs. Just a like a fairy tale."

He bent down, picked one up on a moistened fingertip, touched it to his tongue. "But this was a cookie."

We moved the table aside and found a small triangular wedge hidden under the skirt of the couch. I pulled on a latex glove, took an evidence bag and a pair of tweezers from my pocket, and dropped the cookie chunk inside. "Now we figure out where this came from and who ordered it with a hazelnut coffee."

Mike shook his head in amused disgust. "And learn what kind of lazy pig brings treats and coffee to his own crime scene."

"And spills the coffee and laughs because he knows they'll blame it on the painter."

"Story of my life."

The next part was easy. Michelle at Fast Forward—we'd been friends since I gave her a copy of *The House at Pooh Corner* to exorcise the Disney demons from her daughter's mind—identified my evidence instantly.

She took it on her tongue for a few seconds, wincing at where it had been, then spit it out onto a napkin and gave it back. "That's one of Dany's health cookies. No dairy, no eggs, no sugar. She makes them with tahini. They're totally unique."

"So…does anyone order hazelnut coffee and one of these?"

She thought for a minute or two while she poured a few cups of coffee for nervous customers. I was wearing my uniform and everyone was feeling guilty about something.

Michelle made change for someone and turned to the other girl behind the counter. "Angie? Can you think of anyone?"

"Just Bob Bulmer. The sheriff? But he drinks decaf. Does it matter if it's decaf?"'

"Not really."

"Is he in trouble?" Michelle asked.

"No, no. Though you have to wonder about someone who drinks hazelnut decaf."

"Now what?" Mike asked me later as I drove him back to his jobsite.

I looked up at the imposing three-story shingled pile, dormers lined up on the steep roof, presided over by the freshly painted widow's walk. "Now we stake out this place—and catch him in the act."

But we were too late. Mike had been working downstairs and hadn't ventured into the finished bedrooms for weeks. A quick walk-through of the second floor told the tale like a tour guide: picture hooks where paintings had hung, end tables with circles in the dust, dents in the carpet where an antique dresser had stood.

Mike looked like he was about to cry. "If we don't find this stuff before the Binghams show up…Jesus. Someone hates me."

"Someone's stalking you," I said.

"What?"

"It's the only way they could get in to these houses. You unlock the doors. You disable the alarms."

"Yeah. But I'm always—oh, shit."

"What?"

"I drive into town for lunch, or to pick up some supplies from Marine, and sometimes I—it's a hassle locking up and setting the alarms if I'm only going to be gone for half an hour. And also…they monitor the systems. I don't want my customers knowing when I'm gone or how long I take for lunch. It's none of their business."

"And who's going to know? Or notice?"

"Exactly! This isn't inner-city Detroit. What is a burglar supposed to do? Try every mansion and hope for an unlocked one and then try every unlocked one for a disconnected alarm?"

"No, Mike. He's supposed to choose a house painter, track his movements, and use the time, however long it is, when he leaves the house open, to do the burglaries. Then the burglar just waits. The homeowners come back in the summer and the painter gets the blame. If he really does hate you, it's a win-win."

"So this is about the Bradley?"

Bulmer had pushed a warrant through Town Meeting the year before. He wanted the town to buy him a U.S. Army surplus Bradley Fighting Vehicle. Some prominent citizens took his side in the debate, including Jonathan Pell, the new CEO of Logran

Corporation, and a consortium of real estate brokers who were concerned about property values.

But you have to see a Bradley to realize how crazy this idea was. It's a small tank, perfect for enforcing martial law in a conquered city—a deranged and surreal choice for Nantucket.

Mike had said some harsh things about Bulmer, calling him a would-be tin-pot dictator and a fascist blowhard. David Trezize ran Mike's guest editorial in the *Nantucket Shoals*, and the link on the little newspaper's website had been shared more than a thousand times.

The Bradley was voted down by acclamation.

A bad defeat; and Bulmer was famous for his grudges. That sounded like a motive to me. And as sheriff, Bulmer's main job was driving around; mostly he delivered summonses. He had plenty of free time for surveillance.

But some wild conjectures, a coffee stain, and a handful of cookie crumbs weren't enough to arrest him for.

And I had another suspect to deal with.

The next day I took Tim to Something Natural. We got a pair of lobster salad sandwiches, some Matt Fee tea, and a couple of bags of chips. We drove out to the new standpipe on Washing Pond Road. The gate was open and we cruised past the giant white metal water tank to the grassy verge that overlooked the jumble of houses edging the western moors. I explained the situation while we ate. The strong south wind nudged my cruiser.

"I didn't take those books," he said. "I swear. Where would I even put them? Someone would see them. Carrie would tell on me."

I nodded, finished my iced tea. "So what were you doing out there?"

"Nothing."

"Come on. That's a long bike ride for nothing."

"Dad!"

"Tell me."

"It's private."

He stared away, out the car window, following a red-tailed hawk as it circled the valley. I was going to have to put this one together myself. Jane had seen him at the bookshelf. The comment about the fore-edge book must have been a hasty improvisation to cover whatever it was he was really doing there. The sudden interest in antique endpaper watercolors had struck me as a little odd anyway. I had studied Jane's library myself and there was no adolescent contraband there, nothing racy beyond a copy of *Lolita*. But Jane kept some photographs her ex-husband had taken of her, the only ones she had ever looked good in, or so she said. She was planning to crop one of them for a new dust-jacket portrait. "The whole picture might sell more copies," she had joked when she showed it to me. She was topless, coming out of the water at Pickle Beach, our informal nude bathing strand. And Jane was right. She looked great in the photo—sea nymph, slim and girlish, perfect fodder for a seventh-grade crush.

Tim would never admit to finding that picture and I would never force him to. I needed a new tactic.

"Okay," I said. "I have to tell Jane something, so let's think of a reason you might have been out there. Not the real reason—whatever it was. That's none of my business. As long as you didn't actually steal anything."

"Are you kidding? I would never do that."

I keyed the ignition and started backing up. "Here's a lesson from the adult world. If you're suspected of something, confess to something else. Something not as bad but maybe…a little embarrassing?"

"Like what?"

"Well…Jane has a collection of vintage Barbies at the cottage. Maybe you were playing with them."

"But those are girls' toys!"

"Exactly. So you wouldn't automatically admit it, the initial denial is explained…and no one ever thinks about whatever it was you were really looking at."

He thought about this as we turned off Washing Pond Road and headed back into town. "You're sneaky," he said.

"But for a good cause."

"Barbies? Really?"

"It'll be great. Jane will think you're a budding feminist."

"I am a budding feminist."

I patted his knee. "Good for you."

I was on a roll that week. Mike Henderson's case came together the next day.

Pat Folger called to tell me he had found squatters in one of the houses he did caretaking for. The illegal tenants were brothers from Ecuador who worked for Quidnet Land Design, one of the biggest gardening firms on the island. Pat knew I was interested in squatters and their stories. These three had been evicted from Bob Bulmer's house on Essex Road. The area was known for its barracks-style housing, with as many as twenty people crammed into three or four bedrooms, all paying a thousand dollars a month for the privilege of heat, running water, and a roof over their heads. It was a great deal for the landlord, though.

So why would Bulmer have evicted them?

Maybe he had an even more profitable venture going. Maybe he needed the space for storage.

But how to find out? I decided to reverse the tactic I had shared with Tim. Bulmer's barracks housing scheme was illegal, but fairly common, and we cracked down on the worst offenders from time to time. Bob knew he got a free pass from the town because of his law-enforcement position. But that was going to change. I called Paul Higgins, our building inspector, and he agreed to make a surprise visit to the Essex Road house, looking for safety violations or an overtaxed septic system.

I'd be there to check out the real crime.

Bob had no idea I suspected him of anything beyond some building-code violations, and so he was happy to give us a tour of his now-empty house.

I found Jane's fore-edge books prominently displayed on the mantel, between two of her sitting-dog bookends.

Bob waved a pudgy hand around the living room. "No illegal tenants! Are we good?"

I hefted one of Jane's books. "I'm good, Bob. But you're busted."

When I told Jane the story later that night she said, "Bullmer, ugh. I think he was rifling through my photographs, too. They're all in different order now."

"Does it bother you? Him seeing, you know—the uncropped versions?"

She shrugged. "A little. But what the hell. Boys will be boys."

"Right, you are."

I remembered my boy as we sat by the water tower, his face turned away in shame, and thought, you'll never know how right.

But that secret was safe with me.

Sunday Drive

James Sallis

Years ago I wrote a novel titled Drive. *New York publishers didn't want it. Too short. Too quirky. Too pulpy.*

Rob at Poisoned Pen Press did. And so, as it turned out, did a lot of others.

When Poisoned Pen Press knocks at the door, I hitch up my pants and answer.

—J.S.

• • ● • •

Because it's the weekend, traffic is light, and once we get out of downtown, where I parked on the street quite a ways off, having made the parking-lot mistake once before, we've got smooth sailing, calm seas, all that. Caroline stares out the window, talking about how much this area has changed, the whole city, really, that you can hardly recognize it from what it used to be. Mattie, in the back, is texting one-handed on her new iPhone, nibbling at a Pop-Tart in such a way that the edge is always even. She holds it away from her mouth every few bites to check.

When I suggest that we take a little drive, not hurry home, Mattie groans, then looks away as I glance in the rearview mirror. "Whatever you want is fine," Caroline says.

I jump on I-10, then the 202 out toward Tempe and all those other far-flung lands. Back years ago, when Caroline and I were first married, I worked these roads, running heavy equipment, backhoes, bulldozers. Knew every mile of highway, every block of city street. Then I went back to school and got my degree. Now I program computers and solve IT problems all day long. Now I can barely find my way around out here in this world.

"The music was lovely," Caroline says. "Back there."

"Puccini, yes."

"The story was dumb," Mattie says, leaning hard on the final word. So at least she was paying that much attention.

We drive out past the airport and hotels to the left, cheap apartments, garages, and ramshackle convenience stores to the right, past a building that looks like a battleship and that I swear was not here the last time we came this way, past the two hills near the zoo that look like humongous dung heaps. Wind is picking up, blowing food wrappers and blossoms from bougainvillea in bursts across the road.

Caroline fidgets with the radio, cakewalking through top forty, light jazz, classical, country. Trying to regain something of what we felt momentarily, by proxy, back there? Trying to muffle the silence that presses down on us? Or just bored? What the hell do *I* know about human motivation, anyway?

On impulse I exit, loop around, and get on the 51 heading north. Soon we're cruising through the stretch of cactus-spackled hills everyone calls Dreamy Draw. Caroline has something peppy and lilting about a lost love playing on the radio. Ukulele is involved. Mattie leans forward to listen to the music as three Harleys come up on our left, their throaty *raaaa* like a bubble enclosing us. All three riders have expensive leather jackets and perfectly cut hair.

At the 101, the Harleys swing right toward Scottsdale. We head west for I-17 to begin the slow climb out of the valley, through Deadman Wash, Bumble Bee, Rock Springs. Where clouds hang above hills, the hills are dark. Nascent yellow blooms sprout from the ends of saguaro arms. Caroline stares off, not toward the horizon or into green-shot gorges, but out her window at dry flatland and cholla. Mattie is asleep.

In the distance, out over one of the mesas, hawks glide on thermals.

• • ● • •

Close to the end of the second act of *Turandot*, about the time Calaf was getting ready to ring the gong and lay his life on the line for love, the old geezer sitting in front of me, the one whose wife had been elbowing him to keep awake, began weeping uncontrollably. She elbowed him again, more English on it this time, and after a moment he struggled to his feet and staggered up the stairs and out. I followed. When I caught up, he was standing motionless by one of the windows. He could have been part of a diorama, twenty-first-century man in his unnatural habitat.

"You okay?"

He looked up, looked at the window, finally looked at me. I could see the world struggling to reboot behind his eyes.

A minute ago I was thinking how all these people paid sixty or a hundred dollars to spiff themselves up and sit through two hours of largeness and artifice—grand emotion, bright colors, carnival—before going back to their own small lives. Now I was thinking about just one of those people, and how sometimes we find expression for our pain, how it can just fall upon us.

"I didn't want to come to this. My wife's employer, she works for a doctor, he gave her tickets he couldn't use. She insisted we come. I knew it was a bad idea."

"Because…?"

He shook his head.

"Let's get some air," I said.

We stepped outside, where life-size sculptures of dancers, canted forward on one leg, arms outstretched, had found refuge from time and the Earth's pull. A beautiful day. Across the street an old woman stood behind a cardboard podium singing arias much like those going on inside. Poorly dyed gray hair fell in strands that looked like licorice sticks. Her dress had once been purple. My companion was watching her, no expression on his face.

He took out his wallet, pulled something from one of the photo holders and began unfolding it.

"Nineteen seventy-six, when I was working the pipeline." He held it out for me to see. "Twelve hundred and ninety dollars. One week's work."

It was a check. You could make that out, but not much else. When I looked back up and smiled, he looked at the check.

"Guess you can't make it out too good anymore."

He folded it carefully, put it back. Glanced again at the diva, who had one foot in the door of *Nessun dorma*. The strangeness of hearing the piece as a soprano aria matched perfectly the strangeness of the setting.

"Well, young man," he said, "we should go back in now."

We did, and even before I retook my seat I sensed that something had changed. The audience seemed poised, expectant. And was there a void onstage? One of several court scenes, better than a dozen attendants and functionaries in place. The patterns were wrong. What, I asked, sliding in next to Caroline, had happened?

A cast member—the forester, she thought—had collapsed and been spirited out, with barely a breath's hesitation, by two others. Made quite a rattle and bang when he hit the floor. It was a major aria for the ice princess, of course, and with but a moment's glance toward the commotion, the soprano had flawlessly continued, inching toward the inevitable high C or whatever it was. A woman two rows back had asked her companions, loudly, if this was a part of the show.

The rest passed without incident, building inexorably to its grandly happy, unrelenting conclusion, soprano soaring like a seabird, tenor stolidly tossing his voice to the rafters, chorus dug in and determined to hold its own, orchestra a clash with horns and percussion.

Turandot had been wrong.

Now the riddles were solved, the gong would sound no more.

And we were outside, moving within moving corridors of other opera-goers, past the bronze dancers, past the diva with her cardboard podium, reclaimed by our lives.

• ● ● ● •

Just this side of Sunset Point, Mattie has one of her seizures. Doesn't happen much anymore, with the medication, but we're used to it from the old days. Something starts thumping against the seat, I look back, and it's her legs spasming. I edge off the road, get in the back with her, and hold her till it stops. From the first, right after Mattie was born, Caroline never was much good at handling that. She'd fall to pieces or just kind of go away. As the seizures got worse, so did the going away. I don't blame her. Or anyone. Things just happen.

We're back on the road in four, five minutes, Caroline looking out the window, Mattie sleeping it off. We inch up the hill and around a long curve behind three semis. Our speed drops to 55, 48, 44, 40. Atop the hill we're able to pass. I roll down the window. The air is fresh and cool. Something with that unmistakable pulse of baroque music—strings, horns, keyboard continuo—plays on the radio. It begins to cut out, like a stutterer, as we gain altitude.

Mattie wakes, rattles a box of Jolly Ranchers to see how much is left, pops one in her mouth and sucks away. We're ten thousand feet up and there's a pinpoint puncture, our air's hissing slowly out. That's what it sounds like.

"What do you want to do about dinner?" Caroline says.

I'm thinking about a movie I'd like to see. There's this family. The father goes off to his job every day, it's exciting work, all about people and solving real problems for them, and he comes home and talks about it over the dinner table, where they all eat together. The mother's a teacher, so she tells what went on at school, funny things her kids said today, how much better some of them are doing, how others still have problems with fractions or irregular verbs or something like that. The daughter talks about school, too, and her friends, and about track-team practice this afternoon. She's healthy, vibrant, and isn't going to die before she ever gets to be an adult.

"We can pick up burgers at the corner on the way home," Caroline says. "That work for you?"

I think of Montezuma's Castle just miles from here, an entire city built high into a hillside, accessible only by long ladders. Back in the day we'd go on picnics at a little park not far from there. I want to say, "There's no magic left in my name, little one. No magic anymore in these hills. In the sun, yes, and in the sky. But those are far away." I don't, of course.

We're into the thick of it now, hill and curve, hill and curve. The drop-offs have shifted to the right, Caroline's side. In a minute we'll be there, the highest point, the deepest drop. I pick up speed and Caroline looks over at me. Upset that I'm going too fast? Or does she sense something more?

I look in the rearview mirror. Mattie has gone back to sleep. Good.

This is where we get off.

The Paternoster Pea

Priscilla Royal

I blame Mary Reed and Eric Mayer for leading me to Poisoned Pen Press. Discovering their wonderful Byzantine mysteries made me think their press might not reject a series because the sleuth and era were a bit different. Thirteen years ago, I was a very rejected writer...

And the Press allowed e-mail submissions! Having paid a small fortune in postage, this won my bank account's heart. The next pleasant surprise was encountering the man I later called The Gatekeeper to the Dream, Monty Montee. He was responsive, encouraging, and professional. When PPP turned down my first quirky modern cozy, I e-mailed to ask if I could submit a medieval. His positive reply arrived almost instantly. I sent even faster. Soon after, Prioress Eleanor and Brother Thomas found a home. I had four glasses of wine that night (I rarely drink) and never felt a thing! Years later, things haven't changed much. I am still in love with Poisoned Pen Press and all the wonderful people who work there.

—P.R.

• • ● • •

Robert Wynethorpe smiled as he walked through a flock of loudly squawking, colorful fowl and stepped over piles of greenish manure in the castle courtyard. He shouldn't be in such a good mood on this chill East Anglian afternoon, not with the task his father had set for him just ahead, but he never could stay in bad humor for long.

Ever since his elder brother, Hugh, had gone off on Crusade, Robert had been in charge of the estate. He loved the land, he did, everything that grew in it, and the beasts that grazed it. And, unlike his warrior brother, Robert was good at farming, something their father appreciated because it left the good Baron more time to play his beloved political games in the court of the aged King Henry III. Robert hated politics; he hated fights; and he especially hated having to host this meeting between his best friend and another man, of near equal rank but greater rancor, to settle a nasty quarrel.

At least he had had the good judgement to seek advice from his younger sister on this dangerous conflict between two men who owed fealty to their father. Eleanor was now prioress at Tyndal Priory, and he was much relieved when she offered to help resolve this issue between the noblemen. Despite her youth, she was gaining quite the reputation as an equitable judge of disputes. Some were even suggesting she was divinely inspired. Having grown up with her, Robert rather doubted she was exactly *divinely inspired*, but he had always respected her common sense.

It was her arrival that had just been announced and brought him into the castle courtyard. As he made his way through a small herd of goats, Robert saw her at the gate with her usual attendant, Sister Anne.

Eleanor was a tiny woman, dressed in virtuous simplicity, who sat serenely on the humble donkey she had named after their beloved father. He wondered why she'd done that, but knowing his little sister's wicked wit, he decided he might not want to learn what specific parental quality the small gray beast had brought to mind. To know and perhaps laugh would make him feel disloyal to their father, and Robert was nothing if not loyal to family and friends.

His good mood now vanished like a summer sun behind thunderclouds. Entering the courtyard just behind the two women was the colorful party of Sir George of Lavenham, a man well known for superb horses, fine attire, and profound appreciation of the feminine gender. Robert might love George like a brother, but the man's occasionally injudicious admiration of women had brought his childhood friend into this conflict.

Some weeks ago, Sir Thomas Edwardston had accused George of seducing his older sister and getting her with child. George had denied the charge. In this case, Robert believed him, but not out of naïve belief in his friend's virtue. He knew that George avoided virgins, preferring to play with married women who had more experience in the pleasures of the bed. Indeed, had Robert been married, he would have feared far more for his wife's virtue than for his sister's even in her pre-convent days. Not that Eleanor hadn't been a match for any man even in those tender years.

His good humor returned with the thought.

"Dearest Sister!" He stepped forward to help Eleanor down from her small mount. Then in an overly bright tone he added, "And Sister Anne! What a joy to see you."

Robert did not like Sister Anne and failed to understand why his sister invariably required her company on these journeys outside the priory. The woman was almost of a man's height and never hesitated to speak her mind on medical matters. Her reputation for scholarship in herbal cures and potions was well known, and Robert had both grown up with and liked educated, intelligent women. But he still preferred them to maintain a modest behaviour in public and to have a softer form than this angular companion.

Robert looked at Sister Anne riding astride the gray beast with her feet dragging inelegantly just inches above the ground and stifled a snort. Glancing at him, Sister Anne slid off her own donkey without his assistance.

"Had Father not chosen you to care for the estate in our eldest brother's absence, Robert, you would have made a fine courtier with that too-silver tongue of yours."

"Ah, Eleanor!"

"And your steward's dear wife? Will she be preparing the usual room for Sister Anne and me?"

Robert grinned. The steward's "dear" wife was a termagant who had long been a source of humor between them. "As we speak. With the requisite water for bathing and fresh rushes for the floors, strewn, at my command, with rosemary and lavender for my dearest sister and the most welcome Sister…"

The prioress put her hand up to her brother's mouth. "Shush, Robert. More such lies about Sister Anne and no priest will have time to shrive you of all your sins." Little escaped his sister's notice, including his dislike of her chosen companion.

Before Robert could reply, a muscular arm swung around his shoulder and jerked him backward. "And what has your incomparable steward arranged for your oldest friend?" Robert elbowed George in the gut, which only caused the man to laugh. "It is well Hugh went off to the Holy Land, Robert. A sultan's warriors would need only a puff of breath to knock you to the ground."

Robert frowned. "Less levity, George. We haven't much time. It's a serious business, this charge of Edwardston's. Tonight you and he must come to an amicable settlement. Father was clear he would brook no ill feelings between you two." He hesitated. "Have you given thought to Edwardston's proposal that you marry his sister?"

"I'd sooner marry my best yellow hunting bitch."

"The Lady Sarah is hardly a dog, my friend, and it is time for you to think of taking a wife, in any event," Robert said.

"Indeed, I would not choose to join hands with an Edwardston kin of my own volition. But had his sister been to my liking, I might have at least considered the prospect. But Edwardston has tried to force her on me with false accusation, and her spawn is that of another man. 'S Blood, Robert! I expect to father my own sons, not borrow them."

"But borrow them you will, my lord," Eleanor interjected, "unless you wish to incur the wrath of my father. Or are you able to produce the real perpetrator of this injustice against the poor woman?"

"Lady Eleanor! Forgive me. I have forgotten myself. My language was coarse and nothing a woman of your piety and virtue should hear." George bowed deeply, both to hide his reddened face and to honor the only woman he had ever wanted to marry from the time they were children together.

The loud clopping of hooves announced the arrival of another party of horsemen.

Eleanor and her companions turned slowly and watched them enter.

• • ● • •

Edwardston was dour, a man of wealth and many followers yet increasingly fewer friends. He was a collector of debts, human and pecuniary, and in the collecting saw only the value to himself. Although known for charity, his generosity was calculated and without compassion. As time passed, he found his only true comfort in his priest, who was grateful to Edwardston for his comfortable position, and thrice-daily mass with which he hoped to provide his soul with lodging in Paradise.

Thus it was that his sole male attendants on this occasion were his priest, who also acted as his physician, and the poor son of a lackland knight, Timothy. Some wondered if the young man was an early Edwardston by-blow, for his narrowed eyes and perpetually creased brow closely resembled his master's. Others noted that the young man's expression was not uncommon amongst those who lived with the landed but had nothing of their own.

Behind Edwardston and his men was a litter carrying the Lady Sarah at such a distance that it seemed almost an afterthought. She also was minimally attended. A solemn-faced woman of indeterminate years rode beside her on a dull-coated mare.

"'S Blood! He brings both forger and chain, Robert," George muttered, glancing at the priest, then at the litter.

"I warned you. He means to have her married."

"I swear my innocence! Let me prove it in combat!" George slammed his fist against his chest.

"My lord father has forbidden it," Robert whispered. "He wants neither of you dead for such a thing as a woman with child, who, I will repeat, would make you a perfectly good wife with the lands she'd bring. You would gain in rents and he in status. A good match, methinks."

"I will not have another man's leavings for my firstborn."

"If you refuse the lady and the true father of her child cannot be determined, then my sister must rule on fair recompense that you both agreed upon."

"I respect your sister, Robert, as you know I always have, and will honor my word to your father. But, between the two of us, how can she make such a judgement? A woman given to God can know nothing of men and their ways."

"But much of women and theirs, my lords, which may suit us just as well," Eleanor said as she walked past the two men on her way to the litter.

"Come, my dear," she said, extending a hand to the plain-faced woman, dressed in familial black but beginning to bloom in motherhood. "Let us have some wine to refresh our bodies and prayer to refresh our souls."

Quickly forgotten by the men, who turned to scowl at each other, the women walked off together in companionable small talk toward the stone stairs of Wynethorpe Castle.

• • ● • •

Robert Wynethorpe was a generous host, even under circumstances less convivial than he would have preferred. That night the minstrels played in the gallery above while servants rushed through the hall with trays of swan neck pudding, roast salmon in onion wine sauce, and savory spiced venison pies. Red wines flowed, and trenchers swelled with the sweet fat of rich meats.

Edwardston begrudged a smile when he was presented with a particularly fine slab of salmon. George, who normally reveled in a fine meal, looked pale, but even he picked steadily, albeit dispiritedly, at his food.

The prioress sat with the Lady Sarah and Sister Anne. Eleanor, honoring the Rule of Saint Benedict, refrained from all meat, ate only vegetables and sipped moderately at the wine. Lady Sarah, looking pinker in the cheek than she had upon arrival, spoke softly in the prioress' ear.

And Sister Anne was engaged in a spirited discussion with Edwardston's priest on the subject of whether Galen or Hippocrates had the better treatment for intestinal wind. Robert wished he had seated both of them further away from his own ears, preferably between Edwardston and Lavenham, who were so engaged in their own thoughts that they would be deaf to such a detailed discussion.

After the main courses had disappeared into the mouths of men and two favored hounds, the prioress put her hand on Sister Anne's arm and whispered in her ear. The good sister relayed the message to Robert.

He waved his hand, and the minstrels ceased their play.

"My lords!" he shouted.

The guests quieted with reasonable good humor, wine having been generously but not excessively poured. Indeed, many thought the coming entertainment might be worth the attention now requested by their host.

Robert cleared his throat. "As you know, Sir Thomas of Edwardston has accused Sir George of Lavenham of great insult to his beloved sister and has demanded recompense from him. However, my father has forbidden mortal combat between his liegemen while my brother has taken the cross, thus honoring our Holy Father's prohibition against Christians killing one another during this holy war. And since neither man has been able to agree on a reasonable solution, the Prioress of Tyndal Priory, a woman respected far and wide for wise and God-given judgement, has agreed to arbitrate the problem. The two men have agreed to abide by her decision."

The prioress rose from her chair. A benevolent look crossed her face. Only those closest to her could see the twinkle in her gray eyes. "My Lord Edwardston, you believe your sister has been wronged, and you seek recompense from the man who did it, do you not?"

"Yes, my lady. I expect him to marry her."

"And marriage alone? No other remedy will suit?"

"Such is only right in God's eyes, and I abide by God's will."

"And you are correct, my lord. Yet I do believe that your sister and this man must have betrothed themselves to each other before carnal knowledge took place. The Lady Sarah is both a noble and an honorable woman and would never have allowed sinful converse to take place without such a solemn contract, which can no more be broken without the permission of the Holy Father than marriage itself. You would agree?"

Edwardston nodded in somewhat surprised satisfaction. The Lady Sarah bowed her head modestly. Robert pulled George back into his seat as his friend tried to rise, red-faced, to protest.

"And, my lords, you have agreed to my judgement in this matter as my most noble father has ordered?"

"Yes," replied Edwardston.

"Er, yes," said Lavenham, Robert's elbow in his ribs.

The Lady Sarah, who was not asked, smiled.

"You honor me with your confidence. However, I am but a simple woman and could not judge this matter without the help of wisdom far superior to mine. I therefore propose a trial which will, with the grace and help of the All-Knowing God, reveal the truth in this controversy."

"No bloodshed," Robert muttered in a hoarse voice.

"This will be a holy trial but no trial by combat, as our father ordered, although the man who betrothed himself to the Lady Sarah would die if he were so foolish as to lie about his commitment to her."

A low murmur of approval and anticipation rippled through the hall.

"Death or life is within his choice," continued the prioress, "however, to knowingly take your own life is a great sin in the eyes of Our Lord."

Robert nodded public agreement but privately whispered, "I hope you know what you are doing, dear Sister."

Eleanor raised her hand as if to bless the assembled, and then opened it to display a small pea. "This is called the paternoster pea. It is not native to England, but perhaps those of you who have traveled to Italy are aware of its sacred properties?"

Edwardston's eyes lit up in genuine joy. "Indeed, I do, my lady! It is well known in Venice. While I was on pilgrimage to Rome many years ago, I saw just such a pea used at a trial I attended of an accused murderer. He ate it and died within a few hours. It was God's judgement upon him, for God would have saved him had he been innocent."

"Exactly, my lord. The innocent may eat of it and live, but the guilty quickly die a horrible death. It is this pea, a tool blessed by God with His infallible knowledge, which shall determine guilt or innocence here, not I."

"I agree to the trial, my lady, but I would be satisfied if Lavenham married my sister."

"He refuses, and claims innocence of her condition, my lord." She glanced at the pale Lavenham.

Edwardston's eyes narrowed with anger. "Then let him eat the pea! His death will satisfy my honor, and the exposure of his lie will give legitimacy to the child he planted in my sister."

Eleanor turned to George and held out her hand with the tiny pea. "Will you prove your innocence, my lord, and eat the paternoster pea, or will you claim the Lady Sarah as your lawful wife?"

"Good God, man, take her as your wife!" Robert hissed at his friend.

"I will trust in God's judgement and eat it, my lady," George said, standing and taking the pea from the prioress' fingers, "for I am an innocent man." With that, he tossed it into his mouth.

"Chew it thoroughly, my lord," the prioress said.

His face gray, George noisily and thoroughly chewed the pea before swallowing it.

Eleanor drew the sign of the cross over George. "And God will soon reveal to us the truth in this case!"

"Send Lavenham to his chamber with attendants from our three households to watch him until morning. We shall then reassemble here," Robert said. He turned to look for his sister, but she had already left the hall with Sister Anne and the Lady Sarah. Indeed, the time for feasting had ended for all but dogs, rats, and the poor who would get the evening's scraps.

• • ● • •

"His soul will be in Hell now." Edwardston lounged in his chair and looked around with a smug expression at those who chose to gather the next morning.

Emerging from the hall that led to the chapel, Eleanor seemed to float toward the assembled men, her hands hidden in her sleeves. She was so small of stature that the Lady Sarah and Sister Anne seemed like attendant giants at her side. "You have heard of someone's death, my lord?" she asked in a voice which carried remarkably well from one so seemingly delicate.

Edwardston leapt up and bowed his head in the prioress' direction. "I assume we shall hear of God's judgement on Lavenham shortly, my lady. He would have been wiser to marry my sister than to bluff it out with God. More wine, Timothy. The rushing winds, caused by Satan's minions taking Lavenham's soul to Hell, have chilled me."

Timothy, who was dressed with a somber drabness exceeded only by that of his master, nodded. But his youthful eyes were brighter than usual this morning as he turned away from the trio of women to wait upon the men.

A familiar voice boomed from the hall. "And some for me too, Timothy, for the winds chilled me as well. Although my soul is safe, Edwardston, I dreamed the Prince of Darkness himself came for you. Sadly, it seems both of us have been profoundly disappointed."

As George strode into the dining hall, Edwardston dropped his goblet, the spilled wine turning the rushes dark red. Behind Lavenham came those who had watched him overnight, including Edwardston's priest.

"But God should have…"

"Struck me down? Only if I were guilty. Am I right, Lady Eleanor?"

"Indeed." The prioress bowed slightly in the direction of the almost speechless Edwardston. "And do we not all trust in the perfect knowledge of God?"

"But my sister…"

"…shall be married as duly promised to the man with whom she made solemn promise of holy matrimony, and as you, my lord, have rightly agreed she should." The prioress stood and reached into her robe. "We have another man to test with the paternoster pea." She turned slowly in the direction of Edwardston, stopping to look at the young man by his side. "Timothy, son of Sir Leonard?"

The young man blanched.

"Timothy? Impossible! He is nothing, the son of a landless knight whom I kindly took into my service at the begging of his father on his deathbed. The boy would not dare…"

Timothy coughed. "My lord, it is true. I cannot lie and damn my soul. I am your sister's contracted husband, and she bears our firstborn now."

In shock, Edwardston's mouth opened into a veritable maw. "This is a blasphemy! I will not allow this marriage."

"It would be a blasphemy to forbid it, my lord. You gave your sacred word before both God and man yesterday that your sister would be rightly wed to her betrothed. To marry someone other than Timothy would be bigamy and unlawful in the eyes of the Church. You are a man of his word?" There was just the hint of a question in the prioress' voice.

Edward snorted. "Indeed! But how do I know this isn't a lie made up by a boy cursed with ambition above his station?"

"Because he speaks the truth, Brother, and I swear it on my hope of heaven." The Lady Sarah quietly walked over to the young man and gently took his hand. "When you saw Sir George coming from my chamber, you assumed what you wished. I did not have the courage to tell you the truth for fear of what you would do to Timothy. Sir George had only been passing by and heard my cries. He entered my chamber, as a gentleman, to save me from what he feared was something evil.

I ordered him immediately on his way and told him nothing of what had transpired nor who was hiding behind the tapestry at my window."

"Hiding? This craven cub was hiding in your room while I...?" Edwardston sputtered.

"While you looked at my clothing, the blood on the sheet, and called me whore. You assumed much, Brother, and would not hear me out."

"Yet for a joyous bride, you cried most piteously, madam. I still have good reason to call it rape and conclude this was no contract to marry." He glared at Timothy.

"Brother, you are not a tender woman who may have joy in her bridegroom, yet know pain in becoming his wife. Our mother died when I was young, and we have no near aunts or other sisters. I had none to tell me how a man made a woman his wife. Though I pled my troth to Timothy, I knew nothing of what came after."

Edwardston shook his head, acknowledging a rare defeat. "I will allow the rites of marriage, but it will last as long as it takes to get the Holy Father to annul such an unprofitable union."

"Then bring forth your priest, my lord," the prioress said, "and let us celebrate with public rites the lawful union of Timothy with the Lady Sarah."

"He will get the marriage annulled, Sister." Robert was sitting at the head of the deserted table. From outside, they could hear the sounds of departing horses and men.

"Not unless he is willing to pay much for it. More likely, the Holy Father will order Timothy to Jerusalem as a penance and a much-needed sword on the Crusade, but he will not waste time on a petty quarrel between minor lords. Perhaps such a judgement would be best. I fear Timothy adores his new wife most for the lands she brings, yet she loves him dearly. Perhaps the young man will never return to shatter her illusion of his love, but she will still have his child to comfort her."

"You seem so certain of this."

"As certain as we can ever be in this life."

"And how did you learn of this Timothy, anyway?"

"As I said, Robert, I know the ways of women, and I know George's taste in bed partners. It could not have been him."

Robert blushed. "How could you...?"

"I am a nun, dearest Brother, not a saint."

"Nonetheless..."

"The Lady Sarah told me it was Timothy. A woman will not lie to another woman about love if she knows the other will help her gain it."

"But when did you talk?"

"After we left you all to the horses, the three of us rested and then went to the chapel to pray. One always speaks one's heart in the presence of a kindly God."

"But what about the paternoster pea? It would have killed George had you been wrong."

"A simple English pea, Robert. Dried with age. I have no paternoster peas in the convent, nor access to same. As a young girl, I overheard the story of the Venetian trial when Edwardston returned from his pilgrimage. I eavesdropped sinfully in those days." Eleanor smiled mischievously at her brother. "Knowing him well, I realized he would have cared more for the results of God's peculiar justice than what the pea actually looked like, and Sister Anne did assure me that Edwardston would never be able to tell the difference at a distance. She also told me that one had to chew the paternoster pea to release the poison, which is why I told George to do so in case someone knew the secret of its properties. We did assume he would bring his physician priest with him, as he always does, who could confirm the nature of the deadly pea, should Edwardston doubt the word of a mere woman, however much she may call upon the results as God's judgement."

"You never cease to amaze me, Sister."

"And may that always be the case, dear Brother," the prioress said, as she laughed with a pleasure as earthy as the land itself.

The Olive Growers

Jeffrey Siger

I published my debut novel with Poisoned Pen Press by ignoring my (now long gone) agent's recommendation to do otherwise. After signing with Poisoned Pen Press, that novel (Murder in Mykonos) became Greece's #1 best-selling English-language book, landed on the radar list (top 50) of The New York Times *hardcover best-sellers, and presented me with the opportunity of switching to a publishing giant. But the Poisoned Pen Press family gave me what I wanted out of the writing life—unfettered time on the Greek island I called home, writing mystery-thrillers I wanted to write, and wonderful editorial support. So, I stayed, and together we're up to eight Chief Inspector Andreas Kaldis novels, with a ninth on the way. Thank you, PPP.*

—J.S.

I never knew my mother, and she barely knew my father.

I knew only public orphanages, shunned warehouses for society's unwanted children of the poor and the damned. Places where you measured your life by how well you survived as prey or thrived as predator.

I learned to respect predators and expected them to return the honor. Those who did not were a threat to be dealt with swiftly, for surely that was how they would deal with you.

I never wanted to kill. I warned those older boys to stop raping the younger ones, the ones who'd turned to me for protection. They refused. They disrespected me. They left no choice.

That's when I received my first lesson in political justice.

The government apparatchiks charged with overseeing the institution saw widespread rape within its walls as a far greater scandal than an isolated murder, and portrayed the killings to the nation as the unprovoked slaughter of two exemplary young men by an unhinged, ruthless savage.

But at twelve, I was too young to go to prison, though not to be unrelentingly vilified in the press and ordered to spend my next five years alongside other minors deemed in need of reformative measures. The system succeeded in making me a celebrity among my aspiring criminal peers, and utterly unemployable in the outside world.

Everyone knew my name, and no one dared hire me. Only the military wanted me. They refined my predator skills, trained me for tasks they asked few to perform, and praised me for my service. But once back in civilian life, I found the same shuttered minds each time I sought work in my own name. That's when I went to work for my childhood associates, doing jobs consistent with my reputation.

And when they called me, they did so by a different name. One charged with respect for what I did. They called me Kharon, the same name the ancient Greeks used in speaking of the mythical ferryman of souls from the place of life to one of death.

But now a decade has past, and much has changed. I live along the slopes of Delphi's Mount Parnassus, amid the mountains, valleys, and seemingly endless olives, myrtle, and pines of an omnipresent spiritual essence far greater than myself. Tens of thousands of hundred-year-old olive trees spread out for miles in rows running from the Gulf of Corinth's harbor town of Itea, northwest to the town of Amfissa, and northeast to the picture perfect village of Chrisso. Here, in a broad fertile valley of endless green, I grow my olives in peace and anonymity, and live a different life.

Harvest time is coming. That means readying the olive press, not just to process the fruit off my trees, but the olives of my neighbors who come to me to turn their crops into oil. I'm always busy at harvest time because I charge a fair price, and my press is the only one left in the valley that does.

The other press owners sold to foreigners who came to take advantage of Greece's collapsing economy. With taxes doubled, redoubled, and doubled again, and banks no longer lending or renegotiating old loans, they sold to save what they could. Many growers did the same, selling their trees to the same foreigners.

A foreign owner tried buying me out a few years back, but I wouldn't sell. Then he asked me to raise my prices to match what he and the other foreign owners charged the growers. I take a traditional fifteen percent share of the grower's crop, while they charge twenty percent. He said I'd be a fool not to charge more. After all, what choice did the growers have but to use *us*? I told him I viewed things differently: those who worked the land deserved a fair shake from those of *us* who profited off their labor.

When I refused to raise my prices, the foreign owners tried luring away my customers by offering to press olives for a third less than I charged. Their lowball scam didn't work, so they went back to charging their higher prices and began bad-mouthing me, saying my old-fashioned pressing methods turned my customers' olives into inferior oil. As proof, they pointed to the premiums their processed oil drew on the market relative to mine.

That last part got a little tricky and I lost a few customers, until word got around that the foreigners secretly reimbursed the oil buyers out of their five-percent-higher processing fees, and growers got a bottom-line better deal from me for their olives.

Yes, it could be frustrating at times, but my true frustration lay not with my competitors' hardball business practices. Mob-like as they were, they'd never tried strong-arming me. They only wanted to monopolize the market, and between the trees they owned, and the additional oil their buyers acquired at pressing time from local growers, they already controlled most of the valley's crop.

No, my frustration came from my countrymen in the valley. They should be creating their own unique brand, their own packaging facilities, and their own foreign markets. Instead, they allowed foreigners to acquire their oil at wholesale and ship it to Italy to be packaged under Italian labels and sold off at premium retail prices into Europe, America, and other lucrative markets.

They plodded along as they have for generations, seeing their only path forward as through the past, and offering one excuse after another for maintaining their old ways—even as they sold their birthrights to practitioners of the new.

They needed a leader. But don't look at me. I am not about to jeopardize my anonymity in service to a cause no one else is prepared to champion. I am secure in my life. I have my trees, my press, and sufficient assets to survive whatever may come. And, should worse ever come to worst, I still possess unique skills very much in demand at a very high price.

• ● ● ● •

"Kharon, are you inside?"

"Yeah, what is it? I'm busy."

"It's Niko. I have a favor to ask of you."

At least he's upfront about it. "Gimme a few minutes."

"Okay, I'll wait in my truck."

I wonder what he wants? Maybe credit? No, he's one of the more successful growers in the valley. Fifth generation, though he doubts his son will come into the business. The son's moved off to Athens to make his fortune. Good luck with that.

I finished what I was doing, put the tools away, wiped my hands, and headed out the door. Niko's decades-old, faded-red Toyota Hilux sat on the far side of the tiny dirt parking lot, over by the beginning of my olive trees. A blond woman sat next to him in the front seat. She wasn't his wife.

As soon as Niko saw me he jumped out of his truck and met me halfway.

"Kharon, I'm in sort of a delicate predicament with that girl in my truck and—"

"Hold on right there, Niko. I'm not judgmental but I'm also not fool enough to get involved in whatever mess you might have with your wife. As far as I'm concerned I never saw you here with that woman, but that's as far as I'm prepared to go."

Niko furrowed his brow, looked at his truck, and back at me. "That girl's young enough to be my daughter."

I raised my hands. "Hey, like I said, I'm not judgmental."

He laughed. "You got it all wrong. She's my niece, the daughter of my wife's sister. She lives in the United States, in California, and just graduated from some big-time agricultural school."

"What's all that got to do with needing a favor from me?"

Niko rubbed his forehead. "Whenever I visited my wife's family in the U.S., I'd brag about my olive operation and big-time connections."

I shrugged. "It's a common experience."

"But I really went overboard. I told her if she ever came here I'd be able to hook her up with major players in the olive business."

"You know everybody in the valley better than I do."

"Not the part she's interested in."

"What's that?"

"Marketing."

"What makes you think that I know anything about marketing?"

"It's not what I think, it's what she thinks."

"I don't follow you."

"I told her you charged the lowest pressing fees in the valley, operated your business with old-fashioned equipment, and still managed to beat back your competitors' efforts to drive you out of business."

I didn't like the sound of where this was headed. "Is she looking to write something about a dinosaur olive farmer discovered alive and well in Delphi?"

Niko signaled no in the Greek fashion with an upward jerk of his head. "Nothing like that. She just wants to know how you do business. Can't you at least talk to her?"

I stared at him. "Sometimes you can be a real pain in the ass."

He smiled and patted me on the back. "Great, I knew I could count on you."

Niko turned toward his truck. "Thalia, come out and meet my friend, Kharon."

If he hadn't told me she was from California I'd probably have guessed it. Long legs clad in denim, big blond ponytail, blue eyes, and well, the kind of figure you had to work hard not to stare at. She came straight at me with her right hand extended and a big smile.

"Hi, sir, Thalia Georges. Pleased to meet you."

I wished she hadn't called me sir. We shook hands. She had a firm grip. "Likewise."

"I hope you'll have some time for me. I'd love to learn how you operate your business so successfully."

"It's easy with loyal customers like your uncle."

Niko smiled.

"When's convenient for you, sir?"

"Please, it's Kharon."

She smiled.

Say good-bye to the rest of my morning. "How about now?"

She looked at her uncle.

"I've things to do back at my place that can't wait."

I jumped in. "I'll drop you off when we're done, if that's okay with you."

Another smile. "Sure."

Niko left and I gave Thalia a tour of the press. She said she'd never seen equipment quite like that before. Whether or not she meant it as a compliment, I decided to take it as one. We did the question-and-answer session while strolling north along a mat of green grass and brown dirt carpeting miles of ancient olive trees.

She told me of her life from birth to now. When she asked about my past, I said I was an olive grower. She didn't push for more, just said she too loved the land, always had, and guessed that's all one needed to know about a person to understand his soul.

She definitely was from California.

Next came questions bombarding me on all things olives, including how I started in the business, overcame a close-knit community's natural resistance to strangers, dealt with less than honorable competitors, and viewed the future of the olive industry in the valley. I answered every one, except for how I acquired the wherewithal to buy my trees and the press.

At the edge of the village of Chrisso we climbed a steep hillside east toward a group of boulders perched above an aqueduct carrying water down from the mountains to the valley.

We sat among the boulders looking south across the valley toward the Gulf of Corinth. From this height, none of the trees we'd just walked among stood out from any other, except for random cypresses spiking the sky. We saw only a broad canvas of olive green, framed on three sides in beige and chocolate brown, with touches of ochre and terra cotta, its far side bordered by sapphire blue sea and bright blue sky.

Thalia leaned back on a boulder, and stared off into the sky. "I can smell the sea."

"If the wind's right, you'll catch a whiff of wild herbs and lavender mixed in."

She shut her eyes. "You've answered all my questions but one."

Here comes the zinger.

"From everything you've said, it's pretty clear growers like my uncle are doomed. It's only a matter of time until the foreigners own it all. So, why do you remain on the deck of the *Titanic* waiting for it to hit the inevitable iceberg? Are you a fan of disasters?"

"That's two questions."

"Okay, answer the first."

"Because I was waiting to meet you."

She tilted her head toward me and opened her eyes. "Are you making a pass?"

I couldn't help but smile. "No, at least not yet. I've been waiting for someone to show up who cares enough about this valley to fight for it."

She sat up. "And you think that's me? You must have taken too much sun on our walk. I'm only here for a few weeks to visit my family."

"This valley's in your heart. The same as it's in mine."

"This valley's not my home."

"Of course it is. Your roots go even deeper into its soil than mine." I waved a hand out toward the sea. "Look out across this valley and tell me honestly whether you believe there could be a more beautiful place anywhere on Earth."

She shook her head. "No, I won't lie. But what could I possibly do to change things?"

I stood up, took her hand, and pulled her to her feet. "That my dear, we'll discuss on the way back."

• • ● • •

Our walk began with Thalia listing the reasons why she could not possibly stay: a lucrative job offer from an international mega-agricultural company, her family, and a new boyfriend. I pointed out that her new job had her moving to Canada, away from her family and boyfriend, but that in this valley she at least had family.

She countered with the difficulty of earning a living in Greece, and that no matter how things worked out with her uncle, she could never expect to inherit his land or business. That would go to his son.

I said her fortune in the valley lay in a different direction, one which involved her using her skills and education to establish a cooperative marketing venture among the valley's growers, aimed at creating a unique brand for the lucrative high-end market abroad.

"Like Sunkist?" she said.

"Sunkist?"

"Everyone in the United States knows Sunkist. Most think it's a company, but it's a not-for-profit marketing cooperative of independent California and Arizona citrus growers."

"That's precisely what I'm talking about. You could be the person who brings that concept here."

She shook her head. "It requires growers willing to work together for the common good, and that doesn't exactly fit the Greek business model."

"I didn't say it would be easy, but look at the upside for anyone willing to take on the challenge."

She smiled. "Stop selling me."

"Nope."

"It takes a lot of capital to get that sort of marketing program up and running."

I smiled. "Not to mention the packaging operations."

"You expect me to do that too?"

"Of course. That's where the real money is."

"So, where in this fairy tale of yours does the wizard appear with the cash needed to make the project fly? And don't say the Greek banks."

"No, but there are investors looking to cherry-pick great opportunities in Greece, and I know you're the perfect one to sell them on this."

She shook her head from side to side. "From the hustle you're running on me, I'd say you're pretty good yourself. Why don't you take this on and leave my life alone?"

I smiled. "I don't have your blue eyes."

"I get it. You don't want to tell me your real reason."

"No, that is the reason. Looking into my eyes draws a very different reaction."

"Meaning?"

"They tend to discourage the sort of long-term commitments we'll need for this to work." I nodded toward my olive press. "We're back."

"Where's your car?"

"That's my ride." I pointed at a vintage BMW motorcycle.

She smiled. "Why does that not surprise me?"

I locked up the building. I'd finish what I'd been working on tomorrow. Ah, yes, Greece's unofficial national motto, *Avrio*. Tomorrow, there's always tomorrow.

The ride to Niko's took twenty minutes. Twenty minutes of Thalia's arms around my chest, her body pressed against mine, the engine vibrating between our legs. I wished Niko lived farther away.

"Call me tomorrow," she said when I dropped her off. "I want to talk with my uncle about your ideas."

"If you want me to speak with him, just ask."

"Thanks." She kissed me on both cheeks and ran toward the house.

I watched her until she disappeared, and thought of her as I drifted back along the road toward my place at the base of Mount Parnassus, mythical home to the nine muses.

Oh, joyful muse of comedy and favorite of Delphi's protector, Apollo, have you returned to once again enchant, dear Thalia?

• ● ● ● •

Not only did Thalia's uncle agree with the plan, it fired him into organizing a meeting of every independent grower in the valley, and cajoling all of them into pledging their oil to the new cooperative. Next, her uncle compiled a list of everyone he could think of who might be interested in funding an independent olives-to-bottle operation in the valley.

Over the next several months, Thalia and her uncle travelled across Greece from one investor meeting to another, gathering enthusiastic commitments to back the project. Delphi Valley Olive Oil Cooperative stood poised to forever change the way business was done in our valley.

The night before the scheduled contract-signing with investors, I heard a horn blaring away in the parking lot outside my press. People didn't honk like that around here, especially in the middle of a chilly March evening. A lost stranger would knock on the door; a friend would just walk inside. I peeked out the window. Niko's truck sat in the middle of the parking lot aimed straight at the front door. I couldn't tell who sat inside. But someone definitely wanted me out there.

I left through a rear window, made my way into the olive grove, and circled around to come up on the truck from behind, the horn still blaring. I recognized the driver and tapped twice on the top of the cab. Thalia lurched forward against the steering wheel. The horn stopped—replaced by her screams.

I stepped to where she could see me. "It's me, Kharon," I yelled.

She didn't seem to hear me. I opened the door and touched her arm. "It's Kharon."

She screamed louder, her eyes clenched shut, her hands locked on the steering wheel.

"*Thalia, it's me!*"

She kept screaming, rocking back and forth in the seat. I stepped back and waited. That's when I noticed she wore no coat…her blouse torn open…she wore no pants…or underpants.

I took off my jacket and draped it over her shoulders. She pulled it off and laid it across her waist, still rocking, but no longer screaming.

When she stopped rocking, I said, "Let's go inside. It's too cold out here."

She didn't look at me. I held out my hand. She reached for it with one hand, clutching my jacket around her waist with the other. I led her inside and sat her in my office chair.

"Wait here."

Her eyes widened. "Don't leave me, please."

"I won't, I'm just getting you a blanket."

I brought her the blanket and a cup of coffee; and sat holding her hand. I didn't ask what happened. She would tell me when she wanted to.

An hour later she did.

Late that morning she'd received a call from a man who described himself as the representative of the valley's foreign press owners. He said he knew the closing on the Cooperative was scheduled for the next day and he had a proposition to discuss with her.

She said it would be a waste of everyone's time.

He said she should contact her investors, and that he'd call back in thirty minutes. She hadn't had time to make the first call when an investor called to apologize for backing out at the last moment, saying unanticipated business developments made it impossible for him to invest. He refused to elaborate.

Within that half-hour she learned every investor had withdrawn, each giving a similar bullshit reason for the change of heart.

Precisely thirty minutes had passed when the representative called back. She agreed to meet him and his foreign press owners at one of their facilities later that afternoon.

Thalia recognized every foreign press owner at the meeting, but not the nattily dressed, self-proclaimed representative. He introduced himself as the chairman of the board of a cooperative venture similar to the one she now advocated for the valley, and said he had an offer intended to address her cooperative's potential competition with his.

She asked if it was the same deal as he'd offered her investors to scare them away. He said they needed no persuading beyond a simple explanation of the terminal risks they faced should they not invest their capital elsewhere.

He offered her one hundred thousand euros to walk away and do nothing further to organize the valley. She said no. He said she should reconsider, as this was no business for a woman.

She told him to go to hell and stormed out of the building. Two bull-like men leaned against a van parked beside her uncle's truck. It was one of many vehicles in the parking lot. One of the men answered a cell phone as she approached the truck. An instant later the other man grabbed her and both men forced her into the rear of the van.

That's when she began screaming. They didn't bother to gag her or drive away, and she didn't stop until they threw her out of the van and drove off.

The only vehicle left in the parking lot was her uncle's truck. Everyone from the meeting had left, ignoring her screams as they did.

That's when she drove to my place.

She sat quietly staring off into the middle distance.

I asked no questions, just drove her home in silence in her uncle's truck. I told Niko I would be away for a few days, and left Thalia to decide what she wanted to do next.

He offered me a ride back to my motorcycle. I said no.

I needed the walk to decide what I'd do next.

• • ● • •

The first of the foreign oil press owners disappeared three days later. The next day another vanished, followed by another. By the end of the week all but one had disappeared from the valley without a trace.

The nattily dressed man now went nowhere without his two bodyguards. He was with the lone remaining foreign press owner when a text message came through on his cell phone:

IT IS TIME TO MAKE A DEAL

WHO ARE YOU? he replied.

LOOK OUT THE WINDOW AT YOUR CAR.

He looked out the window at the black BMW 750.

I SEE NOTHING.

WATCH.

Five seconds later the BMW exploded.

Another ten seconds passed.

THAT WAS A SIGN OF MY GOOD INTENTIONS. IF I WANTED YOU DEAD YOU'D HAVE BEEN INSIDE.

WHAT DO YOU WANT?

I replied:

JUST TO MEET AND CHAT ABOUT A BUSINESS PROPOSITION

WHEN AND WHERE?

I told him, and tossed away a missing owner's phone.

• • ● • •

It was a pitch-black, new moon night when the nattily dressed man drove up to the pressing facility of the first foreign owner to disappear.

I'd watched his two bodyguards arrive an hour earlier, creeping in through the adjacent olive groves, wearing black military camouflage and state-of-the art night-vision goggles, both men armed to the teeth. They took up positions designed to triangulate on me, once their boss drew me out of the shadows.

Nattily Dressed stepped out of his car into a deadly still night, his head swiveling as if on ball bearings, an unlit flashlight in his hand.

"Over here." I said in a stage whisper from a corner of the building.

He swung the flashlight my way, turned it on, and showered me in light.

I didn't react, just stood perfectly still, holding one hand behind my back. "Are you finished with the spotlight? Aim it at the ground and walk toward me. Otherwise…" My hand swung out from behind my back gripping a Heckler & Koch MP5K submachine gun.

The beam went straight to the ground, and he stepped quickly toward me.

At three paces from me I said, "Stop."

He did, his head jerking from side-to-side like a nervous bird.

"Expecting someone?"

His voice cracked. "No."

"Now strip."

"What?"

"Until you're bare-ass naked."

"I have no weapons."

"Well, I do, so you better listen."

He stripped down to his shoes.

"Those too, and the watch."

I took his flashlight, turned it off, and kept him standing there until he shook from the cold. I turned on the light and motioned toward the building with the gun muzzle. "Inside."

The dank smell of old olive oil hung in the air; the only sound the gentle sloshing of oil inside a two-story high storage tank. I shone the light on the tank. "I always wished I could afford one of those modern stainless steel tanks. Maybe someday."

"Is that what you want?" He said, still shaking. "Money?"

"Haven't you learned your lesson yet? Money didn't work on the girl. What makes you think it will work on me?"

"This is about the girl?"

I raised the submachine gun to my shoulder and took aim at the middle of his forehead. "I can't wait to hear how you're going to try to explain your way out of that one. But let me caution you. If you're about to say you had nothing to do with what happened to her, and fail to convince me, I am going to empty this magazine into your balls." I aimed the muzzle at his groin. "Now, what did you want to say?"

"Nothing."

"Good. Now, up those steps to the top of the tank."

He stumbled up the stairs.

I followed him up, and shone the flashlight into the tank. "Say hello."

He looked half at me, as he edged up to the tank and peered in. "They're alive!"

"Yep, every last one of them, including the one I let run free until I could arrange to blow up your car. All nicely packed together like a half-dozen sardines in a half-meter of oil, with duct tape over their mouths and their hands taped behind their backs."

"What do you want from me?"

"I want you down there untying your friends."

"What?"

"You heard me." I waved the MP5K at his head.

He gripped ahold of the tank's edge and swung over the side trying to ease down, but his hands slipped and he fell with a splash into the oil.

"Undo them." I said.

It took him five minutes.

"Okay. Attention, everyone." I nodded toward the front door and an overhead light went on. "We're about to enter into a business transaction and I need your undivided attention. Do I have it?"

No answer.

"I'll need a verbal answer from each of you." I waved the gun above the tank.

"Yes," said a chorus.

"Good. My colleague, who assisted me with the lights, is a childhood friend and an accomplished Athenian lawyer. He's prepared documents for each of you sign. The terms are simple and straightforward. Each of you is selling your press and trees to the cooperative headed by Thalia Georges. In exchange, you'll receive a twenty-year payout based upon the fair market value of your property today, plus annual interest on the unpaid balance, at bank rates."

"That's ridiculous," said Once-Nattily Dressed. "We have no reason to agree to this. Your little olive oil charade isn't scaring any of us. You'd have to kill us all, and you wouldn't dare, because you know you'll never get away with it."

Some nodded, but not all.

I shook my head. "I can't believe you need more convincing, but so be it." I walked around to the other side of the tank.

"Look out below," I yelled, and tossed one of the bodyguards over the side. Fifteen seconds later I tossed in the second, each with his throat cut.

I stared over the edge of the tank. "Convinced?"

Silence.

"Good, and for any of you who might be thinking of later reneging on this deal, or possibly taking revenge, permit me to explain the penalty for such a breach of trust. If Ms. Georges should so much as slip in her shower, or if I ever see one of you in this valley after tomorrow, you all die. In other words, be prepared to keep a close eye on each other, because if anyone of you steps out of line, you're all dead. Period, end of story."

I held up a cylinder. "For example. This is an incendiary grenade." I pulled the pin.

"Should I decide to drop this, you'll all be French fries in a matter of minutes. So, what will it be, folks, fries or good-byes?"

Everyone signed that night, and disappeared from the valley the next day.

When I presented Thalia with the signed agreements she didn't smile, nor did she cry.

I also told her that the two men who'd attacked her had died in a freak accident in a partially filled oil vat. Apparently they'd been using an acetylene torch to repair a crack in the steel lining and ended up frying themselves into harmless crispy critters.

Thalia smiled.

Apollo couldn't have been more pleased than I at such a smile.

Her Mama's Pearls

Vicki Delany

Way back in 2006, Poisoned Pen Press published my debut novel of psychological suspense, Scare the Light Away. *I still remember how excited I was when I got the e-mail from Editor-in-Chief Barbara Peters, saying they liked my book and wanted to publish it—but first I had to cut 20,000 words! In the years since, the press has published two additional novels of stand-alone suspense, as well as eight books in the Constable Molly Smith series, the latest in 2016. And, the excitement continues....*

—V.D.

The town wasn't marked on the map.

I snorted in frustration; this was supposed to be the latest, most comprehensive map available, and it didn't have this two-bit town marked on it. I punched the buttons on the GPS. Nothing but a single straight line showing the highway.

My car radio was tuned into an oldies station, and I was singing along with the Beatles on "Sergeant Pepper's Lonely Hearts Club Band" when, with a burst of static, the song ended. I flipped the dials: nothing but more static and dead air. A brand new car, everything top of the line, and the radio couldn't even get me through the first trip.

It was late November, and although snow had not yet fallen, the forest was drawing in on itself, preparing for the long winter to come. I'd been on the road for two weeks. The first sales trip for my new job, installing and supporting computer equipment to mining companies. It was also the first time I'd been away from home since my marriage. I was thoroughly sick of lumpy motel beds, tasteless diner food, and the endless expanse of Northern Ontario rocks and pine trees. I thought of nothing but getting back to the city.

As the highway became the main street I slowed down, intending to cruise through town and out again. It was a small town, all right; I could see clear from one end to the other, to where the highway opened up again and continued on time-lessly. It looked old, too. The buildings were mostly wooden. Handmade signs swinging in the wind marked the few small storefronts.

Although I'd stopped for a lunch break less than an hour ago I had a sudden urge for a beer and pulled up to the sidewalk before I was even fully aware of making the decision to stop.

I got out of the car and took in my surroundings; a general air of neglect and decay lay over the town. The buildings were in desperate need of a few coats of paint. Loose wooden shingles clattered in the cold wind. A hand-rail on the steps of the tiny white church across the road had broken off and lay like a bar-rier across the front door.

I hadn't yet seen a single person or car. The streets were as deserted as the morning after Judgment Day.

As in most small northern towns, the bar was instantly rec-ognizable. It was the only building on the street that had any appearance of being used.

I pushed open the swinging door and walked into the dusky gloom. I stood in the doorway letting my eyes adjust to the lack of light. At first I thought I was the only person in the bar, but gradually I made out the shape of the bartender wiping glasses behind the counter.

He watched me approach in silence. Before I could place my order, he slapped a bottle of beer on the bar.

"Cheers."

I wiped my eyes and attempted to focus on the bartender. He was an old guy, with a full scraggly beard, mostly gray shot with black, and badly cut hair, wearing a pair of loose dust-colored trousers held up by worn suspenders that might once have been red but were now more of a dirty pink.

"Cheers. Nice little town you have here," I lied.

He grunted and went back to washing the glasses.

"Where is everyone?"

He looked at me.

"I mean, in the town. I haven't seen a single person except yourself since I got here. Where is everyone?"

He put down the glass and turned to face me. "They're all at home, I reckon, at home getting ready. Big night tonight."

"Big night, how?"

"Every red-blooded man in this town has been waiting many a long year for this very night. I reckon they're all at home right now, taking baths and washing their hair and puttin' on cologne. Old John Albright was spotted yesterday buying a bottle of shampoo in the general store." He shook his head and chuckled, "John probably ain't had his hair washed since his mama did it for him."

"Why? What's going to happen tonight?"

He eyed my beer thoughtfully. "It's a long story."

"Let me buy you a drink, then," I said, "and you can tell it to me."

Another bottle appeared. He drank deeply and then pulled a stool up to the bar.

I could tell this was going to be a long story, indeed. I was anxious to get home, and had planned on driving most of the night. But somehow, before the old man even began, I knew I wanted to hear his tale.

"Tonight Mary McConnell is coming back to town."

"Mary McConnell, is she some old-time movie star? I've never heard of her."

"No, you won't know her. But every man in this town does. You see, Mary's the most beautiful woman most of us have ever seen. This here town ain't much, and it's fading fast; pretty soon there ain't gonna be nothing left. But Mary, she always made this town real special. Poor Mary.

"Mary McConnell was the most beautiful girl you ever did see. And not just beautiful, but nice too, real nice. Kind to everyone. Even the other girls, who you'd think would be jealous of Mary, they liked her too. Her parents thought the world of Mary, she was their only child. They loved her so much. Too much maybe.

"They wanted nothing but the best for Mary. They expected her to make a good marriage. I know they was looking over to the next town, to the Barnett boy. Him bein' the only son and his dad the big mine owner. All of us boys, we were all hoping to catch Mary's eye. Any one of us would have given anything for Mary. We would have made her happy."

He stared at his bottle as if the past were playing itself out before his eyes. I expect it was.

"But our Mary, she had a mind of her own, you see. She treated that Barnett boy like he were dirt. Probably because her parents chose him. One day, right out of the blue, it was announced that Mary was going to marry Jack McNeil." The old man spat on the floor.

"Jack McNeil. Even back then he was nothing but a low-down, lying skunk. Never had done a decent day's work in all his life. But he was a charmer, I guess. And he had charmed our Mary. I remember their wedding day as clear as if it was yesterday. Mary, looking as beautiful as only Mary could. Her poor mother's face all red and swollen from crying, and as for her old dad, he looked like he'd swallowed a thundercloud. Jack, of course, was grinning all over his stupid face, like the cat who'd swallowed the cream. The whole town came out to the wedding, of course. Everyone said they wouldn't believe it if they couldn't see it with their own eyes. That was the last time anyone ever saw Mary smile.

"The wedding was organized right quick. We all knew why soon enough. Mr. McConnell gave the best part of his farm to

Mary and Jack, and money to build a house. McConnell had the most prosperous farm in the county in them days. That didn't last long. Little bit o' neglect and a farm goes downhill pretty fast. As for the money for the house," he snorted in disgust, "Jack didn't keep much of it. Nothing but a shack he put up for our Mary and her baby. Mr. McConnell didn't last long after the wedding. He died that very winter; Mrs. McConnell moved away to live with her sister. She would come to town a couple of times a year to visit Mary. She sure aged fast, Mrs. McConnell.

"Then Mary and Jack got the rest of the farm and the big old farmhouse. Three more babies Mary had, all of them girls. Prettiest little gals you ever did see. Took after their mom, they did. Mary looked after those girls real well. She didn't have nothing for herself, but her girls always had bright ribbons in their hair and clean dresses. Real polite they were, too.

"Mary looked after the farm as best she could. Didn't get no help from Jack, let me tell you. See that table over there, the one in the corner? That's where Jack sat, day after day, drinking beer and telling everyone what a great man he was. None of the boys from town would have nothing to do with him, but in those days we got a lot of strangers passing through and they would always let Jack buy them a drink and listen to him talk.

"While Jack was in here drinking and talking all day long, my poor Mary was working on that farm and raising those girls all by herself."

Overcome by emotion the old man fell silent. I noticed that he no longer referred to "our Mary" but to "my Mary." He wiped his eyes and continued.

"Folks were mighty sure Jack raised his hand to Mary more than once. She'd not be seen in town for a couple weeks, then she'd tell the women at the store she'd been sick. She broke her arm, said she fell down the stairs." The old man shrugged, and his eyes slipped away from mine. "No one wanted to interfere. Jack had a temper, we all knew that, and what happens between a man and his wife is their business, right?"

I didn't bother to argue. The old man's guilt was written all over his face.

"To make matters worse, if anything could be worse, the bastard never stopped chasing women. Louise Robinson told everyone in town that on the very day Mary was having her first daughter, she saw Jack arm in arm with some fancy lady. For a few years more, Jack still had the charm. He acted like a randy alley-cat all over this part of the county, never tried to hide it, neither. And when the drink took effect and the charm was gone, Jack paid for it. Everyone in town tried to hide what was going on from Mary, but of course she knew. She said nothing and kept on working the farm and raising those girls. You see, she was just too proud. Too proud to let any of us see how much she was hurting.

"But time passes. Mary's daughters grew up to be fine young women. At her last daughter's wedding, after the bride and groom had left and the younger children been taken home, when Jack was snoring it off under a table in the corner, Mary stood up in front of everyone.

"'I have an announcement to make,' she said, 'Jack McNeil and I have been married for twenty-five years. For twenty-five years Jack has drunk and whored his way through this county, and smacked me around whenever he felt like it. For twenty-five years I have put up with it and raised my daughters as best I can. Tomorrow, I'm moving on.' Now, none of us knew what she meant, but we were thunderstruck, as you can imagine. Mary walked out the door, head high, leaving Jack dead to the world.

"No one knows what happened when he got home. But next thing we knew the police were out at the farm and Mary, my precious Mary, was under arrest. For murder."

"She killed Jack?"

"Yup. With his own hunting' rifle. I went and visited her in the jail in the police station. Her face was mighty banged up, and it was easy to see she weren't able to move well, I can tell you. The trial was the talk of the town. I was there every day, sitting in the front row, letting her know she weren't alone. She told the court Jack had hit her when he got home from the wedding, and she'd finally had enough. She grabbed the hunting rifle he left on the kitchen table and let him have it. She didn't seem too sorry about it. I wondered if she'd planned it—wouldn't have blamed her if she did. If that's what she meant by moving on."

"I hope she got off," I said, "Clearly, she was a battered woman."

"Guilty. She got ten years."

"That's ridiculous. She had the right to defend herself."

"Jury didn't see it that way. Man's got a right to control his wife, or so some say."

I was stunned at the severity of the sentence. This place was such a backwater it seemed that modern legal defenses hadn't reached it yet.

"It coulda been worse. Some folk said she was lucky she didn't hang."

I assumed he was speaking rhetorically.

"Everyone who'd been at the wedding saw how much Jack drunk that night. And we all knew he hit her. I figure the jury took that into consideration."

I shook my head. Finished my beer. "Okay, but you still haven't told me what's happening tonight. Why's tonight going to be so special?"

"When they took her away, off to prison, Mary stood up and made a statement to the court. She said when she got out she was coming back to this town and in one grand, glorious night she'd make up for all of her lost years."

"You think it's going to be tonight?" I said.

"We got word she left the prison yesterday morning. Mary's youngest daughter and her husband took over the farm. They live there and that's where Mary'll be going."

We sat in silence for a moment. Outside, the shadows were lengthening.

"Time to lock up, Sonny," the bartender eased himself off his stool. "I have to go home and have a bath. Get my best suit out of the mothballs."

"What time do you think she'll be here?"

He looked at me in surprise. "After evening chores, of course. Farm life don't stop even for a ten-year vow."

I reached into my wallet but the old bartender wouldn't let me pay.

"I reckon I'll make enough tonight to cover it," he chuckled.

As much as I wanted to get home, I knew I had to see the end of the story. I'd passed a run-down motel a few kilometers outside of town, so I turned my car around. I took a room there and had a short nap.

By the time I got back to town the bar was hopping. They were lined up three-deep at the wooden counter. Two young men were acting as bartenders; the old man sat on his stool and talked to the patrons. All conversation was of the fair Mary McConnell and the evil Jack McNeil.

Not a seat in the place was free. I pushed my way through the crowd and nodded to the old man. Again, no one asked what I wanted to drink but just handed me a beer. The bartender reached into his apron and pulled out an old-fashioned bottle opener and pulled off the cap.

I leaned against the wall in a far corner of the room, where I could see everything. Most of the men were in their fifties and sixties or more. All were dressed in the same uniform of cheap, shiny suit, starched white shirt, and thin black tie. Didn't anyone in this town ever get to Toronto for a shopping trip? The air was thick with the smell of smoke and department-store men's cologne. A few women sat at tables by the door. They wore home-made dresses and clunky black shoes with thick heels. Several of the women sported colorful hats; one even wore gloves. None of the women were drinking wine or beer, rather they sipped daintily at glasses of what looked like lemonade.

They didn't have to tell me she was coming. At an instant the place fell silent. The door opened and a path cleared through the room like Moses at the Red Sea.

When the old man told me his story that afternoon I'd been sure he was exaggerating. Maybe Mary had been a somewhat pretty small-town girl in her youth but after twenty-five years on the farm and four children and then a stint in prison, I was expecting a stout, worn-out old woman. I stared in astonishment. She was outstanding. Fine lines were chiseled in the skin around her mouth and under her eyes, her thick black hair was liberally streaked with gray, her hands were coarse, but Mary McConnell would still be a traffic-stopper anywhere. Her flamboyant red gown was hopelessly old-fashioned, but it gave her an air of ageless glamour and set off her lush figure to perfection. A string of pearls hung around her neck and a red ostrich feather dressed her hair.

"That's the dress she wore to the Christmas party at the mine office with the Barnett boy," I heard one man whisper to his companion.

"Aye, and her mama's pearls."

Mary moved gracefully through the crowd smiling at everyone in turn. She stopped beside the bar and turned to face the crowd. You could have heard a pin drop.

Mary raised her hand. "My daughter's husband kindly presented me with a small check upon my release. I would therefore like to buy a drink for everyone in this town."

A great cheer went up and men pushed forward.

Mary turned slowly to face the old man who had told me her story. They stared at each other for a long time. Not a word was spoken. From across the room I could feel the strength of a love that would never die.

When everyone had a drink (in some cases two), Mary raised her hand again. Again the room fell silent. "Let's drink to Jack McNeil," she cried, throwing back her head and draining her glass, "the foulest man ever walked God's green Earth." With that she hurled her glass against the wall.

"Bartender," she said, "another round for me and all my friends."

It was time to take my leave. I wanted to say goodbye to the old bartender, but when I stood in front of him, he didn't even see me. He had eyes only for his Mary.

"We've lost so many years," I heard him say.

"Yes, and we will never have them," she said, "but we will have this night. I will not try to make up for all that I have lost.

It is too late. But we will party here every year on November 22nd and think of what might have been."

He nodded sadly. "Every year."

As I turned to go, some old fellow, his hair plastered down with goo, bumped into me as he pushed up to the bar. "It's my turn," he shouted. "A round for everyone."

Not until I was in the street standing in a pool of light cast by the bar windows did I realize that the man had paid for a round of drinks for the entire town with a five-dollar bill.

I drove slowly back to the motel deep in thought.

"Big night in town," I said to the desk clerk.

She yawned. "What town would that be?"

"Why, Black River, of course."

"Black River." She looked at me in amazement. "That whole town was deserted before the war, when the mine closed. No one's lived there since. Buildings were all torn down years ago. You must be thinking of another town."

"Are you sure? I was just there. Lots of people around, big party at the bar."

The woman laughed and returned to her magazine. "Not in Black River, there isn't, buddy."

Despite the lateness of the hour, I was determined to prove the woman wrong, if only for my own peace of mind. Clouds had moved in to cover any light that might be cast by moon or stars. As I drove, the headlights of my car cut a thin beam of civilization through the thick darkness of the Northern Ontario wilderness. I don't remember there being any turn-off required to get to Black River, but there must be. In the darkness I must have I missed it, even though I drove up and down that stretch of highway several times.

I didn't go back to the motel. I drove south, all through the rest of the night heading home.

I arrived at the office to the welcome news that my territory had been changed and I would now be working much closer to home.

I never forgot the little town of Black River, but it was a few years before I got the chance to travel north again. In bright summer daylight I drove the highway, taking every turning I could find. The motel was still there, right where I left it, but of the town of Black River? Not a sign.

I'll come back on November 22. Perhaps I can find it then.

Chaos Points

A Young Adult Mystery

Meg Dobson

As an author of young adult fiction, I met the Poisoned Pen's new YA imprint publisher at Arizona State University's Desert Night, Rising Stars writing conference. Although crime fiction/thrillers are my favorite reading genres, I'd never written one. By happenstance, the summer before, I attended Writers Police Academy. It is a comprehensive hands-on police/FBI/forensic/Secret Service conference for writers. I was prepared to write the genre.

I mentioned to the publisher I'd be interested in submitting, but I wanted to write about serious issues that modern teens face every day. I wanted to write the gritty, but not have it be in-your-face violent. (The bodies stay off page, for example.) The publisher said that was what they wanted—YA crime fiction with an edge.

My Poisoned Pencil 2015 debut novel Chaos Theory *dealt with an underage confidential informant. This is my third Kami short story:* Politics of Chaos *released in a 2015 Sisters in Crime anthology, and the 2016 Malice Domestic anthology included* Elemental Chaos. Politics *dealt with the Secret Service and a daughter of a presidential contender;* Elemental Chaos *dealt with bullying and a terrorist threat.*

—M.D.

• • ● • •

In *Nighthawks*, the artist, Edward Hopper, painted people (random chaos points) frozen in time and place. Beyond that, the viewer knows nothing. Yet the *Nighthawks'* characters hold tension, causing the observer to ask questions. *Who are those people? Why are they there? Do they have homes, people who love them, families who care?* The viewer suspects secrets, but can never know them.

I reread my team's e-file on Emma Carson's sister. Margot, a high school junior, had been a chaos point that met another, which resulted in her death. Thorough and organized, the e-file facts are as beautiful to my logical mind as Hopper's *Nighthawks* is to the art critic. My friends and I, we could get hurt—again. *Do we do this or not?*

I bury the painful memories and whisper, "Yes," while closing the laptop.

A high school student in a small Iowa college town, my daily interests are more fitting for Nancy Drew—only my team rides the edge. My crime team deals with the ugly, the horrible, and sometimes the fatal.

● ● ● ● ●

Three Weeks Later

"Earth to Kam-iii!!!" Sandy says with her normal extension of my name and the assumed exclamation marks. From behind me, my best friend grabs my shoulders. "What's up? You don't daydream."

She's right, but I'd been off in Edward Hopper *Nighthawks*-ville again. The artist's work haunts me. I knew why. He left the questions unanswered, and that, I cannot accept. I don't believe in unsolved mysteries. Chaos points become chaos threads. I follow them; it's what I do.

That, and I'm scared about last time—the hurt, the pain. *Nighthawks* is a safe refuge because it never changes. Those people were forever trapped, unable to move forward into their destinies. That has advantages. You know, hide your head in the sand, don't rock the boat—all those trite clichés.

"Stay on point!" Sandy sticks her thumbs into the top of my spine.

"Ouch." I straighten my shoulders back. Under my thin long-sleeved t-shirt, the vile push-up bra crushes the girls upward. Darn angel TV ads. Pain accompanies her second thumb jam, and I gasp in stale cigarette smoke and other gross smells from the motel room. It is dirty, ugly, and disgusting.

The chaos points have built one atop the other, amassing energy and mass. It'll be a tsunami release. There's no stopping it now, right? But the painful memories from last time won't shake off.

I say, "Sandy…"

She eases into professional mode—no exclamation marks. This is serious, Sandy. The Sandy most people never hear or see. She says, "Forget it, worrywart. Emma and her family need answers. We're getting them."

There's a knock on our motel door. Daniel's masculine, "Ready?" slips through the thin prefab.

"Yep," Sandy says.

"Come on." Through the door, Daniel's deep voice ripples along my nerve-endings. He doesn't talk much. In those two simple words he's said: *Everything's set. Everyone's waiting. Let's get this done.* At least, I'm pretty sure that's what he's saying. It's tough communicating with the big silent type.

I slip on the thin hoodie over my tight t-shirt, leaving it unzipped.

Seen from the back, Sandy and I could be sisters—me the older and her the younger, because she's eight inches shorter, but we're the same age. From the front, we can't be more different. Her Vietnamese almond eyes contrast to my black ones. Her chin and brow are wide and delicate. Mine are blocked and strong. I lift the hood over my head.

Stepping outside, the sun is setting. The fading rays highlight the snow-filled gaps between the crop stubble. Nervous, my deep breath draws in the tart and wild air, but it also carries the disgusting taste of rubber tires. Traffic roars by on Highway 30.

I release the air from my lungs and it leaves tiny icicles inside my hoodie.

Daniel lets out a short huff seeing me. In our strange friendship, he's never blatantly focused on my breasts. He does now. Of course, they are on full alert, thanks to this outfit and the freezing temperature. Darn. I mean he's noticed. He's a guy, but this is…gross.

I say, "Get out of here, Daniel. See you there."

"Right." He backs instead of turning toward his car. At least his eyes are on my face, but he has this goofy grin.

I whisper to Sandy, "I'll kill you for this."

"Hey, whatever it takes. We agreed. We get justice tonight, Kami."

For the umpteenth time, Sam the Amateur Graffiti Artist re-inspects our dirt/mud-smeared license plate on the forest green pickup I call the Green Machine. For me, Sam's name, and often others, comes with a descriptive label. The dirt he's smeared on the plate disguises the truck's numbers and the Iowa county ID. Luis Sanchez, our police mentor, insisted on it for our protection.

Sam the Finally Satisfied tosses the keys to Sandy, his girlfriend, and blows her a good luck kiss, jumping into the borrowed four-door sedan with Daniel. They both wave and head out of the motel parking lot. Crossing the highway overpass, they will pull into the targeted Sip N Go. They'll order pizza of whatever kind isn't pre-made and wait for it and us.

I tug the loose ends of the hoodie tight against the freezing Ides of March and shiver. "You should have let me wear my parka. This looks too obvious."

She grins and pops the locks on the Green Machine. "Testosterone never minds obvious."

With my hand resting on the pickup's roof, I blink my eyes and they open to a darkened world. My heart beats hard and fast as I climb into the passenger side. Then Sandy drives out of the parking lot.

Across from the motel is a truck stop packed with cars and semi-trucks. At the entrance sits one car. It's another loaner. Hollywood Gavin and Luis, our police liaison, lean against it. Hollywood is handsome—think Robert Pattinson, and you'll get the nickname. He's private-school smooth next to Daniel's hard edges.

Gavin revs my hormone engine when he wants, but Daniel is a never-ending-cinnamon-roll yummy. Our three chaos points bounce around like popcorn kernels in hot oil. How's a woman to decide? My counselor helps me with that. Data sets are so much easier to understand and far more predictable.

Gavin's our computer hacker. We'd brought him on for our January case, and he'd signed up for the long haul.

Sandy the Movie Buff swipes her nose in her con signal. Gavin tugs an ear in reply. Then he flicks his thumb on his smartphone. Hidden in the parked cars and semis, the unseen police cavalry mounts.

She drives the Green Machine south, trailing Daniel and Sam's path over the highway. Nervous, I wish I'd peed back at the motel.

Sandy's purse sits on the armrest between us. I pull out her driver's license. The birth year is crudely altered. She'd used the edge of a steak knife and black ink to do it.

I say, "This is too fake. He'll know."

"If it's over-the-top altered, it will be easier to convict him. Now, shut up and concentrate."

Sandy turns into the convenience store parking lot. Inside the store's glass doors, Sam and Daniel stand by the pizza station talking to an older woman with frizzy dyed red hair and "built like a brick outhouse," as my grandma used to say. At the cash register, the dirty-blond guy restocks the cigarette case. He doesn't check out the mud-smeared license plate. Sam the Graffiti Artist will be ticked.

"Let's do it," Sandy says.

Regretting the poor bathroom visit choice, I replay my police training on avoiding entrapment. I'm not letting this case die on a technicality. My stage fright vanishes. I'm riding the chaos thread now, enjoying the addictive thrill of the chase.

• ● ●

Inside, we ignore Sam and Daniel who are our undercover protection and head for the cold drink cabinet doors. Sandy's a cool pro. The creep behind the register focuses on me. So I twit beautifully: hoodie unzipped, shoulders back, boobs at attention. We grab two six-packs of beer, and head for the register.

Sandy grins and her boot taps my tennis shoe. I square my shoulders even more.

"That's a lot of beer for two girls," Dirty-Blond says.

Sandy says, "Pity party. She broke up with her boyfriend."

I try to look dumped and semi-interested in the jerk. He scans the stuff, but Sandy doesn't offer her driver's license.

"I need your ID."

"Sure."

My best friend pulls it out while I lean over the counter. When Sandy hands him the dummied driver's license, he lifts it below my boob level so he can peek at both.

"What's your birthday?" This time his voice has a threatening quality to it. He's spotted the alteration.

Sandy gives him the fake date without a qualm of guilt. He doesn't buy it, but he doesn't stop the sale.

Instead, he asks, "Where are you partying tonight? I get off in half an hour. Been a bit lonely myself."

I drop both elbows onto the counter top with boobs popping. "At the motel. We'll take cigarettes too; whatever you like."

"How about I join you later?"

Sandy goes Southern with her voice. "You do that, sweetie."

That seals the bargain. He reaches back and pulls out a carton, scanning them. Sandy runs her credit card through the reading slot. He passes the fake ID back, and his hand glides against my angel-lifted boobs. I want to slug him.

Daniel, now in line behind us, holds two pizza boxes. His large muscled hands tighten and loosen on them with a crunch.

Crunch. Crunch. I brush against him as we leave. My look says, *Ignore the creep—focus.* I can talk big-silent-guy too.

Sandy and I dump the beer in the backseat and drive back over the highway bridge. She swipes her nose again at Gavin, who thumbs his phone and climbs in the passenger door. Luis in the driver's seat plops a blue cherry bubble on the car's roof. Then they peel out and head over the bridge.

Black-and-whites stream from behind semis and RVs. Lights spin. Sirens blare. You'd think it was a police Memorial Day parade. Sandy makes a U-turn and follows, returning to the scene of the crime.

I punch in a number on my smartphone. "Emma?"

The girl on the other end answers fast, with a breathy, "Kami?" We've talked several times.

"It's done. Police are arresting him now."

There's a scream. No, it's more cry than scream. Then she says, "Thank you. Thank you."

Although she lived two hours away, she'd heard about our team. Sam's blog post about our confidential informant case had gone viral in Iowa. Emma had contacted us via our high school's website link, wanting our help.

Emma's older, but underage, sister, Margot, died a month prior in an alcohol-related car accident. There was physical evidence that she'd been abused and beaten before it happened. No one knew who did it or how Margot got the alcohol, but the high school rumors pegged this Sip N Go guy. There was DNA evidence but no criminal database matches. Authorities had been frustrated with no true leads.

I say, "Under the new state law, now that he's sold alcohol to underage customers, he'll be arrested. His DNA and fingerprints will go into the system. If he's the guy, we'll have him."

Over the phone, the sobs continue as Sandy pulls up behind the flashing cop cars.

I say, "I hope it helps."

"It does. It does. Thank you!"

In the long term, I doubt it will. Grief is grief.

Gavin, then Sam and Daniel, come to stand by the Green Machine. Sandy and I get out and join them. Highway traffic sounds are an unending drone, and the ground rumbles beneath my feet. The tire taste bites my tongue, and the smell twists my nose in disgust.

The sun has set; no moon has risen. Overhead in proper *Nighthawks* style, the giant retro orange and green neon Sip N Go sign burns down on us, mixing with the red-and-blue police lights.

But I'm not Edward Hopper. Whether it's good or not, I must have answers. Chaos points lead somewhere, and I must follow.

• • ● • •

Two weeks after the arrest

It's snowing, again. It's been a long winter and spring isn't knocking very hard. My laptop is open to my final update on the Margot case. Although we wait for the DNA analysis report, Sip N Go guy's fingerprints matched those on several empty beer cans found in her totaled vehicle.

Better yet, after the arrest became public, those high school rumors turned into witness testimonies. Two young women came forward. They had bought alcohol and been abused by the same man.

I close the e-file and poise my finger over the inbox messages from Sam the Case Feeder. *What bashing chaos points will emerge? Where will the threads lead my team?*

Two Bits, Four Bits, Six Bits...

Frederick Ramsay

About a dozen years ago I was in a critique group and trying, with little success, to pitch a book I'd written (Judas) to agents. One of the members of the group knew Robert Rosenwald, publisher at Poisoned Pen Press, and said the Press did not require an agent but specialized in mysteries only. I happened to have an old mystery I'd written years before. I rewrote it and sent it off. It was nearly a year before anything happened, but then, one Sunday afternoon, Editor-in-Chief Barbara Peters called and said they liked the story, and so the first Ike Schwartz mystery, Artscape, *moved off the hard-drive into print.*

—F.R.

• • ● • •

Charlie had no right to say the gun was his. Just because he'd been the one who saw it first and picked it up, didn't make it his. Hadn't they both found it in the weeds next to the creek? Charlie said if he wanted it, he'd have to pay him four dollars. Jake didn't have four dollars. He had a pocket full of change that added up to, like, two dollars and a quarter. He hoped if he threw in his Matt Wieters rookie card, Charlie would let him have it.

"It's probably some crook's gun," Charlie had said.

"We should turn it in to the sheriff's office, Charlie."

Charlie shook his head. "No, that won't do any good. Murderers always wipe their fingerprints off their weapons and anyhow this is probably from someplace a million miles away. I think I'm going to keep it."

"We both found that gun."

That's when the argument started about possession being nine-tenths of the law and what it would take to buy him out. Charlie's dad was a lawyer, so he would naturally know all about that.

Jake patted his pocket with the money and kept walking. Charlie's house had a long walkway which led to the big porch that stretched all the way across the front and wrapped around the side. Jake liked that porch. He'd asked his dad why they didn't have a porch. His dad only grunted, "You sound like your Ma. Hand me that nine-sixteenth open end," and kept on working on the car he kept in the garage which he said would sell for "big bucks." It was a "classic," he said. It looked like a pile of junk to Jake.

"Besides, them Livingstons never sit out on that porch from one day to the next. You could park a damn Volkswagen on it and them people wouldn't notice it for a month of Sundays."

Charlie would notice. Good weather or bad, he always sat on the porch around the side of the house. He said it was his office. Jake veered off the path and headed toward Charlie's office. When he heard the first gunshot, he stopped dead in his tracks. The next two sent him hot-footing across the lawn and into the woods.

• • ● • •

Billy Sutherlin had the crime scene tape in place and the crime scene techs going when Ike arrived.

"We all set here, Billy?"

"Pretty much. Miz Livingston is in the front room. She's all shook up, like. We don't know where the boy is, but we're looking."

"Where's the husband?"

"According to her, he's in Roanoke for the day. She expects he'll be home for supper."

"Anybody tried to reach him?"

"She don't know where he's at exactly, so, no."

"Call his office and see if they know. Okay, what have we got?"

"Samuel Purvis, thirty-five, white male, shot three times here in the hallway. The shooter got him once in the chest, twice in the back. Blood spatter suggests that whoever shot Purvis nailed him the first time and twice more when he tried to run away."

"Who is he?"

"Not too sure yet, friend of the family, the wife said."

"No witnesses?"

"Wife says she was upstairs, heard footsteps, guessed Purvis came on in, and then the shots. She says her son, Charlie, might or might not have seen something. Kids run pretty wild out here in the summer, so no telling where he might have been at the time."

"Okay, show me what you have so far."

●   ●   **●**   ●   ●

Jake hightailed it to the woods and crouched down behind a clump of sassafras. When he dared to take a look back at the house, he saw Charlie careen around the back of the house and disappear in the woods twenty yards away. Jake worked his way over to him.

"Charlie, what happened? Who got themselves shot?"

For a ten-year-old, gunshots emanating from a big house could only mean one thing: somebody had been murdered. Charlie sat in the brush, his arms locked around his knees. He didn't look too good, glassy-eyed, sort of.

"Charlie, are you okay? What's wrong?"

"Oh, my God. He's dead, Jake. My Uncle Sam is shot dead. I was on the porch like I always am. Oh, God. I...the shots. Bam, and then bam, bam. I run in the house and there he is in the front hall. He's dead, Jake, and our gun is what killed him."

"Holy cow! Wait. When did it get to be *our* gun?"

"Your gun, then."

"Mine? Charlie. You been telling me it was finders-keepers, and nine-tenths of the...whatever, and now all of a sudden it's mine? How'd that happen?"

"Well, I agreed to sell it to you and so that makes it yours, see?"

Jake frowned and studied Charlie close up. He always deferred to Charlie because he was older by a year and generally believed to be smarter. At least that's what his teachers said, so it must be true. At this exact moment, however, Jake wasn't so sure. Charlie was looking less like a fox and more like a weasel.

"You know what that makes us, Jake?"

"What?"

"Accessories to the commission of felony murder."

Charlie learned all that talk from his dad. Jake wasn't sure he knew what he was talking about most times, but this sounded serious.

"We are accessories to murder? How are we? What's felony? I ain't aware we done anything. Oh, you mean because we didn't turn the pistol over to the sheriff. I told you we should have and—"

"It's not that, stupid. My Uncle Sam is lying in the house shot dead with…okay, with our gun."

"I got that. You didn't shoot him, did you? If you did, that don't include me. I don't even know your Uncle Sam. Heck, I didn't even know you had an uncle. How can the murderer have killed your Uncle Sam with our gun?"

"I hid it in that big flowerpot out front like always, and he musta found it, walked in, and shot Uncle Sam."

"How did that happen if it was hid?"

"I don't know. The only important thing is, it was took and we are accessories to murder. What are we going to do?"

"I don't get it. Someone shot your uncle with the gun we found and that makes us accessories?"

"Cheese and rice, Jake, are you that dumb? Our fingerprints are all over that gun. When the police find it, we're sunk."

"Charlie, if someone took our gun to shoot your uncle, don't it stand to reason that they'd keep it or, if they didn't, you said yourself, they wipe their fingerprints off before they throw it away?"

"Not if they were wearing gloves. Then they wouldn't wipe it in case there might be somebody else's on it. That would lead the police away from them."

"And straight to us. Cripes, Charlie, I told you we shoulda turned that gun in to Sheriff Ike. Now lookit what we got to deal with."

"Shut up, Jake. We need to find that gun."

"Charlie, how the heck we going to do that? We don't know if he threw it away or, if he did, where he threw it at."

• • ● • •

Ike Schwartz thought of himself as the "Reluctant Sheriff." He'd run for office the first time to rid the town of a truly corrupt sheriff, the second time to foil the return of the same. Now it had become a "'hard to break" habit. His dilemma was: If he wasn't the sheriff, what else would he do? His wife, Ruth, had a career. They had no children. What would an old CIA hand, out-of-work sheriff do?

Billy Sutherlin leaned around the door. "We might have something, Ike. There's a rumor going around that Miz Livingston was having an affair with the dead guy."

"And?"

"Well, Lawyer Livingston is supposed to be in Roanoke, but he coulda drove back, caught Purvis, and shot him. Then all he needed to do is scoot back to Roanoke and make hisself seen around town and come home for dinner and be all shocked and surprised his old buddy is bumped off in his front hall. He has motive and opportunity."

"And assuming he has a gun, the means. Okay, it's a possibility. Put out a BOLO on him and bring him in."

"Already done. You want to talk to the lady again?"

"Yeah, only let's talk to her here. Any luck locating the boy?"

"Not yet."

"Okay, send a couple of deputies back out to the house and search the area. Kids and woods and summertime, he'll be in there somewhere. While they're at it, tell them to keep an eye out for the weapon. It's not likely the shooter tossed it, but we might get lucky."

"Right. Anything else?"

"Samuel Purvis, our vic. What do we know about him besides what you told me earlier? Is he married? Kids? What?"

"He's married and has a real estate office in Lexington. Don't know about family. His wife has been notified and is on her way here."

"That sort of suggests another possibility, doesn't it? If she suspected the affair, she could drive down here from Lexington, which you know is a whole lot easier to do than driving up from Roanoke. She catches him in flagrante, plugs her husband, and pops back up the road before anybody even knows she's gone."

"You think she knew about the affair?"

"Billy, we don't even know if there was an affair. If there was, we don't know if either of the spouses being cheated on knew about it. That said, if there was, and one or the other of them did know, we have at least two possible suspects with a motive, but zero evidence any of this happened."

"So, where's that leave us?"

"Right now, we are six bits short of a dollar."

"Six bits short of a…what?"

"A dollar. In the twenties, my granddad had a haberdashery. He always bought an ad in the local high school yearbook. I was looking through them a while back and noticed a football cheer they printed in the book.

"Two bits, four bits, six bits, a dollar.
"If you're for the Tigers,
"Stand up and holler."

"Right. What's bits?"

"Come on, two bits is a quarter, right? So, four bits would be two quarters or fifty cents, like that."

"So, you're saying we're a far piece from closing this one out."

"You got it."

• • ● • •

"How in the heck are we going to find a gun which we don't even know he threw away, Charlie?"

"I might have seen him do it."

"Scout's honor, Charlie, you didn't see no man run out here, did you?"

"I…okay, I just guessed he must have. I mean you were out front. Did you see anybody go that way?"

"No."

"So, there you are. He had to come through here, right?"

"So, let's say he did. Where'd he throw the gun?"

"If he's left-handed, over there." Charlie pointed into the trees to their left and then those to the right. "If he's a righty, over there."

The area to the right was mostly grass and finding a pistol would have been easy. No gun. They worked their way left toward an oak, poking the shrubbery aside with sticks. Jake almost missed it.

"I got it," he hollered. Over here."

The pistol was almost hidden by leaves. Jake leaned forward to pick it up.

"Don't touch it, Jake,"

"Don't touch it? How are we going to get rid of our fingerprints if I don't? Unless you have some gloves or something in your back pocket, one of us is going to have to."

"I don't but, wait. I saw on TV how the detective sticks a pencil in the barrel and kinda lifts it up."

Neither of them had a pencil. Jake had to try three twigs before he found one that didn't snap under the weight of the gun. He held it up and Charlie wiped the pistol, barrel, cylinder, and grip, with his shirttail. Jake didn't think he'd ever stop and the pistol seemed to get heavier every second.

"That's got to be enough," he said. "Now what do we do?"

"I guess we put it back where we found it."

"Where we found it first, or where we found it just now?"

The twig snapped and the gun dropped to the ground. Before Jake could fit another twig into the barrel and lift it up again, a deputy crashed through the underbrush.

"Hey, you kids. What are you doing here? Don't you know this is a crime scene?"

"Yes, sir," they both said. Charlie added, "I live here, so it's okay, right?"

"What do you mean you live here? Is your name Charlie Livingston?"

"Yes, sir, it is and my Pa is a lawyer, so you'd better be careful."

"Ha! That's a good one, kid. We been looking all over for you. You come with me. The sheriff wants to talk to you,"

"We found the gun," Jake blurted.

"Shut up, Jake."

"You found the…sure you have."

But Jake couldn't stop. His fingerprints were no longer on the gun. He could not fairly be accused of being a felony accessory, and he needed the thing over with. He pointed at his feet "Right the Sam Hill here."

The deputy stepped over and whistled. He turned and spoke into his shoulder radio. Within a minute two other deputies joined him. The gun disappeared into an evidence bag and the two boys were hustled into a police cruiser and whisked to the sheriff's office.

• ● **●** ● •

Ike spent a half hour with the two boys. Charlie Livingston did most of the talking. The other boy, Jake Baker, listened, his eyes fixed on Charlie. Occasionally he'd frown, but he did not interrupt. Their story in a nutshell was that Charlie and Jake were exploring the woods and heard the gunshot. They didn't think too much of it. No, he didn't hear anyone calling him. When they came near the house they veered off the path and found the gun. When asked why they left the path, Charlie paused. Jake started to say something and Charlie jumped back in.

"We had to pee."

Both of you?"

"Yes, sir, and that old oak tree is our peeing tree."

"Your what?"

"It's good luck to pee on that tree so, we do whenever we can. Ain't that true, Jake?"

Jake didn't seem too sure, but nodded his head. Ike sent them home with a caution not to talk to anyone about what they'd seen or done.

• • ● • •

At five-thirty, Billy stepped into the office. "Ike, we got a 'hurry up' done on the ballistics and prints from the gun. I reckon we have good news and bad news and one odd thing. There was a piece of a twig jammed in the barrel. It must have got there when he tossed it. Hard to figure, though."

"The bad news?"

"It was mostly wiped clean, but the killer forgot to wipe the shells in the chamber. There were prints on them."

"What's bad about that?"

"The prints don't belong to anybody even remotely related to the crime. They belong to a Chako Hernandez who is in the cooler over in Lynchburg for murder in a stick-up last week."

"So, he isn't our shooter?"

"Nope, and there's more. The ballistics came in and the bullets in the Lynchburg shooting and the Purvis killing are from this here gun."

"So, Hernandez hands off the gun. Someone else sells it on to our killer. How many spent shells in the cylinder?"

"Five."

"How many shots fired in Lynchburg?"

"Two."

"And three here. What kind of person doesn't reload a gun for a week and then sells it along?"

"Well, maybe he just wanted to get rid of a hot weapon."

"And not wipe the thing clean. Is anybody really that stupid?"

"I met a few heading off to jail who were."

"And the person who buys a 'hot weapon.' Why doesn't he wipe it and reload it?"

"You got me there, Ike."

"Okay, we're done for now. Tomorrow, I want to re-interview the two Livingstons, Ms Purvis, and I will want the two boys,

Jake Baker and Charlie Livingston, brought back in. You set that up for me, will you? I'll want the kids separate from the adults first, though, and make sure Jake's parents is with him."

"What're you going to do now?"

"You call Roanoke again about that BOLO you put out on Livingston. Me? I need some alone time with a little sipping whiskey and a chance to think."

"We're still six bits short of a dollar?"

"As it now stands, maybe four. Have those people here for me at ten sharp."

• • ● • •

Ike turned up at the office early. He made several phone calls. He drummed his fingers on his desk. After another brief phone call, he downloaded a file to his computer and spent the next hour studying whatever he'd been sent. The Livingstons, and Mrs. Purvis arrived a few minutes after ten. Billy ushered them into Ike's office and stood in the corner. The three adults sat and waited. Ike squared himself to his desk and placed his hands flat on its surface.

"Thank you all for coming in. Mr. Livingston, before you say what you are about to say, I know that none of you are either required to be here or answer any questions. You may caution any of the two women, if you please, but I urge you to be patient and let me proceed uninterrupted."

Livingston frowned and nodded.

"Good. Now this may hurt, but I have to ask. Mrs. Livingston, it is alleged that you were having an affair with the deceased. Is that correct?"

Louise Livingston paled and began to protest. Her husband stood up and started to yell something at Ike about having his badge. Mrs. Purvis sat mouth agape. Louise Livingston slumped down in her chair and shook her head. All three began to speak at once.

Finally, Ike slammed his fist on the desktop. "Everyone be

quiet. Actually I don't need an answer. It's true, isn't it? I have a witness, so you needn't deny it."

Billy's eyes widened, "Ike?"

"But we'll get to that in a minute. See, here's the thing. Because of that, two of you have motive and opportunity to commit the crime. Mrs. Purvis, all you had to do is drive down here from Lexington, walk into the house, and shoot your husband."

"I never did. You can ask anybody. I was at the market and then...No!"

"We found the murder weapon a few yards from your back door, Mr. Livingston. And you also have motive and opportunity."

"Me? I was in Roanoke all day, but you already know that."

"Yes, but no one remembers seeing you. You need a better alibi. As do you, Mrs. Purvis."

Livingston turned. "My advice to you, Emily, is not to say another word. I have several criminal lawyers I can recommend."

"Lawyer? Why do I need a lawyer? I didn't kill my husband. If what you said is true, Sheriff, I might have considered it, by God, but I didn't know."

"Not even suspect?"

Emily Purvis' mouth snapped shut with an audible click.

"You, on the other hand, had a very good motive to shoot Sam Purvis, Mr. Livingston."

"Stan...did you?"

"Shut up, Louise. You know as well as I do that this is, at best, circumstantial, Sheriff."

"I do. I do. Wouldn't it be nice if you had an iron-clad alibi, though? See, you went to Roanoke. You must have had a reason. So why doesn't anyone remember you being there?"

"I was meeting with a client. The identity would be privileged information."

"Even if it meant clearing your name?"

"I have done nothing to be cleared of."

"No? Hmmm. The thing is, it turns out that you do have an alibi. We put out a BOLO when we wanted to find you. A street cop in Roanoke saw it after he finished his shift late yesterday afternoon and reported seeing a car with your license number parked outside an apartment complex."

"There, you see?"

"Well, yes, I do see. There was surveillance TV on that street and I just spent an hour or so reviewing it. Would you like to see it?"

"That won't be necessary."

"Oh, it's no trouble." Ike opened his laptop and turned it so the three people opposite could see the screen. "Here you are pulling up and parking at nine-fifteen. You get out and disappear into the building. Okay, I advance it and here you are at noon leaving the building. So, you could not have been at your house to shoot Sam Purvis."

Louise Livingston leaned forward and squinted at the screen. "Who's that with you?"

"A client. As I said, privileged—"

"That's Marcy Dunlap. You handled her divorce last year. She's the one with the sad story and those big doe eyes. How is she a client now?'

"Just wrapping up some details and—"

"Play the rest, Sheriff."

"Oh, if you say so,"

"Stop this, this minute, Sheriff. You are way off-base here."

Louise Livingston was on her feet. "Twice a week, you have to go to Roanoke. What a dope I was. You were seeing that bitch."

"And while I'm away, you're shacking up with Sam."

"You two sit down and be quiet. Mrs. Purvis, It looks like we're back to you."

• • ● • •

Jake and his mother sat with Charlie and Essie Sutherlin in the cubicle next to the glassed-in office used by the sheriff. They could hear the shouting, but the words were muffled.

"What're they yelling about?" Jake asked.

Charlie shook his head and sighed. "It's just grown-ups being themselves."

"Your folks yell like that?"

"All the time."

"You hush now," Jake's mother said. "What goes on in Charlie's house is none of your business."

"Why are they holding us out here, Miss Essie?"

"Well, Jake, I reckon they want to talk to you two, but need to have some time with your folks and Miz Purvis first. Hey, don't you worry. You just tell Sheriff Ike the honest truth and you'll be fine."

Jake shot Charlie a look.

The door opened and Billy Sutherlin poked his head in. "Hey, Essie. These two boys behaving?"

"They are and it sounds like they are doing better than the adults."

"Yeah. Well, it got pretty hot in there. Ike wants you all now."

They traipsed into the office. Chairs were arranged so that the two boys sat directly in front of Ike and out of the Livingstons' line of sight. Mr. Livingston was not pleased.

"I insist on knowing what my son is doing here, Sheriff."

"Take it easy, Counselor. I talked to these two boys yesterday and they told me how they came to find the murder weapon. I wanted them to repeat it with their parents present so that there can be no question about whether the story was coerced and/or subsequently distorted."

"I still want to state here and now that I object."

"Noted."

"Mrs. Baker, thank you for coming today. Jake's dad?"

"He's at work."

"Thank you. Now, Charlie, you told me yesterday that you and Jake were exploring, is that correct? Exploring in the woods and you didn't know what was happening back at your house?"

"Yeah."

"Okay, you heard the gunshots but didn't think anything of them. Then, later, you were walking home and veered off the path and stumbled on the gun. At that time a deputy showed up and retrieved the gun and brought you two in. Right so far?"

"Ummm, yeah."

"Jake, you okay with this? You don't seem so sure."

"It's what Charlie said."

"I see. Boys, do you know what perjury is?"

"Lying when you swore to tell the truth."

"Exactly."

Livingston cleared his throat. "Sheriff, these boys are not under oath and what makes you think they're not telling the truth?"

"Right again, Counselor. Good thing you're here to represent them. Now, boys, lying to a police officer, whether you are under oath or not, is different. That is, if you say this or that and he says you said it, then, if it isn't the truth, you have a problem with obstructing justice and judges don't like that. You understand?"

"Yes, sir"

"So, we're clear, then. Jake, what time did you go over to Charlie's house?"

"Must have been about ten-thirty, maybe."

"And you walked up the path?"

"Yes, sir."

Did you see any cars parked in the driveway?"

"Charlie's Ma has a big old car. It was there."

"Any other?"

"There was a car with a sign on the door."

"Mr. Purvis. Any other?"

"No, sir."

"Now Jake, remembering what I said about telling the truth, what did you do next?"

"Me and Charlie went exploring and found the gun, like he said."

"Okay. Let's try another approach. Charlie, where were you when Jake started up the walk?"

"I was on the side porch where I always am."

Louis Livingston bolted upright. "You were where?"

"Side porch, Ma."

"Why?"

"I always am."

"I didn't know."

"Charlie, look at me." Ike fixed Charlie with what his deputies called the thousand-mile stare. "Was the window open?"

Charlie swallowed. "Maybe, I don't remember."

"Oh, my God," Louise Livingston slumped back in her chair.

Ike sat motionless for what seemed an eternity. "See, here's what had me confused. The gun was all wrong. Who sets out to kill someone with a partially loaded gun? The pistol, by the way, was used in a stick-up in Lynchburg a week ago. I'm guessing the perp tried to toss it in the creek but didn't understand the laws of physics and when he tossed it out of his car window, it did not drop straight down but landed on the bank. That's where you two found it, didn't you, boys?"

Jake looked at Charlie. "Charlie?"

"Never mind Charlie. You tell Sheriff Ike the truth, Jake, or your Pa will tan your rear so's you won't sit for a week," his mother said.

"Yes, sir, we did."

"Okay, Charlie, you with us? Here's what I think happened. You were on the porch and heard something going on in the room next to you. It upset you."

"I peeked in the window." Tears rolled down Charlie's cheek.

"You peeked and…?"

"Nothing."

"Charlie, I need the truth."

"Ma and Uncle Sam were…doing it."

"Doing what, Charlie?"

Livingston bounced up again. "Charlie, don't say another word."

"Sit, Counselor. Doing what, Charlie?"

Charlie leaned forward in his chair and sobbed.

"It's okay. You take a minute. Get yourself together."

Charlie looked up, tears streaming down his face. "He said he was going to kill me."

"Who said he was going to kill you?"

"I walked in the front door and Uncle Sam was there. I said, 'I saw you,' and he said if I ever told anybody he would kill me. He started to come at me. I had the gun and I pointed it at him."

"And?"

"He just laughed and started to grab for me. He said a bad word and 'You're dead, Charlie.' I didn't know…he…I pulled the trigger. He kind of spun around and the gun went off again."

"Then you ran out of the house and threw the gun in the bushes."

"Yes."

"And you had your friend, Jake, help you find it later?"

"Yes."

"Why?"

"Fingerprints. I had to wipe them off."

"Thank you, Charlie. That's all. Mr. Livingston, your son will need an attorney. A clear case of self-defense, I would say. Jake, you stick around. You might have to testify, but I'm guessing this will never go to court. Mrs. Purvis, I am sorry to put you through all of this, but it was necessary. Okay, people, we're done here. You all can leave now."

Red-faced, afraid, or confused, they filed out. Billy poked his head around the corner.

"Two bits, four bits, six bits, a dollar
Looks like our Sheriff
Done got hisself a collar!"

"Knock it off, Billy. There is nothing to cheer about here."

Dodo

Melissa Tantaquidgeon Zobel

I'm a Mohegan Indian writer from Connecticut. You don't see a lot of Native American stories getting published in New England. That's why I sent my first nonfiction manuscript to the University of Arizona Press. When I completed my first spine-tingling tale of murder, I was naturally drawn to the fabulous Poisoned Pen Press, also of Arizona. The hearts, minds, and spirits of these folks are as big as the Grand Canyon. Happy twentieth anniversary, Poisoned Pen! May you continue to kill it for many more years to come.

—M.T.Z.

I

Growing up, the best guys I knew were the ghosts of the dead soldiers that hung out by the Vietnam Veterans Monument. I always gave them packs of Marlboro cigarettes because they complained about the lousy Chesterfields and Pall Malls in their C-rations. It wasn't charity. They told great stories about the dangers of messing with the evil god Yêu Quái and the Goo spirits of Southeast Asia. Go ahead and laugh; my brother, Dodo, always did. He only saw the butt obvious in this world, like everybody else in my hometown—except my Uncle Rennie.

I don't know what I would have done without Rennie. He taught me important mystical stuff about ghosts, angels, demons, precognition, past lives, and afterlives. He even proved one of his beliefs by visiting me in a dream yesterday to invite me back home to his funeral reception. So here I am in Pettipaug, Connecticut, for the first time in thirty-five years.

I shuffle through slick rusty leaves en route to the American Legion Hall for my uncle's reception. The fading foliage reminds me how Rennie always said this is the time of year when spirits come to visit us. Thanks to his recent postmortem appearance, I'd say he solidly proved that one. In life, he couldn't convince many people to adopt his way of thinking. In fact, he spent a few years locked up at the state loony bin in Norwich, due to his freaky premonitions. I nearly wound up in Enfield Prison, for the same reason.

Beyond our mutual mystical interests, we shared a love of nicknames. Rennie was short for Lorenzo. My name's Oscar, but he called me Oz because I'm a wiz at dodging trouble. Rennie nicknamed my brother, Dorian, "Dodo" because he was just the opposite. My late sisters, Sadie and Theresa, were known as "Shady and Trixie," due to their love of dangerous pranks. He referred to my dad, Lucio, as "Loosero" because he made fun of all the supernatural stuff we cared about.

I check out the dull-eyed crowd entering the American Legion reception hall. Man, it sucks that honoring Uncle Rennie's memory means I have to hang with so many losers who didn't understand him, like my brother, Dodo. I could sense his slimy vibe the minute I got back to town. What's worse is that I'm feeling something awful is about to happen to him.

II

I amble into the crowded reception hall and pass a table covered with tuna fusilli, baked ziti with sausage, meat lasagna, and chicken pesto tortellini. Too bad I'm a vegetarian. A love of pasta and bad women are two things that Dodo and I actually share. We sure don't share the same fashion sense. He always loved New England's morbid navy, gray, and black clothing. Meanwhile, I'm sporting a sunny yellow, orange, and white shirt that reminds me of candy corn. It's impossible to miss me. But the locals I pass keep their eyes glued to their cell phones, fingernails, and the cracks in the vinyl floor.

Granted, I haven't kept in touch since leaving here in a hurry all those years ago. My decision to skip town wasn't personal. I never would've left if Officer Cieco hadn't tried to chase me down, simply because I defended myself against my demon landlady. Once I took off, I kept going until I hit another ocean. It wasn't long before I fell in love with Southern California's eternal sunshine and lack of questions.

A woman with skulls tattooed on her mounded cleavage turns her back on me when I try to say hello. This final cold shoulder makes the bar in the next room look heavenly. I grab a seat on a torn red vinyl stool between two prune-faced guys whose tee-shirts show through their thin white dress shirts. Their bottomless-pit eyes tell me they've recently been bitch-slapped by grief, which means they're Rennie's friends, for sure.

The glue-on wood paneling behind the bar is decorated with black plastic frames filled with photographs of buck-toothed soldier kids, chomping at the bit to ditch this town. The guys on either side of me stare at those bar-back pictures like they're some kind of magic mirror, transporting them back to their grunt days in Vietnam. Dodo's unlucky 1951 birthday got him drafted, whereas my 1956 birth year kept my face from sitting on this veterans' wall beside that of my brother.

I should point out that Dodo's picture is not a photograph. His image stands out from the rest because it's a sketch. When he returned from 'Nam, he carried a lean hungry look that one of Rennie's artist friends captured for the cover of a comic book version of some novel. Dodo put a cropped copy of the cover on this wall instead of his military photo. Too bad the bargain pulp paper it was printed on has yellowed, not to mention frayed and curled inside the cheap frame. You can hardly make out Dodo's pretty face anymore.

I feel a thunderous slap on the back. I turn and face a mug that's as free of wrinkles as the day the artist sketched it. Dodo's still-thick brown wavy bangs dangle over the rims of his oversized nineteen-seventies glasses. His face looks like it should be on the cover of *Tiger Beat* or *16 Magazine*. Yet he just celebrated his sixtieth birthday. I can't help but think that Dodo might be an incubus who sucks the life out of women to maintain his youthful appearance. Rennie could have verified this for me. He knew how to spot every kind of demon. He told me some of them even disguise themselves as angels. That kind of fraud reminds me of those pristine white Colonial homes in the old part of town that are all rotten at the core, just like my older brother.

I lick my lips as Dodo puts a near-empty plate of spinach-and-mushroom manicotti on the bar. I wonder how I missed this dish.

"'S been a while, bro," he hisses. "You're looking good." He speaks these words with his upper lip curled, in a wicked expression the Italian men in my family seem to master at birth. Women love it. Guys want to punch it off their faces.

And seriously? Me looking good? What the hell is he talking about?

My hair is thinning on one side. I'm missing two teeth from a bar fight. My left eye is droopy, and my back is starting to bow. What I'm looking like is a funky Quasimodo. This baby-faced jerk knows I'm fifty-six and can easily pass for his dad.

"I'm living the California Dream," I snort back at him.

I turn away and check out the leggy twenty-somethings who are lingering around the entrance to the bar. It's obvious they're trying to catch Dodo's wandering eye so they can enjoy all the empty humiliation he has to offer. It's a good thing he's never been married or had a kid. I've tried both. Neither decision was great, especially the kid bit. My son likes to think of rehab as his second home. But that's nothing compared to what a kid of Dodo's could be. That hellcat could bring on the apocalypse.

I glance outside at the boarded-up brick building where Dodo's Comic Book Store used to be. You can still see the tufted bottom half of the Dodo bird decal that was once featured on his storefront window. My brother worked for my dad's electrical business during high school to save enough money to open that store after graduation. Dodo worked so hard his junior year that he stayed back and didn't graduate until he was nineteen. Then in 1971, Dodo turned twenty and was drafted for 'Nam. His business had barely been open a year. Funny how nobody's redone his storefront. I suppose they figure the place is bad luck.

One of the leggy babes edges closer to my brother. She licks her full ruby lips. My shoulders twitch.

I point at Dodo's old building. "Too bad you lost your comic book store," I say, loud enough for her to hear.

Dodo swipes a palm over the bangs on his unwrinkled forehead. "Too bad? Losing my store sucked royally. My timing's the worst. Comic books used to be for kids. Now everybody reads them. I could have been a zillionaire. Instead, I'm a grease monkey at a garage that forever borders on bankruptcy and pays me diddly-squat. Meanwhile, you live in the land of bikini babes, great weed, and eternal sunshine."

He raises his arm. I duck, thinking he's taking a swing at me. But he's only offering me an imaginary toast, as the bartender hasn't yet served us any real drinks.

"Here's to you, Oz!" Dodo winces at his risen invisible glass, like he's actually jealous of me, which is flipping hysterical.

III

I feel bad, for like a millisecond. Then Dodo shoves the guy next to me off his stool and snatches it for himself. The barkeep snorts like a bull over his rudeness. I'm thinking I'm about to get stuck in the middle of another bar fight. But the uprooted guy swats the air lightly, like he's used to Dodo's insults. Nothing but Uncle Rennie's passing could've brought me back together with my brother. Nothing.

The barkeep leans into me, his gold cross dangling over the bar. Slivers of well-combed silver hair rake across his liver-spotted pate. "It's good to see you, Oz," he says, "despite the circumstances." He offers me a respectably calloused hand. "I'm Buster Nowicki." He squeezes my knuckles too tight. "You remember me?"

"Sure." I smile, grateful for the recognition. "You were Dodo's buddy back in high school. Then you wound up in his unit in Vietnam. Lucky you."

"Yeah." He rolls his bloodhound eyes. "Lucky me." Buster pats my shoulder. "Your Uncle Rennie was a great man. He knew the secrets of the universe. Plus, he was a guy you could trust." Buster's eyes shift sideways, toward Dodo. "Unlike some people." He pounds the bar top. "You ready to drink a Gansett in his honor?"

I nod lightly, noticing he doesn't ask Dodo if he wants a beer, even though my brother is patting his hand on the bar, in the universal gesture for requesting a drink.

Nowicki passes me a can of Narragansett lager.

"Hey, No Dicky," says Dodo, standing. "What about me? Did you forget about the time I saved your ass on the Ho Chi Minh Trail?"

Nowicki chuckles, "You didn't save my ass; you nearly got it shot off, trying to sell fake American cigarettes. You were a jerk then and you're twice the jerk now." He bends to rummage under the back of the bar like he's randomly decided to start spring cleaning in October. Buster finally emerges with a red face and an open beer which he slams in front of Dodo with a shaking hand. Beer sloshes onto Dodo's forty-year-old "Dressed Up to get Messed Up" band tee-shirt.

My brother puts his palms up in surrender. "Oh, c'mon, Buster. Your daughter is a grown woman. Lay off me. Will you? You know Angie ain't no saint." He smacks his lips. "But I'll admit she's a great cook. Everything is all natural. Picked from the garden and the woods, or bought at local farms. Look at me. I'm the picture of health."

Nowicki grinds his crooked teeth into his words. "Yeah, she's great, and you're trying to break her heart."

Here it comes...

"No way," Dodo leans into the bar. "I told Angie I didn't care if she kept the baby or not. I never told her to get rid of it." My brother lifts his chin. "Truthfully, I think it's about time I had a kid. Don't you? Wouldn't you like a good-looking grandbaby?"

I hold my breath as Nowicki turns his back on us and faces the veterans' photos. I'm afraid he might be crying. I lower my head, respectfully, not wanting to stare at a guy when he's down. I imagine myself back under the pretty pink lights of the Pechanga Casino poker room, enjoying a winning hand of five card stud. My eyes are following my favorite waitress' ass, when I feel the thump and hear the crash. I bolt upright and see shattered glass glistening across the back of the bar. Buster Nowicki is holding Dodo's broken picture frame, tearing the paper picture inside it into narrow strips.

My brother has one arm frozen stiff on the bar, like he's about to leap over it, when his elbow crumples. He falls back toward my side of the bar. I lunge too late to catch him. His neck whacks the stool and then hits the ground with a crack. He's out cold.

The guy Dodo kicked out of his seat yells, "I'm a medic," and pushes me aside.

Buster Nowicki stands motionless, gray-faced and bloodless. The medic guy shouts, "He's got no pulse. He's not breathing."

I grab my thinning hair. "No way!" I dial 911 on the burner phone I bought at the airport. "Dammit," I mumble, as I can't seem to hit the right buttons. I should've paid more attention to my premonition. Maybe I really am as much of a bad luck charm as my late parents claimed. I've come home for the first time in thirty-five years, and my brother collapses at my feet.

IV

Buster tosses the dirty paper plates, plastic utensils, and half-drunk beer cans from the bar top into the trash. He wipes the bar down, like fifty times, as if he's stuck in some kind of psychotic loop. A parade of hotties follows the ambulance gurney as it rolls Dodo's body away. The paramedics continue to work on him, so I guess he's still alive. My brother's ageless form makes me think of the dead boy soldiers at the monument. Only, Dodo isn't young. I need to remember that. I overhear a teenage girl ask her older friend why I couldn't have collapsed instead of Dodo.

My Uncle Joe staggers into the bar from the main room and points at Buster. He's half the size he was the last time I saw him, and he calls out in a raspy squeal, "What the Sam hell did you put in my nephew's beer?"

My eyes widen at Joe's accusing words. I figured Dodo simply had a heart attack.

Buster stares past Joe into the main hall, eyeballs bouncing, like he's searching for somebody. His eyes halt and soften, like he's found who he was looking for.

He turns to Joe. "What can I say? I admit it. I killed the bastard. I'm not sorry, either."

"What?" My jaw drops.

Joe pokes a twisted arthritic finger at Buster. "I knew it. You poisoned my nephew for knocking up your daughter."

Buster runs his hand across the broken glass in front of the whiskeys, cutting his fingers. He smears his dripping blood on the shredded cartoon image of Dodo beside the broken frame. "Guilty as charged," he says, with a quavering voice.

Uncle Joe storms toward Buster, huffing. His head flies back when he sees me and realizes who I am. "Oz! You're home! What'd this bastard do to your brother?"

"I didn't see anything," I reply.

Buster puts his hands to his heart. "You know why I did it, Oz. Somebody had to end that guy. You know he's unnatural."

"Why you dirty..." Joe lunges at Buster.

I step in front of Uncle Joe and haul back my arm, preparing to punch Buster Nowicki on behalf of the entire Grigio clan, when I feel a meaty arm pull me back.

V

"You remember me, Oz? I'm Officer Cieco," says the neat silver-haired policeman who is gripping my pulsing bicep.

A young cop muscles past him and starts to read Buster his rights.

"I'm surprised to see you back in town." Cieco flips open a notepad. "Can you make a statement about what just happened here?"

"Hell, no. My head is spinning." I lean on the bar so I don't collapse. "I can't make a statement about what happened because I don't know what the hell happened. One minute my brother was alive and the next he wasn't."

Cieco sneers. "It doesn't really matter. Buster Nowicki has already confessed to killing Dodo. The toxicology report will reveal what type of poison he used."

"Why do you assume that Dodo was poisoned? Buster said he killed him. He didn't say how." I feel the balding side of my head starting to sweat.

Cieco strokes his chin. "How else could he do it? Did you witness something?"

I start to pace, back and forth, along the short distance of the bar. "I don't know what I saw. Why don't you examine the evidence? You didn't bother looking at it before you put out that warrant for my arrest. Rennie said you wrongly judge people because of your limited view of the world. You don't believe in demons, so you tried to jail me for tying up my demon landlady, even though she was about to fatally curse me. You don't believe in premonitions, so you punished Rennie for his foresight. He told that guy his brakes were bad because he saw the future. He didn't sabotage that car, like you claimed. Sure, Rennie and the guy were in love with the same girl. But if Rennie was his killer, why would he warn him?"

"Your parents didn't believe in any of that mystical nonsense."

"You're right, and look what happened to them. Their friend, Hannah, had a powerful demonic doll that protected her home. Mom and Dad didn't believe in it. After they pocketed Hannah's jewelry, they wound up in a deadly car wreck. You put a drunk driver in jail for their deaths. But Rennie and I both knew the doll was the one that really killed them."

"Oz," says the cop, "enough with the crazy. You only dodged doing serious time because the statute of limitations ran on what you did to that nice old lady. You want me to arrest you now for drunk and disorderly?"

"Always looking at the small picture, aren't you?…Wait a minute. The picture! That's it!" I point at the broken picture frame behind the bar.

I move closer to read the piece of paper glued on the back of the frame. It shows the comic book novel title that used Dodo's face, back in the days before graphic novels.

"*The Picture of Dorian Gray!*" I exclaim.

Cieco sighs. "What are you jabbering about now? Did Buster use that picture frame for self-defense? Is that how the glass got all over the place?"

"Open your mind, man," I say. "Buster didn't use this itty-bitty frame for self-defense. He smashed it to supernaturally murder Dodo."

I hear the click of handcuffs. "Of course he did. As far as I can tell, you're drunk and disorderly. Shades of decades past."

My voice climbs an octave. "You've got to be kidding. I always knew you had a puny brain but I assumed you knew how to read. You really don't get the connection between Dodo's death and that picture?"

Ceico writes fitfully on his notepad. "Don't know. Don't care."

"Then I'll spell it out for you. Dodo is short for my brother's full name of Dorian. *Grigio* means 'gray' in Italian. The Dorian Gray character in the famous novel by Oscar Wilde dies after his picture is destroyed."

The younger cop bites his lip to keep from laughing. "So you're saying that breaking your brother's picture killed him?"

"Sort of. In the story, Dorian dies because his damaged picture no longer supernaturally protects him from the ravages of age, illness, poison, and injury. His years of bad living suddenly take their toll. The same is true of Dodo."

"I don't get it," says the young cop.

"Neither do I," mutters Ceico.

I raise an eyebrow. "Doesn't anybody in this town read?"

Cieco tightens my handcuffs. "I think we'll be adding a psych eval to your processing at the station, Oz."

I hear a loud "Aha!" and we all turn. Uncle Joe's jet black hair pops up from behind the bar.

"Hey, Cieco. You gotta see this." He points downward.

The cop lets go of me and slips behind the bar. He squats to see what Joe's yapping about. I hear him snap on a pair of evidence gloves.

Cieco lifts an open box of rat poison into the air and shakes it at me. He places it inside an evidence bag.

"Thanks, Joe," he says. "This should wrap it up."

VI

Cieco herds people from the main room out the front door. "Time to go home, folks," he growls.

I feel hot with rage. "Buster didn't kill Dodo with rat poison," I yell, making one last effort. "The man's a decorated combat vet. Poisoning's not his style. Buster killed Dodo by breaking his picture."

Nobody's listening to me.

A sweet-faced woman in her thirties slips out of the unisex bathroom that's behind the bar. She's holding her very pregnant stomach. Her long brown hair is piled neatly atop her head, and she's dressed angelically, in white pants, white patent-leather heels, and a sheer, ruffled white chiffon blouse. Naturally, she ignores me. She bends down beneath the bar, pulls out a near-full aluminum pan of spinach-and-mushroom manicotti and scurries back into the bathroom.

Someone snaps their finger in my ear. I turn and see Cieco.

"Hey, Oz," he says. "The hospital just confirmed that your brother, Dodo, was declared DOA. I need to find that cute girlfriend of his and give her the bad news." He scans both rooms. "She's waiting around here somewhere because I told her she shouldn't drive. Have you seen her?"

I shrug. "I got no idea who the hell she is."

He extends two open palms. "Of course not. She's the mother of your future nephew. Why would you care about meeting her? You'll never see the kid, anyway. Right?" He removes my cuffs and returns to the main room, saluting with his back to me. "You're free to go. If I don't see you for another thirty-five years, that's fine by me."

A weird fog rolls into the room. I rub my eyes and see it's my ghostly soldier buddies. This is the first time I've seen them indoors. It's also the first time I've seen them hanging their heads. I figure it's because they knew Dodo in 'Nam and want to pay their respects. I pull out some smokes but they back away, cowering, staring past me, bug-eyed. I turn around and see they're looking at the woman in white. She looks like an angel, except for the wide succubus quality of her mouth. I find it odd that she has exited the bathroom for a second time and is still carrying her manicotti pan, which is now empty and squeaky clean. It occurs to me the soldiers may be freaking out because they've seen people compulsively clean things as a way of dealing with heavy grief.

Could this be Dodo's girlfriend, Angie?

She steps behind the bar, puts down the pan and picks up the bloody shreds of Dodo's picture, staring at it blankly.

Yup, it's her, all right.

I hope she doesn't know the story of Dorian Gray and is planning to do something pathetic, like tape the paper bits of his face back together to bring him back to life or something. I shiver at that thought.

She gathers up all the shredded paper and rolls it unto a ball, and then tosses it in the bar sink and sets it on fire with a Bic lighter. Flames flicker in her bulging green eyes. I glance toward the soldiers to see what they make of her actions and find they've gone.

A thin rope of smoke rises from the bar sink. Dodo's torn paper face is now reduced to charred flakes. The woman in white examines the burnt remains and cocks her head, curiously. She parts her wide mouth into a demonic grin. Holding this expression, she rinses the burnt bits of Dodo's face down the drain, shakes off her smile, and pats her stomach.

I point a finger gun hand in her direction. "You must be Angie Nowicki."

She points to herself with both hands. "I must be."

"I'm Oscar Grigio, Dodo's brother."

Her eyes narrow. "The fugitive."

"At least I'm not a demon, like you."

She pops a hand on one hip. "Wow, you really are as crazy as they say."

I rise and get in her face. "Not crazy, just clairvoyant. I knew something bad was going to happen to Dodo, today. At first, I thought he died of a heart attack. Then I figured he kicked it because your dad broke his picture. Now I'm considering the possibility that you poisoned him. Murder by manicotti, perhaps. I noticed there were mushrooms in that dish you made." I fold my arms. "Dodo said you forage in the woods for your own cooking ingredients. I know death cap mushrooms taste delicious. But nobody dies that quickly from mushroom poisoning. However, the Dorian Gray in the book was protected from poisoning and ailments, only as long as his picture remained intact. So I'm guessing that once your dad ruined Dodo's picture all the poisons you'd given him kicked in at once."

She lifts an evangelistic finger over her head and stares into my one good eye. "*Better for him that each sin of his life had brought its sure swift penalty along with it. There was purification in punishment.*"

I grab the balding side of my head. "Whoa. That's from the ending of the *The Picture of Dorian Gray*."

She claps. "You're such a clever fugitive."

I lunge in and grab the thin chiffon sleeve of her blouse. She pulls away, ripping it at the shoulder. "I know a demon when I see one," I say, shaking. "You won't get away with this. I'll force the cops to test Dodo for mushroom poisoning."

"They won't listen to you." She bolts for the main room, pointing behind her. "Help!" she cries. "Officer Cieco! Anybody! That creep in the orange shirt just attacked me!"

I fly out the back door. I still know the fastest way out of town. I'm headed back to Southern California, where everybody understands the power of ageless Dorian Grays, precognition, angels, demons, past lives, and afterlives.

La Corazonada

Warren C. Easley

How I Almost Didn't Become a Poisoned Pen Author: In the spring of 2012, I finished a manuscript I was very proud of. The title was Matters of Doubt, *and it featured my protagonist, Cal Claxton, coming to the aid of a young homeless man accused of a brutal murder in Portland, Oregon. This was the fourth manuscript I had competed in the series. The first I wisely put in a desk drawer, and the two before* M of D *I shopped around. Both manuscripts caught the attention of Annette Rogers at Poisoned Pen Press, at least to the extent that she wrote me a couple of rejection letters that gave me hope!*

I took the critiques in those letters to heart, and when I submitted Matters of Doubt, *figured I had a real contender, my best work by far! I heard nothing back. Not even a friendly rejection from Annette? I was hurt, maybe a little mad. Meanwhile, the manuscript was getting a lot of attention elsewhere. Almost as an afterthought, I e-mailed Annette because, well, I wanted to write for PPP. The same day, I got back a note from her saying "Resubmit. We changed our process and you got lost in the shuffle." I resubmitted the manuscript and signed a three-book deal with Poisoned Pen Press three months later. Whew.*

—W.C.E.

• • ● • •

On a gorgeous May morning, Albert Kleinman decided he would take the afternoon off at his law office in Southeast Portland.

Albert practiced alone, doing a little criminal defense, mainly DUIs, some divorces, and a lot of *pro bono* for people in his neighborhood whose boats had not been lifted by the tide of the so-called recovery. He was placing a *Closed* sign in the front window of his office when a young woman came in carrying a small briefcase. She wore a hat with a broad rim, large dark glasses that concealed her eyes, and delicate black gloves. Her legs were slim and pretty. Albert invited her to sit and chuckled to himself. She reminded him of Holly Golightly in *Breakfast at Tiffany's,* and he wondered if one of his friends had sent her as some kind of joke.

But the woman was all business. "Are you Albert Kleinman?"

"In the flesh," he said, suppressing a smile. "You can call me Al."

"Okay, Al. My name's Stephanie Nicholson. I'm a personal representative of Ms. Johnson. We need your help in closing a business transaction, and we understand that you know how to handle…um, things of a sensitive and confidential nature."

Albert nodded, still half expecting a joke to be sprung. "Go on. I'm all about sensitive and confidential."

The woman sat up a little straighter, smoothed the skirt on her lap, and when she spoke her lip quivered perceptibly. "A man has some photographs we wish to purchase. We would like you to negotiate with him and secure the best price. And by no means do we wish the deal to fall through."

Albert frowned. Clearly, this wasn't a joke. "That sounds like a job for the police. Extortion's a felony, you know."

The woman's slender neck contracted as she swallowed, and a muscle rippled along her jawline. "We just want to purchase the photographs and the digital record. You can call the photos art treasures, whatever. There's no crime involved."

Albert leaned forward and opened his hands for emphasis. "Look, Stephanie, the police know how to handle this sort of thing. You can have this guy put away for a long time."

She folded her hands in her lap and summoned a look of fierce determination. "Ms. Johnson must have the photographs back."

Albert paused for several moments and the woman sat there watching him from behind her dark glasses. Finally he said, "What price range are you talking about for these art treasures?"

"The seller is asking two hundred and fifty."

"*Thousand?*"

"Yes."

Albert snapped his head back and whistled. "They must be very valuable, these treasures."

"Ms. Johnson will give you five thousand in cash now and another five when you close the deal. In addition, you can keep anything you save off the two-fifty."

Albert knew he should have halted the process right then and there, but there was something about this young woman that drew him in. A protective instinct born of her apparent vulnerability and fear, or was it the fact that she was pretty and reminded him of one of his favorite movie characters? A little of both, perhaps. In any case, he was also behind a month in his rent.

He agreed to help her, and after she signed a hastily drawn-up contract she said, "I'll let you know when and where to meet this man for the negotiations." Then she picked up her briefcase. "There's, um, one more thing. Ms. Johnson's afraid of this man. She purchased a gun for protection, but she doesn't know the first thing about it." She opened the briefcase and handed him the gun, her gloved hand trembling ever so slightly.

Albert examined the weapon. "This is a street gun." He pointed at the barrel. "See? The serial number's been filed off. Where did you get this?"

"Um, Ms. Johnson bought it from her gardener."

"This thing's bad news. Tell your Ms. Johnson to get rid of it."

Instead of responding, the woman reached into the briefcase and produced a box of cartridges. "Can you show me how to use it, please?"

Albert shook his head, but it was clear there was no changing her mind. While the young woman watched, he loaded the weapon then unloaded it and showed her how to snap the safety on and off.

He knew it was a foolish act, and he pushed down a feeling of having been manipulated. After she left, he took a beer from a small refrigerator, sat back down with his feet on the desk, and exhaled a long breath. The encounter stirred up thoughts of his ex-wife. She left him for a young pro-golfer, and, accustomed to the better things in life, demanded half of everything, including his big salary at the most prestigious law firm in Portland. Albert's response was to resign his partnership in the firm, sell the house and most of their belongings, and write a very big check to his favorite charity, Mercy Corps.

Even now, three years later, he laughed aloud thinking about what happened next. She flew into a rage, broke off the affair with the golfer, and returned to Portland, threatening to sue. But it was too late, the assets were gone. Being a resourceful woman, she gave up on the suit and took up with and married one of Albert's previous partners, a man of considerable means.

Alfred considered this his finest hour, and the truth was his wife had done him a great favor. His new, more authentic life brought him great satisfaction and even a few moments of happiness.

The next day Albert met the man with the photographs in a small park in downtown Portland. He had an eastern European accent and the nervous manner of a drug addict. After heated negotiations during which the man repeatedly raised his voice, they agreed on a price of two hundred thousand, to be paid in cash upon receipt of the photos and the digital card they came on. Albert understood why he was hired as a go-between. The man was unstable.

Things happened very quickly after that meeting in the park. The young woman called that night, and Albert told her the terms of the deal. She said she would bring him the money the following evening so that he could arrange the exchange. Albert was to wait for her alone at his home.

But she didn't show that night, and she didn't call to explain.

While having his morning coffee the following day, Albert saw a grainy picture in the newspaper of a man who looked very much like the blackmailer. The caption read—*Man Slain in Pearl District Apartment*. The victim was forty-one-year-old Sergei Kuznetsov. He'd been shot in the head. The motive appeared to be robbery.

A feeling of alarm gripped Albert, and he thought about contacting the police. But he wasn't certain that the murder victim was the man he'd met in the park, so he did nothing. The young woman still hadn't called the next day, and by that time Albert was pretty sure she wouldn't. He was just leaving for his law office when the police arrived. They'd received an anonymous tip that he'd been seen with the murder victim at Overton Park two days earlier. They produced a clearer photograph of the victim, and Albert admitted that was the man he'd met with.

"What was the nature of your meeting?" he was asked.

"I was negotiating a business matter on behalf of a client."

"What caused the argument?"

"Argument? There was no argument. Just a business negotiation."

Albert was pressed for the name of his client and the subject of the meeting. He said he would have to get back with them after speaking to his client—something he knew wouldn't happen because by now he was certain he'd been set up.

The next morning the detectives arrived again, this time with warrants to search Albert's office, car, and house. They started with his car, and in the trunk behind the spare tire they found a gun and fifteen thousand dollars in cash. Although he pointed to scratches on the driver's side door, the police seemed skeptical of Albert's claim that he didn't know how the items got there and noted his lack of an alibi for the night Kuznetsov was killed.

Crime lab confirmation that the gun found in his car was the murder weapon was swift, as was the discovery of his prints on the weapon. Albert was arrested, formally charged with murder, and held without bail. Sergei Kuznetsov, it was revealed, was a high-roller who supplied drugs to the wealthy and was famous for flashing cash around in the bars and restaurants in the Pearl

District. The motive was robbery, and the police were confident that they had arrested his killer.

• • ● • •

Albert was in denial about the seriousness of his situation, and it wasn't until he found himself in jail that he called his good friend Hernando Mendoza, a private investigator. Nando—as he was called by his friends—was a Cuban American who had made his way from his island homeland to Florida in a makeshift raft of his own making fifteen years earlier.

"How are you? Nando asked as Albert was led into the interview room and shackled to a steel chair bolted to the floor.

"I'd be better if you'd brought me a *plato comunista* from Pambiche. The food in this place is inedible."

Nando laughed as he was prone to do, a deep, baritone rumble that filled the room. "When we get you out of here, my friend, I will take you to dinner, my treat."

Albert filled Nando in, and when he finished sighed deeply and shook his head in disbelief. "I was a fool to have trusted her, Nando. I read her wrong. I figured she was the one who wanted the pictures back, and I felt, you know, some kind of obligation to help her."

"What is done is done, my friend. Have you thought about a lawyer?"

Albert laughed bitterly. "Two old colleagues of mine have called already. But they don't work for free, do they? No, I'm going to represent myself."

"Is this wise, Albert?"

"Hell, no, it's not wise. You know what they say about a lawyer who represents himself?"

Nando shook his head.

"He represents a fool, that's what. But I don't have the money for a lawyer. It's you and me, Nando."

They came up with three things that afternoon for Nando to investigate. First they wondered if the woman had driven to

Albert's office. If so, had someone in a neighboring shop noticed what kind of car she was driving or if someone had dropped her off? Second, they wanted to know where the woman got the pistol used to kill Kuznetsov. The police would also be looking at this, but Nando knew people on the street to ask who would never talk to the police. Third, they wanted to see if they could find an alibi for Albert. He had been tricked into staying home alone the night of the murder, but perhaps one of his neighbors had seen him through a window? Or perhaps they had seen someone breaking into his car that night?

The list was a short one, but the friends parted sharing a sliver of hope.

• • ● • •

They met again in the jail three days later. Nando said, "My friend, you do not look so good. Are you getting enough sleep?"

Albert shook his head. "Hell, no. This place never quiets down. If it isn't a fight or someone snoring like a locomotive, then they're bringing in some drunk at three in the morning. Christ, Nando, I've got to get out of here."

Nando frowned and cast his eyes down. "I'm sorry, but the news is not so good. I visited every shop for five blocks on either side of your office. No one noticed a woman like the one who calls herself Stephanie Nicholson. I put the word out on the street that I wanted information on any handguns sold recently, but I have not heard a word back."

Albert shook his head. "Damn. I was hoping you'd get a line on the gun. Did my neighbors see anything?"

"Nothing. I talked to all of them. In Cuba a car break-in like this would not be possible. People live on their front porches there. You Americans are either on your little phones or watching the TV."

After more discussion, they decided Nando should focus next on the victim, Sergei Kuznetsov, his background, his friends, and his hangouts. Perhaps this would provide a lead. Other than that, their only hope was that someone would come back to Nando with information on the murder weapon.

It was hard for Nando to leave his friend that night. He knew Albert's heart was heavy with worry. But he had an idea. In Spanish, it's called *una corazonada*. A hunch. But he didn't mention it to Albert. He didn't want to raise his hopes until he was more certain.

Two days later Nando was sitting in the conference room when they brought Albert in. There had been no word on the murder weapon and no leads on Kuznetsov. Albert slumped down in his chair, looked at his friend, and raised his eyebrows as if to say, *why did you come?*

Nando took an envelope from his briefcase and slid it over to Albert. His heart was beating like it had the night he launched his raft for Florida. "Do you recognize this woman?"

Albert opened the envelope and slid out a photograph. He looked down at it and then back at Nando. "My God, where did you get this?"

"Is she the one who visited you?"

"I think so. Who the hell is she?"

Nando let out the breath he had been holding. "Her name is Nicole Stephan. The woman who visited you said her name was Stephanie Nicolson. Do you get it? It's a play on her real name."

"My God, Nando, you're right."

"She has been missing for five days. Her car was found at a trailhead up on Mt. Hood. They are looking for her as we talk."

Albert studied the photo more carefully, then nodded with firmness. "Yes, I'm certain it's her. She's the right age, the nose and mouth are right. She had those huge dark glasses on, but I'm still certain. How in the hell did you find her?"

Nando smiled with modesty. "It was not difficult. One thing I know about you, Albert—you are a *very* good judge of character. After all, you chose me as a friend. So I asked myself, what if the woman didn't know she was setting you up? What if she thought she was helping someone, a friend, perhaps? Then her sincerity would have seemed genuine, am I not correct?"

Albert nodded. "I suppose so."

"Such a person could have fooled you, no?

He shrugged. "Yeah, I guess."

"And *if* she was being used by someone, then these bad people might want to get rid of her, too."

"Alright. I'll give you that."

"So I looked in the newspaper for any crimes against young women, and there she was, missing. I got the big print of her from a friend at the paper."

Albert's face lit up. "Brilliant, Nando. Brilliant."

The newspaper article mentioned that Nicole Stephan worked as a personal trainer at a private health club in the Pearl District of Portland. "You should go there, Nando. See what you can learn," Albert suggested. "You can buy a one-day membership if you tell them you're interested in joining."

Nando gave his friend an uncertain look. "There are no private clubs in Cuba."

Albert laughed. "Don't worry. Just act like an arrogant SOB, and you'll be fine. A lot of the jerks I used to work with hang out there. Oh, go out and buy yourself a good workout suit and some new cross trainers. You'll need to look the part."

Nando left the jail that day feeling good about his detection work and the faith Albert placed in him. Albert was not a man prone to high praise. Being called "brilliant" by his friend was a first.

• ● ● ● •

The Summit Health Club was located on the second floor of a restored warehouse on Couch Street, behind the city block occupied by Powell's Books. Nando was an avowed capitalist but a thrifty one. The cost of a one-day pass, fifty dollars, made him yearn again for communism. After paying a young girl at the counter, he said, "I am looking for Nicole Stephan. I understand she is your best personal trainer."

The girl's face clouded over, and he thought she was going to cry. "Nicole's not here this afternoon. I can let you talk to the manager, if you'd like?"

Manager Troy Davidson had broad shoulders and arms that rippled with muscles. He looked up at Nando from a stack of papers and without smiling said, "Can I help you?"

"Yes. I would like to use a personal trainer for my workout today. I understand Nicole Stephan is not available."

Nando's words must have surprised Davidson because his eyebrows rose slightly and his eyes got a little bit larger. "You know Nicole?"

Nando smiled. "No. I have not had the pleasure. A friend recommended her."

Davidson looked at Nando again as if his mind was turning something over—some question about him, or maybe he was just deciding whether or not to mention that Nicole was missing. Nando continued to smile. "She's not here this afternoon. I think Jennifer's available. She'll do a good job for you."

Nando was six feet, four inches tall with black, wavy hair, dark skin, and a smile—like his mother used to say—that shamed the morning sun. Maybe it was his smile or the fact he was raised the only boy in a family of six sisters that caused women to confide in him. He didn't really know why, but it had always been so. Jennifer was worried sick about Nicole, but she was optimistic because her friend would never go hiking without being prepared. She told him everyone in the club was upset, and that several employees were up in the mountains helping in the search effort. He also learned that Jennifer had two cats, loved cooking and taekwondo, and had just broken up with her boyfriend.

After expressing his sympathy about the breakup, Nando asked, "Does your friend Nicole have a boyfriend?"

Jennifer laughed. "Not at the moment. She was in a relationship, but she got dumped, too. Trouble is, she's not over it."

Nando's father used to say *una corazonada* is a whisper from God. As he lay back on the bench to prepare for a set of presses, he said, "Your boss is a handsome man. He must be popular with the ladies here."

Jennifer got in position to spot him. "Oh, yeah. Troy's quite the lady's man, alright, just ask Nicole."

Nando squeezed off twenty repetitions and eased the barbell back in the rack. "Oh, so it was he who dumped her?"

"Right," Jennifer answered with a smirk. "He's hit on just about every woman on the staff."

Nando wiped his brow with a towel and looked indignant. "Not you?"

"Oh, yeah. He came on to me a couple of times." She laughed. "I told him to take a cold shower…"

Nando knew gossip was like an addictive drug. He waited.

"…But he's gone up-market now."

"Up-market?" he asked with a puzzled look.

"Uh huh," she said, nodding her head.

"Not a client," Nando said with more feigned indignation.

"You guessed it. He likes 'em good looking or rich. This one's both. Then she laughed and added, "She's Nicole's client, actually."

"*No,*" Nando replied, his heart beating faster. "Let me guess— this rich woman has a husband."

At this point, Jennifer furrowed her brow and cocked her head at him. "You've got me talking too much, Nando. Let's see how many crunches you can do."

Jennifer was a gossip, but she was also a smart woman. Nando finished his workout without asking any more questions, although he wanted very much to know the name of Davidson's current lover. Afterward, he took a shower, dried off, and busied himself packing his gear and then combing his hair until he was sure no one was in the adjoining restroom. He entered and stood with one foot on the sink and one on a paper towel dispenser to unlock the latch on the small, high window that faced the back alley. He left the club by the front door after saying good-bye to his new friend, Jennifer, and having convinced himself the club had no burglar alarms.

• • ● • •

At three o'clock the next morning Nando stood in the alley behind The Summit Health Club looking up at the restroom window, hoping it was still unlocked. Albert had said to him many times, "Nando, when you're working for me, I don't want you breaking any damn laws. Do you understand?" But this was different. He was sure his friend would forgive him for what he was about to do.

He took a deep breath, leaped up, and grasped the window ledge with both gloved hands. Then, aided by the traction of his new cross trainers against the wall, he scrambled up, leaned his forehead into the windowpane, and to his relief it swung inward. He wound up draped over the ledge like a sack of rice, half in and half out. The paper towel dispenser hung on the wall below him. He worked his way down until both hands rested on it, lowered himself until his feet just cleared the window, and then swung into the room like a gymnast.

He went straight to Troy Davidson's office. It was locked, but he found a key in the middle drawer of the receptionist's desk. In the top drawer of a filing cabinet behind Davidson's desk Nando found what he was looking for—a series of folders with personal information and workout schedules for each of the manager's clients. When he read the name on the third file in, his heart beat a little faster: Sergei Kuznetsov. He rifled through the other eight files, all women, and copied their names into a small notebook he'd brought with him.

Nicole shared an office with Jennifer. It was unlocked. Nicole's client files were tossed carelessly into a file drawer in her desk. Nando fished them out one by one and wrote down the names of her female clients. The last name he copied rang a bell, but he didn't know why. As he was leaving the office, it came to him. It was the *first* name of the woman that was familiar. He would have to double-check the last name, but he was pretty sure what he would find.

Building a raft in Cuba to escape to Florida was good preparation for being a private investigator. In those days, the Cuban authorities were watching carefully for signs of such activity, so Nando learned to plan carefully and work with stealth during the five years it took him to prepare his escape.

So it is in the PI business. He went back to Davidson's office and used the flat blade in his Leatherman to unscrew the plate covering an electrical outlet on the side wall. He had the bug—a matchbox-sized microphone and transmitter—installed and the plate back on in under two minutes. He preferred room bugs to telephone bugs, because most people talk more freely behind closed doors than on the telephone.

• • ● • •

Nando was pretty sure Jennifer would agree to help him. He got her undivided attention when he guessed the name of the woman Troy Davidson was having an affair with, the name she had withheld from him the day before. When he told her about the blackmail plot and the scheme to frame his friend, Albert, she said, "That figures. Nicole would do anything for that rat, Troy Davidson." When he told her that Davidson and his lover probably had done away with Nicole, she was horrified and wanted to immediately go to the police.

"I understand your concern for your friend," Nando said, "but I do not yet have enough evidence." He met Jennifer's eyes and held them. "I have an idea for a trap, but I will need your help."

Jennifer nodded eagerly. "Whatever it takes."

"It could be dangerous."

She laughed. "I'm not afraid. Nicole would do the same for me."

After Nando filled her in on his plan and coached her a little, she was even more enthusiastic. As Albert would say, Jennifer had *chutzpa*.

The next afternoon Nando was in the back of his van with his headphones on, his receiver tuned in, and his tape recorder running. He could hear Troy Davidson handling papers on his desk and the squeak of springs as he shifted in his chair. He called Jennifer and said, "We are going."

A few moments later he heard her enter Davidson's office and close the door. "I know what you're up to, Troy."

"I beg your pardon?"

"Nicole told me how you had her go to this lawyer to get some pictures back that a guy named Kuznetsov took of you and your latest fling. The pictures were no big problem for you, but that bitch sure as hell didn't want her wealthy husband to find out she was jumping your bones. Now Kuznetsov is dead, the lawyer's in jail, and Nicole's missing."

Davidson stayed calmer than Nando hoped he would. He laughed. "That's nonsense, Jennifer. Nobody's going to believe that. From what I read, that lawyer shot the Russian and robbed him."

Nando's heart began to hammer in his rib cage, but Jennifer didn't miss a beat. "Nicole may be stupid in love with you, Troy, but she isn't as gullible as you think," she said, cool as an icicle. "She gave me a letter to be opened if something happened to her."

Nando held his breath and imagined Jennifer's hand extended with a copy of the letter in it. She had typed it on the computer the way she thought Nicole would have written it. He began working on forging Nicole's signature based on some papers Jennifer brought from the club. On his ninth try, Jennifer cried, "*That's it!* You nailed it, Nando." The back-dated notary seal was an added touch, something he procured from a friend of his in Southeast Portland.

Nando waited. Finally, Davidson sighed heavily and said in a low but audible tone, "She was well paid for her little errand, Jennifer. She's gone off to start a new life somewhere, I suppose." He laughed and added, "She'll be calling you in a few days, you wait."

"That letter's going to cost you, Troy. I'd like some traveling money, too, so I can join Nicole."

"I'm sure that can be arranged," he answered. The words sent chills running down Nando's back.

"I want twenty thousand in cash. Then I'll give you the letter and forget all about this."

Another long pause. "You drive a hard bargain, young lady."

"I'll give you two days to get the money."

Nando heard a door open, then shut. He continued to listen, hoping Davidson would be tempted to call his lover, but that didn't happen.

• • ● • •

Although the evidence they had would not be admissible in court, Nando hoped it would be enough to get the police to listen to him. He called the detectives working the Kuznetsov murder and got their voice mails. He punched off his cell phone angrily and said to Jennifer, "In Cuba, there is not so much voice mail. One can usually reach a human there."

They were both famished, so he took her to his and Albert's favorite Cuban restaurant, Pambiche, for dinner. Afterwards, he tried the police again without success, so he suggested that she stay at a hotel that night as a precaution. She made a face, so he said, "I have a big couch in my living room. You can have my bed." She agreed.

Jennifer had gone to bed. Nando selected a Hoyo de Monterrey and stepped out on his porch to smoke it, thankful that good Cuban cigars could be purchased on the Internet. When he felt the barrel of a pistol on his neck, he thought of what his father used to say, "If you stir up a hornet's nest, don't be surprised if you get stung."

"Back in the house and keep your mouth shut or I'll blow a hole in you." It was Troy Davidson. He stayed behind Nando, pulled the door shut, and said, "Where's Jennifer?"

"Who?"

Davidson hit him hard with the pistol, and he dropped to one knee. "You know who. You come in the club asking about Nicole, you spend the afternoon with Jennifer—"

"It was your idea to give me Jennifer."

Davidson hit him again, knocking him to the floor. "I checked you out, Mendoza. You're a PI, and I know you're mixed up in this somehow." Out of the corner of his eye, Nando watched him take a cushion from the couch and wrapped it around his pistol. "Last chance. Tell me where she is or I'm going to put a bullet in your head."

Jennifer was a strong woman. When she hit Troy Davidson with a piece of lumber that hung on the wall in Nando's bedroom, he hit the floor—as Nando later described it—like a ripe mango. She stood there, her chest heaving, and looked at the stout piece of hand-carved wood in her hands. "What's an oar doing in your bedroom?"

Nando beamed a smile despite his injuries. "It is a souvenir from another life."

• • ● •• •

The charges against Albert Kleinman were dropped and Troy Davidson and his lover were arrested and charged with the murder of Nicole Stephan, whose bludgeoned body was found two weeks later. Nando and Jennifer were waiting for Albert in the lobby of the police station. When Albert saw his friend, who sported two large bandages on his head, he said, "Oh, God. Does this mean you're going to charge me extra?" Nando laughed and filled his friend in on the final details leading up to his release. When he finished, Albert said, "You left one thing out, Nando. Who the hell is Troy Davidson's lover?"

Nando laughed again. "Your ex-wife. Who else?"

Time's Revenge

Mary Reed and Eric Mayer

We arrived on the doorstep of the Press via an unusual route. Having read the then-infant Poisoned Pen Press had been nominated for the 1998 Edgar Award for Best Critical/Biographical Work for their title AZ Murder Goes…Classic, *we wrote to congratulate them, and at the same time asked if they would eventually be considering fiction. We learned later that Editor-in-Chief Barbara Peters had commented on the lack of a mystery series set in Byzantine times not long before our note showed up. An encouraging reply arrived and* One For Sorrow *was accepted in due course. The rest, as they say, is historical mystery….*

—*M.R. and E.M.*

• • ● • •

The clock filled the room with the drip, drip, drip of water dropping from its wide basin into a receptacle below. For the old wine merchant, Laskarios, lying on the mosaic grape clusters decorating the floor of his study, time had run out.

As the palace physician, Gaius, examined the body, John, Lord Chamberlain to Emperor Justinian, looked on. A tall, lean man with a military bearing, he wore plain dark blue robes unbefitting one of his exalted position.

Gaius propelled himself to his feet with a grunt. "No signs of violence, John." He smelled as if he had been kneeling in real

213

grapes, having been drawn away from one of his long conversations with Bacchus.

"Senator Honorius spoke of murder. I know him well enough to respect his word."

Gaius shook his head. "No blood. No wounds. No signs of poisoning."

John silently looked round the study, the wooden desk and chair in front of the window, the water clock with hourly markings engraved inside its ceramic basin, the frescoed vineyards on the walls. The open second-story window faced south over a courtyard with a distant view of the Sea of Marmara. Below the window sat a sundial, its gnomon a miniature obelisk. It was one of many such timepieces. The paths in Laskarios' extensive gardens did not wind between flowers, shrubs, and statuary but between a bewildering variety of shadow clocks.

Laskarios, frail and bald and clothed for the oppressive August heat in a thin white tunic, resembled an ancient infant curled up for a nap.

The physician ran the back of his hand over his damp forehead. "My head's pounding. I wish that infernal dripping would stop, John. Never mind. I'm off now. I'll send someone from the palace to deal with the body. Tell the senator that Laskarios died because he was an old man. Death is time's revenge."

• • ● • •

Time's revenge for what? John wondered as he made his way along the corridor from the study, passing by one clock after another. Revenge for wasting so much of it?

If Gaius was right, John had wasted his time coming here. However, if Senator Honorius was right, he owed it to Laskarios to find his murderer. The wine merchant had helped John survive his early days in the city.

John had arrived in Constantinople years earlier as a palace slave. Housed in a barracks, worked as hard as a farmer's mule, but not as well fed or treated, he had all but lost faith in the world and might have sunk into a life of hopeless servitude. Then he was lent to Laskarios for several weeks after one of the wine merchant's servants broke a leg while helping to haul a large bronze sundial to the house roof.

Laskarios treated John, like the rest of his staff, with a kindness the young slave had almost forgotten existed. That respite had renewed John's strength and helped him to endure until Fortuna offered him the chance to escape his servitude.

The wine merchant explained the basis for his philosophy of kindness one chilly autumn day while John adjusted the wedges in the apertures of a water clock, changing its flow to account for the shorter days of approaching winter.

"Time is the one thing rich and poor possess in equal measures, John. Nor can the rich accumulate time as they can wealth," Laskarios lectured, a Plato of time with a single student. "So then, in the end, we are all equal."

Yet hadn't he attempted to hoard time by filling his house with clocks?

Perhaps not. As he grew older he became an object of gossip and derision at court because he rarely left his home, unwilling to be out of sight of a clock. Did he fear that if he could not keep a constant vigil over time it would slip away from him all at once?

As it had today.

As John entered the atrium downstairs he was greeted by an elaborate timepiece he hadn't seen during occasional visits in the past. Unlike the simple study clock where the water level dropped inside its basin to indicate the hour, this clock featured a small figure pointing a wand to a pillar on which the hours were engraved.

"Ingenious, isn't it?" The speaker walked over with a sailor's rolling gait and placed a big weathered hand on the clock's marble base. "It was built specially for Laskarios by a craftsman from Greece. The master took great pleasure in explaining to guests how a flow of water from the upper part turned a system of cogs lower down, causing our little winged goddess to fly upwards hour by hour."

"Indeed. And you are Menas, the steward?"

The man made a perfunctory bow. "Lord Chamberlain. I apologize that you have been drawn away from your usual duties. Senator Honorius was understandably shocked and distressed. However, the master has been ailing for months. Indeed, this morning he was too weak to show the senator around the grounds himself and delegated me to do so. The master's death is a tragedy for all of us."

Did the man's tone strike John as transparently insincere only because Senator Honorius was convinced the steward had engineered Laskarios' death in some fashion?

"When were you with the senator?"

"Between the third and the fifth hours."

"You are certain?"

Menas allowed himself a smile. "How could I fail to know the time? We were in the garden, looking at the sundials."

"I understand Laskarios intended to move to his country villa," John said. "He was selling this house?"

"That is correct, Excellency. And I must tell you that the senator's offer for it was much too low. I advised the master we could surely get a better price but he has—*had*—some sentimental attachment to Honorius."

"And this is of interest to me because…?"

"Because I believe Honorius did not appreciate my giving business advice to the master. But, after all, I am steward. I do not expect aspersions to be cast on me, and yet, one must be careful."

"Of course." John glanced toward a marble bench occupied by two servants, both of them clearly afraid.

"The young man was the last person to see Laskarios alive," Menas said. "The girl is the one who found him dead."

"Remain nearby. I may need to speak with you again."

The waiting servants stood and regarded John with obvious unease as he approached, which struck him as odd. The Laskarios

John remembered would not have treated his household in a manner as to make them fearful of authority. But since Laskarios had been unwell, Menas might well have taken over much of the running of the place.

Was he being unfair to Menas to imagine he would make a harsh master?

"Albia, your Excellency sir," as she introduced herself, was a slight young girl who should have been pretty except for a vagueness about her features, as if a sculptor had given up just before finishing his task.

"Cook sent me up to ask what the master wanted for the evening meal." She spoke hesitantly and so softly John had to lean toward her to make out the words, causing her to retreat a step.

"You found Laskarios lying on the floor?"

She nodded and bit her lip.

"And what did you do?"

"Oh, Excellency sir, I screamed and then Martha ran in and then…I don't remember."

"Martha?"

"The gardener."

Martha had seen Laskarios dead almost as soon as Albia. Why hadn't Menas brought her to the atrium for questioning? John would have to speak with her, especially since Albia had nothing much to add. She was now approaching a state of panic.

Before dismissing the girl, John asked the obvious question in a house filled with timepieces. "Did you notice the time when you found your master?"

"It was about the fourth hour of the day, Excellency sir."

When she had departed in haste, John turned his attention to the other servant. Like everyone under Laskarios' roof, Timothy had a keen awareness of the hours. He had delivered a pitcher of wine to his master in the study shortly after the third, which meant Laskarios had died between then and the fourth.

Timothy's looks and manner would have made him as noticeable as a chair in the course of his duties. A perfect servant. Which is what made his fury, betrayed by the flush on his cheekbones, the edge in his voice, and his partially clenched hands, so surprising.

"Why are you angered, Timothy?"

"Angry?"

"It is obvious. What is the trouble?"

Timothy licked his lips and his gaze darted from side to side as if looking for an escape route.

"Your master was very kind to me some years ago," John told him. "If you believe there is something unusual about his death, I want to know it so I can put matters to rights."

"It's not for me to say whether his death was unusual, sir. If the Lord called him in the natural way, we all expect as much. But for those of us in the house it would cause a wrong. The master would never turn us out into the street and we fear…" he paused and then blurted out "…that the senator will."

"Did Laskarios tell you he planned to sell his house to the senator?"

"He did not confide in any of us, but everyone knew. The master insisted the senator had to keep us all on here, there being no need for us at his country villa, but the senator refused to agree."

"Who told you that?"

"No one, sir. It was just in the air, as you might say."

Watching the young man's agitated face, John detected no sign he was hiding anything. "But it is common knowledge the senator was trying to drive a bargain your master would not accept?"

"I…I'm a servant, sir. I empty chamber pots. What do I know about business?"

• • ● • •

Senator Honorius sat alone, eating the meal he'd been expecting to share with Laskarios hours earlier. The room's painted screens had been removed for the summer, opening the dining room to the inner garden beyond.

As John entered, the senator looked up, a stuffed grape leaf positioned in front of his lips. "Any theory on how the steward killed his master, John?"

John sat down and regarded the gaunt, white-haired man over a silver platter heaped with what John—veteran of so many imperial banquets—recognized as pork broiled with honey and wine. He didn't feel hungry. "The physician said there was no indication Laskarios was murdered. And even if he was, Menas was with you touring the grounds between the third and fifth hours, and Laskarios died some time after the third and before the fourth."

Honorius waved his hand in a dismissive manner. Despite the heat he wore heavy embroidered robes with decorative roundels stitched on front and back. Was it a matter of affectation overriding comfort, or had the senator reached that age when he was continually chilled by drafts from death's nearby realm?

"Two different servants have confirmed the time during which he must have died," John continued. "Naturally, I'll seek corroboration, but they gave me no reason to doubt them."

"That's why I asked you investigate. Otherwise, Menas will go unpunished. You have a reputation at the imperial court for getting to the heart of things."

Honorius dug into the pork with a gusto that belied the circumstances.

John's gaze drifted to the dining room's clock, a huge cornucopia trickling water into a bowl whose outer surface was decorated with bas reliefs of fruit.

"For banquets, that was filled with wine," Honorius remarked about the clock.

"Why do you think Menas killed Laskarios?"

"He's going to lose his post, isn't he? I don't intend to employ Laskarios' servants, although he expected me to agree to do so. They have no loyalty to me. For that matter, it may surprise you to learn that Menas has no loyalty to Laskarios."

John remembered what the steward had said about aspersions being cast on him. "What makes you say that?"

"Laskarios confided in me. He suspected Menas was robbing him. Had the notion he planned to abscond when he stole enough. Menas was a sailor, you know. It wouldn't bother him to set sail for a new port."

"Why did he suspect Menas?"

"Laskarios wasn't very clear about that. I fear his mind might have been growing as feeble as his body. No doubt you are unconvinced. Menas has been pouring lies into your ears, hasn't he? He's a cunning rascal."

Between the senator and steward, John would have picked Menas as the rascal. "I gather you and Laskarios had not come to a formal agreement?"

"I suppose we would have eventually, but Laskarios drives a hard bargain. He over-values the place from sentiment. A businessman would have been eager to take what I offered and have the necessary documents drawn up for signature."

"Will Menas as executor agree to your offer with more alacrity?"

The large bite of lamb Honorius was swallowing descended with difficulty. He reddened and grabbed for his wine cup. After taking a gulp he wiped watering eyes. "Surely you cannot think Menas and I are working together in some fashion?"

"Of course not. It was you who insisted he be investigated."

"Yes, well…in response to your question, Lord Chamberlain, no, Menas will not be quick to agree to my offer. He needs time to loot his master's estate thoroughly while no one is supervising him."

• • ● • •

John went to the garden at the side of the mansion in search of Martha, who'd been drawn to Laskarios' body by Albia's screams. Beyond the garden wall loomed the distant Hippodrome. He paused at yet another timepiece as he looked around the beautifully kept grounds. Constructed of a wooden T attached to one end of a long narrow base, it was attended by a servant whose duty it was to place it to face east in the morning and reverse it at noon so the time was indicated by the position of the shadow of the T on the hourly markings on its base.

Laskarios' obsession with time had been foolish, but what harm did it do?

Except perhaps to himself if while so fixated on the menace of time he may have been blind to dangers around him.

And yet, Gaius had insisted there were no signs of murder. And John knew that as physician at Justinian's court, Gaius was an expert on every form of murder, no matter how subtle, even when he was intoxicated.

John spotted a sturdy woman kneeling by a flower bed, watering seedlings. Seeing John, she rose, brushing ineffectually at her soiled tunic. Her eyes were sea blue and her mouth a red rosebud.

"Yes," she confirmed, "I heard Albia's screams and ran to her. The poor child's humors are afflicted, sir. Her thinking is not clear. Despite his kindness, she was always afraid of the master and to find him dead…well…"

John asked why the girl had been afraid.

"He was always making advances to her. But we shouldn't speak ill of the dead, sir," Martha added quickly. She went on to explain that Laskarios had richly rewarded her for suggesting the pleasant conceit of a time garden, where flowers opening and closing at various hours marked each day's passage. She indicated the flower bed beside them. "The work on the plantings has begun, as you see, but he'll never see it in bloom."

"It is possible Albia might have been mistaken about her master's behavior," John observed.

"It may be so, sir." Martha sounded dubious. She ran her hand over her sweating face, leaving a streak of dirt.

"The household knew Laskarios was selling his house. Who told you?"

"I don't remember, sir. No, wait. It might have been Timothy."

John ended their conversation. As he was returning to the house, Martha called after him. "Come back next summer when the garden is in bloom, sir." Her face darkened. "If we're still here then."

• • ● • •

"Martha says I told her about the master selling this house?" Timothy shook his head. "I am afraid she's just trying to cause trouble, sir."

"Why would that be?"

"Oh, who knows? She is a vicious woman." He looked fearfully at John and quickly averted his gaze.

Timothy's third-floor room was humid and hot enough to bake bread on the sill of its one inadequate window. John regretted wearing even a simple robe rather than a tunic but a Lord Chamberlain—even one who had been a slave—could hardly be seen in public dressed like a laborer. "I'm not here to cause difficulties, Timothy. I'm seeking information."

"But, sir, I told you everything I know when we spoke earlier."

"Then why are you afraid of me?"

"Do I seem so?" Timothy sighed. "I suppose I do, don't I?"

"Think carefully now. Who told you about Laskarios selling the house?"

Timothy looked at the ceiling and pondered the question. "No one told me, sir," he finally said. "Now I recall I overheard Menas and Martha talking. Menas knows everything, being the steward."

John took a breath. It was like inhaling warm broth. "Why would Menas talk to Martha about his master's business?"

"Menas and Martha are sleeping together, sir."

Yes, John thought. Of course. Was that why Menas had neglected to mention Martha coming to Albia's aid? Had he been trying to protect her, lest suspicion fell on her? A gardener, after all, would know a great deal about poisonous plants. Yet Gaius was positive Laskarios had not been poisoned. He started to leave, then stopped and looked around the room. "No clocks?"

"I hate them, sir. The hours are always snapping at my heels. This is the only room in the house I can get away from them. Everywhere else it's like being chased by the Furies. Do you know the master had the clock in his study specially designed so he could hear time slipping away?"

• • ● • •

John found Menas in another part of the garden, standing in front of a sandstone pillar casting a finger of shadow across an open grassed area set with a semicircle of stones representing the hours. The shadow clock was echoed by a more elaborate marble obelisk some way off. Decorated with carvings of Chronos, the personification of time, it announced the hour in similar fashion.

The steward folded his brawny arms and greeted John's question with an expression of smug arrogance. "Yes, Martha and I are close friends. It was that worm Timothy who told you, no doubt. He would like Martha for himself, as if there were any chance of it. He spies on her, sir. Disgraceful behavior, I call it."

"I'm not here to look into domestic scandals. What I want to know is why you didn't bring Martha to the atrium so I could question her. She joined Albia right after the body was found."

"Martha wasn't the person who discovered the body. I didn't think she'd have anything to add."

A much younger John would have been tempted to plant his fist in Menas' smirk. He was suddenly certain Menas was a murderer as Honorius claimed, even though Laskarios had not by all appearances been murdered. And yet, John reminded himself, the court teemed with unpleasant and dishonest people who stopped short of murder, while some of the worst villains were the most plausible.

"Lord Chamberlain, it seems to me the senator imagines he'd get a better price on the house from me as estate executor."

"Then why did he tell me Laskarios suspected you of stealing? If shown to be true, you'd be removed as executor."

Menas shrugged. "I cannot say. I am sure you will be able to unravel his motive, sir." He continued to smirk. He was mocking John and enjoying it.

"And if I have come to the conclusion you murdered your master?"

Menas didn't flinch. "Surely that is impossible, given Laskarios obviously died of old age. Not to mention your questioning of Albia and Timothy showed he died between the third and fourth hours. Senator Honorius will have to admit he was by my side as I showed him round the gardens from the third hour to the fifth, so I cannot have been indoors during that time."

John stalked off without a further word. Crossing the grass he noticed his shadow had joined those of the pair of shadow clocks.

He paced the gardens. He thought best on his feet. Never had he come upon so many motives in a single afternoon.

If Menas had indeed been stealing from Laskarios he would want to forestall discovery and give himself extra time to loot the estate. He and Martha could then run off together.

Could Martha have served as his accomplice or had she acted alone, afraid Laskarios was about to take legal action against Menas?

Albia, with her clouded mind, could hardly be blamed had she chosen to exact revenge on Laskarios for his unwanted advances, if he had actually made any.

Timothy, or any of the household servants, might have killed Laskarios purely from anger, believing he was about to throw them into the street by selling his house to Honorius. Or might he have thought that by killing Laskarios the sale to the senator would be halted and a more compassionate buyer found?

Then there was the senator himself. Honorius might have decided Laskarios would never sell to him but Menas would, or even that he could get a better price from Menas in return for sharing his savings.

John came to the front gate and an imposing clock formed from a massive stone block with a half hemisphere scooped from its side. A thin gnomon, projecting horizontally over the curved depression, cast its shadow over the hour lines engraved there.

So many ways to mark the hours and yet, take away the moving shadows, the falling water, the turning wheels, and where was time itself? For all that it could be seen or felt, it might as well not exist.

• • ● • •

When he entered the kitchen, John was surprised to see Gaius lounging there, a half empty jug of wine in front of him. He was telling a rotund woman John took to be the cook a scandalous tale about Empress Theodora. The cook's assistant, Albia, peeled garlic bulbs at the other end of the table. Their pungent odor filled the long room.

Gaius looked up at John with a guilty expression.

The cook gave John a nervous sideways glance, emptied a bowl of vegetables into a pot on the brazier, then checked one of a series of tiny water clocks of various sizes arrayed on the shelf over it. Each one, John surmised, held a different amount of water to indicate cooking times for various dishes.

"How do you calculate meal times?" John asked the cook.

"Well, Excellency, the master was very particular about that so we use that to make certain they are not late." She pointed a ladle to a nondescript example similar to the one in the study. Her round face clouded as she remembered Laskarios was now beyond caring what time the evening meal was served.

"What time did you send Albia to Laskarios' study?"

"The same time I always send her to ask what to prepare for the meal, Excellency. At the sixth hour."

"Albia." John sharply addressed the girl who was chopping her garlic, apparently oblivious to the conversation.

She stopped chopping and stared at John in confusion.

"You told me you found your master dead at about the fourth hour, but the cook says she sent you to his study at the sixth."

The girl's expression turned to fear. "But I'm sure the clock said it was about the fourth hour, Excellency sir."

"Are you certain? Did you look at the kitchen clock?"

The cook glared at the girl, who was screwing up her face in a painfully visible effort to gather her thoughts.

"No. I looked at the clock in the study. I don't usually look at clocks," Albia finally said. "Why would the likes of me need to? I do what I'm told, whatever time it might be. But the master's room was so quiet. It was as if he had sucked all the sound out of the air when he died. All I could hear was that horrible drip, drip, drip, from the clock, so I couldn't help but look at it,"

• • ● • •

Laskarios' body had been removed from the study but John, Gaius, and Menas nevertheless skirted the spot where it had lain.

Menas continued to look smug, but now his smirk was a rigid mask concealing whatever his real feelings might be.

John walked to the window and looked down at the shadow cast by the miniature obelisk two stories below, then over to the water clock. "The water level indicates one time but the sun, strangely enough, does not agree."

Menas' features remained frozen.

Gaius looked on, bewildered and not entirely sober.

"When I was a young mercenary in Bretania," John continued, "before I came to Constantinople, a colleague drowned in a swollen stream." He controlled the quaver that threatened to break into his voice. Deep water frightened John more than all the concealed knives at the imperial court. "When we pulled him out, almost immediately but too late, he might merely have been sleeping. For drowning leaves no signs."

Menas laughed. "I'd wager you've never encountered a bloated corpse floating by the docks, sir."

John shot a glance at Gaius. "The Lord Chamberlain is correct," the palace physician said. "What are called the signs of drowning are mostly the effects of long submersion in water."

"As a former sailor you would know that," John told Menas. "Which is why you pushed Laskarios' face into the bowl of that water clock. He was too feeble to struggle. There were no marks. Any dampness would soon evaporate in this heat or be mistaken for sweat. Like my dead colleague, he looked as if he had slipped off to sleep. Forever. Not uncommon for old men in failing health."

Menas' smirk twisted into a smile. "But it makes no sense, sir. Remember, Laskarios died after the third hour and before the fourth. The senator was with me between the third and fifth hours, as he will confirm."

"And the senator was telling the truth. You left Honorius in the garden at the fifth hour, came up to the study, and killed your master. The cook's assistant, Albia, thought she discovered the body at the fourth hour because she looked at the water clock in here. But it was showing the wrong time because when you drowned him Laskarios inhaled water. About two hours' worth."

Menas' laugh was not convincing. "But—"

John cut him off. "Your initial plan was for the death to appear natural. You should have kept to it. Perhaps you noticed the missing water, or it may be that you didn't and only realized what had happened when Albia told me in your presence what time she'd found Laskarios. In either case you decided you might as well show you were innocent to be doubly safe. You're a clever man, Menas. Too clever for your own good, trying to use your murder weapon to demonstrate your innocence."

Menas' gaze darted around the room. He took a step toward the doorway, which had suddenly been blocked by two imperial guards.

"I took the precaution of sending a message to the palace before summoning you to the study," John said.

Menas whirled around. Gaius stepped into his path and Menas knocked him down.

Before John or the guards could react, Menas had flung himself out the open window.

• • ● • •

No doubt the steward had intended to escape. It was, after all, only a two-story drop. Unfortunately for his future schemes he had forgotten the sundial below the window.

By the time John and Gaius got to Menas he was dead, impaled on the sundial's sharply pointed obelisk, his blood spreading across the dial.

"There are few who were as devoted to the hours as Laskarios," John observed with a thin smile. "Now time has taken its revenge."

Taking the Waters

Kerry Greenwood

What we look for in publishing is people who love books. I had an American publisher once, but they decanted my first two novels into the USA as though they were bargain counter Christmas crackers at a dusty, down-at-heel Two-Dollar Shop. They came and went without discernible impact, so I forgot all about it. Much later, Allen & Unwin (my Australian publisher) alerted me to Poisoned Pen Press, and I resolved to investigate. Everyone I spoke to encouraged me, so I signed up. PPP is the ideal press for mystery writers, because they love books, and actually want to sell them. This makes all the difference. They are charming, enthusiastic, and more like a family than a corporation. The writers talk to each other. I do not know of any other publishing house where this happens. I have never regretted my decision. Thank you all!

—K.G.

• • ● • •

Miss Dorothy Williams (assistant and companion to The Hon Phryne Fisher) was sitting in the embrace of the leather-cushioned passenger seat of the Hispano-Suiza. She was terrified, as usual. Her lips moved as she sat, but silently. She was protected from the early spring chill by her cable-stitch cream cricket jumper, heavy worsted jacket, brown woollen skirt, lisle stockings, and boots. She also wore an Improved Freda Storm Veil for Frightened Passengers, but it was not helping as much as she had hoped. It was grey, like Dot's mood, with double elastic, and further anchored by two vicious-looking hatpins stuck into her brown plaits, one from each side. In her mind, she was re-checking the luggage. Her own (a small suitcase and the picnic basket), and Miss Fisher's two enormous valises which occupied the remainder of the car boot. She realized that if anything had been left behind, it was now far too late to worry about it.

Her eyes remained resolutely shut. Phryne's lips would purse when Dot exclaimed at passing barrows, bicycles, carts, and assorted vehicles. Words Had Been Exchanged in the past, and it was better if Phryne pursued her imperious path through Melbourne's traffic unobserved by her prayerful companion. Dot was now invoking the succour of St Christopher, patron and guardian of travellers. A small silver medallion hung from her neck, and both her neat hands were clasped around it.

While her eyes remained closed, her ears were receiving a good deal. Curses, shouts, car horns, police whistles, and the rebuking clangour of a passing tram. Better not to know, she decided, and continued her novena. When she had finished, Dot inhaled deeply. The passing air was astringent, but clean; and there was no sound but the roar of the eight-cylinder engine and the wind. She opened her eyes to find herself careening down a steep hill into what appeared to be a valley of apple orchards.

'Where are we, Miss?' she ventured in a timid voice.

'Just heading into the Avenue of Honour in Bacchus Marsh, Dot,' Phryne informed her. 'Where there is a thirty-miles-per-hour speed limit, with which I intend to comply.' She eased the motor back to a gentle purr, and Dot looked at the road with interest. Flourishing elm saplings lined both sides.

'There are plaques there, Miss,' Dot observed. 'Were they planted in memory of those fallen in battle?'

'Yes, Dot. Most of them brutally murdered by incompetent generals.'

Dot, who knew well that Miss Phryne had played a consider-able role herself in the Great War, decided to let this pass. 'You don't mean Sir John Monash, surely, Miss?'

'Indeed not. He and General Allenby were the only generals commanding who seemed to have any idea how to win a war without getting half their own men killed.'

So many dead, from one small town. Dot crossed herself. 'And where are we going, Miss?' Phryne silently handed Dot a book, with a bookmark. It appeared to be the Victorian Government Tourist Bureau guidebook. An envelope marked page 196. It was addressed in firm, cursive script to The Hon Phryne Fisher, 221B The Esplanade, St Kilda. Dot turned the envelope over. The return address announced itself as Capt Herbert Spencer, The Mineral Spa, Hepburn Springs.

'Read it, Dot. Captain Spencer wants our assistance.' Dot read as follows, written in what she decided was a firm, manly hand.

Dear Miss Fisher

I know that you served with distinction in the War, and you will be aware that all too many of our brave survivors suffer from shellshock. The Army and the Ministry show them little sympathy, and even less help. You will know well that they are not shirkers or cowards; but men who have endured more than flesh and blood can manage. At my spa I am attempting to provide my patients with the rest, recuperation, and care they so badly need. I hope that, when you have seen my establishment for yourself, you may see your way clear to supporting my endeavours.

If I may trespass a little further on your patience, I may say also that a local girl has gone missing, and I have reason to believe that the local police (in whom I have little confidence) suspect that one of my patients is to blame. I do not believe this for one moment, but will cheerfully abide the result of any investigations you may wish to undertake. Would you care to join me for dinner this coming Thursday?

I remain, Honourable Miss Fisher,
Your most obedient servant

Herbert Spencer (Capt, retd)

'So there we have our case, Dot,' said Phryne, as they passed by a most impressive Town Hall and began to climb out of the snug valley again. 'Captain Spencer intrigues me. And he may prove to be a most attractive young man, or so I hope. I am delighted to discover that one Herbert at least remains alive and helpful. So far as I knew, the War had killed off every Herbert, Albert, and Clarence in the nation. The girls are back at school, Mrs B has gone off to visit her sister, Mr B and Tinker can mind the house and the domestic animals, and I can feel a small adventure coming on. And I have never been to Hepburn. Doctor MacMillan recommends it highly. The roses should be out, and I hear that it is a most beautiful village.'

Dot perused the page on Hepburn Springs, and discovered that it was two miles the other side of Daylesford, and promised a most invigorating climate more than two thousand feet above sea level. The curative properties of the mineral springs were extolled at length, although sinusoidal electric baths sounded a bit extreme, even for her headstrong and fearless employer. Dot made a firm vow to herself that having electricity applied to her bath would happen only over her lifeless body. And a shilling a time? A mere sixpence would purchase a hot or cold mineral bath without high-voltage shocks being applied to her person. A hot bath sounded like a splendid idea.

'Dot, I am a little concerned about the girl. If I like the good Captain and his work, I shall certainly give him a reasonable sum. The problem with these small country towns is that the police feel they have to keep the local movers and shakers happy. If there is crime, and convenient incomers to blame for it, then they are all too prone to bend the facts to suit their convenience.'

'Miss, it says here that one of the springs is sulphur? That can't be right, surely?'

'Indeed it can, Dot. The idea of a brimstone bath is appealing, in a strange way. And the others sound wonderful.'

The remainder of their journey was so pretty that Dot sometimes kept her eyes open, despite the throaty roar of the engine. What she could see of the countryside fleeting past her looked quite green and attractive. To Dot's immense relief Phryne turned off the highway and began to head up into a forested woodland. This meant slowing down enough so Dot could enjoy the view properly. They climbed steadily, driving through a small town which appeared to be Daylesford. Halfway down the main street, a loud whistle sounded. Phryne pulled over on the brow of the hill and observed a very large uniformed policeman. His puffy right hand was held palm outwards, right in their path. Phryne stopped in the middle of the road and leaned over the side. 'Good afternoon, Officer,' she announced brightly. 'How may I be of assistance?'

His flabby, porcine features frowned horribly at her. 'Hold it right there! May I see your driver's license, Miss?'

The Irish brogue was unmistakeable. So was the exasperating air of self-righteous stupidity which accompanied his shiny sergeant's stripes. *Just what I need,* Phryne considered. She handed over her license, and wondered if he would need any help with the longer words. He frowned again. 'Miss Frinny Fisher, is it?'

'Something like that, yes.'

'And where would you be off to, then, Miss Fisher?'

'Hepburn Springs. And if you would be so kind as to give me my license back, I would like some afternoon tea. I am staying at the Mooltan, if you think that is any of your business.'

The Sergeant started, as if he had been bitten by a snake. 'You don't want to go in there, Miss! Some very dubious characters there. A young woman has gone missing, and the one who abducted her is staying right there. But I'll be having him, don't you worry. And some of the others.' Phryne held out her gloved hand, and with reluctance the Sergeant handed her license back and stood aside

'Thank you, Sergeant. And I hope you have a really annoying day.'

Dot gasped as the car roared off down the main street. Soon the Hispano-Suiza purred gently down a hill into a village which announced itself as Hepburn Springs. Suddenly Phryne turned off the road and puttered around a curving gravel pathway flanked by rose bushes (partly in flower) and lavender. As they drew near the house, Dot regarded what was evidently Mooltan. It was a snug two-storey bluestone house with an iron-laced slate roof and two windows on each side of the front door, and five on the second storey. Balconies with potted plants lined the upper storey. It would be warm in winter, and cool in summer. Phryne engaged the handbrake and stepped out of the car, dressed in black trousers, black leather flying jacket, helmet and goggles, and black boots with sturdy flat heels. She inhaled deeply. 'Smell that country air, Dot!'

Dot did so, and unobtrusively kissed her St Christopher medallion, giving devout thanks that she would not have to be driven anywhere for a few days. As they emerged from the Hispano-Suiza, a youthful figure came from the front door and walked towards them. Phryne smiled at her.

'Hello, You must be Miss Dulcie. I'm Phryne Fisher, and this is Dot. Doctor MacMillan's friend. She sends you her best.'

Dot realized that she had mistaken the men's clothes and haircut. Dulcie grinned. 'Yes, we were expecting you,' she said, with broad Australian vowels. Another young woman appeared (in a long, grey skirt and woollen jumper). 'This is Alice.'

'Afternoon tea's ready,' said Alice. 'I hope you like scones, cream, and jam?'

'Yes, we really do. And some tea, to wash away the grime of roads. And policemen.'

Alice coloured. 'You've met our Sergeant? He's a bit…abrupt.'

Dulcie patted Alice's hand. 'Stupid and offensive is what you mean. His name is Sergeant Offaly.'

'Never mind him. Come inside.' Dot looked back at the car boot, but Alice shook her head. She was pretty, in an Irish fashion: dark, waved hair framing a delicate face with dark green eyes.

'Dulcie will get your luggage. Come inside and have tea.'

As they sat down to feather-light scones, mulberry jam, and thick, fresh cream, Alice poured the tea and Dulcie hustled their bags up the wooden staircase. 'This is wonderful,' Phryne approved. 'Who made the scones?'

Dulcie reappeared and leaned on the back of a chair. 'Alice did. And the jam. We're not usually open till September, but any friend of Doctor MacMillan is welcome. She stays here a fair bit. It's comfy.' Dulcie's light blue eyes flickered. 'Business or pleasure, Phryne? And will you be dining in?'

'Both, I hope. And possibly to solve a mystery. I'm here to see Captain Spencer, and I'll dine with him. Dot will be delighted to have dinner here, though.'

'I might have an idea or two about this, if it's what I think it is. So what did our cop want with you?'

'He stopped me in the middle of the road in Daylesford. And when he found out I was staying here, he warned me off.'

'He wouldn't know if a tram was up his backside till the conductor rang the bell. And he's got it in for my brother. But let's talk about that later. You'll want a rest, I'm sure.'

Dulcie disappeared again, and Phryne made small talk with Alice. Dot admired the strong tea and had three cups. Then they retired to their rooms, and Phryne sat on the balcony, smoking a cigarette and admiring the quiet, elegant village below her. The room was tasteful, well-furnished, and unobtrusive in the right way. And the whole house smelled deliciously of lemon floor wax and lavender. She could hear the small river in the distance, buoyed by early spring rains. Phryne wondered if Dulcie's brother might be Sergeant Offaly's suspect for the girl's disappearance. It seemed likely enough. She sighed, and went inside for forty winks. The bed was magnificent, and she was asleep in a moment.

• • ● ● •

Dot and Phryne came downstairs shortly before dinner. Dot was dressed as before, but Phryne had attired herself in cream-coloured trousers, a white Russian *blouson* with pearl buttons on the left, and a French biretta stuck at a rakish angle. She considered that she looked not only beautiful, but also visible. Since she had noted the dearth of streetlighting, this might be advisable in Hepburn Springs by night. She found a distrait young man lamenting quietly to Dulcie. He looked gentle, but easily broken. His face was pale, and his dark eyes darted back and forth without rest. Dulcie sat him down. 'A drink, Phryne? Dot?'

'A gin and tonic, please.' Phryne looked at Dot, who shook her head.

'This is my brother, Aubrey, Phryne,' announced Dulcie, shaking gin, ice, and tonic into a glass. 'He's one of Captain Spencer's patients. And that Sergeant—'

'He's watching us!' Aubrey's hands clenched in his lap.

'I've met him,' said Phryne, patting his arm. Aubrey shied as if he had been stung like a wasp.

'My girl is lost, and he thinks I killed her! I'd rather die than hurt her! We want to get married! And I don't know what's happened to her.' Aubrey buried his head in his hands.

'Tell me about her.' Aubrey looked at her, and his sister.

'Miss Fisher is a private detective, Aubrey. I'm sure she can help.'

Aubrey laid both hands on his chair and seemed to calm down. 'Helena is one of the masseuses at the spa. She's only seventeen, but she loves me, and I love her.'

'How did you meet?'

'I've been taking the waters, and she was looking after me. Captain Spencer is doing really well with us. And the nurses—well, they're not really nurses, but you get the idea—are so kind. When they massage you, and speak softly, and you feel the bubbling waters around you, then you can forget—the guns. And she started spending more time with me. I have shellshock, you know. I managed Gallipoli, but…the Western Front—we're not cowards, no matter what they say. It's just—'

Aubrey's lips started trembling, and Phryne spoke soothingly. 'It's all right, Aubrey. You don't have to explain. I was there, driving an ambulance. I remember. It was the guns pounding for days on end. And one day you can't bear it any longer.'

Dulcie was at Aubrey's side, hugging him. 'Take your valerian drops, Aubrey. Come on.'

Aubrey rummaged in his pocket and brought out a small bottle. Dulcie put a glass of water on the wooden table in front of him, and he shook several drops into it. He sipped carefully at it, and when it was finished he replaced it on the table. Then he leaned back in his chair and sighed. At that moment, a silver tabby cat entered the room, sniffing. 'Hello, Tamsin,' said Dulcie. 'Come for your fix?'

Tamsin flowed upwards and landed on the table without a sound. Her red-brick nose sniffed at the glass. Soon she was rubbing her head around the rim of the glass, purring in ecstasy. Finally the little cat put her head right inside the glass and began to roll around the table on her side. The glass rolled off the table, but Dulcie caught it dextrously in mid-air. Dot giggled, and Dulcie placed the glass on the floor. 'Come on down, Tamsin.'

The cat thought about this, and leapt down, resuming her love affair with the empty glass. 'Not all cats like valerian,' Phryne observed, 'but she certainly does.' Aubrey's hunched shoulders began to relax, and he managed a smile. Phryne began to sing:

'Take a sniff, take a sniff, take a sniff on me; I've got the Valerian Blues.'

Aubrey laughed, and Phryne stood up. 'Have fun, Dot. I am off to see Captain Spencer.'

'You know the way?' Dulcie asked. 'You can't miss it. Straight down the road to the bend. It's on your right.'

'Take care, Miss Phryne,' Dot called after her.

'I will.' It was a cool twilight, but the walk to the spa was barely a hundred yards. Yellow lights shone from several houses, and there were small, cosy movements in the trees. Nocturnal possums were probably foraging already. And the sound of water was soothing. She knocked at the door of the red-brick building, and waited. Almost immediately the door opened, and soft light welled out into the valley. Phryne drew in her breath. Captain Spencer (or so she must assume) stood before her and shook her hand. 'So good of you to come,' he said. He was everything she could have wished for in a dining companion: taller than some, but slender-hipped, with firm shoulders; impeccable evening dress; steady hazel eyes; clear, slightly tanned complexion; and a friendly smile. His navy blue suit, white shirt, and starched cuffs were impeccable. He took her hand, led her inside, and conducted her into a small, carpeted alcove at the edge of a larger dining room. A silver(ish) candelabra with three beeswax candles stood in the centre of a spotless tablecloth. The table was set for two, with treble wineglasses on each side. 'Please, sit down,' he invited.

It was indeed most inviting. But Herbert fixed Phryne with a steady eye. 'I am afraid I have a confession to make. We are all vegetarians here. All of us have seen too much blood, and we cannot abide it. But humans do not require it. Legumes are an endless source of sustenance. And of course Australia has magnificent vegetables and fruit.'

This promised to be a dreary meal: with everything boiled to extinction. Every remnant of taste and nourishment would be expelled from the sad remnants of whimpering vegetation, and the cadavers would be reanimated with bicarbonate of soda. She smiled brightly, but her heart sank. As soon as they were both seated, a youngish woman in a plain black dress with a spotless white apron appeared with a bottle. She filled two of the glasses, nodded to Phryne, and disappeared back into kitchen. Herbert grinned shyly. 'I hope you like this. It is herbal wine, such as I give my patients.' Seeing her eyes flicker with momentary dismay, he added hastily: 'I have a Barossa valley red and a Taltarni dessert wine to follow.'

Mollified, Phryne drank. It was unexpectedly sweet, and strongly flavoured with mint, thyme, sage, marjoram, basil, and some others that she could not identify.

'There is a romantic story attached to this wine,' Herbert expounded. 'A monastery was in desperate straits, and a monk dreamed that a stranger would come and save them. Next day a shipwrecked sailor was cast ashore, and they took him in. They shared what little they had with him, and told him of their direst poverty. When they showed him their herb garden, the mariner laughed and showed them how to make this wine. They kept his secret, and sold most of what they made at a high enough price to pay their debts, and prosper ever afterwards.'

Phryne drank a little more. 'It is more subtle than I expected. Well done! I take it the recipe is a secret no more?'

He smiled. 'I found it in *The Gentle Art of Cookery*. So I did not break any confidences. But my poor guests find it most restorative.'

'Tell me about them,' said Phryne, as the silent woman reappeared with two bowls of potage Lorraine. It smelt delicious, and was: onions, carrots, celery, and haricot beans in a fine stock.

'*Merci*, Violette,' said Herbert. As the woman disappeared again, Phryne lifted one eyebrow. 'I found her in France, and brought her here. Her fiancé and all her family were killed in the war, and she wanted nothing more to do with Europe. Or men,' he added.

'But she likes you.'

'Oh, yes. But not in that way.' He dropped his eyes for a moment, and resumed. 'You know that shellshock is a disease, and not malingering?'

'Indeed I do. I have seen brave men lying in their beds inert, unable to respond.'

'The term is dissociation. They see without seeing, and hear without hearing. Sometimes they even lose the power of speech. It took a long while for anyone to understand. They are beaten down by blood, gunfire, and accumulating horror. And it can only be cured by prolonged rest and recuperation.'

'Which you provide. I understand you use baths, massage, and quiet? Have you tried music?'

Captain Spencer looked pleased. 'Yes. We encourage them to sing, individually and together. You are staying at the Mooltan, I hear? Then perhaps you have met Aubrey? He has a fine tenor voice. I am encouraging him. Violette plays the piano and accompanies him.'

'Yes, I have. Speaking of Aubrey and his beloved; could Helena have run away?' she inquired. 'Maybe she hitched a ride on a passing truck and ran off to Melbourne?'

'No. She's happy here. And her grandpa is very ill, and needs help. She wouldn't run away. And Aubrey really does love her. They will do well together. If she can be found.'

Violette cleared away the soup plates, and brought out a bottle of rich, red wine. Herbert drew the cork, poured little into his glass and sniffed it, nodded, and filled two glasses.

The main course was laid before her. 'And what do we have here?' Phryne inquired.

'Vegetarian loaf, potatoes Lyonnaise, glazed onions, *épinards au sucre*, and *navets glacés*,' Herbert announced.

'It looks wonderful,' Phryne enthused, and stuck her fork into the épinards. If Violette could make spinach and turnips fit for a civilized dinner table, then she really was a cook in a thousand. Soon Phryne stared at her miraculously empty platter, and laid down her fork. A slow smile crossed Herbert's manly features.

'You are surprised?'

'I am.' Violette appeared again as if by sorcery. Phryne smiled at her. '*Mille remerciements, Madame. C'etait magnifique.*' Violette smiled briefly, and exited. Phryne turned to the Captain. 'What was in that vegetable loaf? 'It was wonderful, but—'

'Eggplant, celery, cottage cheese, breadcrumbs and—sundry other things.' He gestured vaguely in the direction of Madame. In due course Violette brought out the dessert wine, *crème chocolat*, and surprisingly excellent coffee. They chatted easily of the sights of Paris. It seemed that he had met Violette there. The sweet, fruity wine was excellent. Herbert's eyes began to shine, and Phryne noticed his eyes constantly upon her. This did not displease her at all. As Violette came to clear away the plates, Phryne spoke with her quickly in low voices; but as the conversation was in the patois of Montparnasse, Captain Spencer did not catch a word until Phryne's smiling *Bon, d'accord!* and Violette's *Oueh!* At length Herbert rose to his feet.

'Phryne, that was wonderful. Thank you for your charming company.' Phryne nodded, embraced Violette and kissed her in the French fashion. To Herbert she extended her gloveless hand for him to kiss, which he did with enthusiasm. At the same time Phryne leaned forward and kissed him on the cheek.

'Thank you, Herbert. I would love to see more of the spa in the morning, if that it is convenient. Shall we say nine o'clock?'

'Perfect. Shall I walk you home?' He conducted her to the door, and Phryne shook her head.

'It's not far, but I'd like to listen to the forest for a little.' *By myself,* she thought silently. *Not that you aren't extremely pleasant company.*

• • ● • •

Next morning dawned bright, still, and cold. Phryne rose late. Over a splendid English breakfast she outlined her evening with Herbert, and Dot frowned.

'Miss Phryne, I wonder about this tonic he's been giving his patients.'

Phryne speared a piece of bacon with her fork, and paused. 'What about it, Dot?'

'Miss, what about the licensing laws? You said it had alcohol.' Phryne looked questioningly at her companion.

'I never even thought about that, Dot.'

Dot smiled faintly. 'No, Miss. I suppose you wouldn't. But it's serious. He could go to prison for this, couldn't he?'

Phryne put down her fork and stared at her companion. 'What are you suggesting, Dot?'

Dot folded her napkin. 'Miss, what if Helena threatened to tell on him, so he kidnapped her?'

Phryne ate a little more eggs and bacon, considering this. 'He certainly has a strong motive, in that case. I wonder? Can one smile, and smile, and yet be a villain? If so, why would he have dragged me into this?'

'Well, Miss, maybe he likes Aubrey and hopes to put the blame on someone else.'

'I suppose it had to happen one day. The villain calls in the detective, hoping to outwit her. But there is another problem. The only policeman around here is Sergeant Offaly. Can you see Helena wanting to tell him anything at all? And what's her motive?'

'Money?'

'It's possible. We will have to bear your theory in mind, Dot.' Phryne felt a shiver down her lower back. She had been sorely tempted by the Captain. Rule One of Detection: never get romantically involved with suspects. 'All right, Dot. I'll go and have a look at the spa by daylight. You scout around town, see what they think of Helena, if you can. And anything else you can find out.'

Dot walked easily around the corner to the main shopping strip. She bought a pint of milk (twopence) from the general store, and received the information that Helena was a good girl who would never run away. She bought an apple from the greengrocer (a penny), who deplored the absence of Helena and what a good girl she was. The baker was more forthcoming. Mrs Simpson (for so the wooden sign proclaimed her) sold Dot a half-loaf of fresh bread and a meat pie (sixpence).

'My pies are famous, you know,' she volunteered. 'I sell lots to Paddy the publican.' As if giving away state secrets, Mrs Simpson leaned forward and divulged in a stage whisper, 'Those poor soldiers live upstairs at the pub, you know. And that nice Captain Spencer won't let them eat meat. But when they can't stand any more of the Captain's vegetables, Paddy lets them eat my pies!'

'Have you heard anything about that missing girl?' Dot ventured. Mrs Simpson looked downcast.

'She's so sweet. And I don't believe that Aubrey had anything to do with it, either. He's a good man, the poor soul!' Dot hovered by a tray of cakes, since Mrs Simpson seemed inclined to talk. 'Did you hear? Vern is going to stay at the pub in future!'

'I'm sorry, but I'm new here. Who is Vern?'

Mrs Simpson looked maternal. 'He's a big man: a bit simple, but kind as anything. He lives with his brother at the bottling plant, you know; but he'll be better off in the pub. That brother of his—that Sid—he's a bad 'un: mean and spiteful.' The baker leaned forward confidentially. 'But I should tell you about Vern. You'll know him when you see him. He likes looking at girls, so he'll want to look at you. But mind: he won't offer you offence. He's gentle as they come, is Vern. Can I help you with one of those sponge cakes, Miss? They're fresh this morning.'

Dot declined politely, and took her purchases back to Mooltan for a cup of tea and a lie-down.

• • ● • •

Captain Spencer met Phryne in the vestibule of the spa. It was red-brick—long, low, and exuding comfort from every cornice. Herbal scents filled the atmosphere, and Phryne inhaled deeply.

'We use many different scents,' expounded the Captain. 'We discovered that lavender is very good for asthma. And others are sovereign for different ailments.' Phryne looked steadily at him. He wore the same navy blue suit as he had worn the previous night. His face was steady, grave, but good-humoured. Was this kind philanthropist a kidnapper, and possible murderer? He showed her everything: the massage cubicles, the little bathrooms with their bathtubs, the big, heated pool in the centre.

'Would you care for a bath and massage yourself?' he concluded.

Not even a hint of tension, Phryne considered. *If he really is the culprit, then he is a dangerous adversary.* She undressed in one of the cubicles and had a sumptuous bath, scented with lavender. The water was unlike anything she had ever encountered: warm and spritzig to the touch. She could feel the mineral salts gently scouring her skin, and smoothing away the tension in her limbs. She arose, threw her wrap around herself and was conducted by one of the masseuses into another alcove. 'Hello,' said a pretty girl in a white dressing gown. 'I'm Sheila. Just lie down on the bed, Miss, and I'll do the rest.'

Phryne lay on her front in silence while strong hands kneaded her back, shoulders, arms, and legs. This would be the standard massage for the soldiers, she assumed: personal without being indecorous. 'You've probably heard about Helena,' Sheila volunteered. 'A terrible business.'

'Could she have run away, do you think?'

Both Sheila's hands began to drum on her back in a jazzy rhythm. Phryne considered that being treated as a percussion instrument was a little over the odds, but Sheila should be encouraged to talk.

'Never, Miss. She couldn't have been happier here.'

'Tell me about the Captain.'

The drum solo ceased for a moment. 'He's very kind, Miss. Self-contained. But he means well. We'd know if there was anything wrong, Miss.'

This seemed only too likely. 'Any ideas, Sheila?'

'Wish I did.' And that appeared to be it from Sheila, who finished the massage in silence. Phryne stood up.

'Thank you. And now I think I would like a swim. There appeared to be splashing noises, and someone began to sing "Walking My Baby Home," One or two other voices joined in. Phryne doffed the wrap in one movement and walked out of the cubicle.

'Miss, the pool's full of soldiers! You can't go in there—'

But it was too late. The singing stopped dead as eight young men, entirely without clothing, stared at the naked goddess who entered the water and began to swim towards them. Then one of the men began to sing "My Blue Heaven." Some averted their gaze. Others did not, and goggled at her. She waved, and swam in a curve around them. Nobody so much as moved. Phryne nodded to herself. She swam for around three minutes, and stood up in the pool, her porcelain breasts bobbing in the water in front of them.

'So where does a girl go for a smoke around here?' she inquired.

One of the men pointed. 'There's a courtyard next to the tea-house, Miss.'

Phryne inclined her head, swam back towards the cubicles, and dressed carefully. She waved at the men, found the courtyard, and lit a gasper. There were several men there smoking at their ease. They nodded politely. Phryne suddenly noticed a large tin placard on the back of the tea-house. She read the following: *Pharmaceutical tonic, Hepburn Spa. This product carries the approval of the Chief Medical Officer of the State of Victoria.* One of the men watched her, and spoke out of the corner of his thin mouth.

'Yair, Miss. It's all aboveboard. I run the still. It's a beauty. Want to try some?'

He was a wiry, middle-aged man with a face scored with lines, and cheerful grey eyes. He held out a small medicine bottle, and poured out a measure into a teaspoon. Phryne accepted it, and tasted. *Very like green chartreuse,* she thought, and far stronger than the herbal wine the Captain had given her last night.

The man looked conspiratorial. 'Jeez, the old biddies love this stuff. 'Specially the Methodists. They're s'posed to be dry; but nerve tonic doesn't count.' He held out the bottle for her to read. *Spencer's Nerve Tonic. Take one teaspoon as required.* Phryne smiled.

'Yes, I can see that they would. Thank you.'

Cautiously, one by one, the men introduced themselves. There was a Jonno, a Bert, two Daves (Big Dave and Tiny Dave—who was, inevitably, the taller of the pair), a Stevo, a Billy, and a Kevvy. Some worked the still, some were masseurs, and one—a slim, elegant man called James—appeared to be the dance instructor. All seemed well-content with their lot, and praised the Captain highly. In Australian, this was expressed as 'A good bastard.'

Suddenly there was a tremendous sound of an engine. It seemed to be in pain, and roared like a hippopotamus with a toothache. An ancient, dirty white truck had pulled up, and Phryne watched, fascinated, as an enormous man climbed out of the cabin. Wooden barrels, presumably filled with mineral water, were stacked in a tidy row along the back of the tea-house. The giant leaned over and picked up one under each arm, and carried them to the tray. They must have weighed a hundred pounds each, but he seemed not even to notice the weight. Sitting in the cabin, and glaring through the window, was a thin-faced, cold-eyed man. He did not deign to assist, but wound down the window. 'Come on! Get on with it, ya big idiot!' Then he wound the window up again, and stared forwards at nothing.

As the huge man returned for the next pair, Phryne looked him over. Six and a half feet tall, and several axe-handles across his shoulders. He was not so much fat as exceedingly well-armoured. In the Middle Ages he might have been used as a battering ram. But his strangely unlined face was mild and gentle, and his brown eyes were kind and filled with simple wonderment, as if looking at everything for the first time. Sheila stood beside Phryne and lit a cigarette herself. The man looked adoringly at both women for a long moment, smiled, and hoisted two more barrels. 'He's harmless,' James pronounced, blowing a smoke ring.

Soon the tray was full. The man secured his load with thick rope to the back of the cabin and climbed aboard. The protesting motor roared back into life, and the truck slowly chugged back up the hill.

'That's Vern,' said James. 'Quite a specimen, isn't he?'

'I see. Tell me about the bottling plant.'

He looked surprised. 'There's nothing much to tell. Vern drives the truck. He picks up the barrels from here and delivers them to his brother, Sid, who's in charge. He was the moody one in the truck. We're not happy about Vern being cooped up there. We don't trust Sid. Vern's going to live at the pub, I hear. He'll be happier there. He likes looking at young girls, you know. But he never does anything untoward. Why, do you think they might have something to do with Helena's disappearance?'

'Probably not.' Phryne spoke abstractedly, thinking hard. Dot's theory seemed to have sunk without trace. But…something about the scene she had just witnessed triggered warnings in her head. She would have to be very careful. Helena was probably alive, but in peril.

Phryne returned to Mooltan, listened to Dot's account of her investigations, and sat in the library, working out a plan. Alice offered them a simple dinner of ham and cheese sandwiches, a slice each from a fresh apple pie, and unexpectedly good coffee.

'Dulcie,' she announced, 'you, Dot, and I are going on an expedition tonight.'

Dulcie put down her coffee cup. 'Where we going?'

Phryne outlined her plan. 'Comfortable clothes and boots, black if you have them. We will require secrecy. And I will bring my flashlight. Country nights are so surprisingly dark.'

'Is Aubrey coming?' Alice asked. Phryne shook her head.

'Men get over-excited in rescues. And other delicate moments. We will manage.'

'Be careful,' said Alice in a melting voice, staring at Dulcie. Dulcie clasped her hand for a moment and stroked her hair.

Half an hour later, the light had drained out of the sky as they set off up the road towards the bottling plant. It smelled eerily of mineral springs and wattle. 'All right,' Phryne grinned at them. 'Over the top!' Dulcie smiled. Dot gritted her teeth and looked stoic. Phryne switched off the torch. Her jacket pocket contained her gun, and a spare box of ammunition in case Vern needed more suppression than six bullets could provide. The plant was nothing more than three large galvanized iron sheds spaced apart from each other. Phryne waved the others back, and crept up to a lighted window in one of them. She peered in to look.

Vern was filling bottles from a keg by the light of a kerosene lamp, quietly and slowly, with concentrated efficiency. Sid sat lounging in a wicker chair, watching him. There was no-one else there. Phryne tiptoed back to Dot and Dulcie. 'Try the other two.' They slipped away and Phryne went back to the window to keep watch there.

Dulcie tried the door of the second shed. She pulled the door open with agonizing slowness. 'Hello?' she said in a low voice. 'Anyone there?'

There was no answer. She did not dare look inside in case she tripped over something. 'Dulcie,' said Dot next to her ear, 'the other one's locked from the inside.'

Dulcie led the way to the third shed, a little apart from the others. She knocked gently. 'Helena? It's me, Dulcie. We're going home now. Come on.'

There was a sound of a rusty bar being pulled back. The door opened. In the faint light, there was Helena, still in her white nurse's dress. Her feet were bare. 'Dulcie?' said the girl. 'Thank God for that! But he took my shoes. I'll have to walk barefoot. And I don't care!'

Slowly, they began to slip away. Back at Shed One, Phryne

heard Sid speak, but she could not catch the words. Vern's reply was loud, and emphatic.

'No! Mum said not to play with girls! And I won't!'

A vast realization flooded Phryne's brain. She'd been right about the place, but all wrong about the villain. Now Sid raised his voice. 'Vern, I got yer the girl so she and you could stay here with me! Mum told me to look after yer. Youse don't need to go live at the pub!'

At that moment, bright moonlight appeared above the hill. Sid chanced to look out another window, and saw the ghostly girl flitting across the yard with two black shapes beside her. He ran out the door and yelled. 'You come back, ya little slut! You live here now!'

'No!' said Vern. 'Don't hurt her, Sid!'

Phryne moved quickly around the shed, drew out her pistol, and pointed it directly at Sid's head. 'Stop right where you are, Sid. Hands in the air!'

Sid gaped at her, froze, and put up his hands. Phryne turned to Vern, who had emerged from the door. 'Hello, Vern,' she said. 'I'm Phryne Fisher. Why don't you mind the girls while I deal with Sid?'

Vern blinked at her. The yellow light spilling out of the open door showed a slim, black-coated figure holding a gun to his brother. He nodded. 'Thank you, Miss. I'll do that.'

Dulcie, Dot, and Helena climbed onto the tray of the ancient truck. Vern mounted the cabin and opened the window to look at the girls. 'Got to wait here for the lady,' he explained, and sat immobile. His three passengers watched in admiration as Phryne advanced on Sid.

'I'm not going to shoot you right now.' Phryne steadied her hand so the gun was pointing between Sid's eyes. 'Because we don't want any trouble for the Captain. But you're going into the shed where you locked up Helena, and I'm going to lock you in. Or you can receive, at no extra charge, several more holes in your worthless body. Of course, if you have violated Helena, then I'm going to shoot you anyway. I've nothing else to do with my evening, you horrible creature.'

'Nah, I got her for Vern. He likes lookin' at girls.'

'And you don't, of course. Well then, in you go.'

Obediently, Sid marched into the shed. There was no light inside, and Phryne did not offer him any. There was a separate lock on the outside, and she shot the bolt home with a loud snick. 'Have fun!' she exclaimed, and then joined Vern in the truck's cabin.

Vern started the engine, and the truck galumphed its way down the hill towards Hepburn Springs. 'Where are we going, Miss?'

'Mooltan. We want our supper. Would you like some too?'

'Yes, Miss. But Sid says I eat too much.'

'Never mind Sid. But your Mum would be proud of you, Vern.'

He thought about this. 'Can I have apple pie, Miss?'

'As it happens, Vern, you may. There's half a pie left. And you can have it all.'

The truck groaned to a halt in front of Mooltan. The front door was open, and Alice stood beside a frazzled-looking woman in a brown overcoat. The newcomer gazed at the truck, and her face glowed with relief. Helena leapt down and embraced her. 'I'm back, Mum!' Tears ran down her mother's cheeks, and she wrapped both arms around her daughter, and did not let go for a long moment.

• • ● • •

Phryne surveyed the dining room with satisfaction. Everyone was talking excitedly except for Vern, who sat at the table with a napkin tucked into his grimy shirt-front, methodically working his way through three-fifths of an apple pie, with extra cream. She let them talk themselves into a lull, and tapped a teaspoon on the side of her coffee cup.

'I think we need to take note of local sensibilities tomorrow, Helena. You, your mother, and Dulcie should go and visit Sergeant Offaly and explain that you had experienced a bridal argument, and as a result, you'd come to stay here at Mooltan and gave strict instructions that no-one was to know where you were. Does that suit, Helena?'

Phryne looked the girl over. She was very pretty, with short hair cut in a bob. The grimy nurse's uniform suited her well. There was a sweetness in her manner, but Phryne detected a whim of iron beneath it. Helena took Aubrey's hand in hers and held it tight. Then she fixed her penetrating blue eyes on her mother's face, and nodded.

'Yes, Mum. That's what we'll tell him. Because we don't want the village gossips talking about me, and what goings-on there might have been up at the bottling plant, do we?'

Her mother (a thin, mousy woman with faded hair) stared at Helena. 'A bridal argument?' she ventured.

'Yes, Mum. Because Aubrey and I are getting married this summer.' The maternal face turned to Aubrey. His face was set, his jaw was square, and he looked like a man who had been offered two separate lifelines: his beloved's rescue, and the chance to secure parental permission at pistol-point. He had no intention whatever of letting go of either of them.

'Yes, we are,' he stated, with finality.

'And Vern will stay at the pub in future,' Phryne added, to head off any more dispute. Vern gazed adoringly at her for a moment, and bent his head to the last of the pie. Phryne continued, 'What this was all about was that Sid didn't want to have to pay for Vern's keep at the pub. So he kidnapped Helena so Vern could look at her instead of the women he would meet at the pub. A mad scheme, you may say, and you would be right. But Sid is not a nice person.'

'Mean as a dunny rat,' Dulcie pronounced.

'Miss, are you going to let Sid out?' inquired Dot.

'No. He can find his own way out. Or someone will rescue him, in due course. And he won't say anything. He can't. Not without getting arrested for kidnapping. I think he will be a new man when he gets out.'

'A penitent sinner?' Helena's mother looked sceptical.

'I doubt it. But being locked up overnight in his own prison isn't going to be pleasant. He's a small, mean bully. He won't recover from this.'

'I'll keep an eye on him, Miss,' Vern offered. 'What he did was bad. Mum wouldn't've liked it. I'm not gonna listen to him anymore.'

Phryne inclined her head.

• • ● • •

Next morning, Phryne awoke from a restful sleep. She threw open the doors to the balcony and looked out over the peaceable valley. It was a golden morning. Birds sang and twittered in the sweet-smelling wattles. Today she would visit the Captain again and offer him money. And he would offer her dinner. Then she would seduce him, if it seemed to be a good idea at the time. After that, she considered, it would be Violette's move. *Bon appetit, Madame.*

The Reading
by the Polish Author

Vasudev Murthy

Sherlock Holmes in Japan *was originally published by Harper-Collins India. Poisoned Pen Press acquired the U.S. rights and published it with the new title,* Sherlock Holmes, the Missing Years: Japan, *with some amount of additional editing.*

I had a simply wonderful time working with PPP. I'd say they actually helped me look at my book with new eyes. Their editorial and support staff are an author's dream; the whole process from editing to production to marketing was transparent and extremely collaborative.

PPP then gave me excellent advice in planning my next book, Sherlock Holmes, the Missing Years: Timbuktu; *the end result was something I couldn't have come up with on my own.*

Working with PPP has been the Nirvana moment of my writing life.

—V.M.

● ● ● ● ●

[Editor's Note: The following is an excerpt from Mr. Murthy's unpublished manuscript titled *The Ramgarh International Literary Festival*, which is a parody of his experiences with literary festivals in general, though this one is set in a remote village in India. It is written in the style of one of his favorite authors,

P.G. Wodehouse. Consider it comic relief from all of the sur-
rounding murder and mayhem.]

• • ● •• •

Meeta looked at the schedule.

'Hmm, choices, choices. Hall A has the little-known Oriya
poet Mohapatra speaking about his little-known poems.'

'Fascinating,' I said, and I meant to be very sarcastic.

'Hall B has a panel discussion on The Importance of Panel
Discussions at Literary Festivals.'

'Profound,' said Abhishek, also in a cruel mood.

'Hall C has Meditation Camp by the famous meditators
Singh and Singh. Complete silence is expected. They expect
standing room only, though everyone is expected to sit down. I
heard there is elaborate security.'

'Let's skip that.'

'Hall D has a reading by the famous Polish writer Władysław
Czartoryski. Sheelaaa Dey is going to speak with him about his
magnificent work.'

'I don't know how you pronounce his name.'

'Never heard of him.'

'He's famous.'

'This sounds intriguing. Let's go.'

And the three of us ran six kilometers to Hall D, hoping to
get good seats.

There were many smarter than us and so we found Hall D
already packed. I wondered how it was that none of them showed
up at our session but were always available for other sessions. We
sat on the laps of some guys in Row 2 and waited expectantly.

Sheelaaa Dey was on stage, wearing a sheer dress that had
not much to contribute. Everything about her was absolutely
crystal clear. She smiled gorgeously at the audience and said *Hi*
to several people she knew.

Władysław Czartoryski was announced and he came on stage,
waving at the audience, which greeted him with thunderous
applause.

He was a small, slight man with a beard, rimless glasses, a grey shirt, and grey trousers. It was obvious that he wore grey underwear too. He had a stoop. He looked very sad. It was clear he was from Poland.

Mics were adjusted and Sheelaaa Dey smiled at the audience and batted her eyelids. Władysław Czartoryski sat quietly and expectantly.

Sheelaaa picked up his book. It was a good nine hundred-fifty pages thick and required some effort to handle. She showed it to the audience, her muscles rippling.

'Folks, this is the book that has made waves in the world of literature. They say Władysław Czartoryski will almost definitely win the Nobel Prize this year. So we are really extremely honoured that we have you here, Mr. Czartoryski.'

Władysław Czartoryski looked blankly at Sheelaaa.

The audience was at the edge of their seats.

Sheelaaa spoke. "Let me begin by saying, sir, that your book is quite remarkable. It must have taken years to write it.'

Władysław Czartoryski looked blankly at Sheelaaa.

'Critics have said that the book weighs on their shoulders and conscience. Remarkable words of praise. What is this book about?'

Władysław Czartoryski looked blankly at Sheelaaa.

The audience moved further to the edge.

Sheelaaa smiled and smiled but we could see that she was getting nervous.

I suddenly realized that Władysław Czartoryski couldn't speak a word of English. No wonder he was a best-selling and famous writer.

So I yelled out from the audience in Polish, which I speak fluently.

'Władisław, co jest wasza książka o?'

Władysław Czartoryski's face brightened. I had guessed correctly.

Sheelaaa winked at me gratefully.

The crowd went wild.

Władysław Czartoryski spoke. 'Moja książka jest historią o pisaniu w zupełnym. Co zdarza się kiedy wy nie możecie widzieć co wy piszecie? Robi słowa przyjmują różne znaczenie? Robi one przybył do życia. badam, depresja, łza, wydać, szary nadforma dla odlewania niebiosa, piękność samobójstwa, rozpaczliwy, tortury, wina, napięcie, rozdzielenie i tak dalej napiszę książkę w skończonym.'

The crowd broke out in frenzied applause. Already it was clear that this would be the event of the festival, perhaps its defining moment.

Sheelaaa gestured at me, asking me to interpret.

'He says that his book is a story about writing in utter darkness. What happens when you cannot see what you're writing? Do the words take on a different meaning? Do they come to life? He explores darkness, depression, misery, sadness, tears, pathos, utter hopelessness, grey overcast skies, the beauty of suicide, desperate miserable longing, grief, torture, meanness, guilt, grimness, tension, wrenching separation, and so on. He wrote the book in complete darkness.'

Once again the audience broke out into furious clapping. Some louts even whistled loudly. Władysław Czartoryski smiled wanly and nodded in acknowledgement, enjoying another moment of international recognition.

Sheelaaa had to hog some of the limelight. 'And really, that is what great literature is about. It is about exploring utter misery and sadness. My books are also very sad and I'm hoping to win the Nobel sooner or later.'

'So now, may I ask you to read from your book? Perhaps pages 750 onwards? I understand that the book is particularly sad at that point.'

Władysław Czartoryski looked at me, bewildered.

'Tak teraz, może pytam was ogłaszać od waszego książka? Prawdopodobnie Numeruje strony 750 do przodu? rozumiem co książka jest szczególnie smutna przy takim punkcie.'

'Ah,' said Władysław Czartoryski, his face brightening. He was planning to enjoy his own sad and miserable writing about misery. He opened the huge book at page 750 and started reading with dramatic flair.

"Ink-czarna noc wirowała o mnie, szarpiąc moim piórem, moją duszę, moje spodnie, kamizelka, moich moich rzęs. Nigdy nie było moim bardzo odczuwalne tak całkowicie zgnieciony. Ciemność docierane w samych komórkach mojej wątrobie i żal nie znaleźć żadnego sensownego wyrazu. Nawet śmierć nie byłabyodpowiedź. Noc nadal mocno, skręcanie i obracanie, odparowanie ciekłego istotę jakiejkolwiek nadziei, że może być jeszcze istniał. Tak, nie ma nadziei. Rzeczywiście, smutek i beznadzieja zdefiniowane mnie i oznaczałoby mnie teraz na wieczność. I napisał w czarnym tuszem na białym papierze, a ja nie wiedziałem, co demon smutku odbyła moje pióro i napisał wszystkie możliwe synonimem smutku. Warszawa była daleko i nigdy nie będzie żadnego światła, które przypomina mi się w tym kierunku. Żadnych pytań może zostać poproszony. Ona odpowiedziała. Nie było się bez kolacji kiełbasy i kaszanki dzisiaj. Jutro. I dzień po. Spojrzałem po mojej lewej stronie. Było ciemno. Potem spojrzałem na prawo. Było ciemno ponownie. Byłem sam. Pisanie ciemne słowa w ciemnym pokoju. Wypełniłem mój żołądek z żalu."

There was a stunned silence. A few sensitive girls in the first row started crying. It had been deeply moving.

But someone had to say it and he did. 'But what did he say?' Sheelaaa looked at me, and I, getting the hint, spoke:

'The ink-black night swirled about me, tugging at my pen, my soul, my pants, my vest, my eyelashes. Never had my very being felt so completely crushed. Darkness lapped at the very cells of my liver, and grief did not find any worthwhile expression. Even death would not have been an answer. The night continued forcefully, twisting and turning, vaporizing the liquid essence of any hope that might have still existed. Yes, there was no hope. Indeed, grief and hopelessness defined me and would mark me now for eternity. I wrote in black ink on black paper, and I knew not what demon of sorrow held my pen and wrote every possible synonym of tragedy. Warsaw was far away and there would never be any light that would point me in that direction. No questions could be asked. She had answered. There was to be no dinner of sausage and blood pudding today. Tomorrow. Or the day after. I looked to my left. It was dark. Then I looked to my right. It was dark again. I was alone. Writing dark words in a dark room. I filled my stomach with grief.'

This time, the crowd went absolutely mad, having finally understood the genius. Never before had they heard a Polish writer speak with such feeling about his book—in fact, reading from his book. They understood the original, and my translation had turned out to be quite good too.

I beamed at Władysław Czartoryski, and Władysław Czartoryski beamed at me. We were the heroes of the moment, happy that we had made more than a thousand people utterly miserable with his tale of woe.

The reading had been a massive success and I was called on stage to share the happy moment. Sheelaaa actually kissed me and said she appreciated my inputs. Władysław Czartoryski shook my hand and handed over some blood pudding and sausage that he had kept in his trouser pocket. He took me aside.

'Thank you Mr. Murthy. That was nice of you,' he said in English.

I was taken aback.

'Hey, how come you can speak English, Władysław Czartoryski?'

'Haha, one needs to have a flair for the dramatic, Mr. Murthy! Who reads English novels anyway? This is a good marketing gimmick! I can make fools of hundreds of people pretending to be a depressed author. Now people will buy tons of my book in the original Polish. I'll be rich and I'll get the Nobel Prize! Hahaha!'

'Hahahaha! Really clever, Władysław Czartoryski!'

'Call me Wlady!' said the man, with a twinkle in his eyes, slapping my back.

'Call me Vasu!' I said, coughing and choking and slapping him with love.

'I wish you absolute misery and many awards, hahaha!' said Wlady, having a good chuckle.

'I hope you get the Nobel Prize posthumously, hahaha! That would be really miserable!'

'Hahaha!'

'Hahaha!'

'What are you guys laughing about?' said Sheelaaa, coming up to us and trying to reclaim Władysław Czartoryski.

'Just remembering my wild time in Warsaw and Bydgoszcz.'

'I never knew you had been to Bydgoszcz,' said Władysław, in Polish.

'I haven't but I wanted to confuse her!' I said, also in Polish.

'Hahaha!'

'Hahaha!'

Sheelaaa tried to join in the laughter but somehow her 'hahaha' in English just didn't make sense, and she knew it.

I left Władysław Czartoryski busy signing the hundreds of copies of his nine-hundred-fifty-page Polish book to his adoring fans in India who would never be able to read even a single page but would still adore him anyway.

Wild by Name, Wild by Nature

Jane Finnis

Ever since I became a Poisoned Pen Press author in 2003 I've been an oddity…no, a rarity, that's a better word. I'm English, living and writing in England. How did I find my way from here in Yorkshire to there in Arizona? Through another English mystery writer, Rhys Bowen. She's settled in California now, but we go back a very long way, to the days when as fellow students at London University we both vowed to write fiction. Rhys got there considerably ahead of me, and when I asked her advice about the U.S. market, suggested I submit my first Aurelia Marcella novel to PPP. "They're fairly new," she said—this was 2003, remember—"but they're already among the best." I was thrilled when the Press took me on, and still feel very lucky to be published by a team that, though no longer new, is still definitely among the best. Here's to the next twenty years!

—J.F.

• • ● • •

I haven't told anyone about this for ten years. But I think it's safe enough now. We have a new Caesar in Rome, and there's more respect for law and justice in the Empire nowadays, even in outlying provinces like ours. Mind you, law and justice aren't always the same.

It was in our early days in Britannia. My sister, Albia, and I had moved here from Italia, after Pompeii…no, you don't want to hear all that, do you? The point is that the Fates gave us the chance to be innkeepers, and we found ourselves running the Oak Tree Mansio. We took to the work like ducks to water. Albia was my housekeeper in those days, and together we were building up a good trade, and loving it. Succeeding, too, because of our excellent position on the main road from Eburacum to the coast.

We had an amazing mixture of customers. Some were just changing horses or having a drink and a bite to eat, others stayed overnight. There were government officials, traders, soldiers, couriers, a sprinkling of private travellers, and a few striving so hard for anonymity they must have been spies. We made them all welcome. But until that August afternoon we'd never had a gladiator as a guest.

I wasn't in the bar-room when he arrived. I was in my office trying to sort out the accounts, which is not my favourite occupation. So I was delighted when Albia came flying in, wearing a smile as big as the Circus Maximus.

"Aurelia, guess who's asking for a room here tonight. Ferox the Wild Man!"

"You mean Ferox the gladiator? *Here? *Are you sure?"

"Come and see for yourself. He's in the bar-room now, large as life and twice as gorgeous. Isn't it wonderful? One of the most famous fighters in Britannia, under our roof!"

There were a dozen or so men drinking in the bar-room, and Ferox the Wild Man stood out among them like a stallion in a field of mules. He was tall and broad, with muscles on his muscles, and a crescent-shaped scar below his left eye. His golden hair was cropped short, his jaw stuck out, and his pale-blue eyes were sharp. He was a slave, like most gladiators, but he was richly dressed; he wore a tiger-skin cloak and his belt had silver studs. He wasn't carrying his weapons, of course, but he looked every inch a formidable trained killer, "wild by name, wild by nature," as his supporters called him. But now and again his fearsome appearance was softened by a wonderful boyish smile which made him look about eighteen, and as handsome as a young god. Albia and I and all the barmaids fell for him immediately.

"Welcome to the Oak Tree, Ferox," I said. "I'm Aurelia Marcella, the innkeeper. I hope our girls are looking after you properly?"

"Pleased to meet you." He gave us his dazzling smile, just for a couple of heartbeats. "Yes, everything's fine, thanks." He indicated the man sitting next to him. "This is my trainer, Durus."

Durus didn't smile. "That's me. Hard by name, hard by nature." He was also a big man, presumably an ex-gladiator like most trainers. He was in good shape and well-dressed, but much older than his fighter, with grey hair and a world-weary look to him.

"Welcome, Durus. You're wanting accommodation for tonight?"

"We are." He took a drink, and I noticed they both held mugs of beer, which surprised me, because I'd always heard that gladiators only get water to quench their thirst. "Rooms for Ferox and me and one servant, and stabling for our carriage and horses. How much?"

I told him our room charges.

"Expensive," he grumbled. "But we can't make Eburacum tonight, so we've no choice."

Albia asked, "Are you on your way to the games at Eburacum?"

They both nodded, and the trainer answered, "My boy's come north to show your local lads how a real champion fights. He has the opening bout."

"Congratulations," I said. "Everyone's looking forward to the games, even people like Albia and me, who can't get away to be there in person. We have so few gladiator shows round here, you'll get a very good crowd. Are you taking on our local hero, the Lion of Brigantia?"

"Yeah. And when I've done with him, I'll be able to call myself Lion-Tamer as well as Wild Man."

There was a jeer from the other customers, who had been listening to every word. One of them called out, "That's fighting talk in these parts, Wild Man. Nobody's ever beaten the Lion."

"Nobody *yet*."

This provoked an even louder jeer and a comment about cocky foreigners being too big for their helmets.

"I'm no foreigner," he answered. "Born and trained here in Britannia. Down south, though, where folk are a bit more civilised."

Our customers continued to trade insults and boasts with the Wild Man, and I felt a twinge of alarm. The Lion is a native Brigantian boy, born and trained only a few miles from us. He has a legion of devoted fans, and I didn't want any trouble. But I needn't have worried. The banter remained quite good-tempered, mostly because Ferox had the sense to answer cheerfully and with, for a gladiator, fairly moderate bragging. Durus didn't join in, preferring to sit quiet, watching and listening. I couldn't help thinking what an odd couple they made. Ferox, a slave who faced death in the arena in a couple of days, was laughing and joking, while Durus, who'd survived long enough to win freedom and safety, looked thoroughly miserable.

Eventually Durus said to me, "I'd like a few words about the Wild Man's meal requirements, please. You know how important diet is for keeping fighters in top condition, and my boy is on a special regime at present."

"Of course. Let's go into the kitchen."

Cook was getting the evening meal ready, and he eyed Durus somewhat warily when the trainer raised the subject of Ferox' food. Some gladiators have the most weird and wonderful diets. This one was relatively straightforward, thank the gods—bread and fresh vegetables, and plenty of bull's meat. This last might have been a problem because we hadn't any; it isn't popular hereabouts, and we don't serve it often. But Durus had brought a supply with him, and insisted he'd cook it himself, with his own special mixture of herbs for the sauce.

He agreed that Cook should prepare onions and carrots and provide plenty of fresh bread, and some of his famous sweet honey cakes to follow. Cook can be temperamental, but he was in a jovial mood and took it all in his stride.

While Durus began his cooking, I went back into the barroom, which had filled up in the short time I'd been away. There were more customers than usual "just dropping in," and several of the servants kept finding jobs to do around the bar area. News of our celebrity guest was spreading.

By suppertime Ferox had won over most of our customers by his easy good humour, but all the same he and Durus ate their meal in the private dining-room, probably glad of a bit of peace. Albia and I would have loved an invitation to join them, but it wasn't forthcoming.

They came back to the bar later, and the evening turned into an impromptu party. Everyone was fascinated by Ferox' tales of life as a gladiator, even the Lion's supporters. Durus still refused to be drawn into telling stories of his own, but sat morosely drinking and watching that Ferox didn't have too much beer. He cheered up a little when one of the barmaids made a point of paying him special attention, and when the party broke up and the guests went to their rooms, he took her with him. *Rather you than me, Pluma*, I thought, *but it's your choice*. And, of course, nobody went with the Wild Man. His training regime meant a life without women in the run-up to a contest. Doubtless he'd make up for this afterwards.

I got to bed about midnight, delighted with a pleasant and profitable evening.

I woke with a shock just before dawn. There was a loud hammering on my door, and my sister was shouting my name. Then the door opened and she came in, looking flustered.

"What is it, Albia? Is something wrong?"

"Yes, something awful, Aurelia. You'd better come straight away. The Wild Man's been taken ill, he may even be dying. And the trainer says he's been poisoned."

I didn't waste time on questions. I grabbed the nearest tunic and sandals, and we rushed to the guest wing.

Ferox wasn't dying, in fact he was awake. But he was a sorry sight as he sprawled on his bed, his head and shoulders propped up on pillows. His face was a washed-out grey colour and his eyes seemed to have shrunk into his head. From the unpleasant smell in the room, it was obvious he hadn't kept his supper down. He'd flung back his blankets and his light night-tunic was soaked in sweat. Anything less like a Wild Man would be hard to imagine.

The trainer was standing by the bed, looking, if possible, gloomier than ever. "Try and drink some more water, lad. It'll help your body get rid of the poison, then you'll feel better."

Again that word poison. I didn't like the sound of it.

"Ah, there you are at last," Durus snarled at me. "This poor boy's been sick all night. He's as weak as a kitten now, just look at him. It's your fault, you or your staff. Someone's poisoned him."

"Poisoned? Of course we haven't," I snapped back. His anger was making me angry too, and I made an effort to stay calm. "Look, I'm sorry he's poorly. This sort of attack is horrible. But surely it's just an ordinary stomach upset, the kind of unlucky mishap that can hit anyone. It's really unpleasant for the person who's got it, but there's no question of poison."

"What else can it be? He was fine until he got here. It must be something he's eaten, and the food came from your kitchen."

"You cooked his food yourself. You made a point of it, you even brought the bull's meat with you. Perhaps it had gone bad on your journey?"

"No, it was perfect. Your cook tried some, ask him. But he or his people prepared the vegetables and baked the bread and the cakes."

"We all ate those. Are you suggesting *all* the food was poisoned?"

"Of course not, but there was something wrong with some of it. There must have been." He glanced down at Ferox. "He was in peak condition when we got here yesterday. One meal and a few mugs of beer, and he's half dead. I seriously doubt whether he can fight tomorrow."

The gladiator stirred for the first time. "I can fight. I *will* fight." His voice was weak, but his words were strong. "I've never missed a bout yet, and nobody's going to accuse me of trying to get out of this one. I can't have people saying I've lost my nerve."

"Nobody will," Durus reassured him. "I'll see to it there'll be no questioning your courage. And if someone has deliberately tried to put you out of action and you're too sick to face the Lion, everyone will understand. That's what I think has happened. This local Lion has a lot of supporters, including here at the Oak Tree, I've no doubt. My guess is someone saw you and realised that their own lad doesn't have a cat's chance of beating you...so they decided to give him a helping hand."

Ferox gave a kind of growl. "If someone's tried to poison me, I'll kill the swine with my bare hands." He swung his feet to the floor and stood up, glaring round the room as if he wanted an opponent to take on there and then. "I still intend to fight tomorrow. So let's get moving."

"Good boy," the trainer said. "But we'll have to see. I won't have you risking yourself if you're not fit. Now drink some more of your water."

"Water's no good. Get me some wine, that'll ease my guts."

Durus shook his head. "You know the rules. No wine. Water's what you need."

"*Get me some wine!*" Ferox looked like a fighter then, even in his weakened state, and Durus backed down.

"All right, all right, just this once. But I'm not leaving you alone here. You may still be in danger." He went to the door and called their servant, who was waiting just outside. "Fetch some of the wine we brought with us. I'm not letting him touch any food or drink from this place."

"But you surely don't think...?"

Durus interrupted me. "By the gods, you'll be sorry for this. Trying to hurt my gladiator! Your poxy mansion won't get another customer ever again."

I kept my temper, but it was an effort. "Nobody's trying to hurt him. He's got a horrible stomach upset, either from your meat, or more likely it's a sickness he could have caught anywhere. For all I know half the people here are down with it too."

"You think so? That's easily proved. If other folk here have the same symptoms, maybe I'll have to accept that this is an illness, not deliberate poisoning. But frankly I don't believe that.

After all I'm fit enough, and so are you and your sister. But then you're not due to fight in the arena tomorrow."

"That's outrageous!" Albia objected.

"Prove it. Go and find out whether anyone else has been ill overnight."

We hurried out, glad to be away from his terrible accusation, not to mention the foul stench and the sad sight of a magnificent athlete laid low. And I was worried by Durus' threats. If I couldn't find out what had made Ferox ill, and the trainer started spreading rumours that we poisoned our customers, we were in deep trouble.

We summoned the bar servants into the empty bar-room, and discovered they were all fit and well, except for a few sore heads from over-indulgence last night. They were all concerned about poor Ferox, and none of them had any idea what could be wrong with him. I didn't mention the trainer's theory, but I realised I must start considering it seriously. Suppose he was right? Suppose someone at the Oak Tree, staff or customer, had decided to try to make Ferox lose at the games? Perhaps someone with a large bet on the Lion of Brigantia? No, it just wasn't believable. And yet…

Albia and I went into the kitchen. Everything seemed normal there, all the servants busy getting breakfast ready, the room full of the wonderful early-morning smell of new bread. Everyone stopped as we entered, and Cook came over, frowning. "This is a bad business. They're saying that trainer thinks his boy has been poisoned. In his dinner, if you please. In other words he's accusing *me*!"

"He's accusing all of us," I said, "if that's any comfort. Of course it's nonsense. But if he goes all round Eburacum saying it…We must discover what's really happened. I've been assuming Ferox is suffering from a bad stomach sickness, and I've been hoping some others might have gone down with it too. Well, not hoping, exactly, but you know what I mean."

He nodded. "The sort of trouble that if one person gets it, everyone does. None of my lot have had it."

"You're sure?" Albia glanced round the room at the kitchen boys and girls. "Let's be clear: have any of you been ill overnight?"

They all shook their heads, and Cook said, "Gavo complained of stomach pains first thing this morning, said he couldn't work in here because the food smells made him queasy. That was just a hangover, though. I've sent him to help in the vegetable garden. That'll teach him. Everyone else is fine."

"Well, then," I said, "we're back to what the Wild Man had for dinner."

"Or to drink," Cook suggested. "He was on the beer, wasn't he?"

"He was, but not much, and anyway lots of other customers drank beer too. Ferox had bull's meat, which nobody else did. Could there have been anything wrong with that? The trainer said you tasted it, Cook."

"I did, just before supper, I was asking Durus about the fancy herbs in the sauce. He said would I like to try some. It seemed all right to me. I mean, as all right as bull's meat ever is. And I'm feeling fine."

"Nobody else tried the beef?"

"No, Durus was guarding it like a purse of gold coins."

But I noticed one of the girls looking uneasy, and I spoke to her directly. "Did you have some, Crispa?"

"Not me, Mistress," she answered, a little too virtuously.

"Then who? Come on, girl, this is important."

"Gavo did," she admitted.

"Gavo?" The boy with the stomach pains. Gods, sometimes I'm so slow I'd have trouble catching a tortoise. "Go and fetch him, please, Crispa."

He came in looking pale but not really ill. He was one of the brightest of the kitchen-boys, and he gave me and Albia a rueful smile. "I'm afraid I'm in trouble for eating a bit of the gladiator's food. Only I've never tasted bull's meat, and the Wild Man had all he wanted. The trainer brought the pot back in here after their supper, and there was a bit left in it, and he said to throw it out, but I thought that was a waste."

"What did it taste like?" I asked. "Did you think there was anything wrong with it?"

"Not exactly wrong, but sort of funny. I suppose it was all the herbs in the sauce. I didn't like it much, really. I only had one spoonful. I gave the rest to the black cat, but she didn't like it either, so we did throw it out in the end. I'm sorry, I didn't mean any harm by it."

"Luckily for you, no great harm was done. But I believe it was the meat that has made the Wild Man ill, and that's why it made you feel ill too."

He frowned. "Could be, I suppose. I just thought I'd had too much beer. I wasn't anything like as bad…they say he nearly died. I just had gut-ache and felt a bit sick."

"But you only had a small taste. The Wild Man had a bowlful."

Cook said, "Still, it didn't hurt me, did it? I ate a good couple of spoonfuls. Why didn't it make me feel bad?"

Suddenly I saw the answer. "Because the meat was all right *before* the meal, but not after."

Albia said slowly, "So if poison really was added, it was during the meal itself. Who could have got at the pot of beef after it left here?"

Cook scratched his chin thoughtfully. "Nobody except the trainer. He served them both in the private dining-room. He wouldn't even have their own servant there."

"Did the trainer eat the meat too?" I asked.

"No idea," Cook answered. "The vegetables were in a separate dish. Maybe he didn't touch the meat. Because he'd tampered with it? No, look, that's a daft idea. Why would Durus poison his fighter, who was about to win a very important bout?"

"Then there must have been someone else involved. My guess is the servant. Does anyone know where he spent last evening?"

Gavo said, "He told us his boss had given him the evening off, and he asked where he could get a beer and a game of dice. I took him over to the stables to eat with the horse-boys, and he must have stayed there till bedtime, because he never came near the kitchen again."

"Which means," I said, "that if anybody really did poison that meat—and I still don't know if I believe it—then there's only one man it could have been."

"Two," Albia corrected. "It's true Durus could have wanted to kill the Wild Man, though the gods alone know why. But what if Ferox wanted to poison Durus? He put something in the meat, but accidentally got the bowls mixed up and…"

"Oh, come on now, Albia. If you decide to poison someone, you don't accidentally get the bowls mixed up. And I don't believe Ferox would poison Durus. He needs him."

She nodded. "They need one another. You'd think so, anyway. But I was watching them in the bar, and they didn't seem to be all that friendly together. Perhaps they'd fallen out."

"I noticed that too. They were hardly on speaking terms. I thought it was just that Durus was stopping Ferox from drinking too much, and making him go to bed alone."

The barmaid Pluma came in just then. "Please, Mistress, Durus says he and the Wild Man are leaving very soon."

"Already? Ferox is fit enough to travel?"

"He says so, although if you ask me he's still very weak. But he's had a hot bath, he's getting dressed, and he insists on setting off as soon as he can, because he means to fight tomorrow."

"Right. I'll come and see them off." We walked out into the empty hallway. "Albia, will you come with me? I'd like a witness. I don't think it'll be a very friendly interview."

"Of course I'll come. Will you tell him what we've found out? That it was definitely the meat that caused Ferox to be ill?"

"I certainly will. But whether I dare go one stage further and tell him I suspect he might have poisoned it himself…what do you think?"

"Please, Mistress." I hadn't noticed that Pluma was still in the hall. She was shifting from foot to foot, looking worried. "I don't want to speak out of turn, but there's something not right."

"What is it?" I remembered suddenly that Pluma was the girl Durus had taken to bed last night.

"I was with Durus when he heard the Wild Man had been taken ill. And, Mistress, you just said you suspect Durus poisoned the Wild Man's meat." She took a deep breath. "I think you're right"

"Why?" I felt sudden rising excitement. Were we at last getting to the truth?

"Something he said which didn't mean anything to me last night, but it does now. He was pretty far gone when we went to bed. Some men get happier when they're in drink, but he was the sort that gets grumpier."

"He seemed fairly grumpy to begin with," Albia commented.

"Yes, he was. I felt a bit sorry for him, with Ferox getting all the attention, so I did my best to brighten him up. But he just got more miserable. He kept on complaining how he had no money, he was in debt, the great lord who owns Wild Man never paid his bills, he worked so hard and yet nobody appreciated him. I tried to cheer him up, saying what a brilliant fighter Wild Man is, and how they'd make a fortune at Eburacum. And Durus said, 'Oh yes, after Eburacum everything will be fine. I'll have money enough to get out of the fight game altogether then. And listen, don't bother betting on Ferox, girl. He isn't going to tame any lions.'"

We must have looked sceptical, because she went on quickly. "I couldn't believe it either. I thought I must have heard wrong. I started to ask him what he meant, and he sort of pulled up short, as if he'd said too much, and told me he was just a silly drunken old fool and to take no notice. But he did say it."

Albia frowned. "But surely he said it because Ferox was ill and far too weak to fight properly."

"No, that's the whole point. This was *before* he heard Ferox was poorly. It wasn't till later on that their boy came in and told him Wild Man was in trouble."

"And then what happened?" I could hardly get the words out.

"I offered to stay and help, but he gave me a silver piece and told me to run away and say nothing to anyone about his drunken nonsense. And I thought that's what it was. Only now I think different."

"By the gods," I said, "well done, Pluma. That's the missing piece in the mosaic. Durus poisoned the meat…but not to kill Ferox, only to make him so weak that he can't defeat the Lion."

It was Pluma's turn to look sceptical. "He's trained a winning fighter, and now he wants to make him lose? What for?"

"For money," I answered. "Suppose, despite all that boasting in the bar, Durus has his doubts about whether Ferox really can beat the Lion? He can't admit them, of course, but he's afraid his fighter might lose. He's desperate for cash, and he can only make money by betting on a winner—a *certain* winner. So he's decided to make certain the Lion will win."

We all stood silent and shocked for a few heartbeats. Eventually Albia exclaimed, "What a dreadful thing to do! How *could* he?"

"Quite easily, I'd say, if he's ruthless enough. And if he's sure the Wild Man will fight however ill he is, rather than pull out and risk being called a coward."

"He won't pull out," Albia said. "And if he fights, he'll be killed. It's horrible."

"Unless the spectators feel generous and allow him to live, even if the Lion wins," Pluma suggested. "It can happen."

"It's unlikely in Eburacum, though. The place will be packed with the Lion's supporters. No, Durus is sending Ferox to his death."

The door from the guest wing opened behind us, and we turned to find Durus and Ferox standing there. They were both blank-faced, but somehow I had the feeling they hadn't just arrived on the threshold. We hadn't heard them. Had they heard us?

Ferox still looked ill. His skin was greyish, his eyes were sunken, and he leaned on a stick. But at least he was standing up.

"I'm glad to see you on your feet again, Ferox," I said.

"I'm sure you are!" the trainer sneered. "Not to mention relieved that you haven't killed him. It's a tribute to the boy's courage that he's ready to travel today. Whether he'll be in a fit state to fight tomorrow, we'll just have to see."

"I've told you I'll fight," Ferox snapped. "So let's get started."

"All right, we're going. And, Aurelia Marcella, I hope you're not expecting us to pay any bills."

"No, there'll be no bills."

"Good. Because you're responsible for what's happened to Ferox. I hope he can fight tomorrow, but if he doesn't perform at his best, we'll know who to blame. And we'll make sure everyone else knows too. You'll have no reputation at all left by the time I've finished."

Finally I lost my temper. "Listen, Durus, I know what happened last night...."

To my surprise Ferox interrupted me. "So do I. I had my suspicions, now I'm sure. Don't worry, Aurelia. I know you're not to blame."

Without another word he strode out, Durus trailing along behind him. They mounted their carriage, and we watched from the bar-room doorway as they trundled up the short track onto the Eburacum road.

They never got to Eburacum.

Durus' body was found that afternoon on the roadside about seven miles west of the Oak Tree. He'd been strangled and robbed. The carriage and the servant had disappeared, and so had Ferox.

The death was reported by other travellers, and the authorities investigated in their usual desultory fashion. They questioned Albia and me, and we confirmed that Ferox and his party had stayed with us for one night (we could hardly deny it!) but we saw no need to volunteer anything else about the visit. Eventually they concluded the travellers had been ambushed by outlaws, the trainer killed and the others abducted and probably sold. It happens.

But Albia and I were pretty sure we knew the true story. We'd heard Ferox threaten, "If someone's tried to poison me, I'll kill the swine with my bare hands," and then his farewell remark, "Don't worry, Aurelia. I know you're not to blame." Murder is horrible, but cold-blooded betrayal is equally vile. If Ferox had taken his revenge, whatever the law might say, we felt justice had been done.

So we kept our suspicions to ourselves. Until now.

This morning the first traveller to call in for a bite to eat on his way to the coast was a prosperous-looking trader. He had good clothes, a fine horse, and a large string of pack-mules. When he introduced himself his name was unfamiliar, but with his fair hair, the crescent-shaped scar on his face, and, above all, his dazzling smile, I'd have recognised him anywhere.

He gave no sign that the recognition was mutual, so I didn't speak to him. Discretion is as much part of an innkeeper's stock-in-trade as wine and beer. But as he was leaving he beckoned me over and said very softly, "I owe you thanks, Aurelia Marcella. You did me a favour once."

"It was nothing, Wild Man."

"Exactly. You said nothing, and gave me the chance to get away and make a new start."

"And a successful one too. I'm glad. May the gods go with you."

"And with you." He smiled and went on his way. That wonderful beaming smile has stayed with me all day.

The Customer

Laurie R. King

I've known Barbara Peters for nearly as long as I've been writing, with an early event followed by a life-changing invitation to join the 1995 conference "Arizona Murder Goes...Classic" and talk about Sherlock Holmes. This is the background to my story here, of course—although I'd always thought Barbara found me all on her own.

That means I've been with Poisoned Pen Press since its first project, the collected papers from that conference. Later, PPP became my UK publisher (I try not to take responsibility for that division's closure) and has co-published a number of my other projects, from A Study in Sherlock *to the booklet Barbara and I wrote (with Rob's photos) about our trip to Japan called* Not in Kansas Anymore, TOTO, *and on to the 2016* Mary Russell's War. *Their skill and generosity of heart gives lie to the maxim that one shouldn't do business with friends.*

—L.R.K.

• • ● • •

Luck plays an outsized role in the life of a writer—luck, and friendship. If the two come together, a career can be carved out of nothing. In 1992, out of the blue, I received a number of handwritten manuscripts that purported to come from one Mary Russell, partner and—yes—wife of one Sherlock Holmes. Three years later, Barbara Peters hosted my first Poisoned Pen book signing in Scottsdale. Then the following year, in 1996, I participated in the extraordinary

Classic Crime conference, which led to Poisoned Pen Press. Only recently has the conspiracy between these two formidable women, Russell and Peters, come to light, when I received the following account:

May is a time of brief flowering in Scottsdale, Arizona. Tourists have moved on to cooler climes, while residents have yet to retreat behind twenty-four-hour air conditioning.

On an early May morning like this one, when shorts-clad, sunburned visitors have given the streets back to leisurely locals, Main Street might almost look like an actual vestige of the Old West were it not for the public art. Shops begin to open, galleries pull some of their less fragile art out in front, servers bring lattes to outside tables.

The sun reflected off a shiny black limousine as it turned onto Main from Goldwater Boulevard. It passed slowly down the first block to the intersection, where a huge bronze statue of a man on a bucking horse drew traffic into a circle around it. The limo obediently followed the curve into the next block, where the driver began to pull into the first space—only to change his mind and continue down the block a few spaces before turning in.

The driver jumped out, but his passenger did not wait for his services, leaving him to close her door and hover beside her, hand half-raised, as she walked toward the sidewalk. She ignored him, but made the sidewalk without mishap, so he tugged at his hat-brim and returned to the car. The sound of voices came through the open window. After one rather sharp exchange, the engine died, along with its air conditioning.

The woman standing on the sidewalk was old enough to justify the driver's outstretched hand. Nonetheless, her spine was straight, her white hair neatly tamed into a bun, and the blue eyes behind her thick glasses were focused tightly on the shops across the street. She took a more general survey of her surroundings—palm trees, white Grecian-style porticos, ornate lampposts overhead—before nodding to herself and setting off up the sidewalk, stepping down to move surely across the intersection beside the frozen bucking bronco. On the other side of Main Street, she turned back in the direction she came, moving under the shade of the low portico in front of a series of shop windows.

In her hand was a small package wrapped in brown paper and twine.

Tucked in between cafés, art galleries, and vendors of tee-shirts and turquoise necklaces was a shop of a different kind. The sign declared it The Poisoned Pen, and its windows were filled with the cheerful covers of books about murder.

The tall, thin, white-haired woman paused to study the display before her hand came out to open the door. The short blond woman behind the desk looked up and greeted her, but the old lady just smiled and wandered on toward the shelves.

"Let me know if there's anything I can help you with," the shopkeeper said.

"Thank you," replied the customer. Her accent was English.

Another customer came in to ask for something she'd seen that had a black cover, or maybe red, with the letter K in the title. The shopkeeper was aware of her other visitor listening with a bemused expression as this vague description evolved into the most recent Sue Grafton novel. After the other customer left, *K is for Killer* in her bag, the Englishwoman returned to her browsing, pausing near the small signing table at the back to study the spines of books waiting to be shelved.

When she had worked her way back up toward the front, the visitor commented, "I was impressed by your detective skills, on locating that woman's book."

"It can take a bit of work to figure out what a customer wants," the younger woman agreed. "Ah, I see you've discovered Laurie King."

The old blue eyes looked down at the hardcover book she had taken from a shelf: *The Beekeeper's Apprentice*. "I see the author has signed it."

"Yes, she was in for an event a few weeks ago, so I had her sign some of those, too. I think it's going to be a popular series."

"It would not surprise me in the least. I understand Ms. King has a background as an academic. Theology, if I'm not mistaken."

"No, you're right. They're not religious mysteries, although she seems to incorporate religious elements sometimes."

"Religious mysteries," the old woman mused, studying the author photograph on the inside flap. "You know, as an academic myself, I often think it's a pity that a writer's serious research is not sufficiently explored. People like this often spend years investigating their characters and situations."

The shop owner gave her visitor a curious look. "Odd you should say that. I've been wondering recently if anyone but me would be interested in a more…substantial sort of conference than the usual fan get-together. Talking about research, and influences."

"Modern writers giving papers on their Golden Age counterparts?"

"Exactly. Harry Keating—H.R.F. Keating, that is—could talk about Dorothy Sayers. Or Michael Connelly on Hammett or Chandler."

"Ms. King on Sir Arthur Conan Doyle and his…characters."

"Excellent idea! Are you on our mailing list?"

"I do indeed receive your communications, and I look forward to seeing what you come up with. In the meantime, I shall buy this, if you will."

"I'm sure you'll enjoy it."

"Oh, *The Beekeeper's Apprentice* is a tale I know quite well already. But I do not have a signed copy."

The shopkeeper rang up the sale, added a bookmark, and slid the book into a bag. As she made change for the bills the old woman handed her, she asked, "Are you just visiting Scottsdale?"

"We were here on business, my husband and I. We live in England."

"I do love England! What part?"

"The Sussex Downs."

"Ah, Sherlock Holmes territory—how lovely. Well, I hope you travel safely. And any time you want an American book, we're happy to do shipping."

"Thank you," said the woman. "And thank you, too, for your ongoing support of writers such as Ms. King."

"It's completely my pleasure," the shopkeeper said warmly.

She watched the erect old woman walk out of the shop and turn right. Curious, and just a touch concerned at the fragility of age, the blond-haired woman moved closer to the window, watching her customer briskly cross the street and turn back down the opposite side of Main—three sides of a square when she might simply have crossed directly. A uniformed driver popped out of the glossy limousine parked opposite the shop and trotted around to open the back passenger-side door. When the old lady was settled, he shut the door and went back to the front. The engine started, the car reversing into the street. As it paused outside her window, the shopkeeper caught sight of the customer's partner: a man even older than she, but equally firm and sure of himself. A pair of piercing gray eyes stabbed across the street at where she stood, three seconds of X-ray—and then the driver shifted gears and the limo pulled away.

As the shopkeeper turned, she suddenly realized that the old lady had been carrying a small package when she came in, but only the King book when she left. She hurried down the stacks and spotted the old-fashioned brown paper-and-twine parcel on the signing table. But before she could hurry with it toward the door, to call after the departing limo, she saw the writing on the front:

To Ms. Peters, a mutual friend of the Beekeeper's 'biographer'.

With sincere thanks from her admirers.

Curiously, the shopkeeper pulled one end of the twine and unfurled the paper, revealing a gorgeous little book bound in Moroccan leather. It bore the title:

A Practical Handbook of Bee Culture,
with some
Observations upon the Segregation of the Queen

Puzzled, she flipped it open to the title page, to see the author's name.

By Sherlock E.L. Holmes

And in vivid black ink, just beneath the printed name, was the author's signature.

Sherlock E.L. Holmes

Reciprocity

Catherine A. Winn

I'm a writer in Texas who has always loved reading mysteries, which led me to try my hand writing them. Some of my favorite writers were published through Poisoned Pen Press, so when my mystery novel was ready for submission, I sent it to them. To my amazement and joy, Poisoned Pen Press offered me a contract!

—C.A.W.

• • ● • •

Adelaide Hays sat across the conference table from her husband, Vance, and studied her nails while he glared. Her attorney, Kent Jamison, argued with Vance's attorney, Everett Howell, over the validity of the prenuptial agreement.

"Now Everett, you and I both know Mr. Hays is simply divorcing his wife before the five years are up so he can walk away without paying anything. In my opinion that's fraud. She had no idea the marriage was in trouble."

"Oh, please," Vance said with a sneer at her. "You lied to your own attorney?"

"Don't address my client directly, Mr. Hays," Jamison warned.

Addie put a hand on her attorney's arm. "He's right, Kent. I haven't been exactly honest with you."

Jamison looked at her sharply and started to rise. "You and I need to talk."

"That won't be necessary. I think it's time we invoked the deal-breaker clause."

Jamison frowned. "Mrs. Hays…"

"Gentlemen," she said, rolling her chair back, "I'll only be a moment." When her knees didn't buckle the minute she stood, she smoothed her skirt and strode to the door. What she was about to do would send Vance over the edge.

"She's probably going out to burst into tears," Vance said with derision.

In the outer office two men in business suits each took an arm of the beautiful young woman who had jumped to her feet. Her glance darted from the receptionist at the desk to Addie. "I changed my mind," she said, shaking her head. "I can't do this. He'll kill me."

Addie hurriedly pulled the door closed behind her. "Karla, just hold it together for a little longer. Everything's going to be fine but only if you do exactly what I told you to do."

Karla sank back in her chair and chewed her bottom lip. "He's *really* going to kill me."

"Don't be silly." Addie nodded at the two men. They each took one of Karla's elbows and lifted her to her feet. "Everything has been planned carefully. You'll be perfectly safe from Vance."

Karla shook her head. "I wish I had never agreed to this."

"You have to stay strong to get your money because that's the only way I'll get mine. And remember, once we get in there, don't say anything and don't let him bully you. The boys here will take care of you."

"Okay." Karla took a deep breath and blew it out slowly. "Okay, I'm ready. You'd better be right."

The satisfaction Addie felt at the look on her husband's face was worth all the heartache and pain. When Karla walked in his jaw dropped. His loose jowls and double chin sagged even lower. An ugly shade of red flushed his face but he managed to control himself. Addie took a few brisk steps, retrieved her large tote from a vacant chair, and pulled out a laptop.

Vance's eyes locked onto the laptop as he drummed his fingers on the table.

Addie glanced at the group near the door. The men were actually holding Karla up. Minutes mattered. Addie moved to the end of the table and opened the laptop. She had everyone's attention as she clicked the keys. It was ready to play. She turned the laptop so the screen faced them.

Jamison squinted at her as he leaned back in his chair. Addie knew he didn't like being surprised any more than her husband. Howell, on the other side of the table, appeared bored but the pen he rolled furiously back forth between his thumb and forefinger said otherwise.

Addie felt the pulse throb in her neck as she addressed her husband. "Vance, why do men your age think girls her age really find you more appealing than your money?"

Vance's attorney pushed his chair back and stood. "Now, *I* want a moment with *my* client."

"Sit down, Mr. Howell." Addie was surprised at the authority she heard in her own voice. She needed to get this over with before her courage failed. "You want to see this *before* your private little chit-chat."

Vance gave Addie a withering look that promised revenge. "Just show the damned thing."

Addie moved the cursor, clicked play, and stepped back. "I believe this entitles me to half of our marital assets."

As the video played Vance screamed at Karla. "You taped us!" He shot clumsily out of his chair.

Howell grabbed him. "Get yourself under control right now or I dump you as a client."

Vance shook off his attorney, ran a hand through his hair, and sat back down. "I'll get you for this!"

Karla broke free and ran to him. She wrapped her arms around his neck. "I'm sorry, Vance. I love you! She said you were going to dump me! Please forgive me!"

He disentangled her arms from him and shoved her with all his strength. One of the two men helped her get off the floor and then had to restrain her from trying to get back to Vance. It took both of them to drag a screaming, begging Karla to the other side of the room. This time one of them snatched a chair and pushed her into it. Each of them gripped Karla's shoulders and held her there as she dissolved into sobs.

Addie saw the fight had gone out of Karla and indicated the computer. "Shall I start this over?"

"I'm going to make you sorry you did this to me, Addie." Vance threatened. She knew he meant it.

Twenty minutes later, Karla ran, still sobbing, from the room with her two bodyguards fast on her heels. Addie gave a flash drive, containing a copy of the video, to Howell. "I'm sure Vance will do the right thing, now."

Kent Jamison escorted her from the room but not before she took one glance back at her husband. Vance's jaw worked as he sat with two white-knuckled fists on the table. He was already planning her punishment.

"Do I want to know how you went about getting this video?" Jamison muttered in the elevator on the way down.

"No," Addie said. "Now make this happen and fast."

"First we need to get full financial disclosure."

"Fine, but don't be too demanding. Take their word for everything."

Jamison blinked at her. "That's ridiculous. You know what kind of man he is. There will be millions in hidden assets."

"Look, Kent…" Addie said as the elevator stopped and they stepped out. She faced him. "…things went very well in there. Your next move, your *only* move, is to get me a hefty cash payout. That's all I want. Don't mess things up by trying to best Vance, because we'll lose." Addie strode forward. "And let him have the house, free and clear, no strings."

Jamison growled. "You're not letting me do my job, Mrs. Hays."

"You're doing fine. I'm happy. Make this divorce happen, Kent, before Vance cools off and has time to think."

In the parking garage, Addie kept glancing around as she ran to her car. Vance had not exploded in rage as expected. Seething in silence was a dangerous sign. She and Karla were both in for it. Right now, Addie wished she was boarding the same plane.

On the drive back to the house she kept checking her rearview mirror. It would be like him to try and run her off the road. Ten minutes later she beeped the iron gates open, raced up the drive, and dashed into the house. She set the alarm for immediate response, which would be enough warning to hide or grab her Bersa. It would also send for the police. In this neighborhood they came without delay when an alarm sounded.

She had packed her personal things the night before, knowing he wouldn't spend one more night in that hotel once she presented that video. All she wanted was her clothes, her freedom, and enough money to enjoy it. As she raced up the stairs, she thought how funny it was that all the bravado she had shown in the office failed her when she had left Jamison in the lobby. The terrified feeling that she and Karla shared flooded back. Karla. She had slipped only once with that stupid scene, but she was proud of her for sticking it out and following her instructions.

Addie grabbed the two suitcases and duffel from the closet and set them in the hall. Everything else, the gowns and furs, could be replaced. Let Vance have fun destroying them tonight. The jewelry didn't interest her but it did him, no sense in antagonizing him even more. She checked her watch. Time to go.

She carried her things downstairs, checked the video of the grounds, and with trembling fingers she turned off the alarm. She drove out of the gates without a backward glance and straight to the condo that Vance didn't know about—yet.

The valet helped her unload her things and while he drove her car to the parking garage the doorman put her bags on the elevator. "Don't forget to watch out for my husband," she warned.

"Security has been notified, Mrs. Hays," he said. "We'll take care of you."

Around midnight Jamison's call woke her. "The police think Karla's been murdered."

Addie's hand went to her throat but kept her voice steady. "Think?"

"Blood was found in her apartment," Jamison told her. "Someone called 911 and said they heard screams coming from her floor. By the time the police arrived, she was nowhere to be found."

"She wasn't supposed to go back there. Why would she do that?"

"Will you be safe at your new place?"

"I'll be fine," Addie said. "With video surveillance, security guards, and paying huge tips, I'm more than safe here."

"I'll turn another copy of the video Karla gave you over to the police. Will you be available for an interview?"

Addie hesitated. "Yes, if Vance did this, he should be behind bars."

When she disconnected, Addie immediately notified the lobby. "My husband may show up. I just got word he may have already killed someone, tell everyone to be alert and very careful."

"Yes, Mrs. Hays. He won't get past us."

Around four o'clock Caller ID showed Vance calling from the house. Everything she left behind was probably burning in the fire pit out back. Addie thought it best to answer. "Hello, Vance."

"Howell called me after a cop called him. Something bad happened to Karla." Vance's words were slurred. "Where did your men take her?"

"They were only hired for the day. Once we left the office she was on her own," Addie said, then steeled herself to ask, "Did you punish her, Vance? Someone called the police because of a racket coming from her apartment. They found blood."

"No! It wasn't me," he said with a sob. "Addie, I'm scared for her. She won't answer her cell."

Addie could hear pounding on his door.

"Go away!" he yelled.

She heard the door bang open, voices identifying themselves as police, and then the phone hitting the floor. Addie smiled as she disconnected. Vance in jail meant safety for her. She slept soundly that night. The first good sleep in weeks.

Jamison arrived with the morning paper. Vance's arrest was front page news. Jamison helped himself to coffee while she read the article.

"Why did they arrest him?"

"I have no idea." Jamison sipped his coffee. "I do know they did a quick print analysis and his were all over the place."

"That's not exactly evidence, he spent a lot of time there. Kent, I'm sure he didn't do anything. Vance called me last night right before the police broke in. He'd been drinking and wanted to know where the bodyguards took her."

"What exactly did he say?"

"Howell notified him like you did me. He told me he'd been calling her cell with no answer and he sounded honestly worried."

"Don't give him another thought. Howell got Vance a good criminal attorney," Jamison said. "Addie, they'll want to know who those two men were so they can point the finger at someone else."

Addie nodded.

"I know you'll be on the prosecution witness list to give evidence of his violent side." He gave her a funny look. "Are you hiding anything else?"

That startled her. "No, why?"

"How did you find about Karla in the first place? And who are those men?"

Addie put the newspaper down and smoothed it with both hands. "Kent, I think maybe you should stop asking questions."

"I'm your attorney. You need to be totally honest with me because the police are going to ask the same questions."

Addie sighed. "Karla chose the men and asked me to hire them. She didn't trust anyone else, so I agreed. I have no idea who they are and I wouldn't pay for any protection after she safely left the building. What her plans were after that…" Addie shrugged.

"So how did you find her?"

"It was easy. Vance thinks I'm clueless so I just had to follow him. It only took one time." Addie laughed. "One day Karla and I had a very long talk over lunch and I convinced her that it was in both our financial interests for her to cooperate with me. He'd slapped her around a few times so it was easy. But, Kent, I refuse to testify that Vance ever hurt me. If he manages to get out, he'll come after me."

"You don't actually believe what you said earlier. That he didn't do anything to her?" He couldn't hide his scorn. "You know him better than that."

"As I told you, he sounded like he was being truthful." She squinted at him. "If I do protect him as far as the abuse goes, and there's not enough real evidence, could he get off?"

Jamison shrugged. "He could. Apparently they have enough evidence right now to arrest him and I'd love to know what that is. If they discover more at his house, then he would likely get a long sentence."

"So they're searching the house." Keeping him behind bars was the goal here. "Except for the divorce, I don't want him to have any grudges against me. Remember, he can always hire someone to do his dirty work."

The way Jamison studied her made Addie feel uneasy. "What?"

"Nothing," he said, smiling warily at her. "I better go. One question, how are you going to pay the bodyguards?"

"Cash in advance." Addie raised her eyes. "Karla said to trust them and they obviously didn't disappoint."

• • ● • •

On the witness stand Addie was more than fair. "No," she told the jury. "He was never violent with me." She unconsciously rubbed the scar on her palm where Vance had shoved her hand into shards of a broken wineglass because she had chosen the wrong bottle.

"Oh, come on, Mrs. Hays! Your neighbor testified you told her you were afraid of him," the assistant district attorney insisted.

Addie dabbed at her eyes with a tissue. "When he threw things or hit the walls, I would run next door until he cooled off. But he never, ever laid a hand on me."

During the trial, she watched Vance turn into an old man. Fifty years on him now looked eighty. He was thin, weak, and sagging. His spirit was almost as beaten as his body. It was time to visit him.

• • ● • •

"They tape everything." He held the black phone on his side of the glass. "Anything we say can be released to the public."

"I understand," Addie said softly. "Are you okay? Can I get you anything?"

Vance gave her a defeated smile. "No, but thanks for what you said in there."

"I'm your wife." It didn't hurt to use the words he repeated over and over justifying his abuse.

"I miss Karla. She was always so sweet. I never thought she would work with you against me. You had something on her, didn't you?"

"No, Vance. It wasn't like that. I fooled her."

"Doesn't matter now," he said, wiping his eyes. "I didn't do it, Addie. I didn't kill her, I loved her."

Just another example of how little he cared about Addie's feelings. "I'm sure you didn't."

"There were lots of girls," he confessed. "But Karla was special."

"Oh, Vance, you were so stupid."

"Don't say that." Vance balled a fist.

Camera, she mouthed.

His eyes darkened but he kept himself in check.

"I knew about the others but you never threatened to leave me," she said. "Not until Karla came along. I had to protect my interests."

"Are you saying you were smarter than me?"

"Of course not," Addie lied.

"Yeah," he said, mollified. "Did you see her resemblance to you? I mean the new you I created." He shook his head, smirking. "You didn't look like that six years ago but Karla already had red hair and style."

"I noticed immediately." Addie smiled icily. "She had everything you liked. Do you remember how you met? She told me but I wonder if you remember."

Vance chuckled. "It was your fault we met. She came to my table after you walked out on me and left me all alone at the restaurant."

"Walked out on you?" Addie shook her head. "I forgot to wear the dress you picked out for me. When I arrived at the table you...expressed your disappointment and told me to wait for you at home."

Vance laughed. "Before you got there, I saw this beautiful girl, wearing my favorite shade of green at the bar and she kept looking over at me. I had to find a way to make you leave and you came in wearing the perfect excuse."

"Almost like I deliberately threw her into your arms," Addie said with a grimace.

Vance's laugh was spontaneous and loud. The guard said, "Time's up." Vance hung up his phone and left without a backward glance.

The D.A.'s office came through. With blood traces found in the trunk of his car and a couple of women who stepped forward claiming he had beaten them, the prosecutor's summation was more than convincing with the new slant. "When he got mad at his society wife, Vance Hays took it out on the other women. Because of Karla, the prenuptial agreement became null and void. He owed his wife a lot of money and Karla Swan had to die."

The guilty verdict came back that evening.

The divorce went through as planned and Vance asked to see her. Addie decided it was best to go.

He lifted the phone. "Just wanted you to know, I've forgiven you," he said. "You had my back at trial and that's what mattered."

"Thank you, Vance, I appreciate that," Addie told him. "This is my last visit. I'm going away for a while."

"That's okay." Vance shrugged. "My attorney said I'll be getting out while the case is appealed. I'm going to search for Karla's real killer. I've been set up and I'm going to prove it."

But he didn't get out. Addie closed her condo and flew to the Caymans where she opened up a couple of accounts. Back at the hotel, with some keystrokes on her laptop, she emptied his Cayman account into those new ones. She left a small amount behind as punishment. He would be angry over a zero balance, but insane over a piddling amount. His attorney or the bank officers would be blamed for allowing his account to be hacked by foreigners because his ex-wife was much too stupid to even know about those accounts, much less know how to empty them.

In Costa Rica, she took a cab to the oceanfront house, and pushed open the door. "I'm here!"

"Yay!" Karla came running out of the kitchen. "We're home free!"

"How's the wound?" Addie asked, carrying her bags to a bedroom.

"Healed and worth the pain and the scar." Karla showed her hand. "The blood poured like crazy. I had fun flinging it on the walls. Putting some in the trunk took some doing. He heard us and came outside. Good thing you gave us the gate opener."

"Here," Addie said, tossing a small ledger at her. "Your own personal bank account with everything you earned. Keep that well hidden. You can change the password as soon as you want."

Karla whistled. "Even more than you said."

"Vance is a very clever investor." Addie walked out to the living room and poured a glass of wine. "I couldn't empty out the account until he had no access to a computer. It will be months before he discovers he's broke."

"Pour me one. I'll be right back." Karla went to her bedroom. "By the way, I flew out of Florida a few days later with no trouble."

"I wanted to call you," Addie said. "But didn't dare, in case I was being watched. My attorney was a little suspicious but he's moved on to other cases."

Addie poured another glass and carried both of them to the balcony overlooking the ocean. She stretched out on a lounge chair. It was at this very beach where she had first spotted Karla and come up with the plan. Vance had agreed she could vacation alone in Acapulco. He trusted her subservience and had no idea she had flown to Costa Rica and signed a long-term lease on this secret getaway. Karla was the second generation of American immigrants here and was eager to make a lot of money.

"It's time you went back to your own hair color," Addie said when Karla joined her.

Karla took the glass and wrinkled her nose. "I'm glad. I hate constantly doing roots. I waited, in case you notified me to come back because things fell apart. I kept up with the trial on the Net."

"Your cousins, are they satisfied?"

"Yes, they've become big shots in the city," Karla said, grinning. "And they're making money."

"They bought the bar, then?"

Karla nodded. "A lot of tourists flock to it."

"My plan is to leave at the end of the week. The lease runs out in a few months. Stay until then or lease it in your name."

"Thank you, Mrs. Hays," she said. "I may buy it, since I'm a very wealthy woman now."

"You deserve it, you earned every penny." Addie lifted her glass.

"We both did," Karla said as the glasses clinked.

The Price of Belief

Dennis Palumbo

I knew I'd found the right publisher for my Daniel Rinaldi series when editor Annette Rogers said she enjoyed reading about "the mean streets of Pittsburgh." I'd always believed my hometown would make a great setting for gritty, complex mystery thrillers, and was pleased that Poisoned Pen Press agreed. Since accepting that first book in the series, Mirror Image, *and for each novel that followed, both Annette and Editor-in-Chief Barbara Peters have offered unwavering support (and no small measure of candor) for my work. And my psychologist hero's adventures have been much the better for it.*

By the way, in interviews about the series I've done over the years, I almost always quote Annette's comment about the mean streets of Pittsburgh, and how gratified I was that a publisher had "gotten" what I was trying to do. I guess you could say it was love at first sound-bite.

—D.P.

• • ● • •

Nothing like a guy threatening to jump off a roof to get the public's attention.

"'Bout time you showed up, Rinaldi." Shielding his eyes, Sergeant Harry Polk offered me his trademark scowl as he peered up at the tiny figure barely visible on top of the tall building, standing precariously at the roof's edge. Behind us, uniformed officers struggled to keep a crowd of curious, chattering onlookers away from the scene, although they were still close enough to record the event on their cells and mini-cams, blithely shooting up into a blinding summer sun.

"I left the office as soon as I got your call." A quick glance up at the harrowing sight above. "Thankfully, the traffic out of Oakland wasn't bad. I was afraid I might be too late."

The veteran detective grunted. "Maybe you are."

In this heat, and given his size, Polk's wrinkled blue suit was blotchy with sweat. As was his florid, drinker's face.

"You know about this crazy shit?" he asked wearily.

"That Andrew might be at risk? Of course. So did you, practically from the moment you charged him. He was immediately referred to me, remember? After his *first* suicide attempt."

"Well, looks like he's tryin' again. 'Cept I think the poor bastard's gonna pull it off this time."

I followed his gaze up at Andrew Morrison, who appeared to be swaying slightly, as though readying himself. Behind us, I heard a sudden, excited gasp from the people gathered on the street. Waiting. Perhaps hoping…

The collective silence lasted only a few seconds before morphing into another chorus of murmurs and nervous giggles because Andrew had abruptly stepped back from the lip of the roof, disappearing from our view fourteen floors below.

"Hey, man, where'd ya go?" someone behind me shouted.

Another voice rang out. "C'mon, you pussy! Jump!"

I glanced back at the crowd milling behind the semi-circle of cops, but couldn't tell who'd spoken.

Meanwhile, eyes still riveted on the roof's edge, Polk asked me, "Think Morrison changed his mind?"

"Hell, Harry, I don't know what to think. I gotta get up there and—"

"You gotta *what?*"

For a long moment, I didn't reply, my mind racing. Then I gripped his arm.

"But I'm going to need something first."

"Dammit, Rinaldi!" Polk called after me as I hurried across the pavement and approached one of the uniforms. Sweat gleamed in rivulets from his hatband down the chiseled planes of his smooth black skin.

"Listen, Officer, I'm Dr. Daniel Rinaldi. I consult with the Department and—"

"Sure, Doc, I know who you are. I've seen ya on the news."

"Great. Can you do me a favor? I need to borrow these..." As I reached for his belt and unclipped his handcuffs.

• • ● • •

I'd first heard about Andrew Morrison a month before, in early June. Just before the summer heat wave that would turn Pittsburgh's cobblestone streets into a blanket of hot coals, its air as stifling as the inside of a steel mill's blast furnace. Though the city had few remaining cobblestone streets and no steel mills at all, having in recent decades changed from an industrial powerhouse into a hub of state-of-the-art medicine and pioneering technology. With many of its old neighborhoods newly gentrified as well, the Steel City now represented an amalgam of the past and the future.

As do I. The son of an Italian-American beat cop, I was the first in my extended family to attend college, pursue a profession, go from blue collar to white. Which left me standing with a foot in both worlds. And probably always will...

It was mid-afternoon, and I was just finishing a session with a young woman named Cheryl Rhodes. A junior at Pitt, she'd been viciously raped late one night on the edge of campus. Soon after she reported it to the police, she was referred to me.

Why me? Because I'm a clinical psychologist who specializes in treating people like Cheryl. Victims of violent crime. Those who've survived the assault, the kidnapping, the robbery—but who still lived with the resultant trauma. Crippling anxiety, the torture of self-blame, the ever-present dread of something like it happening again.

Or, perhaps even harder, lived with the guilt of having survived at all when a loved one hadn't.

Something I could relate to. Years ago, my wife and I were mugged by an armed thug outside of a restaurant. Barbara was killed and I was seriously wounded. Since I'd done some amateur boxing as a youth, part of me believed I should have been able to stop the mugger. Save my wife. As a result, during my months of recovery, I struggled with a lacerating survival guilt that still visits me on occasion to this day.

Between that experience, and my highly publicized work treating a victim who'd escaped the clutches of an infamous serial killer, I was hired as a consultant to the Pittsburgh Police Department to help crime victims move on, to the extent possible, with the rest of their lives.

Victims like Cheryl, whose painstaking work with me during our many months together seemed, that late spring day, to be finally paying off. Sitting across from each other in my office, she even managed a pensive smile.

"Guess what, Dr. Rinaldi?" She was a slight woman of medium height, with intense, intelligent gray eyes. "I'm able to start watching *Law and Order* reruns again."

Before the sexual assault, the old TV series had been one of her favorites. Cheryl was interested in a law career.

I smiled. "Sounds like progress to me." And it did.

After we'd hugged good-bye—another breakthrough of recent weeks, given her previous unwillingness to be touched in any way since the rape—I went to my picture window and looked down at Forbes Avenue, which cut through the Pitt campus five floors below. Cheryl had been my last scheduled patient for the day and I was looking forward to beating the traffic home.

That wasn't going to happen.

My desk phone rang and I picked up. It was Angela Villanova, Pittsburgh PD's community liaison officer. We were also distantly related. Older than me, smart and blunt, she'd once tutored me in high school. And rarely let me forget it.

"Is this an official call?" I asked.

"Ya mean, am I referrin' someone to you? Yeah. But it's not a crime victim."

"Then who is it?"

"His name's Andrew Morrison. But here's the thing, Danny. Looks like he murdered his wife."

• • ● • •

Angie was wrong.

From the moment Andrew Morrison stepped into my office less than an hour later, it seemed clear that the thin, chalk-faced software engineer was indeed a victim. The hand that shook mine was moist and tentative, the eyes behind his rimless glasses pinched with anxiety. Even the guarded way he took in my office's furnishings—the matched leather chairs, the old marble-topped desk, my battered Tumi briefcase propped against the wall—gave the impression of a man on the lookout for the next disaster to befall him.

As he took his seat opposite me, I couldn't help but notice his difficulty moving. Though we were both in our early forties, he seemed markedly older. Shoulders slumped, cheeks hollow. Given what he'd just gone through, I wasn't surprised.

We sat in silence for a full minute, his glance flitting nervously about the room, as I went over the details of his case in my mind. The details that Angie had shared with me.

A week before, in the bedroom of their split-level house in Wilkins Township, Morrison had had a fierce argument with his wife, Debbie. One of many arguments, according to the couple's next door neighbors. It ended when Andrew stormed out of the house. Something I confess I had a hard time envisioning, judging by the demeanor of the man sitting across from me.

Some hours later, at nightfall, Morrison returned to find Debbie sprawled across the floor in their bedroom, covered in blood. Viciously stabbed to death. Panic-stricken, he called the police and soon found himself surrounded by uniforms, homicide detectives and CSU techs. After the medical examiner pronounced, the woman's body was taken to the morgue.

Meanwhile, Morrison was in hysterics, so distraught that he had to be sedated on-scene. When the detectives questioned him downtown, he claimed that he'd just driven around for a couple hours after the couple argued, then came home to discover his murdered wife. Due to his continued agitation, the cops arranged for him to be taken to his sister's place in Churchill.

The following day, with no forensics to indicate the presence of an intruder, nor any sign of forced entry to the home, Andrew Morrison was arrested and charged in his wife's murder. His sister immediately hired a lawyer to get him released on bail following his arraignment the next morning. Till then, he'd just have to spend one night in the county jail.

He did and, late sometime after bed-check, Morrison tried to hang himself in his cell. Which prompted Angie's urgent call.

Now, having been freed on bail, he was back living with his sister. And beginning therapy with me.

"I guess you know about the botched hanging." These were his first words to me since shaking hands. "Debbie would have a field day with that. I couldn't even manage to kill myself."

"Well, I for one am glad you turned out to be bad at it."

His returning smile was bitter. "I don't know, Doc. Like they say, practice makes perfect."

I took a breath. "If you're planning any practice sessions in the future, we'll need to make a verbal contract that you have to call me first."

He shook his head. "No promises."

I spent the rest of the session getting a brief history, then asked him about his mood swings, his sleep patterns, his level of anxiety. Most of these I could guess, of course, but I've found that listing certain symptoms can have a palliative effect on a distressed patient. Give them the sense that they at least have some measure of control over their inner states.

I saw Andrew each day after that, fitting him in during lunchtime when necessary, so that we could work on behavioral approaches to managing his anxiety. It wasn't until our fourth session that he could bring himself to talk about that night.

"I'd been driving around for hours, and all of a sudden felt like an idiot. It wasn't that we hadn't fought before, dozens of times. I mean, it started pretty soon after we got married. Debbie found me...I don't know, unexciting, I guess. Not aggressive enough at my job, or in our bed. As for me, I thought she was too demanding. Her expectations of me, too...unrealistic. You know what I mean?"

I nodded. Letting him tell things in his own way, in his own time.

"Anyway, when I got home I found the front door unlocked. I thought this was strange, since Debbie was always so paranoid about crime. Break-ins, that kind of thing. Then when I called out and she didn't answer, I knew something was wrong. Then..."

His voice caught. Tears edged his eyes.

"When I saw her lying there...blood everywhere...I've never seen so much blood. Her body was all slashed up. Cuts all over. Horrible...just horrible. Like a nightmare. Like it couldn't be happening. Couldn't be real."

He dropped his head in his hands.

"And it's all my fault...my fault..."

I leaned forward in my chair.

"How is it your fault, Andrew?"

"If we hadn't fought...if I hadn't stormed out of the house like that...like some coward. But I just couldn't deal with her contempt anymore, you know? I just couldn't stand it...."

There it was. What I'd been waiting for. Andrew's survivor guilt, holding him accountable for the sin of still being alive. Moreover, of the possibility that he might have prevented what happened. If only he hadn't argued with his wife, if only he hadn't left her alone and vulnerable in the house.

If only, if only...

Unless, I thought. Unless it wasn't guilt at all.

I waited another thirty seconds. Then I asked the question.

"Did you do it, Andrew? Did you kill Debbie?"

He looked up at me, his face streaked with tears, his eyes tinged with anguish.

"Me?…Kill Debbie?…I *loved* her. Despite everything. I *couldn't* kill her. I couldn't kill *anyone*…Not in a million years." His gaze found mine. "You have to believe me, Doctor. You *have* to…"

"I do."

But did I?

• • ● • •

As a licensed clinician, I'm of course obligated to maintain my patients' confidentiality. What they say in session never leaves the confines of my office, except for those rare times when a judge revokes the patient's privilege—usually in the course of a criminal trial.

This confidentiality even extends to a patient's name, and the very fact that he or she is in treatment with me. However, in my peculiar position as a police consultant—to whom a patient is referred by the department itself—the person's name and current legal circumstances are known by the authorities.

Which is why, the next time I happened to be talking with Angie on the phone, Andrew Morrison's name came up. By now, it was mid-July and the temperature was nearing one hundred almost daily, pushing my venerable office building's air-conditioning unit to its limits.

"How's he doin', Danny?"

"You know I can't discuss that, Angie."

"Yeah, yeah. Name, rank, and serial number. I'm only askin' 'cause his case ain't goin' so great. For him, I mean."

"How so?"

"Homicide dicks canvassed the guy's neighborhood, talked to his colleagues at work, the pastor at his church. They all say he's an odd duck. Hell, even the padre said Morrison gave him the creeps. Like he's always about to jump out of his skin. Scared of his own shadow. But in a weird way."

Despite the A-C, I was slick with sweat. Having already shed my jacket and tie, now I rolled up my shirtsleeves and reached in my desk's bottom drawer for a bottled water.

"You know none of what you're saying proves anything."

"Maybe not. But the guy's got no alibi for the time of the murder. Nobody who can confirm his whereabouts. I mean, shit, Danny. 'Drivin' around for a couple hours?' My six-year-old niece can come up with somethin' better than that."

"Unless it's the truth."

"Don't matter. With no forensics to say otherwise, and no alternative suspect, the D.A.'s gettin' ready to present to the grand jury. To indict Morrison for murder."

• • ● • •

At our next session, Andrew seemed more agitated than he'd been lately. Fidgeting in his seat. Making a big show of taking out a handkerchief and mopping the sweat from his brow.

"Hot as hell out there today." His voice tinny, tremulous. "Not much better in here, either."

"That's for sure." I regarded him evenly. "So you want to tell me what's going on?"

He drew a long breath. "My lawyer thinks the D.A.'s about to take my case to the grand jury. Second-degree murder."

"I'm sorry to hear that, Andrew. Really."

He looked down at his bony, manicured fingers, nervously twisting in his lap. His unkempt hair blocking his eyes.

"I can't go to trial, Doctor. I won't be able to…"

"Listen, Andrew. No one can predict the outcome of a trial. Any trial. And if you know you're not guilty…"

I couldn't believe how foolish, how inadequate my words sounded. As though justice always triumphed. As though the innocent always escaped the workings of a determined, seemingly implacable law enforcement system.

I tried another tack. "Perhaps your lawyer—"

He gave me a fierce, exasperated look. Voice choked.

"No! Don't you understand? I didn't kill Debbie because I *couldn't* kill her. It isn't in me. I swear, I couldn't kill *anybody*!"

Then his eyes narrowed, and a strange calm seemed to come over him. Even his fingers stopped moving.

"That is, I couldn't kill anybody *else*..."

My heart stopped. "Are you talking about yourself, Andrew?"

He shrugged. "Maybe I am. At least I'd spare the city the cost of a trial."

"I thought we had an understanding. A contract."

"I don't remember signing anything. Do you?"

We sat in silence, staring at each other. It was his calm, measured demeanor that worried me. That led me to fear he'd made up his mind.

Then, to my surprise, he broke into a grin. And climbed slowly to his feet.

"Don't worry, Doc. Everything's fine. If Debbie were here, she'd tell you. I'm all talk, no action."

"Really?"

"Trust me, I don't think I have the guts to do myself in."

"You tried it before," I said carefully. "In your cell."

"Well, as Voltaire said, 'Once, a philosopher; twice, a pervert.'"

"Meaning...?"

"Meaning I made a mess of hanging myself. Just ended up feeling more lame and inadequate than I normally do."

"Dammit, Andrew, you're not—"

"Besides, my lawyer says there's a chance we can make a deal. Give the D.A. something he can live with. That *I* can, too."

I said nothing, though the image of a man as wounded, as broken, as Andrew Morrison spending years in prison was hard to countenance. I seriously wondered if he'd survive.

At session's end, we confirmed the date and time of his next appointment. Then I saw him out the door.

• • ● • •

The call came mid-afternoon the following day. I was in session at the time, so my voice mail took the message. I didn't have a chance to hear it until the patient left.

It was from Harry Polk. I called him right back.

"Doc, I got bad news. About Andrew Morrison."

"What about him?"

"Grand jury indicted him a couple hours ago. When his lawyer told him, Morrison just took off. Ran right outta the guy's office."

"Jesus, Harry. Do you have him? Is he okay?"

"Not exactly. Morrison's up on the roof of the lawyer's building. Down near Point State Park. That office complex there. He's been standing on the ledge for ten minutes. Looks like he's plannin' to jump."

I felt the blood freeze in my veins. Then, rousing myself, I hung up and started calling the rest of the day's patients, cancelling their appointments.

Minutes later, I was barreling down Forbes, heading for the Point. Luckily the downtown commute hadn't yet started, so I made pretty good time.

Soon I was standing with Sergeant Polk on the sidewalk, in the blistering sun, squinting up at Andrew Morrison fourteen stories above.

And then I was speaking with one of the uniformed officers, asking him for a favor.

After which I entered the building lobby, stepped into the elevator and headed for the top floor.

• • ● ● •

There was an unlocked fire door on the fourteenth floor that opened on concrete steps leading up to a second door. Pausing for a moment to collect myself, I turned the handle and went out onto the flat, tar-papered roof.

Cinders that had baked in the sun crunched under my feet as I approached Andrew. Standing just back from the roof edge, he turned at the sound.

He and I merely stared at each other across the ten-foot space between us. A hand in my pocket, I tried to seem as casual, as unthreatening as possible.

Finally, I spoke. "Is this the part where you tell me not to come any closer?"

"I don't know, Doc." He gave a weak smile. "Is that the same part where you tell me I still have something to live for?"

"Well, don't you?" I took a step closer.

"You're kidding, right? If I live, I go to prison for years for something I didn't do. If I die, I'm spared that. Frankly, I don't think you have a case."

"Can you at least back away from the edge, Andrew? You're making me nervous."

"Sorry, no can do. Except for the damned heat, I kinda like it up here. It's quiet. A man can think."

A pause. "Okay, stay where you are. But then can I come over to you?"

He shrugged. "*Mi casa, su casa.* Or whatever the Spanish for 'roof' is."

Steeling myself, I walked slowly across the crinkling tar-paper until I was standing by Andrew's side.

"Actually, Doc," he said, "I'm glad you came up here. Gives me a chance to say thanks in person. You've been a big help."

"Not from the look of things, Andrew. You're a patient of mine who's threatening to jump off a roof."

"Well, there's that. But otherwise, you've done as well as anyone could. In the circumstances."

I nodded. Took another pause.

"Just for the record, okay? Even if the D.A. *had* agreed to a deal, a reduced sentence, you wouldn't have taken it. Right?"

"Right." He sighed heavily. "A man like me wouldn't be able to tolerate prison. Not for one single day. Besides, accepting a deal would mean admitting guilt."

"Not necessarily."

He held up a hand. "Don't get me wrong. I have plenty to feel guilty about. But not for killing Debbie. It's my fault she's dead, no question. I left her alone. Defenseless. But I didn't kill her."

Andrew gave me a sad, almost forlorn look. "Because, as I told you, as I kept telling the police, I couldn't kill anyone."

"Except yourself."

"Exactly. See, you *do* understand me, Doc. It's a real comfort at a time like this."

His relaxed, almost disinterested manner caught me off guard. Suddenly he turned, took two steps toward the lip of the roof, and sat down. Feet dangling over the side.

Hesitating only a moment, I joined him on the roof edge. Sat right beside him, shoulder to shoulder. Hand still in my pocket. My own feet hanging over the edge.

I risked glancing over the side. The crowd below was like a living thing, undulating, people moving about in clusters. Pointing up at Andrew and me. Or aiming their cells and mini-cams. Hoping for something, *anything*, to happen.

I also noted a number of TV news vans parked just beyond the growing throng. By now, too, an ambulance had arrived on the scene.

"We're building quite an audience," Andrew said, peering over the edge as well. "I suspect I'll end up on YouTube."

I said nothing, leaning back a bit. Trying to keep my own anxiety under control. To stay focused.

Andrew turned then, his face as open as a child's.

"Like I said, I appreciate your coming up here, Doc. But I'm going to do it. I'm going to jump. I hope you believe me."

"I do. But I was an idiot to believe what you said at the end of our session yesterday. About hoping for a plea deal. About how you'd never try to commit suicide again because of how you'd botched it the first time."

"Tell you the truth, I was kind of surprised you bought that myself. But other than that, I've never lied to you during our sessions. About myself, my marriage, anything. I'm guilty of many things, Dr. Rinaldi, but lying isn't one of them."

"I know that, Andrew. That's why I believe you when you say you're willing to commit suicide."

"I am."

"But you also said something else in session. Something you said you *wouldn't* do. *Couldn't* do."

"And what's that?"

"Kill someone."

And, with that, I took my hand out of my pocket. My wrist encircled by one half of a pair of handcuffs, the other half dangling. Before Andrew could register what was happening, I snapped the free cuff around his own wrist.

His eyes widened in shock. "What the—?"

"We're handcuffed together now, Andrew. So where *you* go, *I* go. Including over the edge of this roof. To splatter together on the pavement below. If *that* doesn't get us on YouTube, nothing will."

He couldn't stop staring. "You...you're *crazy*..."

"That may be. But I'm not the one with a decision to make. See, if you really want to kill yourself, go ahead and jump. But you'll be killing me, too."

I met his incredulous gaze.

"Now, personally, I'd like to live. But it's up to you."

He could barely form words. "But...but *why*? Why in God's name would you *do* this?"

"Because I believe in you, Andrew. I believe you didn't kill Debbie, just like I believe you can't kill me. A belief whose price I'm willing to pay."

He squinted down at the handcuffs binding us. "Come on, Doc. I know you have the key for these things..."

"Actually, I don't. It's probably still in the pocket of the cop I borrowed them from."

A long, agonizing minute of silence followed as a dozen conflicting emotions seemed to flicker across his face.

At the same time, my own resolve began to weaken. The mad, searing reality of what I'd done flooding over me. All because I knew in my gut that Andrew Morrison wasn't a killer. Or thought I knew. *Believed* it.

Sweat beaded my brow, but not from the heat. My mouth gone dry, heart banging in my chest. I felt my panic rising... Then suddenly, as though from far way, I heard Andrew's deep, heavy exhalation. His voice a whisper.

"I…I can't do it, Doc. You're right. I can't kill you. Not just because of something *I* want. Something that would take my pain away. I can't let you die because of that…"

I gave out a long, relieved sigh of my own.

"Then would it be okay if we went down now?" I met his gaze. "Or do you want to sit up here a little longer?"

He considered this carefully.

"Would you mind if we stayed up here just a bit longer? As you know, there's nothing down there I'm looking forward to."

"I understand. But you won't be alone. I'll be with you as much as I can. Every step of the way."

He nodded slowly. "Guess it's my turn to believe *you*."

We stayed that way, handcuffed together, side by side, on the edge of the roof until it got too hot, and Andrew said he was ready to come down.

• • ● • •

"Jesus, Rinaldi, I knew you had a screw loose, but that was off-the-charts crazy."

Harry Polk was walking with me toward his unmarked, after having arrested Andrew Morrison and sent him off with some uniforms. Meanwhile, a disappointed crowd of onlookers noisily dispersed, as a pair of equally disgruntled news crews packed up their gear and drove off, their hopes for something exciting on a slow news day dashed.

"I'm just glad the cop I borrowed the cuffs from hadn't gone off duty." I rubbed my wrist. "I never got his name, and he was the guy with the key."

Polk grunted. "Yeah, well, it woulda served ya right to be handcuffed to that nut-job for the rest o' the night. Sharin' a cell with him mighta put some sense in your thick skull."

I stopped him at his car door. "Just make sure you keep an eye on him at the jail, okay? He's still a suicide risk."

The sergeant gave me a baleful look. "Listen, Doc. After what you just did, so are you."

I got similar criticism from Angie on the phone that night.

"Jesus, Danny, everybody knows you have a hero complex. Who the hell knew you had a death wish, too?"

"What can I say? It seemed like a good idea at the time."

It was a flippant, facetious remark and she wasn't buying it. She grumbled something unintelligible and hung up.

• • ● • •

Less than a week later, a woman in Monroeville was attacked by a home invader with a serrated blade. He'd been dressed as a gas company employee, and had knocked at her door to let her know he'd be in her backyard, checking her meter. As soon as she'd opened the door, he pushed his way in.

To his surprise, the woman raised German shepherds, and her current four-legged live-in companion tore the hell out of the guy. Thinking fast, the woman locked her assailant in a closet and called the police. Under interrogation that night, he admitted to killing Debbie Morrison as well. Using the same ruse, he'd entered the house and savagely butchered her. He gave no explanation for his actions, and showed little remorse.

The next day, Andrew Morrison was released from jail, with all charges dropped. After which he returned to therapy with me. Still traumatized by the brutal murder of his wife, as well as tormented by feelings of guilt and self-recrimination, he had a long therapeutic journey ahead of him.

And, as I'd promised, I was willing to accompany him all the way. His would be a difficult path, but I believed I could help guide him through it. I guess I had to. I couldn't do my job if I didn't.

Still, for some months afterwards, I had a recurring dream about Andrew and me, handcuffed together on the edge of the roof. The heat of the day pouring down on us. The crowd below waiting expectantly.

We exchange the same words. I make the same argument.

And, in my dream, he always jumps.

The Stranding

Sulari Gentill

Years ago, I set off to university to study astrophysics and came out with a law degree. I'm not quite sure how it happened. Whilst practising law can, on occasion, be creative, they don't like you to simply make things up. Writing fiction seemed liked a better way to indulge my growing fondness for fabrication. Although I came to writing late, and on a whim rather than an epiphany, it soon became as natural as breathing and the thought of stopping as dire.

I was first published in Australia (where I live) in 2010 with the first book of what has become a long-running series. There are now eight Rowland Sinclair Mysteries. The series was picked up for publication in the U.S. by Poisoned Pen Press, which released the first two novels in 2016, with a novel due for release every six months thereafter.

I continue to live with my husband, Michael, my boys, Edmund and Atticus, and several animals on a small farm in the foothills of the Snowy Mountains of New South Wales, where I grow French black truffles and write…a lot. With each book I fall more deeply in love with the craft of storytelling.

—S.G.

• • ● ● •

First light reached shyly across the bay. Her embrace was gentle, as if she knew, as if she cared. He was still, stark against the movement of dawn on the water, dark against the distant wound of a bleeding horizon. His thoughts were lost and he within them—frantically, breathlessly lost. And yet he was still.

The world receded and he struggled once more in mud and blood and terror. But the touch of daybreak was warm. And gradually, the rhythm of the swell soothed the rattling, hammering clatter of artillery and the screams of dying men. It led him back.

A young woman called out to him from the beach. "Ernest!"

The smile began before he turned. It was not for her as much as a response to her, the thought of her, the knowledge of her. May Clarke stood barefoot on the sand, her dress damp with spray, her hair blown wild by the salt breeze. She'd been a child when he'd gone to war. He'd been barely more than a boy himself.

He'd written to her when Jack had died with condolences for the loss of her brother and she'd replied in her careful child-ish hand, but with such strength and compassion that he had kept the pages close through the mire and hell of the years that followed. She'd written to him regularly after that—the letters she might have written Jack, and somehow they had kept him sane. He'd spent his war looking for stories he could tell her in return, funny little accounts of some small thing that wouldn't frighten her, or reveal the horror of what they faced, of how her brother had died. That much he could do for Jack.

She'd met him on the dock when he'd come home—an unex-pected bloom, a beautiful curved transformation of the braids and freckles and awkwardness he'd watched Jack embrace good-bye. May Clarke worked for *The Mosman Daily* now—reporting on society parties and debutante balls—and kept her own small flat at Rushcutters Bay. She cajoled him out of his darker moods, seduced him back to the world, reminded him that he was alive and young and a man.

"Ernest!" May beckoned him quite urgently now.

He ran down from the rocks expecting she'd found a hermit crab or some other treasure in the sand. "Where's the fire?"

She grabbed his arm tightly and pointed down the beach. "Look."

The shape was dark, washed up on the smooth glistening wake of the retreating foam. He tensed. Even from this distance he could make out arms splayed from the crumpled mass.

"Stop here, May," he said moving toward it.

She ignored the direction, following, though she stayed a step behind him. When they were close enough to see, to realise, she laughed. He smiled as she giggled at their fright, their foolishness. It was just an overcoat.

"Oh, we are idiots!" She embraced him in the exuberance of relief.

He heaved up the coat. Soaked, the heavy wool resisted the strength of his arm, clinging to its place on the sand.

"What do you suppose it's doing in the bay?" May mused as she tried to wring the sleeves. The coat was well cut, expensive, at least originally.

"Who knows?" It wasn't the kind of garment one would expect to be left on a beach.

"Ernest—" May pulled his arm again and pointed. Several yards further on…a woman's mantel this time, with a saturated fur-lined collar, and then another, and another. It was the child's coat that troubled May—that unnerved her: a red frock coat with white buttons.

"We should notify the police," she whispered. "This isn't right."

"They're coats," he replied, though the strange stranding perplexed him too.

"Maybe there were people in them once…perhaps the fish have eaten them!" May clutched the child's coat to her breast, distressed by the thought.

He placed his arms around her and kissed the top of her head. "You're getting carried away, sweetheart." Still, he, too, was uneasy. "Perhaps they were cargo that fell overboard."

May shook her head, pulling away to show him the label on the silken lining of the child's coat. *Anna Rosenbaum* in neat, black stitching. "What do you suppose happened to her?"

Ernest frowned. He had no idea, no suggestion to assuage the notions of murder and tragedy that now gripped May.

Two more coats were deposited by the tide, limp empty shadows of the people who might have once walked in them. Ernest dragged the salt-sodden overclothes into a pile while May ran to fetch the police. He waited with his gaze fixed out to sea, struggling to avoid the recollection of more grisly heaps.

Kings Cross station sent two constables. The younger immediately extracted a notebook and licked the lead of a stubby pencil. "You question the duffle," he said grinning broadly at his partner. "I'll get a statement from the tweed."

"We thought...I thought..." May stuttered, colouring. Ernest glared at the young policeman.

"Two bodies found on Sydney beaches in the last week, Kendall." The elder officer frowned, clearly irritated.

"Yeah, but..." Kendall began.

"You can be funny once you've been on the job a month... until then you'd do well to shut-up and listen." Constable O'Reilly introduced himself. May smiled at him and he straightened a little.

"Might these coats be related to—?" Ernest began.

"I really couldn't say, Mr....?"

"Alden, Ernest Alden."

"The bodies on Manly Beach?" May persisted. The newsroom had been full of the corpses which had washed up within a day of each other. A man and a woman...generally thought to be victims of a suicide pact.

But O'Reilly would tell them nothing more. He despatched Kendall to inform the Criminal Investigation Bureau, took their names and addresses and sent them on their way.

• ● ● ● •

May opened the door before he'd had a chance to knock, dragging him into the small flat and kissing him with such force that he stumbled back against the papered wall. He laughed as she loosened his tie.

"My God, you're shameless," he said, dropping his briefcase and wrapping his arms about her. "Marry me."

"Stop trying to make an honest woman of me," she whispered, unbuttoning his shirt.

"You can be as dishonest as you like...I'll help you rob a bank if you want," he replied. "Just marry me."

May smiled, turning away from him and walking into her bedroom. "Are you going to stand around proposing or do you want to hear what I found out about our coats?"

"*Our* coats?" He watched as she unbuttoned her dress and let it fall away.

"Well, yes...they're ours in a way." May stepped toward him, a tantalising nymph in a cotton chemise.

Ernest forgot about the coats, giving himself over to her seduction. May led him to her bed. He followed in awe that fate would have given him something so beautiful, so completely unspoiled. There was a time when he'd thought everything spoiled. Ernest made love to her then, slowly, immersing himself in her. She welcomed him into her body and her self, and the dark recollections which tormented him seemed illuminated and repelled for a time.

It was not until they lay together spent and languid, that May raised the coats again. "Darling," she said lacing her fingers with his, "those bodies they found at Manly Beach—they didn't have coats."

"What?" He kissed the hollow at the base of her throat.

She sighed. "The bodies, Ernest. They didn't have coats."

He groaned. Apparently she was not going to allow him to have her again unless they talked about corpses first. "How do you know?"

"I tracked down one of the journalists who covered the story...I asked him."

"Perhaps they simply weren't wearing coats, May."

"It's July, Ernest."

"Still—"

"What if their coats were among those we found on the beach?"

"You're suggesting someone murdered them for their coats?" Ernest smiled, running his hand along her thigh.

"Who knows?" She pushed his hand away and rolled onto her elbows. "But what if those coats were a murderer's hoard? What if there are more bodies that just haven't yet washed up?"

"Then the police will have their work cut out for them, I expect."

"You know a story like this would make them take me seriously at the paper." May bit her lip.

Ernest frowned, sensing something. "What's happened?" He brushed the hair from her face so he could see her eyes.

"Mr. Casey hated my story," she said, moving to rest her head on his chest.

Ernest put his arm around her surprised. He had read May's article the night before. A story that started with the latest fashion in outer garments, and went on to consider those who shivered in threadbare mantels, long discarded by the stylish, and finished with the poignancy of the coats which washed up on the beach. Ernest had thought it clever and moving…the best of May's writing.

"Mr. Casey said I was getting above myself."

"Casey's an idiot." Ernest felt the warmth of her tears on his chest. She felt his arm tighten about her.

"He said they paid me to cover parties and frocks…that people didn't read the social pages to be preached at. Oh, Ernest…in front of everybody…it was so humiliating…."

"I might have a word with Casey…."

"You will not!" May pulled up and looked him in the face. "He's my boss."

"He doesn't have to be. Marry me."

May smiled. "That's three."

It was the rules, her rules. Ernest was permitted to ask her to marry him three times in a single day, but no more. She could not bear to refuse him more than three times a day.

"I'll just have to show Mr. Casey and the others," she said pressing her naked body against his, seducing him all over again.

"This could be my big break. I'm going to find out what happened to the poor souls who owned those coats."

Ernest drew her into his arms, silently marvelling at the vibrant softness of her. "Just tell me what you want me to do."

• • ● • •

John O'Reilly sighed. "As I explained to Miss Clarke this morning, I'm afraid there's not a great deal I can tell you, Mr. Alden. We've not been able to either identify the rightful owners of the garments in question, or establish how those garments might have ended up in the sea."

"There was a name stitched into the child's coat…Anna Rosenbaum."

"We haven't been able to locate anyone by that name. Certainly no child of that name has been reported missing."

Ernest rubbed the back of his neck. "Do you think the coats are connected to the deaths on Manly Beach, Constable?"

Despite the fact that May's article had been scorned and rejected, other journalists were speculating on the coats. *The Truth* had gone as far as to suggest that each coat had a body which would wash up on Sydney beaches in the coming days.

O'Reilly shrugged. "I really couldn't say, Mr. Alden. There is nothing to connect the two. In my opinion the war's left folks jumpy…we're seeing murder in something that's just a damn shame."

• • ● • •

May stood on the beach, her coat pulled tight and her arms folded against the wind. The midwinter evening had descended quickly, the shadows reaching out to join and merge. May shifted her weight, jiggling to keep warm. Ernest was usually waiting by the time she got away from work. They'd stroll along the sand and have dinner somewhere before they parted. He'd deliver her quite properly to her door by ten, tip his hat to Mrs. Rooney, who seemed always to be sweeping the neighbouring doorstep, and return chastely to his boardinghouse in Edgecliff.

The beach was now all but empty. May's mind returned to the coats, and the people who might have been in them. She needed this story. It was only by virtue of the fact that she wrote for the society pages that she'd not lost her position as the men returned. John Casey did not like her...thought her too bold and impertinent with inappropriate ambitions. He'd said as much as he slashed her work to remove everything but the description of dresses.

The glow of a cigarette on the jetty—the silhouette of a man. May turned away—Ernest didn't smoke. She wished he'd hurry.

She'd dug up all the newspaper reports about the couple found on Manly Beach. The man had been married, a bookkeeper and devoted father. The woman, much younger, an apprentice milliner who lived with her grandmother. Both had been completely dressed but for coats—indeed the journalist who'd reported the story had covered their attire in such detail that May wondered if he'd learned his trade on the social pages. It gave her hope.

There was no glow now, the cigarette stubbed or the smoker gone home. What could be keeping Ernest?

A flash as a match was struck. A face cast into momentary clarity as a cigarette was lit just yards away. Where was Ernest?

Suddenly the beach seemed very dark, and deserted. May decided to move back toward the road and the streetlights. She walked with controlled calm. The smoker paused only a moment before he followed.

May quickened her pace. Her shoes filled with sand as care gave way to haste. The smoker coughed and kept up. May allowed panic to creep upon her with images of bodies and sodden empty coats. She broke into a run slipping in the looser sand.

"Miss," the smoker rasped breathing heavily now.

May screamed, scrambling blindly away from the voice.

"May!"

The chest suddenly before her was familiar, a broad, breathing sanctuary.

"What's the matter, darling?" Ernest asked as she clutched his lapel, shaking.

"There's a man…"

At the moment the smoker caught up, wheezing and gulping air into his laboured lungs.

Ernest tensed, moving May behind him. "Who the hell are—?"

"Percy McRae." The smoker mopped his brow with a large handkerchief. "I'm sorry if I startled you, Miss," he panted. "I noticed you were waiting alone…I thought I'd hang about and make sure you were right. Not a good idea for a young lady such as yourself to be waiting alone after dark…I didn't want to bother you, just to make sure you were right."

May swallowed. "Oh, I thought—"

"I should have realised…."

May smiled, feeling a little silly now. "Thank you, Mr. McRae…it was very kind of you."

Ernest shook McRae's hand and thanked him too. "It was my fault entirely," he said. "I'm late."

McRae bade them a good evening.

"Where were you?" May said angrily when the chivalrous smoker had departed. She caught the hint of whisky on Ernest's breath. "You've been drinking!" she accused.

"I'm sorry," he said trying to take her hand. She shook him off. "Some of the chaps insisted…I'm so sorry, sweetheart."

"You stood me up to go drinking! I might have been—" They passed under a streetlight then, and May saw his face. She stopped. "What's happened?"

He shrugged. "I got the sack today."

"The sack? But why?"

"One of the machines on the floor jammed. It rattled like… it sounded like…anyway I went a bit queer."

"They sacked you for that?" May said, outraged, her anger at him forgotten.

"Not for that…the boss laughed at me and I hit him a few times. Then he sacked me."

"Oh, darling." May had seen the war come unexpectedly upon him before, the way it took his breath. She embraced him tightly, desperate to comfort him, to stand between him and hurt. "You don't want to work for that horrible man anyway."

Ernest said nothing. They both knew he needed to work.

• • ● • •

"I spoke to that constable this morning," Ernest murmured when May lay again in his arms. "They don't seem to have had any luck finding the owners of our coats."

May smiled, noting that he'd said *our coats.* "I know," she said, "but I've an idea."

He kissed her. "Tell me then."

"We'll place a notice in the paper asking anyone who has information on Anna Rosenbaum to contact us."

Ernest's brow rose.

"Someone must know her…or have known her," May insisted.

"Fair enough," Ernest conceded, though he was not entirely convinced. He could only hope that placing the notice would not be too expensive.

"Hey," May said softly, "you haven't asked me to marry you today."

"Sweetheart, I don't even have a job anymore—"

"Don't be silly."

"Are you saying you've changed your mind?"

May stretched out on top of him, placing her cheek against the rise and fall his chest. She could hear his heart. "No," she said, "I haven't. But I don't want you to stop asking."

• • ● • •

The notice appeared in *The Sydney Morning Herald.* The subeditor in charge of the classifieds had given May a professional discount. The notice read: *Seeking information on Anna Rosenbaum or anyone who might know her. Reward. Please contact May Clarke, Flat 3, 42 Bidwell Avenue, Rushcutters Bay.*

The reward was an impulse they could ill afford.

Ernest searched for work without a reference from his last employer, and a disposition too honest to fabricate one. The market was flooded with demobbed servicemen and young women for whom the war had opened vocational doors and who would now not see them closed.

They did not meet on the beach anymore. Ernest would call at the paper's offices and walk May home. They ate in her flat, cooking simple meals on the primus as they shared news and made plans for one day. If Ernest was ever prone to brood, May would not permit it, demanding he make love to her then and there. She'd not allow him to be ashamed, banishing his doubts with her unmitigated belief in him, her undiminished desire for him. Even so, at ten o'clock or soon thereafter, Ernest would quite respectably depart for his own lodgings, in full knowledge that his comings and goings were being observed and noted by the ever-vigilant Mrs. Rooney and her broom.

Nearly a week after the notice had been placed, a letter arrived. Slipped under the door sometime during the day, they found it when they came in. It was written in a precise, neat hand. "I knew Anna Rosenbaum." It gave an address in Darling-hurst. "I will be there between ten and midnight."

"It says *knew*," May said. "Something terrible has happened to the poor little mite. I'm not going to let them get away with it."

"Them?"

"Whoever killed her."

"We don't know that anyone killed her." He studied the note. "We should probably call the police?"

"No—not until I talk to him."

"It's too dangerous—"

"You'll be with me, won't you?"

"Always," he said.

May's eyes softened. "Then what could happen?"

It was after nine when they set out on foot. Darlinghurst was not so far a walk. The clubs were full and the streets of the Cross and Darlinghurst were teeming with those who stepped out at night, who sought and served vice, and who'd chosen this place as theirs. May was not surprised by the choice.

The address to which the note summoned them was near Darlinghurst Gaol, a dilapidated building by an alleyway.

Ernest knocked.

"Are you Clarke?" The voice came from behind them. An old man emerged from the alley.

"Ernest Alden. This is Miss Clarke, Mr.…?"

"You call me Rueben. You come about Anna?"

"Yes, sir."

Rueben gestured toward the alley. "Come…there is a fire here," he said rubbing his arms against the cold. "We will talk."

Ernest took May's hand and they followed. A fire glowed red in the iron confines of a dented drum, casting a weak light into the damp darkness of the alley. Rueben motioned them in to stand around this makeshift fireplace and took his time warming his hands.

"So," he said. "You search for Anna—Anna Rosenbaum?"

May nodded emphatically. "Yes, it's very important that we find out what became of her."

Ernest noticed the momentary movement of the old man's eyes, but too late. They were upon him as he turned. May screamed. A large hand came down across her face, another around her waist. She was turned away from the fight, and so she could only hear the thud of fist against flesh as they subdued Ernest.

May wrenched her face free. "There's money in my purse," she said. "Take it all…just please don't…"

The men beating Ernest stopped. May could see him again now. On his knees, bloodied and gasping.

"Search him," Rueben instructed.

"You can have our money," May sobbed as they dragged Ernest to his feet and went through his pockets.

"Who sent you?" Rueben demanded. "Who uses my granddaughter to find me?"

"Your granddaughter?" May stuttered, trying in vain to reach Ernest. "My God, you've really hurt him."

Rueben lifted Ernest's chin and methodically scrutinised his face. He pushed up the young man's sleeves to inspect his forearms. "You are no Jew," Rueben said quietly. "Who is it you work for? Why do you involve yourself in this?"

"I don't work for anybody," Ernest muttered. "Not anymore. Is your granddaughter alive?"

Grabbing his collar, Rueben shook him furiously. "Who are you to ask? What mischief do you make? There are no Rosenbaums anymore." He raised his arm to strike.

"Stop," May begged. "Please, stop. We found Anna's coat on the beach. We just wanted to help her…to find out what happened to her."

Rueben stared at Ernest and then at May. He recoiled and dropped his face into his hands. "God forgive me." For a moment there was silence and then the old man spoke to his companions in some language which neither Ernest nor May could understand. They argued, the younger men clearly unhappy. Finally Rueben spoke in English once more. "Bring them to the house."

May's captor responded by heaving her into his arms, entirely indifferent to her resistance, her writhing, clawing demands for release.

"Let her go, you mongrel!" Ernest lunged toward them in an attempt to protect May. But he was hopelessly outnumbered. They took him forcibly, too, but it was a more careful restraint than before, more resolute than brutal.

They were taken to a mouldering terrace, externally as decrepit and neglected as any tenement in Darlinghurst. The walls were stained and the ironwork rusted and peeling. Within, however, it was clean and neat though sparsely furnished and as cold as it was outside. A small fire in the grate gave almost no heat. Several people—mainly women and children—admitted them in an uproar of questions, demands, and scolding, all in a foreign tongue. May was allowed finally to go to Ernest.

"Oh, God…" She reached up to touch the split brow above his right eye.

"I'm all right," he whispered as he put his arm around her. "Do you know what—?"

She shook her head. "Maybe they killed Anna."

A woman with a child clinging to her skirt brought Ernest a soaked cloth, folded into a compress of sorts and indicated that he should apply it to his face. They brought him a stool, and then a glass of brandy.

Another woman, older and thin, spoke to them first.

"Will you go to the police?" she asked. "Will you tell them what these fools have done?"

Ernest glanced at May, unsure what answer was the least dangerous.

"We…we don't know," May said. "Are you going to let us go?"

Rueben picked up a little girl. "This is my granddaughter, Annie," he said. "Annie Rosewood. In Poland she was Anna Rosenbaum, but for two months she has been Annie."

May was relieved, but no less confused. "I don't understand." She glanced at the blood on Ernest's shirt.

Rueben sighed. "Before the war, I was a wealthy man, respected. When the Nazis came I was elected to the Judenrat."

Ernest nodded. He'd heard of the Judenrat when he was serving—the councils of Jews who administered the ghettos, who came to be as reviled by their own people as they had been by the Nazis. Some said they collaborated in exchange for small favours, saved their own families at the expense of others.

"We did our best," Rueben shouted as if he could read Ernest's thoughts. "Annie's parents, her uncles and her brothers are all dead. The Judenrat were scapegoats, as subject to slaughter as any other goat!"

"Uncle!" one of the younger women warned. "He did not accuse you."

Rueben stopped. He shook his head. "Yes…you are right, of course. I apologise again, Mr. Alden." He attempted to explain. "We tried, but one cannot administer evil fairly. When first you begin to bargain with lives, you are lost. We saved nothing, no one. After the war, I found my granddaughter, my niece, two nephews...I had so much family at the beginning of the war, and we were all that were left. We came to this country to join my sister and her husband."

"But why change Anna's name?" May ventured hesitantly.

"There are some Jews who hate the name Rosenbaum, who remember the Judenrat only as an instrument of the Nazis. They do not understand that we tried and would not welcome the family of Rueben Rosenbaum or allow us to build a new life free of the past."

"So that's why you threw Annie's coat into the sea? Because it had Anna Rosenbaum's name on it?"

The woman who had asked them whether they intended to go to the police made a clicking sound and slapped her forehead. "No, that was because my brother is a romantic fool!"

Now Rueben looked sheepish. "On the boat they told us, you see, about the wonders of this country. The streets were not paved with gold but bathed in it, because the sunshine here was endless and snow and sleet unknown. A sun-soaked paradise." He looked at his granddaughter as he spoke and they smiled at each other. "As the ship came through the heads we stood out on the deck looking with joy upon our new home"—he danced with the little girl in his arms to demonstrate their elation—"...and in our celebration we threw our overcoats overboard...because we wouldn't need them, you see..."

"And now, now, you are cold!" Rueben's sister spat, arms folded in frustration. "Now you shiver through the winter!"

Silence. Then Ernest laughed. He remembered sailing through the heads on the troop ship...that first glorious glimpse of Sydney, of home, from across the water. He tightened his arm around May. "Mystery solved, Sherlock...not so much murder as littering."

May smiled.

After a time, Ernest stood, wincing as he straightened. "We should go. Mrs. Rooney's probably been sweeping that step for hours."

"Will you go to the police?" Rueben's sister asked again.

Ernest glanced at May and shook his head. "Only to see if we can have your coats returned to you," he said.

May stroked the little girl, now asleep on her grandfather's shoulder. "I'm glad I was wrong."

They took their leave of the Rosewoods, as they now were, amid apologies and gratitude, and set out. Midnight was cold and they were glad that they at least had their coats.

May sighed. "I suppose that's the end of my big story."

"It's a different story," Ernest said quietly.

May leaned into him. "You're right. It's a better story…as awful and as sad, but more."

"You solved the case either way."

She laughed entwining her arm in his. "I suppose I did… well, we did. My investigative skills would have been for naught without you, my dear Watson."

He smiled. "Then marry me."

May gasped. "You rat! That's four times—" She stopped as her eyes met his, became caught and held and lost in his. "Just for that, I think will."

Mabel, Still Gathering Wisdom

Carolyn Wall

Poisoned Pen Press bought my first two novels, Sweeping Up Glass
and Playing With Matches—*on that astounding day all authors
should experience. For years we fantasize the ringing of the phone,
the weakness in our knees, those lovely words: "Are you sitting down?"*

*Quickly I found a chair and began to jot notes—"First published
with us, now sold to Random House," "Other countries, other lan-
guages." "People are going to take your picture. Get a haircut—how
are your teeth?"*

*Rob and Barbara flew me to Scottsdale for a tour and a dinner,
and to speak at The Poisoned Pen Bookstore. I was off and running. Imagination had saved me over and over as a child—who
ever thought its product could be so grand?*

I did.

—C. W.

• • ● • •

When she was eighteen and too old to marry, according to the
custom of her tribe, Mabel Arizona climbed to the highest place
on the dry plain and spread herself facedown on the quartz rock.
She opened her arms to the Great Spirit who saw into her soul,
and read the feelings she kept hidden there.

She called the spirit Simon. With the rock pulsing beneath
her, Simon entered her body through the pores of her dark skin,
and her brain through the follicles of her hair. She offered thanks

to Him with her lips pressed to the warm rock and knew that she had only to think a thing was so, and it would be. When the sun slid exhausted toward the desert, Mabel climbed down from the rock and washed her cotton underwear in the thin stream, and she waited.

It was nearly sunset when Leonard Greely rode into camp, tall and thin with hair like syrup in the last of the sun and his glasses riding high on his nose. Leonard took Mabel's hand, led her into the cornfield and laid her down among the thick stalks. There he gave her the first child.

Because the other Ute women would not speak to her, Mabel married Leonard in the First Baptist Church on Highway 9. To celebrate their marriage, he gave her a small silver box filled with red beans, wrapped in pale blue paper. He built her a hut and bought her a shovel so she could dig a patch for potatoes and another for squash. Before long, there were nine more sons, filling the hut whose renovated dimensions were as ever-changing as the shape of Mabel's breasts. Meanwhile, Simon raced through Mabel's blood, triumphant in her heart and shining in her black eyes.

Although Leonard's house squatted on the edge of the reservation, it was the center of the tribal wheel, for Simon told Mabel all kinds of things—whose son would bring down the season's first deer, which baby would be born dead.

Day after day, Leonard sweated with a road crew that paved its way across the tallgrass land. On Saturdays he brought Mabel his paycheck, and gave it to her with a soft kiss on her weathering cheek, and a new crick in his back. She gave him nothing in return. And now, she was sixty-one.

Having been born in a year that contained an extra day of winter, Mabel measured all things in leap years. There had been two of them since her sons left home—four to live in brick houses in Lincoln, four to make their fortunes along the coast of the Pacific Ocean. Two had driven away in sandals and rusty pickup trucks.

Now Leonard's back was as twisted as a hemlock branch so that it sounded like stones rubbing when he got in and out of bed. Mabel stewed mutton, mixed it with eucalyptus and rubbed his shoulders, and nightly she thanked Simon in advance for easing her husband's pain.

Before long, the last snow melted and the prairie grass greened and grew tall overnight. It had been a wonder to Mabel that most of the beautiful things seemed to happen overnight.

"Perhaps," she said one morning while she was sorting beans for supper, "perhaps, old man, you're too far along in years to be paving roads."

Leonard looked at her over his glasses that were wired at the ear like a gate to its post. "That's a subject best left untouched," he said. "When I die, I'll fall facedown on the stripes I painted that day."

"If I die first, you will come right behind me, dead from starvation and wearing dirty clothes." Mabel hitched herself up in her chair. "And a good thing *that* will be, because one day later, and you would not be able to get up from your bench for the cobwebs around you."

"Listen to you." Leonard eased himself from the straight-backed chair. He took down a string of sausages for her from the larder. "Is this how you talk with the other women? Would the prairie not be itself without the yakking of Mabel Greely?

Mabel smiled. She sliced the pork with an important hand and dropped it in the beanpot. Went to work on an onion. "Never mind, old man. In those first years, I grew tired of hearing my own voice—and answering myself."

"I know." Leonard came around the table. "I should have found you sooner. Then married you first and made love to you second."

"No—" She looked at him. "I would not have it any other way."

And it was a truth. In all the years—divided, of course, by four—she had not wanted for Leonard's gentleness. Even the lines in his face had rearranged themselves to match her own. But she had never been able to take Leonard's hands to the bank; nor would the grocer receipt the lines in her face as down payment on twenty pounds of ground beef.

"And still," she said, "I have given you nothing."

"Say what?" Leonard said.

"Nothing, old man. Get out of here, get into that busted up Jeep of yours and go line the highways."

"The road is nothing without my lines."

From the doorway she watched him crank the Jeep until it backfired and burst down the road like a frightened prairie dog. Then she went out to the grassland, where the blossoms tickled her face and the wind lifted her long hair that had paled to the color of ashes.

She held her arms to the sky. "Ten thousand thank you's, Simon," she called out, "for the strength of the trees that they can give me their branches without remorse." And she bent to gather a few hickory limbs, a crook of willow, a twist of sycamore.

She was wandering the lowland, gathering sticks and dividing her troubles by four when Raven's Tongue limped across the field. Half Ute and half Algonquin, Raven's face was truly a map of the world's rivers and plains. Mabel's friend spread herself on a rock, with her skirts around her.

"You are praying out loud again, Mabel," she said. "Always collecting your twigs and praying. Why don't you come and stitch with us, or weave? Or laugh with us at the peddlers and hitchhikers who pass through with britches stretched across their rumps and fire in their eyes for the young girls?"

"I'm not interested," said Mabel. "Yesterday my sticks bought potatoes and seed corn for the new planting. And anyway, Simon and I have much on our minds."

"Ah. It is bad manners, Mabel Greely, to call the Great Spirit by this nickname."

Mabel added a length of dead cedar. "Nonsense. I also call him Stars and Moon and Wind in My Hair. And Thoughts in the Night, and Words to Music."

"But why *Simon*?" Raven's Tongue's eyes were traveling the horizon, watching for the next piece of meat for the jaws of gossip.

"Do you not remember the game of Simon Says?"

Raven's Tongue snorted. "And what does Simon say to you today?"

"He says Leonard should have a rocking chair."

Raven turned the silver ring on her finger. "Oh, for Heaven's sake. You are wasting the Great Spirit's time and testing his patience."

But Mabel's eyes were on Raven's ring. "He does not test me," she said, "and I do not test Him. It is only that I have no wood and hammer and nails with which to make a chair."

"Then go and buy one. Take Leonard's Jeep tomorrow, and drive to Collinsville, to Mr. Klee's Pawn Shop. There is a rocking chair in the window there."

"You are not listening," Mabel said. "I also have no dollars with which to buy it."

Raven's Tongue looked off to the grassy distance. "Then come to the village, and watch the silly girls with their painted faces and their leather skirts."

Mabel placed her boot on a twist of elm and snapped it.

Raven said, "If this familiar God gives you whatever you ask for, old woman, why don't you ask him to fix this crooked foot of mine?"

"Because it is not *my* foot. I cannot ask Simon to interfere in your life—if you are not ready."

"I am not ready?" Raven's eyes opened wide. "I am sixty-three next month. How can you say that?"

Mabel took a length of string from her pocket and bound up the sticks. "If you were ready for Simon's help," she said, "you would get it yourself."

Raven rose from her rock and stumped away through the grass. Over her shoulder she shouted, "Then Leonard should ask for his own rocking chair!"

Mabel lifted her face to a new west wind, covered her head with her shawl. "What do you think, Simon?" she said. "Are there enough strong sticks in this field to build my husband a chair? Or to sell for a quarter a bundle in the village instead of a dime?"

The wind sighed softly without so much as an answer.

Mabel did not understand. Simon had delivered her ten healthy sons because she had lifted her gratitude to Him in advance, before they were born. Still, she had never asked for an object—not for a pair of shoes or a pretty comb. Perhaps that was why He did not simply plant a rocking chair in the dooryard of Leonard Greely's hut. She must do this herself.

When darkness crept into its private corners, Mabel sat on her bench by the fire and watched the light rearrange her husband's face. She pulled her shawl tight. She would wait until he went to bed and turned once or twice into deeper sleep. Then she would take her shovel and pot holes in her freshly turned earth.

When Leonard snored softly beneath the quilt, Mabel slipped on his workman's coat and crept out to the garden. By the light of the moon, she dropped cut potatoes into the holes, covered them with her hoe and stepped them off. Each tread of her boots packed down the earth and drove the russets into their secret sprouting places. She sat down on a stump to count the weeks until the first green curls would emerge and the yellow blossoms would wither and die. Even divided by four, it was more days than Leonard should wait, for each day bent him more like the limb of an apple tree. Perhaps in her heart, she was afraid he would snap.

Maybe she could borrow the money from one of her sons. From one of her precious children for whom she had traded bundles of sticks for rice and flour—for apples or a rasher of bacon on days of celebration and a handful of powdered chocolate in times of trouble. They owed her naught.

In all these years, she had kept nothing for herself except the silver box Leonard had given her on the day he had vowed to accompany her through sickness and health. It had been a strange ceremony in a strange place, and yet it had felt right. She had promised to love and honor this man with yellow paint on his hands and squinty lines around his eyes from looking into the distance and seeing only more road to be painted.

Before Leonard woke, Mabel filched the keys from his pants pocket, coaxed the first cough of the morning from the Jeep, and drove to town.

In the courthouse square, Mr. Klee was rolling up the awning over his pawnshop. She parked at the curb and sat collecting thoughts about the ladder-backed rocker in his big window. Then she climbed down from her seat and went in beneath the tinkling bell. She did not touch the long glass cases where Mr. Klee displayed other people's treasures that had flown in the face of a need for money.

Had he given his customers enough dollars to pay the light bill or buy new eyeglasses, or a pint of something to ease the teeth from one of life's bites?

"Mr. Klee," she said, "I am Mabel Arizona Greely."

Klee's belly hung over his belt. He hitched at one or the other and spread a smile like butter across his face.

"Yes, yes," he said.

"I am in need of that chair in your window."

"It is one hundred and thirty dollars," he said.

Mabel pursed her lips. "The sign says ninety-nine."

"The price has just gone up. This very morning, and I haven't had time to change the sign."

"I think," said Mabel, "that if I have the money, you must sell it to me as you advertise it this moment—or I will fetch that policeman who just drove past and who also saw the sign."

"Uh-huh." Mr. Klee's tongue crept out to lick away his smile. "And do you have ninety-nine dollars?"

"I would not have come," Mabel said, "if I did not have something of equal value."

She took the bundle from her pocket and unwrapped the square of wool.

The silver box had mottled and darkened, but Mr. Klee was not a fool. His lips came together like pork sausages. "Oh, this is not worth much," he said.

"I am aware of the price of silver," she lied. "You cannot fool me."

"Ah, an astute woman." Mr. Klee said. He picked up the wedding box and turned it over. Pebbles tumbled out, clattering on the glass counter. "And what are these?"

"Why, they're red beans, Mr. Klee!"

"Really. They have petrified and are useless. And, anyway, I do not buy beans."

Mabel laughed. "You would have petrified, too, if you'd been trapped in a little box for ten leap years."

Lines appeared between Klee's eyes, and he gave another tug to his pants. "A waste of good food," he said. "You should have cooked them."

"I did not cook them," Mabel said slowly, "because I never needed them." The little shop did not seem as dark as before.

"Nor did I need more barley for soup, nor salt, nor shoes for my children. My Leonard gave us all those things. And I…"

Klee had already lost interest.

"And I—" Mabel looked at the sparkling rings beneath the glass, at the gold watches and leather wallets, the silver hair clips. "I gave my Leonard potatoes and onions, and a knitted cap each winter. And a quilt for his bed."

Worry lines came to Klee's face. "Don't forget this husband needs my chair—"

"And I have cooked for him his favorite oxtail soup. I gave him a rub on his shoulders. I have wished him my best good mornings and my quietest good nights. My sticks have built a fire that warms him. And, yes, Mr. Klee, I will give him the chair in the window."

Klee took a length of rope and hurried out to lift the rocker into the Jeep. Mabel watched him and laughed. If this pork chop of a man had gotten the better of the deal, it was all right with her. She laid her hands on the glass counter, and Simon blessed the silver box and all its neighbors.

"Amen," she said.

Mabel drove the Jeep and the gently rocking chair out onto the prairie where Leonard waited for her in the dooryard of the hut.

"It's for you," she said.

His blue eyes were quick and bright and watering in the morning light. She held out the stolen keys, but he reached for her hand.

"What?" she said. "Where are you taking me? I cannot play games, I have bread to bake and important things to do—"

"In a while," Leonard said. "In a while you can gather your sticks, old woman, while I rock in my chair."

And he led her gently through the tallgrass to the last dried stalks of the cornfield.

Game, Set, Match

Zoe Burke

I was a happy writer when my agent told me the good news that Poisoned Pen Press wanted to publish my first mystery, Jump the Gun: An Annabelle Starkey Mystery, *which hit the bookstores in August 2013. The second in the series,* No Gun Intended, *came out in January 2016, and the third,* For Beretta or Worse, *is in the works.*

Barbara Peters, the editor-in-chief, and Annette Rogers, the acquisitions editor, are tough cookies when it comes to commas and content—and I say this with gratitude! Their edits are discerning and almost always inarguable. But I was devilishly proud once, when Barbara told me I had to change a scene where my protagonist wrangles her wrists free from duct tape. Her point was that the tape is too strong; it would be at least near impossible to get out of it. Nope, I told her, I had taped my own wrists as a test, holding them in a particular position that I learned from researching self-defense tactics, and busted out myself.

The scene stayed in.

—Z.B.

• • ● • •

Macy Evans was grateful that she could breathe through her nose. The duct tape covering her mouth blocked part of her nostrils and pushed them up like a pig's snout, she imagined. She smiled, or tried to, when she thought about Lucas making pig faces at her. She wondered if he won the spelling bee yesterday. Or was it the day before? Her memory wasn't what it used to be.

The only light in the basement room came from a single overhead bulb. She could see a window high on the wall across from her, but it was covered over with cardboard, duct-taped. She had read that it originally was called "duck" tape, because it repelled water. Then people started using it to repair vents and air ducts. Now everyone called it "duct tape."

Who in the world cares, Macy?

Bitsy, the name she gave her annoying inner voice, was talking. Bitsy was always reprimanding her and ordering her around. She didn't tell her to do things like kidnap a middle-aged woman and lock her in a basement and cover her mouth with duct tape. No, she merely admonished her for foolish behavior—like when Macy tried to take up jogging again and sprained her ankle *(You're sixty years old, not twenty, for heaven's sake!)*, or when she would have one too many glasses of wine *(You laugh too loud when you've had three, Macy; it's unbecoming.)*, or for feeling ignored by her husband *(He loves you like crazy and works his ass off all day long!)*.

Shut up, Bitsy. Just leave me the hell alone. I'm the one tied up and you get to live in my head all the time. Safe and sound and self-righteous as all get-out.

She was sitting on a wooden, old-fashioned schoolroom chair, with her arms around the back of the chair, wrists taped, her feet and calves taped to its front legs.

She was naked from the waist down, except for her socks.

There was a hole in the seat of the chair with a bucket underneath it. "So you can pee," he'd said. But he put a towel over her lap—for modesty's sake, she figured.

He wore a hat and had a scarf wrapped around his face, so she could only see his eyes. His leather jacket was stylish, a brand Macy figured thirty-somethings would wear. He sounded young, too. He even sounded nice.

Nice! Are you crazy? Nice?

I know, I know. He's not nice. He just sounded nice. He spoke quietly and he called me Mrs. Evans. He didn't smell bad. His hands weren't rough. He didn't hurt me much. He didn't rape me. I don't think he enjoyed cutting my pants and panties off so that I could pee.

That just means he's some sort of sexually repressed psycho. Stop thinking about how nice he was and figure out how you're going to save yourself.

Why don't you figure it out, little Miss Smartypants?

Macy shuddered. Not from the cold. An electric floor heater was keeping the room warm enough. Even her feet were fine, thanks to her socks. The cellar wasn't huge. A utility sink, washer and dryer, a couple of big buckets, and a stack of cartons lined the walls.

Macy speculated why she was taken. She and Henry weren't rich. Sure, they were comfortable, and Henry drove a Lexus, but they were strictly upper-middle class. They saved their money and would be ready to retire in another five years. It didn't make any sense.

Is Henry panicked? He must be. He would have gotten home to find me gone, when normally I would be waiting for him, ready to go play doubles tennis at the club, like we always do on Tuesday evenings. We make a good team, with him a power server and me covering the net. Is he worried?

Of course. He's devoted to you. He's too good for you, you know.

Yes, Bitsy dear, you always remind me of that. Macy swallowed. *Has Henry called Susan and Rob, wondering where she was? Are they concerned? Did they tell Lucas that Gramma Macy was missing? He's only six. I hope not. Would Henry have called the police by now?*

Maybe not yet. It has only been a couple of hours, probably, since that bastard kidnapped you. How stupid can you be? You know you're supposed to stay alert in a dark parking lot.

Macy teared up. The man had grabbed her outside of the building where she worked as a copy editor for a publishing company. It was almost completely dark when she left the building at around five-thirty. The supposedly motion-sensitive parking-lot lights never worked correctly. It didn't help that she forgot where she parked her car and ended up walking from one side of the building to the other, hunting for her keys in her purse the whole time. She was finally getting into her Ford Escort when the man grabbed her from behind and held a wet cloth over her mouth and nose. She passed out and woke up in this basement, when he was cutting her panties off. "So you can pee," he'd said.

He hadn't said anything else to her. His voice had been deep and resonant. Kind. A radio voice.

A sound behind her made her sit up straight. A key in the door.

Someone entered and shut it.

She took a deep breath.

Tip the chair over on him, Macy. Knock him over.

Then what? I'll still be tied up and he'll be mobile. Just shut up.

He's going to kill you.

Shut up.

The man came around in front of her. Now the scarf and hat were gone. He was handsome, in a construction-worker sort of way. Short hair, muscular arms, not very tall. His hands were big with fingers that looked too small.

He squatted in front of her. "I'm going to pull the tape off. It's going to hurt a bit. I'm sorry about that. But you have to promise me you won't scream. If you scream, I'll hit you."

Macy nodded.

Scream as soon as it's off, you hear me? Scream as loud as you can!

He stood up, peeled a corner of the tape away, and gave it a quick yank.

Macy gasped.

Scream!

"Thank you."

Are you kidding me? You just thanked him? How stupid can you be?

"Do you want some water?"

Macy shook her head, staring at him. "Why am I here?"

The man looked at her for a moment, then turned away to get a large bucket. He placed it in front of her, turned it over, and sat on it.

"I have some bad news."

The way he said that, so caring, in that comforting voice, made her throat close up and her breath short, and tears flooded her eyes and ran down her face.

"It's your husband."

He killed Henry! He killed him!

"Oh my God. Is he hurt? Did you hurt him? Did you kill him?"

The man closed his eyes and shook his head. "No, he's fine. He's alive. He's not hurt."

Macy whimpered and tried to control her breathing.

He's lying!

"Please, just tell me."

He leaned toward her. "He doesn't love you. Not nearly enough."

Macy recoiled, terrified. She felt sick. Her tears stopped and she held her breath.

You are going to die, Macy. I told you. Henry loves you more than anyone or anything in the whole world. This guy is very dangerous. He's going to kill you.

Macy managed to speak. "How do you know Henry?" She didn't recognize her own voice. It was lower than usual.

"I don't, really, only met him once. But my wife knows him." He paused. "Do you understand me? My wife knows him. Very well."

Macy stared at him, trying to comprehend what he was saying. "Your wife? Who is your wife?"

"Jocelyn Roberts."

THAT'S what this is all about?

Macy took a deep breath and let it out. "I've heard about your wife, Mr. Roberts, and I apologize for my husband. As it seems you know, he doesn't like her, not one little bit." Macy was finding some relief in talking. She managed a little smile. "He complains about her all the time. He has called her 'meddling' and a 'know-it-all'; he thinks that promotion she got was undeserved and that others in their department were better qualified."

Good Lord, Macy! Don't make him angry!

She bit her lip. "I'm sorry. I'm sure this is upsetting to you and to Jocelyn, but kidnapping me? Isn't that taking your anger just a little bit too far?"

Roberts stared at Macy and sighed. "Mrs. Evans, you seem like a very nice woman. But you are a fool. Jocelyn and Henry have been sleeping together for six months. I heard them talking on the phone a few days ago. They're planning on leaving for London this coming weekend."

WHAT? That's nonsense, Macy. Henry adores you. He hates that Jocelyn woman.

Shut up.

But...!

Shut up.

It hit her like the back of her father's hand across her cheek. She knew in her gut that Mr. Roberts was telling her the truth. There were so many signs she had decided to ignore over the past year—no, really, over their whole marriage—that indicated infidelity. She knew he played around. She just didn't want to know.

You can't believe him, Macy. Don't be stupid. Henry just bought you that diamond necklace. He loves you!

"SHUT UP!"

Roberts sat up with a jerk. Macy hadn't realized she had shouted out loud. "I'm sorry. I didn't mean that. I'm a little freaked out at the moment."

He nodded. "I understand."

"Mr. Roberts..."

"Call me Carey."

Don't call him Carey, for heaven's sake! He's not your new best friend!

Macy coughed. "Carey. What did you do to my husband?"

"I gave him a choice." Roberts stood up and walked away from Macy. He took a pack of cigarettes out of his jacket pocket, flicked one out, stuck it in his mouth, and turned to her. "Want one?"

"Actually, yes."

You don't smoke, Macy! Not anymore!

"Today I smoke."

Roberts gave her a little smile, then walked over and placed a cigarette in her mouth. He lit both. She took a drag and started coughing; the cigarette fell to the floor. He picked it up. "More?"

She nodded. "Could you untape one of my hands?"

He squinted at her, and then unwrapped the tape around her right wrist. She shook it out and took the cigarette from him. "Thanks."

Throw it at him! Stick it in his eye! Get out of there!

"What was the choice?"

Roberts sat back down on the bucket. "I love Jocelyn, Mrs. Evans."

"Call me Macy."

Oh, great! Let's friend each other on Facebook, too!

He smiled. "I love Jocelyn, and we've been married just three years. I would do anything for her. When I found out about her and Henry, well, I knew it was all over for me. But I had to know how serious it was. After I kidnapped you, I went to your house. I was waiting for him when he got home."

Macy took a drag. "I still don't understand."

"I have a gun"—he patted the side of his jacket—"and I pointed it at him. I told him I had you—I gave him your purse as proof—and that the address of this place was written on a piece of paper in my pocket. I showed it to him." He pulled it out and held it in front of her, then put it back.

"I'm only a couple of blocks away?"

He nodded. "A friend's house. I'm feeding the cat while he's on vacation. Anyway, I said that I would give him the gun and he could shoot me and rescue you, or that I would come back here and kill you, and he could live the rest of his life with Jocelyn."

Macy froze. They stared at each other.

He's lying, Macy. He's killed Henry. You have a hand free. You need to get away.

"He didn't shoot you."

Roberts shook his head.

"Oh, God." Macy dropped her cigarette on the floor and dropped her chin to her chest. Heaving sobs rolled up out of her chest. Her free hand rubbed the back of her head, as though she was trying to comfort herself, like her nanny used to do.

"What did Henry say, exactly?" She was choking these words out of her mouth.

"He said, 'Get out of my house and take that gun with you.'" Roberts ground out her cigarette with the heel of his boot.

Get it together, Macy. You're about to be killed. I told you. You can't believe all of this. You have to get out!

She lifted her head and wiped the tears from her cheeks. "You would rather *die* than live without your wife?"

He shrugged. "My gun? It wasn't loaded." He took it out of his pocket, pointed it at the wall to his left, and pulled the trigger. Just a click.

Macy stared at him. "So…?"

"So now I know he really loves my wife. And now you know he doesn't really love you."

Macy's shaking became more severe and her breathing was more like gasping. "Mr. Roberts, this is a bit extreme, don't you think? You've kidnapped me and threatened my husband with a gun, all because your wife is having an affair? And now you're going to kill *me*?"

I told you, Macy. You should have burned him with the cigarette.

Roberts stuck the pistol back in his pocket. "No. I don't think I will." He rubbed out his cigarette on the floor.

Macy felt like she was going to vomit. She was hyperventilating now, and folded as far as she could over her knees. Roberts reached out and put a hand on her shoulder.

Macy jolted back up. "Do not touch me, Mr. Roberts. I do not want your sympathy."

Roberts nodded and pulled back. "I understand."

Macy leaned over her knees again until she got control of her breathing. Then she sat up. "Water, please."

Roberts walked over to the sink and filled a glass jar with water. He brought it back to her, and Macy drank in big gulps.

Throw the jar at him!

Shut up, Bitsy! It wouldn't knock him out. It would only piss him off.

She handed the jar back to Roberts. "Why keep me tied up any longer? You found out what you needed to know. You said you aren't going to kill me. So, you can let me go now. Please, Carey. I'll go home and pack my things and head over to my daughter's house. I'll tell her what happened, and then I'll call the police. That will give you time to get away. You must have a getaway plan, don't you?"

Roberts held his smile fixed on his face. "Something like that."

"So, that's what we'll do."

He kept his gaze on Macy for a moment, and then looked up at the ceiling with a sigh. Then he reached into his jacket pocket, pulled out the gun and a handful of bullets, and started loading his pistol.

I told you! He's going to kill you!

"Please, Mr. Roberts," Macy begged. "Carey, please, you said you wouldn't kill me. I don't want anything but for you to get away, now, for us both to be all right..."

"I'm not going to kill you," he interrupted her. "You're going to kill me."

This guy is crazy, Macy. You'll have to get the gun and then run. Just get out of there.

Macy stared at him. "What? Kill you? Why? I don't want to kill you. I don't think you can make me do that."

He smiled. "Now *you* have a choice. Kill me, or I kill you. Same choice I gave your husband, only this time," he waved the gun, "it's for real."

"Mr. Roberts, I think you have gone mad."

"I think you're right."

Do it, Macy. Agree with him. He'll hand you the gun, then shoot him. It will be self-defense.

Macy frowned. "Jocelyn can't be worth dying over. I certainly don't want to become a murderer because of her."

Roberts stood up in the middle of Macy's protests, took off his jacket and tossed it on top of the washing machine. "You won't be murdering me. You'll be killing me in self-defense."

I told you so! You have no choice! Just do what he says!

Macy closed her eyes. "Mr. Roberts, you must be too much of a coward to shoot yourself, seeing as how you want to die so badly."

He spun around, walked briskly to her, and leaned over her, putting both of his hands on her shoulders, glaring at her with wild eyes. "I am not a coward!" He sat back down on the bucket. "Suicide is a sin."

Macy burst out laughing. "You've got to be kidding me! Kidnapping and shooting people are okay, but suicide isn't? What are you, Catholic?"

He slapped her hard, across the face.

Macy choked on her laugh, and new tears sprang to her eyes. She turned her head away from him, trying to find her breath.

Jesus, Macy, will you just listen to me? Do what he says!

I will not shoot this man.

Just like Henry wouldn't shoot him?

I wouldn't be saving Henry.

Macy and Roberts were quiet for a few moments until Macy finally turned back to face him. "You said you wouldn't hurt me."

"I'm sorry."

Jeesh. Yeah, he's real sorry. He's so sorry that he's going to blow your head off in a minute if you don't wise up.

"I'm not going to kill you, Mr. Roberts, so if you're going to shoot me, you might as well get it over with."

Are you insane? He'll do it!

He nodded at her. "I figured it was a long odds, you killing me. You'd probably hit me in the leg or something anyway, even if you did shoot."

"So, what was your Plan B?"

Roberts stood up and looked down at Macy. She kept smiling and reached for his arm, like she would comfort a colleague at work.

He backed away from her, put the gun to his temple, and fired.

Macy had never seen so much blood. It was quickly spreading out over the floor. It had spattered on the front of the washing machine. She was gasping for breath, staring at dead, bloody Carey Roberts.

The puddle grew and crept toward her. She pushed against the floor with her feet to move the chair back. Then she started screaming. "HEEELLLLP! SOMEONE! HELP ME!"

You are so lucky that he's dead and you're not. Stop screaming like a howler monkey.

Macy used her free hand to unwrap the tape from her feet and legs. She stood up and managed to loosen the remaining tape on her other wrist. She was free. She ran to the door, where she saw her cut-up pants. She grabbed the towel, which had fallen onto the floor. It was bloody, but she wrapped it around her waist anyway. She found her shoes and her coat and she put them on, opened the door, and ran out onto the street. It was freezing cold.

"HELP! SOMEONE! HELP!"

You're just two blocks away, remember? Go home! Find Henry!

Macy started running, stumbling, still yelling. The front door to a house opened and a man stepped outside. "Lady, are you all right?"

"CALL THE POLICE! A MAN SHOT HIMSELF ON THE LAST BLOCK!"

When she got to her front door, breathless, Macy turned the knob. Locked. She pounded on it, yelling. "HENRY! HENRY!" No answer. Then she realized that there were no lights on in the house.

Oh God, Macy. He did shoot Henry. Shot him and turned off the lights.

Shut up! You don't know that.

Macy ran around to the back of the house and found the fake rock where they kept the extra key. She grabbed it and ran back around, unlocked the door, and burst in.

"Henry? Henry, are you here?"

No answer.

He's dead. He's dead.

Bitsy, just shut up.

Macy flipped the hall light-switch on, then quickly checked all of the downstairs rooms, turning on more lights as she went, calling Henry's name. She ran up the stairs and checked the three bedrooms, the bathrooms, the closets. Nothing.

She stopped in the hallway, panting, and eased herself down to the carpeted floor, where she put her face in her hands and wept.

He's dead, Macy.

Will you stop, please? He's not even here. He should be here. He should be either dead, or worrying about me, but either way he should be here. And he's not.

He could be dead somewhere else. You don't know that Carey Roberts came here to kill him.

Macy stood up and dialed 911. She told the operator that she had witnessed a suicide and recited the location as well as her address. Then she went into the master bathroom and took off her blouse and bra and the towel and turned on warm water in the sink. She soaked a washcloth and rubbed her face.

She went into the bedroom and dressed in jeans and a sweater and her slippers. She picked up the phone, dialing Henry's office as she looked at the clock: it was eight o'clock. His voice mail message came on. She hung up.

Well, he would have left work. He would have been home by six, so that you could go play tennis.

She dialed his cell phone. Voice mail.

This isn't good. This isn't good at all, Macy.

So, he's turned it off. That doesn't mean he's dead.

Macy went downstairs, poured herself a brandy, and sat down at her desk in the den. Then she called 411 information. She got a listing for Jocelyn Roberts and dialed. On the third ring, she heard a voice.

"Hello?"

"Jocelyn?"

"Yes, who's calling, please?"

"This is Macy Evans."

A pause. "Why, hello, Mrs. Evans. How are you?"

Macy couldn't help but snort a little. "Not very well, actually. Is my husband there?"

Another pause. "Henry? Why, no, isn't he with you?"

"Did he tell you he would be?"

"I don't know what this is about, Mrs. Evans, but before he left the office, he did mention that he was going to play tennis tonight."

You see, it was all a lie, a big lie. He's not having an affair, and you're crazy for suspecting him.

"Are you having an affair with my husband, Jocelyn?"

Silence. "I'm going to hang up now, Mrs. Evans."

"Your husband is dead." Macy hung up the phone.

Well, that was cruel! To tell her like that, and just hang up!

Yeah, I'm cruel, all right.

She hung up and sipped her brandy. Her hands were still shaking. She picked up a framed picture of Lucas and held it to her chest, and then repositioned it on the desk. She arranged a stack of bills neatly, and put a few errant paper clips back in their box. Order, she needed some order.

She grabbed her business cards case and stared at it like it was a priceless artifact. Her tears stopped suddenly. She clenched her teeth, took a large swig of brandy, and sat up straight.

Soon a car pulled up in the driveway and someone banged on the front door. She opened it up to two uniformed policemen.

• • ● •• •

Two hours after the police had left, Macy was lying on the couch in the den, an afghan pulled up to her chin. She heard the front door open and close.

Henry.

Thank God, Macy. He's all right.

Of course he is.

She sat up and looked toward the doorway, as she heard his footsteps move from room to room. He peered into the den, saw her, and stopped.

"Macy?"

She stared at him. "Surprised to see me?"

He frowned. "Lying on the couch at eleven o'clock on a Tuesday night? Yes, I am." He walked over to her and kissed the top of her head. "What's going on?"

"Where have you been, Henry?"

He sat down next to her and put his arm around her. "Honey, I told you that I was going to play men's doubles tonight, and we agreed to switch our tennis to Thursday this week. I had a late dinner with Peter afterward."

Ah. You just forgot about this, like you forget so many things these days.

Shut up and listen.

"What is it, honey?" He stroked her back.

"Jocelyn Roberts' husband killed himself tonight, in front of me, after he kidnapped me."

Henry's eyes widened. He took his arm away from Macy and stood up. "WHAT! He KILLED himself? My God, darling, are you all right?" He sat back down.

See? He's surprised. He's worried about you.

He's surprised, all right. Surprised that Carey is dead and I'm not.

Macy stared at Henry. "He kidnapped me, then he came to see you, here, didn't he? You were going to be home early, and then we were going to play tennis."

"What? Here? I told you, I went to the club from work. I've only just got home now. What are you talking about?"

He's clearly distressed. He loves you.

Macy stood up and walked to the front of the room, staring out into the darkness. Henry followed her with his eyes.

"Henry, you're lying, and you almost got me killed."

"Now, Macy, I don't know…"

"Shut up, Henry. You were here, probably around six."

How do you know that?

Pay attention, Bitsy-boo.

"Darling, I…"

"My purse. Carey Roberts took it. He gave it to you."

"No, he didn't. I don't have your purse. You're not making much sense, Mace."

You certainly aren't.

Macy laughed. Then she reached into the back pocket of her jeans and brought out her card case. She held it up in the air. "I don't know where you dumped my purse, but this fell out. I found it on the floor by my desk."

That can't be. You must have left it there, by mistake.

"Darling, you're in shock. You've been traumatized. You simply forgot your case this morning, just like you forgot about my plans this evening."

"No, I didn't. I always keep it in my purse. Always."

Are you sure? Because, you know, you forget things all the time, and…

Oh, I'm sure all right. So back off.

Henry moved toward her. "You're just mixed up, in shock. I'll call the doctor, get you a sedative. Then you can…"

Macy held her arm out straight to stop him. She pointed her finger at him, shook it, then brought her hand to her chest, covering her heart. "I know everything, Henry. I know you're going to London with Jocelyn this weekend. I know Carey Roberts came here tonight and told you that he kidnapped me. My guess is that you quickly arranged a men's double match so that you could be away from the house and have a great excuse when I was found dead. Murdered."

Henry didn't move.

Macy walked toward him. "You were supposed to be a saint. That's what my father told me. 'He's a saint, Macy.' Why I listened to anything my father ever said, I'll never know. So, here's what's going to happen. You're going to get the fuck out of this house, right now. I'll file for divorce, and you're going to pay me lots of money. I'm going to quit my job, and I'm going to move to New York City, where Lucas will visit me often."

She inched closer to Henry, until they were nose to nose. "Any questions?"

Henry frowned. "This fantasy of yours would be riveting if it wasn't so sick. I'm calling the doctor."

As Henry turned away from her, Macy grabbed a fire iron and swung it as hard as she could against his head. He fell heavily to the floor, unconscious.

Any word from you, little Miss Preachypants?
That's the first time I've heard you say "fuck."
Anything else?
Not a word.
Excellent.

The doorbell rang and Macy froze. She dropped the fire iron and exited the den, shutting the French doors behind her. She looked through the peephole of the front door and saw one of the policemen who had visited her earlier. She opened the door a crack.

"Mrs. Evans? Everything all right?" Macy whispered "yes" and started to close the door. "Wait just a minute, ma'am." The officer held out his hand. "Here's your purse. We found it at the suicide scene, underneath an upside-down bucket. Forensics said they don't need it. You okay, ma'am? Your husband get home yet?"

Hort-head Homicide

Anne Littlewood

Poisoned Pen Press welcomed me as a new author into the "posse" of their mystery writers and into a smoothly functioning, widely praised press that still had the capacity for personal contact. I learned a great deal from writers who had started before me, as well as from the staff. When I say I'm published with Poisoned Pen Press, people in the know raise their eyebrows in respect. The Press publishes such a variety within the mystery genre—historical, cozy, suspense, and so on. They even manage to encompass my Iris Oakley mystery trilogy that features a pregnant zookeeper, an old and possibly murderous elephant, adulterous penguins, and a stolen tiger corpse.

—A.L.

• • ● • •

In world-weary tone, the small woman proclaimed, "The more I actually learn about mycorrhizae, the more twigs I throw into my compost." Her voice trailed off. "Lots and lots…"

"Oh, yes, soil organisms make *such* a difference in root function," my mother said.

"But it *works,*" wee Arlene insisted. "It actually *works.*" Her brow furrowed and she shook her head slowly. "Have to break the twigs into bits. Tiny, tiny bits. Wonderful stuff, actually. In the end."

In a major lapse of judgment, my mother picked up the bottle and sloshed scotch into her own glass, then, after a thoughtful pause, into her friend's. I put a hand over my wineglass before she topped me up, too.

"Um, Mom. I think she's had enough. You, too. Actually."

They both looked at me as if a boulder had spoken. They shrugged it off as one of life's mysteries and went back to soil fungus.

Only a broken ankle (my mother's) and serious emotional indebtedness (mine) had gotten me to this gardening conference at a budget hotel near Seattle. While I was happy to score good-daughter points by driving and nurse-maiding, there was a price. I hate scotch, and the wine could pass for compost tea. Therefore, sadly, I was sober, and yet, after a day spent observing hundreds of slides of flowers in four (or was it five?) presentations, I was nearly as comatose as my companions. I checked my phone for the twentieth time. Ken, my boyfriend, hadn't texted me back.

The two women offered a fashion contrast. My mother wore a wildflower sweatshirt and blue sweatpants with one ankle slit for her orthopedic boot. Arlene was resplendent in a dark purple suit and a blouse of what might be gold lamé—I wasn't sure. It was shiny and looked expensive. Her tiny pointed shoes were also purple and sported spike heels that implied a second broken ankle at this conference in the near future. My own jeans and sweater were newish and clean.

I'd thought my maternal parent and I would hang out in this alcove and enjoy a drink before dinner. We would talk about something of mutual interest, such as my three-year-old son. That would be her only grandson, currently under the care and protection of my father. But she had hailed this elegantly attired miniature to join us and surprised me, but not Arlene Kim, by hauling a bottle out of her tote bag.

"Oh, Gloria, you remembered!" Arlene had said. My mother informed me that it was her turn to bring the Chivas Regal, an old tradition. The plan was to share it with Arlene and others in the hotel room tonight, lady friends she saw only at these conferences.

That bottle was never going to make it.

Arlene had outed me as irrelevant in seconds and ignored me as they pounded back the shots and talked penstemons and loam, plus a long argument about what, actually, was a "gritty mix." In fairness, Arlene did the pounding back and my mother sipped, but the net effect was the same. The three of us had sat here for what seemed like weeks, but was—actually—no more than an eon or two.

I regard plants as food or hiding places or nesting material. But I'm a bird keeper—yes, at a zoo—and I go to conferences with presentations like Guano Harvesting Impacts on Penguin Nest Success and Managing Iron Intake for Toucans, so I wasn't in a position to criticize.

I texted Ken again.

Arlene nudged my mother, nearly upsetting our drinks table. "It's him," she growled. "Can't escape that rat bastard."

My mother looked over her shoulder. I glimpsed a rotund man entering the banquet hall. "You knew Lionel would be here," she said. "The price to pay."

"Pay?" Arlene said darkly. "I'd like to pay him *back*. And I'm actually not the only one."

Gardeners' grievances? I was bored and ravenous and didn't care. "Mom, it's time for the banquet. They're calling us into the ballroom."

"We've got a few minutes. Play with your phone, dear." She leaned toward Arlene, face flushed. "Poor Harold. Lionel ridiculed him for the way he pronounced a Latin name. *Corydalis*, I think it was. Lionel should be horse-slapped."

"Horse-whipped," I said. "Or bitch-slapped. Either one. Um, dinner…"

"Typical Lionel," Arlene said. "I worked with him at the investment firm, and I never understood how he got away with tricking his coworkers and laughing at them. Poor Bunny. I don't know why she stays with him. He's embarrassed almost all of us, actually. I'm surprised you've escaped."

"Not so." My mother's lips compressed. "Last year he told me his secret of success for hardy orchids was burying rusty nails underneath them to add iron. His plants are gorgeous and he was very offhand about it. I passed that on to Fran and Georgianna—you weren't there—and he laughed in my face and told them what an amateur I am." She took much more than a sip from her glass. "I think he has it in for me because my lewisia hybrids are nicer than his."

"Well, they probably are, and he probably does. Actually, if it weren't for what he sells from that nursery of his, no one here would put up with him."

I grabbed the bottle and stood up. Their eyes and then the rest of them followed it, my mother navigating better than Arlene, despite her crutches and a big black boot with Velcro straps. Arlene looked at me and said, "She's *tall.*"

"Oh, I never noticed!" my mother said. "Must take after her dad."

They chortled as I led them to a table in the ballroom. The room was filled with tables set for eight with flowers as centerpieces. I quick-shoved a chair under Arlene's rump, which was descending off-target. When I had my mother seated and the crutches stowed, I tucked the Chivas Regal into her tote bag. "Wait here. I'll get your dinner." I homed in on the buffet line.

When I returned with two plates, our table had been colonized by a mismatched couple. He was the chubby man I'd glimpsed—red-faced, and loud. She was sweet-faced and quiet. "Iris," my mother said, "this is Lionel and Bunny Cutterall. We'll be at Lionel's garden tomorrow for a tour. Maybe he'll show us his nursery as well." I took my cue from her cordial tone and attempted a pleasant face.

"Iris, you better keep up your tetanus shots. Your mother buries rusty nails in the backyard. Heh heh heh."

He sounded like a motorboat overdue for a tune-up. I abandoned the pleasant face. My mother put a hand on my knee, and I swallowed the impulse to plant my plate in his face.

Arlene poured the wine for us, hitting her targets with most of it. I told her to stay put and fetched her dinner, too.

Another couple holding full plates circled near us like geese looking for a landing spot. The man was reluctant, but the woman hissed something about "the only two seats left together," and they chose to alight at our table. Arlene spread her arms in welcome, and I rescued the glassware. My mother tittered.

"Ah, ha!" crowed Lionel. "The novice and the ignoramus. Welcome!"

"Harold and Fran Johnston," my mother said. "Fran, those pots you donated are wonderful." To me, "Door prizes. Fran throws beautiful pots."

"And Harold throws his money around," said Lionel and guffawed. He winked at Harold, who went stony-faced.

Harold recovered and reached over to shake my hand. "Your mother—Gloria—is one of our favorite people at these things. Fran is the gardener. I'm just technical support—don't know a thing about horticulture. We're neighbors of Lionel and Bunny."

"I'm another noncombatant," I said. "Here to provide transportation." That inspired a round of sympathy for my mother. None, however, for me.

Fran was lean and sour-faced. She ignored us all in favor of her plate, eating as though she'd be punished if she didn't. Arlene said something about lilacs and she and Bunny were soon in the thick of it. Or thicket, I suppose, since the topic was new shrub introductions. I wasn't sure what "introductions" meant in this context, and I didn't care. The wine was decent, and that I did care about. Did I dare to overindulge? As a single mother, I didn't often get the chance.

My phone peeped. Ken had texted

To bed now. Luv u.

What did I expect—a sonnet? When she wasn't looking, I finished off my mother's wine. She didn't need any more and it might get me through this dinner.

I noticed with a start that the chair to my right was now occupied and our table was full-up. "I'm Iris," I said, "Gloria Oakley's daughter."

He put down his fork to shake my hand. "Ralph Hernandez. I work for Lionel." He was a pleasant-faced man about my own age, maybe thirty, in a nice shirt and jeans.

"Well, he calls it 'working,'" said his employer. "I keep reminding him to get to it, or I'll have him shipped back to Mexico."

"We've lived in the States for four generations," Ralph said quietly.

"Oh, yeah? I hear one of your family is still pretty damp, if you get my drift. Heh heh heh. Ralph gets to join us because he's speaking about greenhouse management tomorrow."

Why didn't anyone paste Lionel in the mouth for his jokey sneers? The people I hang with would cure him of the habit in a hummingbird's heartbeat.

I was losing my battle with plant coma and grateful that Ralph was willing to tackle other topics. We talked about his kids and mine until he mentioned he'd once worked for a guy who kept exotic pheasants—Lady Amhersts and Reeves, among others. I hadn't any experience with pheasants, aside from peacocks, and mined him for all I could learn, which was lots. Fired up, I decided to talk the zoo's curator into acquiring a few species for the aviary now under construction. After ten hours of pistils and stamens, I was ready to kiss Ralph.

We were engrossed in treatments for feather lice when Lionel suddenly burst out with more of his heh heh hehing. "Got you going! You believe anything I say about Chinese corydalises. Arlene, you guys are just too easy."

Arlene shot him a blood-freezing look. Ralph chewed on his lower lip. "Great boss," I muttered. He looked at me sidelong and said nothing. What a docile bunch.

"You, too, Gloria. Right? You bought it, I know you did! Heh heh heh. You gals are something else."

My mother forced a little smile.

Enough.

I said—sweetly—"The next time you make fun of my mother, you'll wish you hadn't. Just to be clear, you obnoxious blister, I am absolutely not kidding."

Arlene said, "Actually…" and stopped. No one else said anything, although my mother's nails dug into my arm.

I showed Lionel my teeth in what could be mistaken for a smile. "And you need to get your laugh fixed. It's running rough."

The Cutteralls departed in a flurry, or possibly a huff, and I got up to get us dessert.

• • ● • •

Morning found my mother and me and six of the conference participants on a sidewalk outside a ranch house set on maybe an acre: the Cutterall kingdom. The other attendees were on wildflower hikes and walking tours, not options for my mother. We'd been deposited by a tour bus that waited to return us to the hotel. My mother wasn't speaking to me, which was fine since I had a nasty headache. I tried to spot a goldfinch that had flitted into the garden.

Fran and Harold Johnston showed up on foot. Her dour face cracked into a grin when she spotted me. "Here's the Lionel tamer! Maybe we'll get lucky and you'll take him on again."

"Don't simper," my mother muttered in my ear.

The Cutteralls' house was set toward the front of the property, with a Japanese garden—rocks and conifers—leading to the front door. The back was terraformed into humps of raised beds amid gravel paths and islands of lawn, all swooping down toward a creek. Beyond the creek stood two sizeable greenhouses. Behind them, the land rose in a steep hill. Half the hill was denuded, the other half was covered in blackberry vines. To the right—south—a cul-de-sac led to three more houses. Harold and Fran had come from that direction.

My mother crutched toward the front door, narrowly avoiding a pile of smooshed dog poop, and rang the bell. No response. She hitched herself around to face the group. "Did they forget we were coming? Maybe Lionel's waiting in back." She swung along a gravel path into the backyard and we trailed after. No Lionel, no Bunny, no Ralph. We wandered about looking at plants. My mother inspected the place as if she'd lost a pill bug.

Then wailing vehicles began arriving. I hustled back to the front and watched police cars pull up. And an ambulance, then a TV van. My son would have been thrilled. Uniformed personages strode into the house. Gradually the hort-heads caught on and gathered alongside me, staring. A police officer noticed and confronted us. "What are you people doing here?" she asked.

My mother hobbled a step forward. "We're here for a garden tour. What's happening? Is Lionel hurt? Or Bunny? We're friends." She hesitated. "Some of us."

"I'll need your names and contact information, and then you'll have to leave."

"Is this a crime scene?" I asked.

• • ● • •

On the return bus ride, the group, now including the Johnstons, speculated about the Cutteralls with both sincere concern and avid curiosity. The bus smelled nasty and my head still hurt.

We were back at the hotel early since the garden tour hadn't happened. My mother and I sat on the queen bed, and I flicked through TV stations looking for news. The commentators on three channels agreed that Lionel Cutterell had been murdered, stabbed with a gardening implement. "A dibble," my mother said, upon seeing a drawing of the weapon. It was a wicked-looking thing—a wood handle on a pointed metal tip. Designed to poke holes in the dirt to plant small bulbs, per my mother. Robbery was the motive, per the commentator, since some three thousand dollars in cash was missing. "This is awful," my mother said. "It's going to ruin the rest of the conference."

During lunch, Harold announced what everyone already knew. A moment of silence, please, for a talented gardener. Sympathy cards for Bunny were in the lobby for us to sign. His acerbic wit would be missed.

No one contradicted him.

We sat with mini-fashionista Arlene for lunch. She shared that she had nearly fallen to her death on the wildflower hike.

I looked at her cute shoes with slick soles and was unsurprised. When the conversation turned to hybrid something-folia, I checked for news updates on my phone. "Hey, Ralph Hernandez has been arrested for Lionel's murder."

My mother frowned. "That's absurd."

Well, I'd liked him, too, but that didn't make him innocent.

I read, "Apparently Hernandez broke into the Cutterall home at about eight this morning and ransacked Lionel Cutterall's office for cash. Cutterall is believed to have interrupted him. When Mrs. Cutterall returned home from the gym, the attacker ran out the back door and through the extensive gardens. The police found Hernandez' pickup truck at his house with the murder weapon in the bed."

"Ran through the garden? And left the murder weapon in his truck?" my mother said. "Ralph's not that dumb."

"Actually, people do stupid things when they're excited," Arlene said. "Stabbing your boss to death might leave you unsettled."

My mother was uncharacteristically silent during the rest of lunch.

The first afternoon session was about plants that attract birds and butterflies. At last, a presentation I cared about. I was mentally redesigning my yard for swallowtails and hummingbirds, but my mother sat frowning and oblivious. At the break, she sent me to fetch Arlene.

"Arlene," she said, "you're friends with Bunny Cutterall. We need to support her. I want to go out to the house with you. Now."

"Why? What's up?" I asked.

She scowled at me. "A threat to a valued compatriot. Injustice perpetrated by the uninformed."

Arlene said the next session was canceled, since it was supposed to be Ralph talking about greenhouses. Nonetheless, she didn't want to go without Fran and Harold. Fran came quietly, while Harold fretted that he was needed to help the next presenter. My mother urged, his wife commanded, and he complied. The five of us crammed into my car and headed back to the Cutterall house.

The new widow's sister let us in and disappeared to make tea. We sat stiffly on facing sofas with Bunny in an armchair. Botanical drawings cluttered the walls and the carpet was patterned in vines. The room smelled of cleaning products, perfumed ones. Claustrophobia nibbled around my consciousness.

To no one's surprise, Bunny looked shaken and pale. Arlene said, "We're so sorry, dear. Actually we're all pretty upset. Horrible thing. What can we do to help?"

"Nothing, nothing. We had a good marriage. Really we did. I don't know what I'll do without him. The gardens…the nursery…without Ralph…I can't think about it now."

The sister served tea as we murmured sympathetically, then she disappeared to the rear of the house. The group fell silent as we sipped from flowered china cups.

With the exception of my mother. "Bunny, did you see who killed Lionel? Do the police have any real reason to think it was Ralph?"

"Now, Gloria," Harold said, "we shouldn't interfere in a police matter, and this is not fair to Bunny."

My mother set down her teacup. "Listen," she snapped, "it's no secret that Lionel didn't grow those gorgeous plants he sold us. Ralph did. If he's in prison, this entire garden and nursery is likely to perish." An aside—"Sorry, Bunny. Don't mean to be disrespectful." She turned back to Harold and Arlene and Fran. "Ralph is a decent family man who tolerated Lionel for three years, which indicates he is a saint. *And* we know more about this situation than the police ever will. We owe it to Ralph and, ah, to Lionel's memory, to sort this out and not send the wrong man to prison."

Harold subsided and the others seemed willing to try. It wasn't clear which argument carried more weight—save Ralph so the cool plants kept coming, or save Ralph because he might not have done it.

"Bunny?" asked my mother. "What can you tell us?"

Bunny, her thoughts elsewhere, started a little and said, hesitantly, "About Ralph…his grandmother lives with his family. She's illegal. Lionel found out by accident—Ralph's son came over and I gave him cookies. The conversation came around to her and the boy said something about it. You know Lionel liked to tease. He wouldn't have done anything, but maybe Ralph thought he'd get her deported." Her eyes filled. "I can't believe Lionel died because he liked to joke with people."

I could easily believe it.

The friends roosting on the sofas nodded in resignation. Ralph had a fine motive. More sympathetic murmuring.

Except, again, for my mother. "Why was all that money in the house? Who knew about it?"

Bunny explained that Lionel was hiring day-laborers to clear out the blackberries on the slope in back. He paid them in cash. He was careless with it—the money just sat out on his desk. "He liked seeing it. Silly, of course…I have no idea who might have seen it. Certainly Ralph did."

My mother sat quietly for a moment. "Nonetheless, I don't think Ralph did it."

She'd lost her audience. "Actually…" Arlene began, "the police are better…"

My mother flapped a hand at her. "Somebody—we assume the intruder—ran across the garden, all right, but it wasn't Ralph. Whoever it was stepped on that raised bed near the daphnes. I saw the tracks this morning. That person crushed a clump of double Trillium grandiflorum, the pink form, just smashed it to bits. Ralph wouldn't do that. Not in a million years. Irreplaceable."

Arlene and Bunny each raised a hand to their mouth, identical gestures. Harold looked concerned. Fran, of course, looked dour.

Fran said, "Actually, I noticed it this morning. I forgot in all the excitement. Terrible. It may survive, it may not."

My mother nodded. "It's light outside at seven a.m. these days. That clump was big and beautiful and easy to see. Whoever killed Lionel wasn't a gardener."

"But the murder weapon was in Ralph's truck!" Harold protested.

Heads cocked as they pondered this.

"Did Ralph come by before the tour this morning?" I asked.

Bunny explained he would drop by to check the greenhouses.

I considered the layout of the area. "Does he park on the street to the south?"

"Yes, that's closest to the greenhouses."

My mother's eyes narrowed. "The murderer fled that way and dropped the weapon into the truck bed as he passed."

"Or she," I said, but no one heard me.

Fran said, "Ralph would never notice the dibble. The bed of his truck is a mess."

My mother raised her eyebrows and she added, "He parks across the street from our house. I see that truck every day."

"So," my mother concluded, "if Ralph didn't kill Lionel, who did? Someone who broke in before Bunny got back from the gym at eight a.m."

"Water aerobics," said Bunny. "He didn't break in. The door was unlocked. He just walked in. Anyone could have done it…" Her voice trailed off and her eyes filled.

My mother's gaze swept the group. "I'm not buying the random stranger. Robbery could be the motive, but why this morning—when Lionel was home? Who besides Ralph had reason to murder Lionel?"

Fran seemed dourly thoughtful. Arlene looked peevish. Bunny drifted off.

Harold fidgeted. He crossed his legs and uncrossed them. "I suppose Arlene did. Does. Might have."

We stared.

Arlene sat up straighter. "I beg your pardon?"

Harold said, "Um, that situation. You worked at the same investment company. You said, at the Christmas party…"

Arlene's delicate features formed a snarl. "You mean he actually got me fired. Told a stupid joke about me and a new manager grabbed onto it, and I actually ended up 'released to the community.' Yes, I *should* have killed him for that."

Bunny waved her hands. "But Lionel said it wasn't his fault. He said it had to do with commission calculations and that—"

Arlene cut her off. "No need to go into all that."

I said, "You were on the wildflower hike this morning."

"The bus didn't leave until nine. I could have run over here and stabbed him with his fancy dibble and actually made it back in time."

"You're kind of...small..." I said, "to be stabbing a grown man."

Arlene snorted. "Lionel was a lard bucket. Sorry, Bunny. I do Pilates and kickboxing three times a week. I could tie him into knots."

"Um, are you confessing?" my mother asked.

"Oh, hell no. I wouldn't step on that trillium, and I wouldn't implicate Ralph. If I'd killed Lionel, I'd actually be bragging about it. Sorry, Bunny. I didn't really mean that."

Clearly, she did.

"Well, then," said my mother, "where does this leave us? Assuming you didn't kill him." She smiled uncertainly at Arlene.

The room fell silent, investigative energy oozing away. My mother's face shifted toward defeat.

We'd tried the horticultural approach. Maybe a zoological slant would shed some light. "Bunny," I said, "this room smells like some kind of cleaner. Why would you or your sister be cleaning in the living room today? It's not where the...incident...happened."

Bunny looked confused, but she frowned and focused. "Oh. Somebody tracked something on the carpet. My sister—Jeannie—she cleaned it up. She's taking care of everything."

"Dog poop?" I asked.

Bunny nodded. "I thought it must be from Lionel's shoes. But he would have noticed. He is—was—always on the lookout for neighbors who don't clean up after their dogs."

I plowed on. "When we got here for the tour this morning, a pile of dog poop by the front entrance had been stepped in." Little-known fact: zookeepers notice poop.

"Maybe the robber," Arlene said. "The murderer."

I nodded. "When the cops sent us away, we all took the bus back to the hotel. The bus smelled like dog poop."

They looked at me in baffled silence. "And?" Arlene said. Patiently.

"It didn't smell like that on the way here. The return trip included two people who weren't on the trip out. Harold and Fran walked from their house and joined us here for the tour." I let that sink in. "Harold's got dog poop on his shoe. You can still smell it." I couldn't smell anything but pine oil, but it was him or his wife, and he was the non-gardener.

Harold glanced at his sole. "Must have stepped in it when we were here for the tour. Or else just now."

I shook my head. "I watched this morning to be sure no one did. You never went near it. And it's gone now—someone cleaned it up before we came back. You came here before the tour, you stepped in it, came into the house, and tracked it on the carpet. What else did you do while you were here? Before you ran out the back and stomped on the trilliums?"

The others were riveted, teacups suspended.

Harold stood up. "What are you implying? I had nothing to do with this. No reason to kill him. At all." His face had a sweaty sheen.

"Sit down." Fran spoke in the coldest voice I'd heard in some time.

Harold hesitated and then sat.

Fran's eyes pinned him like a butterfly. "At dinner last night, Lionel said something about you about throwing money away. I checked our portfolio before we came here. You've lost even more of our savings. Did he give you another hot tip? Did you fall for it, like all the other hot tips?"

Harold went slightly green. "No, no, that's not what happened. I'll explain the statements to you tonight. You're not reading them right."

Fran went on. "You remember what I said, don't you? That I'm not living with a gambling addict?" She spared us a glance. "Not one who refuses to get help."

Harold shook his head in little jerks. "This is not the time or place. That's *private*. And it's *not* gambling."

"We agreed, Harold—didn't we agree?—that you would leave the finances to me. And you didn't. I'm not going to work like a dog so you can lie around the house and lose money in day-trading. We're done."

"Fran, *stop it*. We'll talk about this later."

Harold stood up, red-faced and frantic, breathing fast. I couldn't tell whether he was going to punch his wife or clutch his chest and fall to the floor.

In a voice that had swapped anger for dread, Fran asked, "Where *were* you this morning? When I woke up, you were gone."

"I couldn't sleep. I took a walk. Why are you asking me? This is crazy."

After a stop-frame moment, my mother leaned toward him and spoke softly, sympathetically. "It wasn't your fault, was it? He swore it was good information, then he laughed at you, didn't he? He tricked you into losing money, and he brought it up at dinner in front of us to humiliate you."

Harold looked at her with eyes showing white like a frightened horse.

"You came here to tell him to give your money back. He only mocked you. The money was just sitting there. So you took it. You did what you had to do."

"That liar owed it to me," Harold said savagely, and clapped a hand to his mouth.

• • ● • •

"Poor Bunny," my mother said. She was in the passenger seat of my Honda, on our way home. A small pot with tiny red blooms sat in her lap, a gift from Ralph.

"Do you really think she'll miss Lionel?" I asked as we pulled onto the freeway.

"Oh, yes. They were close. He never picked on her. I think she was the only person he trusted. He was always trying to be one up on the rest of us. Insecure."

Maybe.

"And will Fran miss Harold?"

She snorted. "That one's been on the rocks for years. I'm amazed they made it this far. I'm also amazed that Harold had the guts to jump Lionel. He's always struck me as a wimp. Fran ran the show."

"She'll be running it alone now." A half mile later I said, "They make you and Dad look pretty good."

She smiled at that. "You weren't too bored by the conference?"

I paused to finish passing a semi. "Not after Harold bolted. That got my attention."

"You were so fast! Chasing Robby keeps you in shape. And your job, I suppose." She shifted the seat back a notch and adjusted her boot. "We make a good team, don't we? We could go into business as Flora and Fauna Investigations."

"Cute. But one detail has me puzzled. That dibble-thing that Harold stabbed Lionel with. What was it doing in his office?"

Her eyebrows went up. "Well, Lionel *was* a gardener. Why wouldn't it be in his office?"

Silly me. This was the woman I'd seen use a trowel as a bookmark. A muddy trowel, at that.

The Cry of the Loon

Janet Hubbard

My agent, Kimberly Cameron, sent my manuscript BORDEAUX:
The Bitter Finish *to Barbara Peters at Poisoned Pen Press, who
immediately said "yes!" to a mystery series set in the wine districts
of France. I was thrilled, of course. Then Barbara said, "Did I
understand Kimberly to say that you have a draft of a novel set in
Champagne?" It turned out that PPP wanted to publish* CHAM-
PAGNE: The Farewell *first. I agreed, but realized too late that
switching titles would require two massive rewrites. Panic—and
Barbara—got me through.*

—J.H.

• • ● • •

Dusk was approaching when the tremolo of a loon brought a
pause to the list-making my friends Sandra and Louise had been
at for over two hours. Sandra was in the process of renovating
the fifties-style camp she had bought at the south end of a pond
in Vermont, around which converged twenty residences, most of
them summer homes. At the other end was a cozy bar that offered
live music sometimes on weekends. Sandra's favorite haunt. She
could paddleboard there and drink as much as she wanted, then
climb on the board to return to camp. She had been warned by
neighbors against this practice but laughed them off.

"Writer John McPhee called that sound the laugh of the
deeply insane," Sandra said. "That must be where the expression
loony comes from."

"I was just reading up on their different cries," I said. "That one curdles the blood, but another sounds like a wolf. The tremolo signals alarm. The male is defending his territory."

"I've been recording them," Sandra said. "The babies should come soon, by the way. It's late May, so maybe mid-June."

Louise said, "Their cries make me sad. They're haunting." She stood and looked out over the pond that one day in the not-too-distant future we knew would no longer be. Sandra had been told that in one hundred years it would not exist.

She had complained. "So what about my grandkids? They end up with a dried-up pond?"

We were on the upstairs screened-in porch that housed a bed where Louise and I would sleep tonight. Sandra would stay in her room with her three dogs, who were all stretched out on the floor nearby.

Sandra was already on her third glass of wine by my count, but then she had probably been sipping since noon. She hid her addiction better than anyone I knew. The only sign that she had crossed over into drunkenness was when she brought up uncomfortable topics. I was often a victim of these; for example, she liked to talk about how I had persevered with my writing career after numerous rejections. By the time she was done, though, her praise sounded more like ridicule.

Louise and I agreed on the thirty-mile ride over that we would exercise more self-discipline this time, and not get inebriated—which is what usually happened when we had our "girls' overnight."

Sandra had lost interest in the list, and began regaling us with a litany of woes: she was turning sixty-five and being booted out of her vet practice, her mother was in a nursing home, her sister had a rare form of Parkinson's that caused her to see double, and to top it all, her sister's son had had the nerve to ask Sandra for permission to marry on her property in town and what could she say but yes, considering her sister's condition. "Anything to take stress off my sister," she said. She lowered her voice when she heard a car turn into the neighbor's driveway. "Bridezilla hates everyone on our side of the family. That's what we're dealing with. A bride who hates her groom's entire family. And on top of that she just charged thirty-thousand dollars to my brother-in-law's credit card. So much for the simple country wedding."

I picked up my glass of chardonnay and sipped. "I'd like to go down and watch the loons while we still have a little light," I said. Sandra had created a viewing station next to the hot tub, where you could squat and peer through binoculars attached to a tripod. Ignoring me, Sandra said, "If I retire, then what? As it is now I exercise two hours a day, and drink the rest. What would I do in retirement? Exercise four hours a day and drink the rest?"

I studied her. Short, athletic build. Not exactly stocky, but certainly not lean. Small eyes like those of a groundhog that didn't balance out her full mouth with slightly buck teeth, yet somehow the overall effect was charming. She pretended not to give a shit, and she swore a lot, which made her seem like one of her aggressive dogs. Louise and I thought it funny that a vet had no control over her pets.

"Do you know how lucky you are to be able to retire?" Louise asked her. "I'll be working the rest of my life."

The desultory conversation bored me. Regret had overtaken me. Another evening that would remain fuzzy in my mind, as I now knew I would drink more than usual, and be tired for two days after. None of us were young enough anymore to sustain a big drinking night. I also realized that I both liked and loathed Sandra.

A sea-change had occurred in our tentative friendship since my Swiss pilot lover, Antonio, and I had driven out to see her eight or nine months ago. He was a real estate junkie, and this particular little camp in the middle of nowhere would interest him. Sandra was in shorts, her hair pulled back in a ponytail. Face alive with curiosity that soon turned to avid flirting. Antonio was amused, and accepted a second beer. I had been laughing along with them, barely touching my wine as I was the desig-nated driver, when she lured him out to a kayak to see the house from afar. She was now hanging onto his every word, adoring his accent, and saying so. He told her how he would transform the little cabin. "Build a log house," he had said.

I stood on the dock, watching them skim across the water in kayaks, looking back at the camp and me, except I suddenly felt invisible. A deep anger welled in me. They returned and popped open two more cans of beer. Antonio glanced at me, and I saw a hint of shame that disappeared before I could name it.

"We have to go soon," I had said.

Sandra's response was to heat up the gas grill and throw a few sausages on it. She looked at me for the first time in an hour, vaguely surprised to see me. "Oh, Rachel, stay for dinner, then go," she said. "I want to get Antonio's advice about the upstairs."

We stayed. She had transformed into a sparkly eyed, rapt listener. I had never imagined her listening to anyone. Antonio had grabbed her interest, and it was clear: she wanted him. I could gauge her level of inebriation when she told him her college SAT scores. A poor girl from Pennsylvania who had managed to become a vet, dyslexia and all. The only way I could dispel the gloom that had overtaken me was to reassure myself that we would never have contact with her again. I would make sure of that.

As we were about to leave, he took out his phone and said, "You two girls stand there and let me get a photo." I hesitated, and then moved closer to her, towering over her, as he said, "smile." He was having the time of his life. Another concern ripened in that moment. I had seen the gallery of photos of women he had "dated" over the years, some of them from the distant past. Was I about to be relegated to the gallery?

I complained a few days later to Louise who said I was being silly. "She was drunk, I'm sure," she said. "And doesn't remember it."

"That's Sandra's excuse for everything," I said.

When I emerged from my reverie, Sandra was looking at me. She said casually, "I had started to think that Antonio was my real friend. At least he comes to see me."

I tried not to let on how her shocking statement had catapulted me into a state of confusion. I stood mute. Was she taunting me? Was she telling the truth?

"I don't know what you're talking about."

"He stopped over a month ago. Out of the blue." She frowned. "I thought it was a little rude, to tell you the truth. To show up unexpected."

Louise interjected quickly, "I'm sure he didn't mean to intrude." I hated the way Louise instantly conjured up excuses for peoples' behaviors that had nothing to do with reality.

"He said he wanted to see the progress on the renovation," Sandra filled her glass with wine, and offered the bottle of red to Louise, who filled hers. "He landed his Piper at the local airport and drove out."

That was a hell of a drive, I thought.

I looked at her now as I would a rival. Hair in dangly pony-tail, visor, no makeup. A pint-sized boxer. But it wasn't about looks, really. It was what she had promised him that night with her gaze, her raucous laughter, her swearing, everything to lure a Swiss-German repressed man into her net.

She turned back to Louise, who said that we should make dinner. I heard Sandra say, "Well, I had to tell her, right? He wasn't going to."

Louise lowered her voice, "I never trusted him. I know it's a cliché, but he's a pilot."

You are the cliché, Louise! I wanted to shout. I wasn't ready yet to let Antonio go. I wasn't even close to letting Sandra snatch him from me.

I stood on the porch and gazed across the pond, exquisitely still as the last light of day was fading into shadow. I stepped out onto the porch and sat on the chair to watch the loons. They were monogamous, I had read somewhere, for at least five years. Exactly the length of time Antonio and I had been seeing each other behind his Swiss girlfriend's back.

I heard swearing inside and went back in. "Dinner's gone," Sandra said. "The dogs managed to eat all the burger. I guess we're meant to go to Brambles."

The bar.

Louise cast a worried look in my direction, and I looked away. I had never felt so trapped. So unsure. I had never in sixty-six years felt my fate so callously unfolding. Sandra marched out and climbed onto her paddleboard against Louise's admonitions. "Let her go," I said. "It's a half mile at most, and we can reach her from the path if we need to."

Sandra arrived at the same time we did, and pulled her paddleboard up onto the bank and dismounted. It was routine for her. We waited, and a twinge of admiration seeped through me. She was a piece of work, as her friends called her.

The bar was packed. The wine was cheap and served in large glasses. The hamburgers were awful. After an hour Louise said she had a headache from too much wine and would walk the half mile home. I offered to go with her, but she said, no, watch after Sandra.

I went to the door with Louise, and she said, "I'm sorry about Antonio. We'll talk tomorrow."

"Hey," I said, in a faux cheerful voice, "I got five years out of him."

"I don't think that's how you feel," she said. "I'm sure nothing happened between them. She told me she didn't feel the lust vibe."

"You *knew*?"

"She mentioned it."

"How are you always so goddamned sure, Louise? You have no idea what they did."

"She told me."

When I didn't respond, she said, "Just climb in bed when you get back. I'm taking a pill for this headache and will be out until morning. I'll leave the light on."

I nodded and went back in.

Sandra raised a glass. "So, what *is* going on with you and Antonio?"

I realized that I was drunk, too. The only way to nip this conversation in the bud was to state a fact. "I love him."

Her head jerked around. "Really? I thought he was a fling."

"Whatever."

The little eyes beaded in on me. "He's defective, you know."

"I need to leave," I said. "I don't feel well. Let's leave the paddleboard and walk the path."

She was as defiant as a teenager. "No. I paddleboard every night."

"We've had too much to drink."

We walked outside. The air was cool, and I wished I had brought a sweater. "What day exactly did Antonio show up?" I asked.

"Oh, get over yourself," she said impatiently.

"See you at the house," I said, stalking off.

I walked, flashlight in hand. A sliver of moonlight fell across the narrow path. I passed a couple of boarded-up houses. The owners would move out over the next two weeks, Sandra had said.

I heard a splash, then Sandra yelled "shit!" I stopped and stumbled to the front yard of the boarded-up house and saw Sandra's head bobbing around.

"Rachel!" she called.

I stood there, unsure.

"Rachel! Goddamn it, my board disappeared. It's floating your way. Hurry up!"

I remained silent.

A gasping sound. She was thrashing around. Desperate. As desperate as I felt when she told me Antonio had come to visit. Everything was still for three beats. Then a soft plea came from the center of the pond. "Rachel? Are you there?"

"Oh, fuck…"

A wail that sounded like a wolf's howl rose and fell. Sandra would be pleased that the loon had cried out at the moment of her demise. I switched on my flashlight and continued walking toward the house.

Judge Jillian

David Moss

After I completed my first novel, This Isn't A Game, I Googled mystery publishers. Poisoned Pen Press showed up on the first page of search results. One site hyped it as a "fan favorite, run by and for mystery fans." That sounded good. But I couldn't make up my mind. Should I submit first to Poisoned Pen Press, or to another place I'll call Publisher B?

I was drinking a glass of Oban at the time, which I'd bought after sampling a few other scotches. That's what I'd do. I'd sample the mysteries. I picked one at random from Poisoned Pen Press' list of authors. Actually, it wasn't quite random. I picked Reavis Z. Wortham for the irrational reason that he had a handlebar mustache and cowboy hat. A few scenes into one of his books, I knew it was better than any mystery I'd read in the past year. Finishing the book cemented that opinion. If Poisoned Pen Press published works of that quality, that's where I wanted to submit my novel. So I did.
—D.M.

• • • • •

A botched poodle-grooming leads to fisticuffs at the kennel club. A couple sues a cake-maker for putting laxative in their wedding cake. A man claims his upstairs neighbor installed a louder vacuum motor to wake him.

Judge Howard got all the best cases.

How was Judge Jillian supposed to compete when her producer came up with snoozers like a landlord tries to add clauses to a pre-existing lease? A woman claims her ex owes her money she lent to repair his van. Former housemates accuse each other of breaking the washer and dryer.

No wonder Judge Howard had leapfrogged Judge Jillian in court show ratings. Even Judge Sheila and Judge Tommy were nipping at her heels.

Finally Judge Jillian had a case to regain her rightful place atop the ratings. She nodded at her bailiff, Chuck, who'd spent thirty years in Court Services, unlike the empty-headed actor who played a bailiff on Judge Howard's show and didn't know the difference between a legal robe and a bathrobe.

Chuck sucked in his belly like he always did when the camera was about to turn his way. "Your Honor, this is case number 422, Gobalt versus Clay."

When the show aired, the voiceover would elaborate: "Ben Gobalt is suing his neighbor, Morton Clay, for vandalizing his lawn ornaments. He's seeking twenty-five-hundred dollars in damages."

Judge Jillian looked over the bridge of her glasses at the two men behind their stands, holding the stapled papers the producer gave disputants as props to make it look like they came prepared.

Chuck placed a blown-up photo on the easel. Two kissing Dutch children statuettes had cigarettes glued to their mouths.

Judge Jillian got things started. "Mr. Clay, did you glue cigarettes in the mouths of Mr. Gobalt's Dutch children?"

Morton Clay slouched like the entire world was created for his amusement. He half-turned to the studio audience. "Not me. But I salute the person who did."

Ben Gobalt slammed his hand on the stand. "You lie. He lies, Your Honor."

Ben was pale and skinny, with a horseshoe of red hair. He'd probably been picked on from the day he emerged from the womb.

Chuck replaced the kissing Dutch children photo with one of lawn gnomes playing cards around a mushroom table.

Ben Gobalt's voice screeched like fingers on a chalkboard. "See for yourself, Your Honor. He painted their beards purple."

Judge Jillian gave the laughing studio audience the first of what she knew would be many reminders this was a court of law, not the Comedy Castle. Judge Howard would have been whooping it up along with them. He presided over a freak show and all the other judges kowtowed to him. Judge Jillian heard through the grapevine that Judge Dana and Judge Arnie told people she needed to lighten up, "have some fun out there, like Judge Howard."

"It wasn't me," Morton Clay said.

Ben Gobalt struggled to speak. "All the time and money I put into my garden, this snake, he dares…"

Chuck took a step closer, just in case. This wasn't Jerry Springer. Judge Jillian put her foot down when her producer floated the idea of encouraging physical confrontations. Still, they'd had tussles during tapings a few times, and Chuck had to break up post-show altercations outside the studio at least once a month.

"You take a lot of pride in your garden, don't you, Mr. Gobalt?"

"Nothing's there by accident. I plan it all out beforehand."

Judge Tina would feign empathy at this point, praising his design skill, sympathizing with the destruction of his treasured ornaments. Judge Jillian had no time for bogus playacting. She wanted the facts.

"Please correct me if I'm wrong, Mr. Clay, but aren't you known in your neighborhood for ridiculing Mr. Gobalt's lawn ornaments?"

"You're not wrong, Your Honor. His ornaments are hideous."

"Is it true that last Thanksgiving you placed a fully cooked turkey on King Neptune's prongs?"

The studio audience howled. A baritone voice called out, "My name is Neptune. I'll be your server tonight."

Judge Jillian broke into a quick but unmistakable smile. That was funny and she wasn't humorless. She just refused to laugh indiscriminately for the sole reason of creating a festive atmosphere. Not that Judge Dana and Judge Arnie could comprehend the distinction, which was no doubt why they languished at the bottom of the ratings.

Morton Clay gave the studio audience an arched eyebrow shrug. "Guilty as charged."

"And did you place a sign next to a retriever with a basket planter that said, 'My fellow ornaments and I apologize for driving your property values down?'"

"I've never denied it," Morton Clay said.

"Yet you claim you didn't vandalize the ornaments this time?"

"I'm not the only one on the street who hates those things."

Ben Gobalt jabbed his finger in the air at Morton Clay. "Liar. He did it. Just like he put the turkey on Neptune."

"He did it last time, so you assume he did it this time?"

"I know he did it. But I wanted another witness. So I called the Astro Man."

"The Astro Man?"

They'd reviewed the list of witnesses beforehand so Judge Jillian knew about the Astro Man. She never would have feigned surprise like this back in the days when she presided over the Santa Monica Municipal Court. But the producer thought the name "Astro Man" added entertainment value, and Judge Jillian liked to throw the producer a bone every now and then.

"That's what I call the neighbor across the street," Ben Gobalt said. "Because he drives an Astro Van. So, yeah, I called and told him to look out his window."

The Astro Man came down from the studio audience and stood beside Ben Gobalt.

"It was late, a little after nine," said Astro Man. "Ben called and sounded upset, so I didn't bitch about the time. He told me to look in his yard. I saw Morton bent over doing something to one of the ornaments."

"You saw Morton Clay? Saw his face?"

The Astro Man shook his head. "He had his back to me and he was wearing that gray hoodie he always wears."

Ben Gobalt shouted, "But I saw him. He had a can of paint and he was painting the gnomes' beards. He looked up at my window and waved and gave me that big slick grin of his."

"My question was for the Astro Man," Judge Jillian said. "We take turns here, just like when you were a child, Mr. Gobalt."

The Astro Man finished up. "Yeah, I saw Morton waving at Ben. The next day Ben asked me to sign a statement about what I saw, so I did. I even lent him my camera so he could take pictures of the ornaments as evidence."

"Now it's your turn, Mr. Gobalt. You say you watched from your upstairs window as Mr. Clay painted the gnomes' beards. He looked up at you and waved. Why not go down and stop him?"

"I wanted to let him finish so I could sue him."

Judge Jillian took off her glasses, pinched the bridge of her nose, put the glasses back on.

"Well, Mr. Clay, Mr. Gobalt and the Astro Man both saw you painting the card-playing lawn gnomes. It seems I have no choice but to award the damages Mr. Gobalt seeks. But we still have ten minutes left in the show and our sponsors wouldn't like it if we finished early. So after the break we'll consider some additional evidence."

Two grips wheeled a big-screen TV into the courtroom, angling it to face Ben Gobalt, Morton Clay, and the studio audience behind them. Ben stood with his back to Morton, looking down at the ground. Morton rubbed his finger over his lips as he watched one of the PAs test the remote to make sure it turned on the TV then hand the remote to Chuck.

The producer called out, "We're back in five, four…"

The studio audience chanted along with him: "three, two, one."

Judge Jillian gave Morton and Ben her trademark glasses-on-the-bridge-of-the-nose stare. "I said before the break we'd consider additional evidence before I give my verdict.…Chuck?"

Chuck aimed his remote at the TV and the monitor blinked on. A Channel 7 reporter stood in front of a house at night lit up by rotating police lights. "I'm outside a Pacific Palisades house where, a few hours ago, the owner was stabbed in his driveway as he got out of his car."

The video cut to a montage of the same reporter outside the same house at different times. "The murder victim is a developer named Evan Oils. Apparently, Mr. Oils was named in several lawsuits for extorting money from investors. The most recent lawsuit, last August, was thrown out.... The police still have no leads in the murder of Evan Oils."

Chuck clicked off the monitor.

Half the audience applauded wildly, maybe out of habit, maybe because of the drama of the unexpected video, while the other half shushed them for cheering a tragedy.

Judge Jillian leaned forward. "Mr. Gobalt, that murder took place the same night at roughly the same time that you saw Mr. Clay vandalizing your lawn ornaments."

Ben Gobalt stared at her blankly.

"Mr. Clay was one of the investors who sued Mr. Oils. Why don't you tell us about that lawsuit, Mr. Clay?"

Morton Clay was gripping the sides of his stand to steady his shaking hands. His grin failed him. "You want me...the lawsuit?"

"Yes."

"Okay. Sure. Nothing to do with anything, but sure. Evan Oils told me he was developing a parking lot. He promised a return of twenty percent a year. He showed me plans and everything. I invested fifty thousand dollars. But there was no parking lot. The whole thing was a scam."

"How did you feel when the lawsuit was thrown out?"

"It was thrown out on a technicality. I wanted to try again. But then someone killed Evan Oils."

"Mr. Gobalt, maybe you followed my line of questioning. Morton Clay had a reason to stab Evan Oils. You're Mr. Clay's alibi."

Ben Gobalt's eyes opened wide. The "ah hah" moment took a while to get there, but when it did, Ben slammed his open hands on the stand. "That snake's not getting out of it this way."

"Getting out of it? I think Mr. Clay would rather pay damages for vandalizing your lawn ornaments than be accused of murder. Isn't that right, Mr. Clay?"

Morton Clay shook his head hard like he had water stuck in his ear. "This isn't right. I'm calling my lawyer. I'm going to sue this show for slander."

Judge Jillian lowered her hand to silence the booing of the studio audience.

"Mr. Gobalt, Mr. Clay couldn't ask for a better alibi than you. One from a friend would be useless. But who would question an alibi from a bitter enemy?"

"I don't know about all that. The news report said there were other investors. And how do you know it was one them, anyway? The snake's going to pay for what he did to my ornaments."

"My producers did a little digging. According to the lawsuit against Mr. Oils, thirty investors put money into that bogus parking lot project. Twenty-nine of those investors joined the lawsuit. Any idea who that thirtieth investor was, Mr. Gobalt?"

Ben Gobalt shook his head. "No, Your Honor."

"Mr. Clay, how did you meet Evan Oils?"

"He used to live near me."

"He used to live near both of you. I still have some friends at the West LA Community Police Station. I asked them to find out if a man named Ben Gobalt wrote a fifty thousand-dollar check to a man named Evan Oils. You did, Mr. Gobalt. You were the one investor who didn't join the lawsuit. You had a different form of justice in mind, didn't you?"

Judge Jillian had to raise her voice to be heard above the screeching sound coming from Ben Gobalt.

"I'm ready to announce my verdict."

Judge Jillian leaned forward, giving the cameraman time to zoom in for the close-up. Judge Kim—the former Judge Kim—had the nerve to crack jokes about a spray-on tan. Judge Jillian thought about sending her a Happy Cancellation card, but she was above that.

"Morton Clay has a history of ridiculing Ben Gobalt's lawn ornaments. He put a turkey on King Neptune's trident and an insulting sign near the retriever with the basket planter. Mr. Gobalt hated Mr. Clay for this. But something happened to unite these two enemies. They were both ripped off by a con artist named Evan Oils. They plotted their revenge. Mr. Clay was the one with enough nerve to commit murder, but he'd joined the lawsuit against Evan Oils so the police could easily discover his motive. He needed an unshakable alibi. Who better than the neighbor he taunted and ridiculed, a man nobody would suspect of helping Mr. Clay by giving him a phony alibi?

"On to the night of the murder. My guess is Mr. Clay hid outside Evan Oils' house and waited for him to come home. When he saw the car approach, he called Mr. Gobalt, and Mr. Gobalt went out to his yard, wearing the gray hoodie neighbors always saw Mr. Clay wearing. He stuck cigarettes in the mouths of the Dutch children. He crouched down and painted the beards of the card-playing gnomes. That's when he made a phone call to the Astro Man across the street telling him to look at his front yard. He waved at his own upstairs window so the Astro Man would think he was inside watching.

"Morton Clay and Ben Gobalt had the audacity to come on this show. Maybe Mr. Clay thought his willingness to deny his own alibi in such a public way would strengthen it. Mr. Gobalt, since I believe Morton Clay murdered Evan Oils, he couldn't have vandalized your lawn ornaments. Therefore, I will not award the damages you seek."

As the audience stomped and cheered their approval, Judge Jillian turned away so the camera didn't catch her saying, "Let's see you and your freak show top that, Judge Howard."

Clear Knights

J.C. Lane

I joined the Poisoned Pen posse in the early 2000s, with my debut mystery, Till the Cows Come Home. *One of my favorite memories is from the 2005 Malice Domestic Convention, when* Cows *was nominated for Best First Mystery. Our illustrious Editor-in-Chief Barbara Peters introduced me to Barbara Mertz, aka Elizabeth Peters, one of my favorite authors of all time. I admit to a major fan-girl moment, and fortunately have a photo of this meeting, so I know it was not just a dream.*

—J.C. Lane

• • ● • •

"You think he was alive when he called?"

Trevor stared at Shaun, who even now was living up to his reputation as the densest accounting major the university had ever seen. "Yes, Shaun," Trevor said, enunciating Very Clearly. "I believe he must have been."

They straddled their motorized scooters and peered into the driver's-side window of the car parked under the streetlight. A man lay slumped over the steering wheel, his face angled toward them, unrecognizable in the darkness.

Shaun ran his fingers through his bleached blond hair. "Claire called me, said this guy was way drunk, but he remembered our ad.

COST OF DUI CONVICTION: $20,000
COST OF CLEAR KNIGHTS: $25
CALL 1-800-GET-HOME

"I grabbed the scooter from my last guy's trunk—pain in the ass, yanking this thing out of a Fit—and rode over."

Trevor took in the surroundings: a curve around the city park, a few houses across the street, dim streetlights offering the only illumination.

A police car coasted around the bend and stopped a short distance away. The front doors opened, and two cops hustled toward the Clear Knights.

"Trevor, Shaun," Gills, the male one, said. "You called?"

Shaun stared at the second officer with undisguised adoration, and Trevor swallowed his irritation. "About a half hour ago Shaun received the order to drive this guy home. He texted me, and when I saw this…"

"So you're the one who called it in?" Officer Shelley Torre pulled out her notebook.

Trevor nodded. "Knew he wasn't going to."

The three of them regarded Shaun, who still gaped at Torre.

"At least he called you," Gills said.

Trevor sighed. "At least."

"You'd think he was the jock," Torre teased.

Gills' radio spewed some police jargon. "Crew's on the way," he said. "We'll need you guys to stick around. I know it's a busy night, but the detective will have questions."

Trevor smacked Shaun on the arm. "Let's back it up so the cops can do their work. *Shaun.*"

They pushed their scooters across the street, parking them in the grass. Trevor gestured for Shaun to stay put, and speed-dialed number one.

"Clear Knights," said a cheerful voice. "Can we drive you home?"

"It's me, Claire. We have a problem." He explained what had happened. "You remember this guy's call?"

"He didn't give me a name. Said he'd started home from the fundraiser—"

"The fundraiser?" Trevor stared across the park. He'd hated missing the dinner, but there was no way he could afford a five-hundred-dollar ticket. Bobby Crandall, the town's very own professional football player, had come home to raise money for the university's new fitness center, and only those well-connected or wealthy would be lucky enough to see him. Trevor's advisor and baseball coach, Dr. Wenger, had offered Trevor a job waiting tables—Wenger had that clout, since he'd been in charge of the event—but Trevor would make more money shuttling drunks from place to place, so he'd reluctantly turned it down. He needed every penny he could scrape up if he was going to make next semester's tuition payment.

"I was expecting him to say he'd had too much to drink," Claire continued, "but he said he thought he *might've* drunk something. He left the fundraiser feeling sick, and got too dizzy to drive."

"The cops will want to hear about that, and anything else you can remember." Trevor heard a hiccup. "Claire?"

"It's just so awful. I mean, a *dead guy*."

"I know. I'll talk to you later, okay?"

Trevor hung up. He was lucky to be dating Claire, a nursing student also working her way through college.

More vehicles arrived, and crime scene techs took pictures and searched the area. A commotion broke out at the car, and Trevor strained to hear what was being said. Nothing coherent reached him.

It wasn't long before a man made his way across the street. Anxiety etched deep lines on his broad face, and veins stood out in his neck. "Detective Barker," he said. "You guys report this?"

Trevor stood. "I did. My friend found the guy and called me."

The detective appraised them. "You're part of Clear Knights?"

"There are five of us. Four riders and one dispatcher."

"I understand you're designated drivers? How does that work?"

"Somebody drinks too much, they call us. The dispatcher contacts a driver, who rides a scooter to the client. Our scooters are collapsible, so they fit into any car's trunk or backseat. We drive the client home, get our bike, and go to the next call."

Barker turned to Shaun. "Tell me what happened."

Shaun watched the cops, his mouth open.

Trevor nudged him with his foot. "Shaun."

Shaun's head jerked up. "What?"

"The detective wants to know what happened."

"With…"

"…the *dead guy*."

"Oh. Right. Claire called me to pick up this dude. I get here and he's…like that."

"You touch anything?" Barker asked.

"Knocked on the window. Tried the door."

"The driver's side?"

"Yeah. And the other side."

"The passenger side."

"Uh-huh. And the back doors."

Barker blinked. "So you touched all the door handles."

"I wanted to see if I could help him. But they were all locked."

Barker took a deep breath through his nose. "You see anything unusual?"

"Like what?"

"Anything."

Shaun thought for a moment. At least Trevor *hoped* he was thinking.

"Nothing's coming to me," Shaun said.

Barker stared at them until Trevor shifted on his feet, like a grade-schooler.

"We have an ID," Barker said.

Trevor waited, wondering why the detective looked ready to explode.

"It's Bobby Crandall."

"*Bobby Crandall?*" The world fell away.

"You know him?"

"Of course. I mean, I know who he is."

Officer Torre trotted up, sending Shaun into near apoplexy. "M.E.'s done. Wants to know if he can move the body."

"Give me a minute. I want to look one more time." He pointed at Trevor. "You guys stay."

Trevor sank to the ground. "I can't believe I didn't recognize him. I mean, it's dark, but it's not that dark."

"I didn't, either," Shaun said. "Anyway, don't people look different when they're dead?"

Trevor glanced impatiently at his friend, then rested his chin in his hands, feeling useless and stupid.

Barker leaned into Crandall's car before gesturing to the M.E. Barker pointed at his own neck, and the M.E. nodded and held his hands against Barker's neck, as if demonstrating. Trevor went cold. Had Crandall been strangled? Who would be strong enough to do that?

Barker re-joined them.

"Was Crandall strangled?" Trevor asked.

Barker looked at him for a beat before saying, "Anything you boys want to add before we get your statements at the station?"

"Yes," Trevor said. "It doesn't make sense he would call us. Bobby Crandall's whole deal is he doesn't drink or do drugs. Doesn't use steroids or even drink caffeine. You've seen his ads, right?" Anti-drinking Public Service Announcements that ran against beer commercials during NFL games. Not exactly a mainstream crusade, but people respected him for it.

"Our dispatcher said Crandall—well, she didn't know it was him then—called us because he thought he *might've drunk* something, not that he was drunk."

Barker turned to Shaun. "Are you sure you can't remember anything else that struck you as odd when you arrived? Lights in the park, a smell, a sound?"

Shaun shook his head, then stopped, his eyes widening. "I guess there was one thing."

"What?"

"A person. Running away."

Trevor thought Detective Barker showed remarkable restraint in not shooting Shaun right between the eyes.

"A person?" Barker said through his teeth. "Running which way?"

Shaun pointed toward the park. "Pretty fast, too. I remember thinking even Trevor would have a hard time catching up."

"Man? Woman?"

Shaun screwed up his face. "Couldn't tell."

"Wearing what?"

"Dunno."

The veins in Barker's neck became even more prominent. He pinned Shaun with a glare. "Stay."

Barker speed-walked toward the crime scene team, yelling and pointing. A technician jogged toward the edge of the grounds, peering at the shoulder of the road and the edge of the grass with a flashlight.

Barker came back. "Anything else?"

Shaun shrugged. "Nope."

Barker gestured to Officer Gills. "Take these two and get their statements." He frowned at Shaun. "Try not to leave anything out."

To Trevor's relief, Shaun kept his mouth shut.

They stashed their scooters in the cruiser and caught a ride to the station. On the way into the building they met Claire, accompanied by another officer.

"Hey," Trevor said, touching her arm. "You okay?"

"Sure. They wanted me to come in now. I forwarded calls to one of the other guys." Her lips trembled. "I can't believe it was him. Bobby Crandall."

Officer Gills spoke gently. "No more talking till your statements are taken."

An hour later Trevor found Claire on a bench, Shaun slouched beside her.

"I'm beat," Shaun said. "We aren't working any more, are we?"

Trevor glanced at the wall clock. Almost three. "No. Go home."

Shaun pushed himself off the seat, looked ready to say something, then clamped his lips together and left, his shoulders sagging.

"Poor Shaun," Claire said.

"Yeah. He can't help it he's so dumb."

Claire's lips twitched. "I meant finding the body. That had to be traumatic."

Trevor wondered for a moment if he should go after his friend, but figured what Shaun really needed was sleep. And a brain transplant. "So, you ready for breakfast?"

Claire shrugged. "I guess."

Trevor pulled her to her feet. "Let's go."

The door flew open and Dr. Wenger burst in. "I just heard. I was finishing up at the Civic Center when the cops came." He swayed, and Trevor led him to the bench.

Claire rushed to the cooler and filled a paper cup. Wenger downed the water in one gulp. "I'm sorry, I'm just…" His eyes teared up. "I wanted to do something."

"Maybe you can. Do you know much about Crandall's movements tonight? Who he was with?"

Wenger twisted a cuff link. "He brought his fiancée, Maria, but others demanded his time, too. Professor Lumley was at his table; she paid to be seated there. Crandall's parents, of course, and his old teammate, George Packard."

Trevor grimaced. "The one who wrecked his knee senior year?" Packard had been hoping for a first-round NFL draft pick, along with Crandall. That hadn't happened.

"So Packard's not playing football?" Claire asked.

Trevor shook his head. "Went into the family business, selling tires."

Trevor caught Claire's eye and knew they were thinking the same thing. Crandall's old teammate had a lot to be jealous of. Was that enough to want Crandall dead?

The inner door opened, and Officer Torre walked toward them. "Who's this?"

Trevor introduced Wenger. "He was in charge of the fundraiser and convinced Crandall to come for it."

Torre's eyebrows rose. "Detective Barker was wondering where you were. Come with me, please."

Wenger stood, buttoning his suit coat. "Thanks, Trevor, and, ah…"

"Claire." She smiled.

Wenger followed Torre through the door, and Trevor took Claire's hand. "Ready?"

Her eyelids drooped. "I'm not really hungry."

"Come on," Trevor said, "I'll take you home."

Claire climbed onto the back of Trevor's scooter and they hummed the three blocks to her dorm. Not the most comfortable ride, but Trevor didn't mind having Claire's arms tight around him.

She kissed him at the sidewalk, and Trevor watched until the dorm's door clicked shut behind her. He knew he should go home and sleep, too, seeing how he'd been up since seven the previous morning, but he didn't think he could turn off his brain yet. A car passed, its lights washing over the street, and Trevor realized there might be others still awake. He eased from the curb and rode toward the other side of campus.

The Civic Center was lit up, and a cop car idled at the entrance. Behind the cruiser were a crime scene van and another unmarked car. It wouldn't be long till news vans started showing up, too. Maybe even ESPN.

Trevor recognized the people on the bench outside the front door, lit up by the building's floodlights. Austin, one of Trevor's baseball teammates, sat curved against the bench's back, his long legs stretched in front of him. DeWayne, the football team's star receiver and Trevor's fellow physical education major, hunched beside him, elbows on his knees, dark face unreadable.

"Trev." Austin yawned, his face pale with fatigue. "Whassup?"

"I think you know."

"Do we ever." DeWayne straightened. "Been getting the third degree for the past hour and a half. You'd have thought we killed the man."

Trevor sat and stretched his neck side to side. "Any idea who did? You see anything?"

Austin snorted. "I was running my tail off. Barely noticed where Crandall was sitting."

"What about you, D?"

"I worked the section beside Crandall's, but couldn't pay attention to him. Too busy."

"Who was serving his table?"

"Who do you think?"

"Don't tell me," Trevor said. "Geena."

DeWayne gave him a look. "Don't think Crandall's lady was happy about it, either."

"Why? What was Geena doing?"

"Nothing," DeWayne said, "'cept being herself. Gorgeous, friendly, you know."

Austin aimed his thumb over his shoulder. "She's getting grilled. That's why we're hanging. Promised we'd wait and walk her home. She's pretty shook up."

"How come you're still awake?" DeWayne asked. "I thought you guys quit driving drunks at two."

"We do, but Shaun found Crandall—he was supposed to drive him home."

"But Crandall didn't drink," Austin said.

Trevor told them what Claire had told him, and what he'd seen Barker and the M.E. doing at the park.

DeWayne frowned. "Who would be strong enough to strangle an NFL player?"

"If he was impaired, it could've been anybody."

"So that's why you were wondering about his table," DeWayne said. "Here comes Geena. You can ask her."

A front-row hitter on the volleyball team, Geena was as tall as Trevor, and her skin glowed with health. This morning her step didn't have its usual bounce.

"That was horrible," she said when she reached them. "Crandall was super nice, treated me like a real person. You know, they don't all."

The guys avoided each other's eyes.

"How about his fiancée?" Trevor asked. "Was she nice, too?"

Geena cocked an eyebrow. "That's a joke, right? Acted like I was serving their table because I was after Crandall. Like I'd want him."

"He was famous," Austin said. "And rich."

"And an amazing football player," DeWayne added.

Geena wrinkled her nose. "The man was fat."

DeWayne bristled. "He was a lineman."

"What I want to know," Trevor said, before the two broke into a fistfight, "is who had the opportunity to put something in his drink."

Geena's forehead scrunched. "He wasn't drinking. The wine was flowing, but for sure not at his table." She paused. "Lots of people could've messed with his lemonade, I guess."

"I saw Dr. Wenger at the police station," Trevor said. "He told me Dr. Lumley paid to be at Crandall's table. Anybody know why?"

"Nope," Austin said. "She hates football."

"She wouldn't drug him," Geena said. "I mean, she teaches health."

"Yeah," DeWayne said, "but she also teaches personal fitness. Maybe she didn't like how fat he was."

"Get off it, DeWayne," Geena growled.

Trevor thought for a moment. "She would understand how fast something could affect him. He was completely unused to drugs; even a little something would get to him. Was she trying to discredit him? Get him caught under the influence?"

"If not her," Austin said, "maybe somebody else was."

"Tons of folks came by the table," Geena said. "It could've been anybody."

DeWayne stood up. "Well, I know it wasn't me. So I'm going to bed. I'm gonna fall asleep here if I don't move."

Austin pushed himself off the bench and stretched. "It wasn't me, either. I was clear across the room. And I'm pretty sure it wasn't Geena, unless she made a pass at him and he brushed her off."

Geena gasped. "You think somebody would turn me down?"

Austin put his arm around her. "Can't imagine who. Coming, D?"

"Fast as my fat butt will let me."

"Will you stop?" Geena smacked his shoulder. "I didn't say all football players were fat. Look at George Packard. Now there's a man."

"Yeah," DeWayne said. "A man who sells tires."

Trevor considered Crandall's old teammate. "Didn't he bust his knee driving drunk?"

Austin nodded. "Nailed one of those concrete mailboxes and crashed into a tree. Dashboard crushed his leg. He was lucky to come out alive."

"Was he?" DeWayne asked.

They looked at him with shared understanding.

"You happen to notice when Crandall left tonight?" Trevor asked Geena.

"Nope. He was upset about something, though, and he and his fiancée got into it good toward the end of the night. And before you ask, I have no idea about what."

"So what happened after that?"

"I took their dessert plates to the kitchen, and when I got back he was gone."

"With his fiancée?"

"No, she left with his parents later on. But Dr. Lumley and George Packard left soon after Crandall did."

Trevor knew that Packard, not nearly as fit now as during college, would still be strong enough to take on the other man.

"Did Packard seem upset during the evening?" he asked Geena.

"Not really. He was quiet. Crandall's dad did most of the talking." She rubbed her eyes. "I just went through all of this with the cops at least five times. I need to go home."

Trevor waved her off. "Sorry."

The trio headed for the street, turning toward campus. Trevor stayed on the bench, his hands shoved in his pockets.

Poor Packard. Was his jealousy of Crandall so complete he followed him out of the fundraiser and killed him?

What about Crandall's fiancée? If she was anxious about other women would she let him leave the fundraiser without her? Or was she the shadowy figure Shaun had seen fleeing through the park?

Trevor glanced at his watch. Almost four. Nobody would be coming out of the Civic Center except cops, and they wouldn't tell him anything. So he had two options since the gym didn't open for another two hours: sleep, or eat breakfast.

He went home to bed.

• • ● • •

Trevor woke several hours later. The mess in the kitchen testified to his housemates' breakfasts, but the house itself was quiet. He pulled on some warm-ups, downed a yogurt, and headed to the gym.

Toward the end of his final set of chest presses in the outdated fitness center, Shaun's face appeared above his. "Want a hand?"

"Nah, I'm done." Trevor set the bar in the rack and sat up, wiping his face with a towel. "You okay?"

"Didn't sleep much. So I had time to think."

Shaun thinking made Trevor a bit anxious, but Shaun surprised him.

"There was a lot of money riding on this fundraiser, right?"

"Tons."

"You think the campaign could be screwed up because of Crandall's death?"

Trevor draped his towel around his neck. "For sure."

"So, what if someone wanted that? Hasn't some guy been protesting since the project started?"

"Barry Smeltzer. The English prof who hates athletics."

"What's his beef with sports?"

"He was always the last one picked on the playground."

"Really?"

"I don't know, Shaun. Anyway, he's been outspoken about how much the university spends on athletics. He forgets it's sports that bring in most of the school's money. I don't see Smeltzer rounding up English recruits and hosting thousands of paying fans."

"And, as any accounting major knows—more money is more money."

Trevor clapped his friend on the back. "Couldn't have said it better myself."

"Well," Shaun said, "you *are* just a phys ed major."

In a short text conversation, Geena answered Trevor's questions. She'd seen Smeltzer briefly at the fundraiser, which confused Trevor. Smeltzer would never support the fitness center by buying a ticket.

Trevor jogged the short distance to the athletics office. He was greeted by the department secretary, whose usual smile was subdued.

"Hey, Alice," Trevor said. "Do you have a list of everyone who attended the fundraiser?"

"Sure."

Trevor scanned the names, and wasn't surprised at Smeltzer's absence. Trevor called the police station. Barker wasn't available, but Trevor left Smeltzer's name with an officer.

"You think he had something to do with Bobby's death?" Alice asked when he'd hung up.

"I don't know. But he's one of the few people I see benefiting from it."

Alice's mouth hardened into a thin line. "I do not like that man. I know you don't, either." Alice spoke past Trevor's shoulder.

Dr. Lumley's eyes were ringed with dark circles. A basketball player, she topped Trevor by a couple of inches, but this morning she seemed somehow smaller.

"I don't what?" she asked.

"Like Barry Smeltzer."

Lumley looked back and forth between Alice and Trevor. "What does that have to do with anything?"

"Trevor thinks he killed Bobby."

Trevor held up his hands. "I just thought Crandall's death might stop the fitness center project, and Smeltzer would like that."

"What do the police think?"

"They're looking into it."

Grasping her briefcase to her chest, Lumley disappeared down the hallway.

"Poor Sheila," Alice said. "This has been so hard for her, with George and all."

"George Packard?"

Alice turned pink.

Trevor waited.

"Sheila was George's advisor. The way his accident was handled…it was pitiful. The football coach told him to drown his sorrows elsewhere. George dropped out of school and never came back." She shuffled some papers on her desk. "Sheila always felt responsible. That's why she asked to be at the head table for the fundraiser. She was afraid George would feel…awkward."

Trevor understood the pressure some coaches put on college athletes. You got hurt and there was nothing more they could take from you, it was all over. Don't let the locker room door hit you on the way out.

Trevor thanked Alice and was walking down the steps when Dr. Wenger barged up. Trevor sidestepped to avoid him.

"Sorry," Wenger said.

Trevor studied the man's face—gray, but with fire in his eyes. "You all right?" Trevor asked.

Wenger's nostrils flared. "I just left the president's office. She wants to put off the fitness center project until Bobby's murder is solved."

"That makes sense."

"Of course it does. But that English professor thinks it's an answer from God that we should shelve it completely."

"Smeltzer?"

"I've put years into this project. Years. Does he think it's easy recruiting athletes when other universities have better facilities? He has no idea how much work it's been to raise money, to organize this fundraiser, to get Crandall to come with all his stipulations—" He clenched his jaw, and stalked into the building.

Trevor watched him go. Something had clicked, and while he didn't like what it told him, he knew it was a possibility. A serious one.

He sent a quick text to Claire, then went back to the athletics office, where Alice peered at him over her glasses.

Trevor pointed down the hallway. "He back there?"

She nodded, and he knocked on Wenger's door. No response.

Trevor opened the door. Wenger sat at his desk, staring at the wall that held his trophies, several signed baseballs, and a bat. Trevor shut the door. Wenger gazed at him with watery eyes, and Trevor's stomach dropped.

"You didn't mean to kill him, did you?" Trevor said.

The tears in Wenger's eyes spilled over.

Trevor spoke kindly. "One of his stipulations was no alcohol at the fundraiser, wasn't it?" But Geena had spoken about the wine flowing freely.

Wenger swiped at his cheeks. "How can he expect that? When people pay five hundred dollars they don't want powdered lemonade. They don't want water!" He pushed his fists against his forehead. "He was going to pull out, said he wouldn't support the fitness center because I'd broken my word." He raised his eyes to Trevor's. "How did you know?"

"Geena said he picked a fight with his fiancée…something had made him angry, and I thought maybe he'd confronted you about the alcohol. Did you follow him when he left?"

"I got into his car. I thought I could talk to him, change his mind, but he wouldn't listen. He stopped at the park and told me to get out. I did, but I'd had too much…there was too much…"

He closed his eyes. "He called somebody, I couldn't hear who. I got back in the car. I just wanted him to *listen*."

"What happened?"

Wenger closed his eyes. "He was acting strange, like he was drunk. Could he have been drunk?"

Trevor shook his head.

"I got so...angry, I just..." He held his hands in front of him. His large, strong hands. "Why didn't he fight back? Why didn't he stop me?"

Trevor pulled out his phone, hoping for a text from Claire. Things could go really bad, really fast. "I think Smeltzer spiked his lemonade. He wanted people to think Crandall had been drinking."

Wenger's eyes sparked, and he pressed his hands against the desk, rising to his full height. "I should have known! He'll stop at nothing to derail this project!"

Trevor took a step back.

"How do you know all this?" Wenger said. "Why are you asking me these things?"

Trevor reached for the doorknob as Wenger rushed him, pinning him against the wall, his arm against Trevor's throat. "Don't you want the new fitness center? You know how much we need it!"

Trevor grabbed at Wenger's arm, but the older man was too strong, and spots danced before Trevor's eyes. He slid his hand along the wall until his fingers wrapped around a trophy. He swung it, catching the side of Wenger's head just enough to loosen his grip. Trevor ducked and grabbed the bat off the wall, holding it as if he were waiting for a pitch. "Stop."

Wenger's lip curled and he took a step forward just as the office door opened. Officers Torre and Gills rushed in, cuffing Wenger. His shoulders slumped and he dropped to his knees, pulling the cops down with him.

"I'm sorry," Trevor said.

Wenger wouldn't look at him.

Barker stepped between Trevor and his mentor. He tilted his head toward the door. "You can go, Trevor."

Trevor took one last glance at his coach before squeezing past the cops.

"Hey," Barker said, stopping him. "You did good."

Trevor gave him a tight smile, and left.

• ● ● ● •

"So what was in Crandall's drink?" DeWayne asked. Their group had met up so Trevor could fill them in. "It couldn't have been alcohol."

"Date rape drug," Trevor said. "GHB."

"Unfortunately," Claire said, "not hard to find on a college campus."

"So it was Wenger I saw running away?" Shaun asked.

"Your scooter's light scared him off."

Shaun's face clouded. "I could've stopped him if I'd gotten there sooner."

"Maybe," Trevor said. "But probably not."

"So now what?" Austin asked.

"The project gets shelved indefinitely, Wenger and Smeltzer go to jail, and Crandall's family—and the town and university—pick up the pieces."

Geena sniffled. "He was a nice man."

Austin squeezed her hand.

The friends sat for a while longer before drifting apart—Claire and Geena to a dorm floor meeting, Shaun to a study session.

Austin, DeWayne, and Trevor looked at each other.

"Wanna work out?" Austin said.

"What?" DeWayne said. "In our old, outdated fitness center?"

"Sounds good to me," Trevor said. "Let's go."

Disguise

David P. Wagner

It was obvious from the beginning that Poisoned Pen Press was different, and not just because they actually would read a manuscript sent directly from an unknown like me. Along with the rejection of my first book, I actually received (gasp!) suggestions on how to make my writing better, and encouragement to try again. That never would have happened in a normal publishing house. But for me, PPP is not a publishing house, it's a publishing home.

—D.P.W.

The priest nodded a silent greeting to the uniformed guard and stepped through the metal doorway back into Italy. Even before the gate clanged shut, he was across the intersection into one of the narrow streets that made up the section of Rome known for centuries as the Borgo. The quarter's history was as long and complicated as any in the city, starting as a burial site during the time of the Etruscans. Now its feel was medieval, giving this side street a scruffy shabbiness, but he preferred walking along it to the clean, wide boulevard Mussolini had cut through the Borgo in the twentieth century. At each corner he caught a glimpse of the wall that connected the Vatican to the Castel Sant' Angelo. Once an escape route for popes, its walkway was now one of the many lesser-known tourist attractions in the city. Perhaps when things were less hectic in his life he would take the tour himself.

Maybe hectic wasn't the correct way to describe his work over the past weeks. It had been slow and steady labor, boring at times, but he'd always kept his eye on the final objective. There were days when it seemed like he'd reached a dead end, and he would have to return to his normal assignments, but he'd stuck with it, and now it had paid off.

At the end of the street he passed four tables on the pavement outside a restaurant. Despite the evening chill, one was occupied by two couples who lingered over a half-empty bottle of red wine. They watched the priest pass, one woman giving him a smiling nod before saying something to her companion. Foreign tourists, he concluded, pulling his jacket tighter. Romans would be sitting inside on a night like this. He turned right and walked through one of the twin arches that breached the wall to allow cars to pass. At this hour the traffic through the wall was light, and it was even lighter where he now walked, a back street that ran between the wall and the rear of the auditorium.

He had no trouble crossing Piazza Pia to reach the sidewalk next to the wide moat that protected the castle. Its imposing ramparts were illuminated by lamps spaced at intervals on the grass of the moat. A feral cat walked slowly in front of one, casting a leonine shadow on the stone walls and causing the priest to stop and watch. After a moment he continued, turning onto the pedestrian street that during the day was filled with tourists. At this hour the tables of souvenir vendors were shut down and only a few souls walked along the cobblestones.

Across from the castle entrance he stepped under the gaze of two angels and onto an ancient pedestrian bridge. Thanks to periodic cleaning, and carefully positioned spotlights, the bridge wore its seventeen centuries well. Beneath one of Bernini's statues a boy and girl squeezed together as they watched a branch float by in the dark water below. She raised her lips toward her companion, but then spotted the white collar of the man passing them, blushed, and quickly returned her eyes to the river. The boy frowned and tightened his grip around her waist. The priest laughed to himself and continued on.

The street on the other side of the bridge was crowded with cars, despite the hour, and the man checked his watch while waiting for the traffic light to change. A pack of motorbikes screeched to a stop with impatient, low-pitched growls as he stepped quickly across the Lungarno and into the maze of streets that made up the Ponte quarter of the city. Cars parked next to the building forced him to walk down the middle of the street, but none passed to squeeze him to the side. Five minutes later he reached a building of indeterminate age on a darkened alley and pulled a key from his pocket. At eye level next to the entrance, eight buzzers lined up with eight names encased in plastic. He inserted the key and the wooden door swung open.

The entrance hallway was dimly lit, partially hiding its need of a good sweeping. He walked directly to the back where cement stairs began their climb to the upper floors. In the center of the stairwell a metal cage bolted to the pavement rose up and out of sight. He pushed a button and a motor groaned to life high above the elevator shaft, causing the heavy cable hanging against the wall to curl slowly upward and disappear. The car arrived, its wood box held together by a metal frame, and the priest got in and chose his floor. From inside the cage he watched as the stairs and floors dropped past him. As always the motor gave the impression that it was reaching the limit of its age and endurance, but it did its duty and grinded on.

When he got to his floor the key chain was back in his hand. Like many apartment doors, this one was equipped with double locks, including a heavy deadbolt. He turned a T-shaped key several times until satisfied that it was open, then fumbled for the smaller key. As he did, he heard a door behind him open.

"Did you get what you needed?" The voice was young and feminine.

The priest smiled, but did not turn around, continuing to work on the lock. Finally it opened.

"If you want to come in and have a glass of wine, I'll tell you."

Perhaps this would be the night that he would get to know his lovely neighbor better. Most of their conversations had been in the hallway or out on the street; only in the last week had she come into his tiny apartment, and then only to ask his advice. She was thinking about becoming a journalist, but she wasn't sure if it was the right profession for her. What did he think? She seemed genuinely troubled, and he'd been glad to help. He'd told her about what had brought him to his calling, his studies, and now the satisfaction that came with the work. He also talked about the frustrations, and explained his latest assignment, if that was the right word for it. She was fascinated, asking questions and listening intently to his answers. He didn't want to admit it, but he enjoyed the attention.

He held the door open and she walked in. She was dressed casually, in jeans and a loose-fitting sweatshirt. Her short hair was wet, like she'd just been in the shower, and as usual she wore no makeup, not that she needed it. He stole a look at her jeans as she passed. He motioned toward his one comfortable chair and walked to the kitchen, an extension of the small living room. She sat on the edge of the chair, her knees touching, and her eyes darted around the room. Fortunately the apartment was relatively neat, and the door to the bedroom was closed. A shelf held a small TV, and the other furniture in the room was a table with a chair, and a wooden desk on which sat his computer, a battered laptop. The desk chair was the twin of the one at the dining table.

"Typical bachelor quarters," he said while he pulled off his suit jacket and folded it over one of the chairs. "All I have is a Frascati. I hope that's all right."

"Yes. Yes, of course. Thank you."

As he walked to the kitchen he pulled off the white collar and tossed it onto the chair. It fell to the floor but he made no attempt to pick it up. Instead he rubbed his neck where it had chafed the skin.

"You're going to get in trouble with that." She was looking at his black, collarless shirt.

"It's a chance I had to take, and now that it's done I don't need to wear it again. Nobody ever stopped me." His hand waved at the white ring on the floor. "The guards never asked me for identification when they saw I was wearing that."

"I don't mean trouble with the guards. I mean trouble later." She slipped her hand from the sleeve of the oversized sweatshirt and pointed heavenward.

He laughed, pulled the bottle from the small refrigerator, and fumbled in a drawer for a corkscrew. "I'm glad you're here so I don't have to celebrate alone."

A row of white teeth bit softly down on her lower lip. It was an affectation he'd noticed before, usually when she was spurning his advances. She was staring at the computer as if she'd never seen one before. Her eyes jumped back to him.

"Are you going to write your story now?"

"I have the last piece of the puzzle," he answered. "So I'm ready to write." He opened the wine and poured it into two glasses he'd taken from a drying rack above the sink. After passing one glass to her he held up his. "To the Church, may this help to change its ways."

As he took a drink she looked blankly at him. The stare continued after he turned the desk chair toward her and sat down.

"To the Church," she said finally, taking the smallest of sips from her glass. "And who was it? If you don't mind me asking."

"Why should I mind? It will be public knowledge in a matter of days."

He told her the name, and from her blank look he decided she'd never heard of the man. But there was no reason she would have known him, the machinations of the Curia stayed inside the walls of the Vatican. As it had been for centuries, nothing was more mysterious to the average Roman than church politics. It was difficult enough for Italians to follow their own government.

Suddenly the girl tossed down her wine, put down the empty glass, and got to her feet.

"I should leave. Thank you for the wine."

He stood up. "But you just got here. I thought we might—"

"No. I really must go. I'm sorry. It was kind of you to ask me in."

"Have you decided to become a journalist? Did telling you about my work help?" He was trying to keep her there, but judging from the look on her face he knew it wasn't going to happen.

"I…I'm not sure. But thank you for your help."

After he closed the door behind her he sat at his desk, the wineglass still in hand. What a strange creature this pretty, young neighbor was. Shy, unquestionably. But it went beyond that. When she'd walked into his apartment tonight he thought it was finally his chance. She knew all about what he did, but had always steered the conversation away from herself. Such a refreshing change from all those self-centered women he knew. But it wasn't over yet. This latest assignment had taught him patience, and it appeared he would need a good deal of it with this neighbor. He smiled and took another drink of wine before opening his laptop.

• • ● • •

She sat on the bed, rubbed her eyes, and stared at the phone. The taste of the wine was still on her tongue, bringing to her mind the look on his face when he told her the name. And such a kind face. She put her hand to her mouth to stifle a shudder and picked up the phone. She knew the number by heart. After three rings a low voice came on the line.

"You have something to report?"

"Yes. He knows."

A moment passed before the man spoke again. "You thought that before. Are you now absolutely certain?"

When she gave him the name she could hear a sharp intake of breath. More seconds passed.

"You have done well. Your work there is finished."

"What will you do now?"

The voice was now hurried. "That does not concern you. Return immediately."

The line went dead.

She got to her feet, walked to the closet, and took out a small suitcase that she opened on the bed. After changing her clothes and packing, she walked slowly around the small apartment, running her hand over the few pieces of furniture. She turned out the lights and opened the door a crack, peering into the dimly lit hallway. Satisfied that it was deserted, she slipped out, closing the door softly behind her. She walked down the steps without looking back, careful that her flat heels made no sound as she descended to the ground floor and opened the door to the street.

It was almost midnight when she turned the corner and walked in the direction of the river. The night had turned cool, but she didn't feel the temperature. A few people passed her, some smiling when they saw her face. Two carabinieri watched her cross in front of their patrol car while they were stopped at the traffic light near the bridge.

"Don't nuns always travel in pairs?" said the one in the passenger seat. "Especially at this hour?"

The driver didn't reply. The light had turned green and he was already shifting into second.

Sage Advice

Kelly Garrett

On a rainy day in Paris, this guy in a fedora and cowboy boots walked up to me and he said "You must submit your work to…" Just kidding. As a lifelong mystery fan, I'd known about Poisoned Pen Press for years. I'd seen their titles in bookstores, and read some of their books over the years. So when they announced in Publisher's Weekly *that they'd started acquiring young adult fiction in addition to their regular fare, I made a note, as I write for both the YA and general mystery market. When I had a young adult manuscript ready, I sent it their way, and just a few short months later had joined the crew at Poisoned Pen Press.*

—K.G.

• • ● •• •

Visions of cold brew waltzed through my mind.

Not any cold brew, mind you. The coffee on nitro from the oh-so-hipster shop around the corner. Something in the nitrogen aspect made it all creamy, with small bubbles or something like that. Other thoughts wanted to invade the image of the world's most perfect drink, but I shoved them aside.

A few people stared as I approached the shop. Maybe 'cause I was wearing a wedding dress. But that can't be too unusual in a neighborhood that prides itself on being weird. Last week I saw a guy outside the same coffee shop, smoking. The cigarette wasn't the quirky part, even if people act like nicotine has cooties. It was his bear costume. Yet no one really paid attention to him.

But wear a wedding dress with a sort of Rita Hayworth vibe? Everyone stares. Maybe next time I'll pick out one that looks more pretty-pretty princess.

"Sage!"

I closed my eyes briefly as my hand reached out for the door to the coffee shop. Two more steps and I would have been free to consume my weight in coffee.

Five feet, three inches of hipster bore down on me. She wore a slouchy cotton beanie in homage to the chilly July weather, but I couldn't really rip on her for the hat. Mainly 'cause it's mine. My sister had pilfered my wardrobe once again, snagging my favorite "Unicorn v. T-rex" shirt as well. My eyes narrowed.

"I need your help!" Rose put her hand on my arm and pulled me away from the door.

"Now's a horrid time. Can it wait for tomorrow? And you agreed you'd stop raiding my closet."

She stared at me for a second and started to motion to my dress. I shook my head, warning her to keep quiet about it.

"I'm calling in a favor," she said.

I groaned. Giving my sister three markers for her birthday had been a dumb idea. On the bright side, this was the third and final request. She'd already had me find a lost goat and fill in for her at the coffee cart so she could go surf for a week.

"Lead the way," I said, sounding as excited as I felt. "And you owe me coffee."

"That's not part of the deal," she countered as I followed her to one of the sidewalk tables. A girl sat there, early twenties, maybe a year or two younger than Rose. Curly blond hair pulled back into a ponytail, big green eyes. Doctor Who tee-shirt. One hundred percent my sister's type.

"Mila, this is my sister, Sage," Rose said as she motioned to me. "She...helps people."

"Helps?"

"Fixes problems. Finds stuff. She's amazing. Totally trustworthy, too. You can tell her anything, like a priest."

Mila raised an eyebrow at me. I plopped down in the chair across from her, feeling like this moment was inevitable. "Tell me, child, how long has it been since your last confession?"

"Sage, seriously," my sister said.

"Mila's out of coffee. Why don't you get her a refill, and get me a cold brew, and we'll talk while you're in line. One pump of simple syrup."

"Just black coffee for me," Mila added.

As Rose walked away, I turned back to Mila. "Really, what's up?"

Mila's cheeks turned red as she squirmed in her seat. "It's embarrassing, but I need you to find a guy for me."

"Lots of guys in Portland."

She pulled a sketchbook out of her Emerald City Comic Con tote bag and slid it across the table. "He left this behind."

The sketchbook had a spiral ring across the top, and scuff marks on the plain black front cover. I flipped through it. Lots of sketches of the St. Johns Bridge, all drawn from the Cathedral Park side of the river, although there were also a few of a stained-glass window. Sadly there weren't any "if lost, return to so-and-so" notes written inside.

"He knows how to draw," I said. "So why do you want to find him?"

Mila looked at the table for a second before looking back up at me. She struggled to meet my eyes. "This is so embarrassing, but my then-girlfriend picked him up one night. I came home and found them…you know."

A small sliver of sympathy snaked through me. "And then?"

"I freaked. Started yelling. Threw both of their stuff around. My ex always carries books like this, 'cause she writes, and I thought I was grabbing her notebook when I stormed out. But when I looked at it later, it wasn't hers."

"Can your girlfriend help you return it?"

"Ex-girlfriend. She can't even remember the guy's name. I just know he has dark hair, is kinda skinny, and about six feet tall. I thought about just recycling it, but I'd feel guilty if I didn't make a solid effort to return it. He didn't know he was getting into the middle of a lover's spat."

Mila smiled at someone over my shoulder. Rose was back. She handed Mila a coffee, and said as she turned to me, "They're having some sort of problem with coffee on draft, so I got you an iced Americano."

I wanted to bang my head against the table. "The thought of that coffee was the only thing that got me through today," I said.

Mila excused herself to use the bathroom, and Rose stared at me. Her eyes flicked back down to my dress and returned to my face. "Care to talk about why you're dressed like a cake topper?"

I shook my head. I glanced to make sure Mila really had gone inside, then looked at my sister. "You sure about this? Do you really want to involve yourself in someone else's relationship drama?"

"I have a good feeling about this," Rose said. Her eyes took on a faraway look, like she was daydreaming about the perfect relationship with Mila unfolding in front of her.

I stopped myself from reminding my sister that her intuition is as stable as a toddler on a tricycle in a glass shop.

Instead, I sighed, picked up my stupid iced Americano, and said, "I'm going to the office. I should have something in a little bit."

• • ● • •

I'd lied when I told Rose I was going to the office. That's usually code for the coffee cart we own and operate in downtown Portland. But I'd seen something in the drawings. The frequent drawings of the St. Johns Bridge meant the guy had to either live or work in that neighborhood. But I was going to start with the second repeated image in the notebook. I knew a guy, so I headed farther into Southeast Portland.

The Tav probably has, or at least had, some sort of unique name. A few decades of neglect had caused the "ern" to burn out of the sign over the door, and they rolled with it instead of fixing it. Unlike some of the faux-dive bars sprinkled around town, The Tav's grit has been earned. Want an on-trend drink of the moment? Go someplace else. But if you want a drink that's strong enough to peel all of the paint off your soul, the Tav is for you. In a neighborhood where gentrification is the name of the game, the Tav's continuing existence defied all sorts of odds.

The bartender nodded at me when I came in, and poured a Maker's Mark without asking. He put it in front of me as I slid up next to a silver-haired guy at the corner of the bar. In a few hours, he'd be holding court amongst the regulars, but for now he was staring at a baseball game.

"Hey, Uncle Jimmy," I said.

"Hi, Pumpkin. So how is my favorite niece?"

"When I left Rose a few minutes ago, she was just fine."

"If I'd wanted to ask about my little Rosemary, I would have," he grunted. "Your face is awfully shellacked today."

"I'm trying a new look." The makeup caked on my face made it itch, like I was wearing a mask that was sucking all the life out of my skin.

As I took a sip, my eyes strayed over to the far wall. At some point in time, the Tav had been classy. Someone had commissioned custom stained-glass windows. But these weren't your usual depictions of saints and martyrs. The center window is the largest, and shows two doors. A woman with hair like a lion's mane stands between them. She holds out her hands like she's asking a question. Something about her draws the eye.

The artist had drawn the center window several times, like he was trying to figure out what makes her so compelling.

I pulled the sketchbook out of my bag and looked at a few of the illustrations before putting it down on the bar. "Recognize this?"

Jimmy spared it a quick glance before going back to the game on TV. "Looks like the window over there."

"I'm looking for the guy who owns the notebook. You seen anyone who likes to draw the chick in the center window?"

"There's a lot of hidden meaning in that window, you know. She's not just a 'chick'..." His voice trailed off as he watched the screen. "Go for a double, you dumbass."

I swallowed my groan. I knew how to get Jimmy's attention, and not just 'cause he favored alternate runlines. "You got money on a five-inning line? Should I drop fifty cents on the action?" I asked.

"No. You don't bet. Don't even think about starting unless you want to answer to me."

"Answer my questions about this sketchbook and I'll leave you to watch the game in peace," I said.

Jimmy pulled the sketchbook to him and flipped through it. "Oh, yeah, I know who you're looking for."

"I'll buy you a drink if you cut to the chase."

"There's an art student who used to work here on Wednesday nights. Three-to-one odds, he's your guy. He was always drawing on the napkins."

"Got a name?"

But Jimmy was looking at the TV screen again. He tore a napkin in half.

"C'mon, focus, please," I said.

Jimmy kept his eyes on the screen as he said, "Bax. He went by the name Bax when he worked here. He lived by a brewery over in NoPo somewhere. He showed me some sketches he was doing for them. This was almost a year ago, mind you. Maybe longer. I'm surprised you don't remember him."

"That's all you got?"

"One of the beers was named after a whale."

"That helps. Here, have this and I'll leave enough to buy your next one," I said as I slid my mostly untouched drink over to him. I slid a couple of bills under the salt shaker.

I put Cinderella's slipper, err, the sketchbook, back into my bag, and headed for North Portland.

● ● ● ● ●

I texted Rose that I was borrowing her car, although I cast a sad glance at my bicycle as I slid into her beat-up Honda. But the trip to St. Johns would take me a few hours by bike.

Uncle Jimmy's reference to the beer named after a whale was the clincher. The oh-so-cleverly named St. Johns Brewing had released "The White Whale" maybe a year and a half ago, to the combined joy and disdain of craft beer-lovers. It had been the Queen Bee beer of its time, with a long list of people wanting to brag they'd drank it. I'd been dating someone who'd acquired a few bottles, and we'd broken up when I'd said it was just an IPA.

But the logo on the bottle had been damn fine.

The sun was starting to set as I turned off of Highway 30 to cross the Willamette, noting the black SUV that had been just within eyeshot behind me since I left Southeast. The St. Johns Bridge looked like a painted scene from a Road Runner cartoon as I crossed the river, trying not to be distracted by either the gothic towers above or view back toward downtown Portland. The SUV turned onto the bridge as well. It was still too far away for me to be able to read the license plate number.

I left Rose's car in Cathedral Park, under the shadow of the bridge, pausing to look at the cathedral-like arches in its base. They looked especially regal in the setting sun.

The drawings had focused on a specific angle. I worked my way up North Baltimore Avenue from the park, keeping an eye on which aspects of the bridge stayed in sight as I passed by a row of orange buildings, a chocolatier, and some assorted housing.

I had to go in two blocks to the left, and then I had it. A newish-looking building faced downhill, looking out toward the river. The apartment units facing the bridge would have million-dollar views.

The front door had an automated system, and I scrolled through it. After a few I hit pay dirt.

C. Baxter.

I hit the call button.

After a few rings, a dude answered. "Bax?" I said.

"Nah, he's down at the pub."

Great. Of course a student would have a roommate or two. Maybe ten.

"Which one? I have something of his to return."

After a moment, I had my answer, so I turned and limped back the way I'd come. I should have switched out of these white sandals before taking the case. The pearls on the straps were cute, but the exactly two-and-three-fourths-inch heels were driving me crazy. Scratch that. Next time I wear a wedding dress, I'm going with ballet slippers. Or flip-flops, as long as they have rhinestones to keep them fancy.

There was a black Toyota 4Runner parked on Baltimore, and I pretended not to notice as I clomped past, trying to walk smoothly on those stupid heels, subtly clocking the guy sitting deep in the shadows of his SUV. It was too dark to make out his features, or even the color of his hair. Only his white tee-shirt was faintly visible.

As far as I could tell, I'd been shadowed since the Tav, maybe earlier, since I'd been too out of it to pay attention. Was it someone from the fake wedding this morning? Or one of my mom's so-called friends? Even after fifteen years in the slammer, people show up a little too regularly, wanting something from her, and expecting I'll be able to get it for them. Except I'm a barista. Officially, at least. The grifter gene skipped my generation. My half-sister was too sweet, my half-brother was too principled, and I was too much my father's daughter to follow in her footsteps.

No one exited the car, and the street behind me was silent as I turned and walked up the driveway of a three-story building built around a small surface parking lot. The brewery was on the second floor, facing the bridge.

After climbing a flight of stairs, I was there. St. Johns Brewing took advantage of the bridge view by incorporating a rendering of it into their logo, which they'd splashed up everywhere, including the brewery tee-shirt of the guy behind the bar. I paused. Dark hair. Even good looks. Could this be the guy? Hopefully yes, 'cause the room was otherwise empty and I was tired of looking for Bax.

"Hey, there," he said as I slid to a stop about a foot away from him at the bar. He eyed my dress and tilted his head to the side. "You meeting anyone here?"

"So, well, long story, but…" I pulled the sketchbook out of my bag. "A girl asked me to return this to you, and say she was sorry." Actually Mila hadn't said that, but it sounded better.

He jumped back from the bar, bumping into the counter behind him. A stack of glasses rattled. "Who are you?" His hand balled into a fist. Great. Just what I needed after a long, stupid day. I held up my hands. "Relax. I'm just doing a favor for a friend. Long story, but my sister met this girl, and she asked me to return the sketchbook on her behalf."

"That sketchbook? The one I lost breaking up a mugging in the park blocks downtown? According to the news, the old guy I helped is still in a coma."

"This makes no sense," I said. If someone wanted to thank him, there were all sorts of public channels. Social media would be the perfect place to ask 'Do you know who this belongs to? He saved my dad from attackers but left before police arrived!' because a story like that, combined with Bax's clean-cut good looks, had viral social-media post written all over it.

"You just helped a guy?" I asked.

Bax squirmed slightly. "Well—"

"Out with it."

"When I checked on the guy after breaking up the mugging, he put a flash drive into my hand and told me to get lost. So I did."

The sound of a car door slamming in the distance made several puzzle pieces fall into place.

"Do me a favor," I blurted out. "Follow my lead, no matter what happens."

"Why?" Bax stared at me.

I stared back. "Trust me. I'm on the side of the angels. Pour me a pint of something, anything," I said as I heard feet climbing the stairs to the entrance of the tasting room. Bax poured a pint, keeping his eyes on me. Wariness covered his face, and hopefully the smile I gave him in return was reassuring.

I sipped but didn't taste the straw-colored beer Bax handed me as a guy came into the tasting room. I scoped him out in the mirror to one side of the bar. White tee-shirt, dark blue jeans turned up at the cuff. Black boots. Bit of a James Dean vibe. He just needed a cigarette and maybe a leather jacket.

"Can I get something for you?" Bax asked him.

"Is this the guy?" Wanna-be James Dean asked.

I turned to face the guy who'd been following me. One of the best parts about being five-foot-one and female is that it's easy for people to underestimate you. You're not physically intimidating when you're standing nose-to-pectoral muscle with a guy. Fake sweetness and girly laughs disarm them.

But you've gotta keep your wits about you.

"Hey, if you wanted to ask me out for a beer, you could have just said something," I said. "Instead of following me around town."

"I'm not asking again."

I turned and picked up my pint, finally tasting the brew, which turned out to be a lager, based on the crisp taste with the perfect light bite of hops. "Hey, this is really good," I said. "And which guy are you talking about? If you're looking for my faux-groom, I last saw him at the Rhododendron Garden…but let's not get into that."

I looked at Bax and motioned to the sketchbook. "Although while I'm here, do you know the guy who owns this? Maybe he draws in here? He likes the bridge."

Bax looked at the sketchbook and shrugged. "I pour beers. As long as people don't start fights, I don't have time to pay attention to what they're doing."

"'Cause you're so busy." James Dean motioned to the otherwise empty pub.

I turned to face the guy. "I'm a little annoyed you're following me. Care to explain why?"

He had to be aligned with Mila, and clearly, her lover spat had been a sham from the beginning. But why had someone decided to drag me into this? 'Cause whoever had started this came at me from an angle I couldn't refuse: my sister. Something told me this guy wasn't supposed to have made contact with me. So would he backpedal, or push forward? More importantly, could Bax keep up? All I needed was to have led a creep to an—as far as I knew—innocent guy. Not to mention the innocent guy had amazing eyes and the sort of perfect nose that it would be a shame to see busted up.

"Sorry," the guy said. He stepped backward, and his eyebrows scrunched like he was thinking hard. "I must have you confused with someone else."

I wanted to tell him to leave my sister alone, and that if he and Mila wanted something, to come at me directly. But so far he hadn't overtly shown his hand, and I needed him to leave. A showdown with him and with only Bax as backup sounded like a terrible idea.

"Yeah, go confuse someone else."

I waited for him to walk out of the brewery and counted to five before going to the balcony to make sure he was leaving. He headed in the direction of his car, probably to report to whoever was pulling his puppet strings.

"What next?" Bax asked. "Is that guy really after me?"

"It's okay," I said. "I know a detective who can help."

Bax bit his lower lip, and his hands shook as he picked up a bottle of water. He knew something I didn't. We were going to have a serious talk after I made my call.

I pulled out my cell phone, scrolled through the contacts, took a deep breath, and hit the call button. "Dad? I have something for you."

• • ● • •

I was waiting on the balcony when my father arrived. Given the dark blazer he was wearing, I could tell he had his side arm with him—or he found the summer weather to be on the nippy side. He scoped out everything as he made his way across the parking lot. I waved and pointed out the stairs, and he made his way up. I met him in the tasting room.

"Beer?" I asked.

"What's with the dress?"

I shrugged. "I was helping someone out today and it just sort of snowballed until I ended up here," I said, not wanting to tell him that I'd ditched my fake groom an hour into the charade. He needed wedding photos to get his parents off his back, but he didn't need to be an overbearing dick about it.

As I told him the story of my hunt for Bax, I could read the ever-present note of skepticism in him. But when I held up the locker key, he reached to snatch it out of my hand. I closed my fist before he could grab it.

"Wait," I said. "Bax is afraid he'll get into trouble for ending up with this. He didn't realize what he had, at least not at first."

"Why didn't he call the police?"

"He was scared. He wouldn't even tell me what was on the flash drive, just that it freaked him out and he was afraid he'd get in trouble for seeing it. He was going to mail it in anonymously, but then I showed up." As I put the key into my father's hand, I said, "locker 231."

I trailed my father down the hallway that led from the tasting room to the bathrooms. A row of old school lockers lined one wall.

"What kind of brewery has lockers?" Dad asked as he opened the door.

"Bax has roommates in a one-bedroom apartment. The locker gives him a place to store stuff he doesn't want his roommates to take."

He put on gloves before opening the locker. After a moment, he held up the flash drive.

"I'm going to want to talk to this Bax."

"I'll make sure the two of you connect." I hid a smile since it sounded like I was setting up a date versus a serious discussion with the police.

My dad sighed and glanced around. "Where is he?"

I could deny the truth my father had already heard in my voice, but instead I half-smiled. Caught again.

"Come on out, Bax. Say hi to one of Portland's finest," I called out. I glanced at my father. "Some nineteen-fifties throwback guy followed me here, looking for Bax. It's probably safer for him to go with you."

Bax emerged from the back of the brewery, where he must have been sitting amongst the tanks, trying not to hyperventilate. He looked young, like a teenager busted for throwing a party while his parents were out of town. When he met my father's eyes, he looked down, but then looked back up and met them straight on. His shoulders tightened and he stood straight.

"So you're the guy who broke up the mugging," my dad said.

Bax nodded.

I slipped away, letting my dad do his thing. No one noticed as I made my way out the door, and then back to the parking lot at Cathedral Park.

I pointed Rose's car toward home. Maybe tomorrow I'll be able to convince my father to tell me what's on the zip drive. For now, I need to divorce myself from this wedding dress. And say "I do" to some cold brew coffee.

Girls with Tools

Triss Stein

Decades ago I published two mysteries with a publisher that dropped its mystery line just about the time I turned in the third. Life kept happening, and it was a long time before I went back to writing. Trying to find a new agent for my new book and new series idea, I had several variations of this actual response, "I love your book but I don't know anyone who is buying literate, non-gimmicky mysteries."

I finally said, "Well, I know who does!" I took a chance and sent it off to Poisoned Pen Press. If all my chance-taking turned out this well, I would have to buy a lottery ticket every day. I am proud to be published by a company with such a strong reputation for quality and professionalism, and happy to be published by people instead of a corporation.

—T.S.

• • ● ● •

Here's how I become a ship builder. A girl with tools. A real-life Rosie, if you want to call me that, though my real name is Philomena.

After the war started, the government had a big campaign to get women to do men's work so the men could all go be soldiers or sailors.

I worked at my grandpa's grocery store then, taking cash and helping at the meat counter as they got short of men. I thought I was gonna die of boredom there. My face hurt from smiling all day.

Then I saw where I could apply at the Brooklyn Navy Yard. It was only a trolley ride away from home. And I could build ships. Repair ships. Use tools. Meet new people. So I said to my pop, who had worked there until he was disabled, and my oldest and bossiest brother, Vito, who was a foreman there, "Why didn't you tell me they're looking for women? I want to do my part!"

Vito said, "You've got to be kidding. No sister of mine is working with those roughnecks. Bad language and worse behavior. Not for you, toots."

And my mama cried, and said, "It's dirty. You have to wear coveralls. You come home with grease in your nails. Not for my little girl."

My pop kept it simple. "Never. I'd rather see you dead."

"I don't care about the grease or the coveralls. Not the bad language, either."

Then Vito said, "Some things there are not right for you to see."

"What things? I don't believe you. You're just bossing me around like you always do."

He did look at me like he always does, like I'm a dumb child, and said, "Yeah? Last year, we had a ship come in where we found bodies below, sailors trapped when the ship got hit. They couldn't retrieve the bodies until we started taking the ship apart. You want that? The sights and the smells were worse than you can guess. Plenty of big, tough welders were sick right there on the dock." He grinned but not in a nice way. "You ready for that?"

Mama crossed herself and I know my face went white, just thinking about it, but I didn't give up.

"If you can do it, I can."

Then came the shouting and the tears and my threats to move in with some relatives. I was eighteen. They couldn't stop me. And mama tried to get me to talk to the priest from Sacred Heart. It went on for weeks.

But then my youngest, favorite brother, Francis, came home on leave after basic training. He couldn't tell us where he was being sent, but anyone who listened to the news on the radio could figure it was North Africa, where there were big battles now.

My other brothers were already in. Mama prayed all the time in those days.

So there was Frankie, all decked out in his uniform, and the whole family was so proud. Mama already made a flag with the third blue star—one each for Frankie and my other brothers in the service—and Pop hung it from a second-floor window.

Mama ordered all of us, everyone, even Pop, to stop our fighting while Frankie was home. He was going to have a good visit before he got on that troop ship! There were threats about the evil eye if anyone disobeyed, but I was so angry I didn't care. Evil eye, big deal! Even Mama didn't really, truly, believe that stuff.

I told Frankie all about our fighting, and he told them. Boy, did he. He smacked the table and said if they want all the boys like him to come home, everyone had to pitch in and do what was needed. Then he looked at our folks and said, loudly, "What's the matter with you? You think you didn't raise a good girl? You think she would play the puttana?"

They all gasped when he said that.

Then he said, "And, besides, I taught her a good uppercut, so she could take of herself if anyone tried anything."

Mama finally said, "How you say no to the boy who's going overseas to the shooting?" I put in my application the next day, with Frankie escorting me downtown to do it.

Well, it was hard work, long hours, exhausting. And I was so proud to do it, something so real. Real tools. Real metal. Real big—really big—ships. It wasn't like making change all day and saying, "Hi, Mrs. So and So" and asking about her arthritis and yes, she needed her ration book for the sausage.

I liked my own paycheck too. I gave it to Mama, but I kept a little back. A girl needed nail polish, especially with my job. And a new hat once in a while.

The first day some guys stared and yelled rude remarks. I gave it right back, loud. Then I smacked my hands together, and got to work. You don't mess with a real Brooklyn girl who grew up in a house full of brothers.

But some of the guys were helpful and nice, once they saw we girls were serious, and I made some girlfriends, too. Then we got a new foreman who was not nice at all. He barked his orders, never wanted to show us anything, was rude to the guys and even worse to us girls. There was some secret crying, lots of days. He really, really did not want women on his crew and he let us know it. Every day. Every hour.

He was an Irish guy. Donelly. Looked it, too, freckles and all. We Italians, we were big at the Navy Yard. I don't know why, but lots of Italian men are ironworkers, so maybe there's a connection to ship work. Being Irish, he wasn't part of the family, so to speak. Maybe it made him grouchy. That's what I thought at first, and I worked extra hard just to show him.

Finally, I'd had enough and I opened my big mouth. "I have three brothers in the service. Three! And a dozen cousins, first and second. Can you even count that high? And I'm doing my part right here 'cause the president says I should. You got a problem with it?"

I happened to have a wrench in my hand when I said it.

Dead silence. Then he laughed and most of the other guys laughed and behind his back a few gave me a thumbs-up.

"Well, well. Look what we got here. A little baby patriot in lipstick! Pretty cute. Now everyone back to work. We got a ticking clock for this job."

A few days later, he sat down next to me at lunch break. Yikes.

"So you got brothers overseas? How are they doing?"

He caught me so off guard that I told him

"My oldest brother is safe. He's here at the yard and looks like for the duration."

"Like me."

"He was one of the guys from here who volunteered to go to Pearl Harbor to rebuild the bombed ships."

"Like me."

"But my next was already in the Navy." I waved my hand around to encompass the whole yard. "He grew up around ships 'cause our dad worked here. He's officially somewhere in the

Pacific now." I had to swallow hard then, to keep talking. The news wasn't good.

"The other one is in England for now." I shook my head. "And my favorite is in the artillery. We're guessing he's on the way to North Africa. Where the Germans are."

I stopped talking, unable to say any more. He kind of chucked me under the chin and said, "So here you are, taking the place of three men. Good work."

A week later he stopped me as I was leaving and said, "We oughta step out sometime. You're cuter than me, but we're both single. Why not? You like to dance?"

Sure, I like to dance. Who doesn't? I didn't like him, not at all, but I faced facts. Men were scarce.

He turned out to be not a bad dancer, and not too grabby, if you get my point, and in the breaks, we talked about my brothers and my cousins, who were all over the map. A real map. My pop had a big one up on the kitchen wall with little pins for all the places the family was. Dark blue for Navy and Marines, green for Army, light blue for the Army Air Corps. Africa, Alaska, a Florida air base, islands in the Pacific we never heard of before. Hawaii. And one in Washington, keeping the generals safe.

Pop was from Naples, and Mama too. They came here as kids, went right to work, got a house and a little vegetable garden and five kids who lived, and one who died. They were proud Americans and they were dead set on proving it every single day, what with Italy being an enemy and all. Besides the service flag, they put up the biggest American flag on the block. When they talked about Mussolini, they only used Italian. That's how I knew they were cursing him.

I told Donelly all of this, different nights, and he nodded and listened and listened. I guess I needed someone to talk to, now that Frankie was off at the war. I couldn't even consider romance with him, and he didn't try too hard. I suppose we were friends. I didn't know you could be that with a guy.

One day I had to help my grandparents clean out the little extra room behind the store. All kinds of junk was needed for the war effort, like old pots and old rubber girdles and paper. My folks sent me over to lend a hand. On my one day off! But they needed my help and it was for a good cause, just like my job.

They had stacks of Italian newspapers. Grandpa used them to wrap tomatoes in the store. And stacks of magazines, too. They didn't read much English so they liked the ones with lots of photos. Grandpa couldn't explain why he kept them except he thought they'd come in handy sometime. Nona just clucked and brought more cookies into the back room while we worked.

A bundle of magazines from the last decade caught my eye. My childhood in pictures! I sprawled on the floor, leafing through them. Glamorous debutante parties and movie premieres, with women in furs and gowns and men in white tie. Adorable, dimpled Shirley Temple. Of course I remembered her! Handsome Errol Flynn, who I had seen in *Robin Hood*, and Clark Gable, taking off his shirt in *It Happened One Night*. I certainly had not seen that when it was new and I was only nine. He looked pretty good in the photo.

President Roosevelt looking a lot younger; the Empire State Building going up in record time. Those men on those girders! Sad photos of farmers losing their homes, and World War I veterans living in shantytowns.

And then I hit stories that sent a chill up my back. Right here in New York there were real Nazis. Used to be. The Bund, they called it. I didn't know that. I was just a kid then, more concerned with saving pennies to buy comic books and staying on the nuns' good side.

Now those Nazi symbols made me sit up straight and look for more stories.

They had a giant rally in Madison Square Garden a little before the war began. How was that possible? And I wasn't a little girl then. I was in high school, in my own little bubble, I guessed, not caring about current events.

I paged through the photos from the rally, a new chill running down my spine. On the next page, there was a photo of a row of men saluting. In uniform. Shouting "Heil, Hitler!" They looked just like the Nazis in Germany we know now, too well, from newsreels.

The article said the organization fell apart when the war started, and their leader went to jail for some kind of fraud. But still. The enemy we were fighting so hard, giving our all, used to be right here, just a few miles from where I sat.

I looked again, and then the chill hit my whole body. I thought I saw Donelly in the front row.

Now this was when Mayor LaGuardia told us, often, to be on the alert for spies. In my house, whatever LaGuardia said was law.

He wasn't just trying to scare us, either. Volunteers patrolled the Long Island beaches, looking for U-boats offshore, and shockingly, they found some. A team of spies had been arrested in Manhattan. Posters everywhere reminded us about loose lips sinking ships. Actually, there was a reminder of it any day at work I happened to look up. The bridge was covered along the sides so no spy could look down and see the battleships and aircraft carriers we were building right there. We were building. We, including me.

And there he was, Donelly, working right next to me, seeing it all. And I realized, with my heart beating faster and faster, I had told him all about my brothers and cousins. Where they were. What they were doing.

Maybe the picture wasn't him. Maybe I was hysterical. Maybe I was just playing I was Nancy Drew. I was only eighteen. I still had all my Nancy Drews under my bed.

I took a deep breath. If I had blabbered to a wrong guy, it was my mess and it was up to me to fix it. I straightened my shoulders. I'd start by keeping a sharp eye on him. I could try to talk to him more. Maybe this fake friendship could work both ways. And I took that magazine with me.

With wide, innocent eyes, I confided in him that while I supported my brothers, I did not understand why we fought with Germany and Italy. The Germans were so civilized. Look at Beethoven! And Italy was my family's own country.

I forced myself to say the lies, looking right into his eyes.

"Yeah, it's tough," he said. "I'm half-German myself. Pretty strange to be at war with the homeland."

For a minute, I forgot he was not really my friend and laughed. "My nona told my brother Frankie that if he got to Naples with the Army, he should look up Uncle Leo. She gave him the address, too. Honest."

"You think he's going to Italy?"

And that's when I knew.

A few days later he gave me something. It was a badly printed pamphlet, all about why we fight. Yeah, well, I knew why. We all did. But this said we shouldn't be fighting and that we had the wrong friends.

"Maybe this will clear up some of your questions," was all he said.

But it didn't clear up anything. It was confusing and… honestly?…what I got from it made me feel creepy. Dirty. And scared. Who was he, for real?

Did I need to tell someone like Yard security? Or the FBI! I had a duty. But what if…? What if it's all innocent, and the photo was not him, and I got a coworker in trouble for no reason? What then?

Before I told anyone, I decided I would have to get some proof. I followed him for a few nights to see what he was up to. I stuffed a light jacket in my work gear, so I could put on something different and blend into crowds, and a cute cloche hat that sort of hid my face.

First night, home to a Brooklyn boardinghouse. Next night, home. Next night, a movie, alone, Humphrey Bogart in *All Through the Night*, at a run-down theater near his home. What a boring life he led.

Then one night after our shift, he got on a whole series of trains and I had to work hard to keep up. We came back out to a sidewalk in Yorkville. That's a long way from home. In fact I had never been there.

I had to ignore the fragrant German bakeries and restaurants I passed, keeping my eyes firmly on Donelly. It would have been a whole lot easier if he hadn't covered his red hair with a gray fedora but I managed to track him weaving through the crowds on the sidewalks.

Finally, he went into a little café, a dump, really, on a little side street, and sat in the back. I muttered bad words to myself, 'cause there was no way I could follow him in and not get spotted. No way I could explain being so far from home.

I stood in front, trying to look casual and…what's that long word? Nonchalant. Too bad there was no bus stop to explain my loitering.

People went in and out, but not many. I got some funny looks from passersby, but most were just hurrying home from work, coming off the Second Avenue El.

Then someone showed up who looked vaguely familiar, a middle-aged man, in a suit, carrying a German newspaper. Well, that was not so unusual. It was Yorkville, the German-American part of the city. But. But.

I pulled my hat way down and took a quick peek in the window, trying to see if he met someone.

Another man went in and I saw, with another quick peek, that they sat with Donelly and seemed deep in discussion. A meeting of some kind.

By then, I started to be scared. I turned, fast, and walked toward the El. I didn't know if it was the best way to get home and I didn't care. It was the nearest. I could disappear, fast, into a packed car.

My hat went into my bag; I shook my hair loose and added a little beret. My light jacket was exchanged for the one that matched my skirt. I almost ran up the steps to the train, and then, safe in the crowded car, I took the magazine out and saw what I was hoping not to see. There were the faces of the two men who went into the café. I dropped the magazine as if it burned my fingers, and didn't relax at all until I was home.

The next day Vito and I worked the same shift for the first time in a while. He came by the house every morning to walk me to the trolley. Because I couldn't possibly find my way there alone. Right.

But the truth? Sometimes a girl needs a big brother, and he was the only one of mine that was around.

So I told him I was scared of Donelly.

He turned red and said, "What did he try? I'll kill him if he did anything!"

"No. Golly. You think the neighborhood boys don't have extra hands? I can take care of that. No. Something different."

And I spilled everything. Even my Yorkville trip.

He grabbed me and just about shook me right there on the sidewalk.

"What the...?" He stopped, took a deep breath, tried to get control. "What the *heck* do you think you were doing? Don't you know those guys are dangerous?"

"It was a public street! Not too late! Plenty of people coming from work! I'm not a baby, ya know."

He took his hands down. "You're an ignorant kid. They were like a mob, the Bund. People got beat up. You gotta stop these games."

"It's not a game. And I need to tell the FBI." I may have weakened the impact, when I added, "So there."

He just said, "You leave it alone. I'll be keeping my eye on you."

What could he do? I asked myself. Nothing. I was going to ignore him.

I tried my wide-eyed innocent approach again with Donelly. I was interested in his pamphlet, I said. I needed to get more understanding, I said. I hated myself, but I did it. Playing a part, like Barbara Stanwyck.

And he bit.

"Let's take in a drink after work, okay? I know a nice quiet bar, real near. Serious talk and a coupla beers?"

Yes, I said. Sure, I said. I even choked out a "Looking forward." He smiled and walked away, not soon enough or far enough for me.

I went, though. Of course I did. Cleaned up after our shift as well as I could. Bundled the coveralls into a shopping bag. Put on my high heels and some lipstick. Took off my headscarf and brushed my curls back in, took a deep breath and said a prayer.

We walked up Flushing Avenue toward the bars that clustered outside the Yard, but then he turned up a tiny side street. What the heck? It looked dark and empty. I was surprised, but he said, "It's not far and I know the owner."

I couldn't see a single store, bar, restaurant. In fact, the street seemed empty even of people. Just as I was getting nervous, he grabbed my arm, very tight. "What are you up to?"

I wasn't faking my surprise.

He repeated it and I stuttered something.

"I saw you following me. What the hell? So either you've got a hell of a crush on me, or you are one nosy little girl."

"Yes, yes." I tried to remember how to do the wide-eyed look. "A crush. Yes." I stammered it out. "Maybe it was immature of me to follow, but I…I wanted to be near…"

He grinned. Not a nice grin. "You're crazy about me? Yeah? So here we are, alone in the dark." He was edging me toward an empty, overgrown lot. "So prove it, baby." One arm was tight around me, and the other hand was where I sure didn't want it. As he dragged me down behind the bushes he muttered in my ear, "You think I don't know? I saw that magazine. I know what you're up to." His grip got tighter with every word. "I faithfully serve the Fatherland, you stupid American child."

What could I do? I did just what my brothers taught me.

My high heel into his instep, a knee where it would hurt the most. And when he doubled over, I hit him with my purse, where they made me keep a metal screwdriver, just in case I needed a weapon sometime when I worked the night shift.

He screamed, staggered back, tripped, and fell. And then he was very quiet. The only sound was my hard breathing.

I was shaking and couldn't think. Running away felt like a good idea but my legs seemed to have turned into spaghetti.

I couldn't hear his breathing at all. Was he knocked out? Dead? I sure wasn't getting close enough to check.

I have no idea how long I was there. Time seemed to stop. The next sound I heard was my name, a whisper.

It was Vito.

I turned and fell into his arms, sobbing. He patted my back and said, "You gotta stop crying and tell me what happened."

I did my best to explain. He stepped fearlessly to the body on the ground, bent over, checked things and turned back to me. "He's dead. Looks like he hit his head on this little wall here."

"He's dead? I killed him? I..."

"You were defending yourself."

He was calm about it. I was not.

"We have to do something. Something. Call the police. Call...I don't know..."

"Are you crazy? He's dead. He had it coming. Leave this to me."

"No, but..."

"Leave this to me! I'm going to hide him now under these bushes, make a few calls for help at the first booth I find, and get you on a trolley. Can you get home? Don't talk to anyone! Don't even look at anyone! Be invisible. You got that?"

I was shaking too hard to argue. I got it. I got myself home, I let myself in, crawled into bed without waking anyone, and that was that.

Donelly didn't show up to work the next day, and no one knew what to do about it, but we were a good team. We did our work without his supervision and the next day, there was a new foreman.

At Sunday dinner, Vito gave me a look over the roast chicken that said as loud as words, "Keep quiet about that night." And then he said, "Pass the gravy my way." So I did. Passed the gravy and kept quiet.

There were always rumors at the Yard. Sure, it was the size of a small city but people know people, made friends, had family, dated. There was one going around, that another ship with dead sailors was in dry dock.

Everyone who heard about it was horrified at what those poor young men went through. Anyone with a sailor brother, like me, couldn't get it out of their heads. That's why it took me several days to connect it to Vito saying, "I'll take care of it."

When I confronted him, he denied everything. He'd never helped me that night. He'd never disposed of Donelly's body. We'd never been on that lonely street. He especially denied the second rumor, that they found a body in the ship's hold that was not weeks old, was not decayed, was not dressed, had no ID.

Some of the guys on our team wondered about Donelly's sudden disappearance. They asked the higher-ups, who had no answers for them. The answer I had, I kept to myself. I didn't go up the official chain; I had a friend who worked in the security office.

She said the body they found didn't match Donelly's fingerprints, but that his fingerprints on record didn't match his name. She couldn't explain it, she just overheard it. Kind of overheard. Through an eager ear at an office door not quite closed, was what I guessed.

I tried to tell Vito all of this, and pry some answers out of him, but he just shook his head.

"Sometimes a brother has to watch out for his kid sister. Ya know? You better leave it at that."

A Fox in the Hand

Tina Whittle

I made my first trip to Arizona in 2011 for a book signing at The Poisoned Pen, my very first ever signing for my very first ever published novel, The Dangerous Edge of Things. *I'm a Georgia girl, born and raised, a child of red clay and cotton fields. The stark deserts and looming mountains and hot dry air were a revelation, as alien as the moon, as exotic as Xanadu. But the people were familiar, as welcoming as any front porch.*

I've been back to Arizona many times since, to Scottsdale and Phoenix and Flagstaff and Sedona. I've hiked those mountains and watched the sun sink in those deserts. And even though my kudzu-entangled heart remains true to the South, something about Arizona always feels like a homecoming.

—T.W.

• • ● • •

The cards were printed on heavy paper, not card stock, and were as delicate and crisp as toast. A genuine Lenormand deck, not a reproduction—circa 1840, I was guessing—and in excellent condition. The antiques dealer two doors down had picked them up at an estate sale and, being the thoughtful chap he was, had decided to offer them to me for what he'd paid. I'd thanked him with a polished citrine hand mala and cleared a spot for the cards in the display counter.

But as I opened the case, the sun caught in the beveled front window of the shop and dappled the cards in my hand. Even through my white cotton gloves, I could feel their energy, layered and potent. Warm.

I got a little prickle. These cards had belonged to somebody who knew what they were doing.

So I took off the gloves and worked with the cards skin to skin, turning the deck facedown and cutting it into three piles. Without invitation, Pythagoras sprang lightly onto the counter and tucked himself into a neat Siamese sit, as precise as a guru. He knew better than to touch, but he put his face right at the middle stack and gave a good sniff. I turned the card over.

"Well," I said, "that's a fine start to things."

The Nine of Clubs. The Little Fox. It warned of close-by treachery and guile, and wasn't exactly the most reassuring card in the deck. But Lenormand decks worked in patterns, not singularities. And the shop was empty except for Py, and he was a big marshmallow, so I didn't see anything to worry about.

At that moment, however, the front door jingled open, and I looked up to see Officer William Davis easing his way inside. He always carried himself tentatively, but respectfully, as if he were afraid he might knock over a potion.

I put my new cards away and smiled. "Good morning, Will."

He ducked his blond head to keep from crashing into a crystal sun catcher. "Morning, Callie."

As usual, his energy was contained and latent, the deep strength of rocks and old trees. But his landscape had shifted since I'd last seen him, some internal tectonics. A fracture line, vibrating.

He inhaled. "What's brewing today?"

"A nice Ecuadorian dark roast. Would you like some?"

He nodded. William was new to the Metro police, new to Savannah, new even to the South. He'd grown up in an insular Vermont hamlet, though, so he was comfortable navigating the eccentricities of a small town. And Savannah was a small town, a fact sometimes lost on transplants. But Will knew not to let the tour buses fool him. He walked his squares every morning, from Troup to Pulaski and up to Chippewa, and he knew to call everyone on his beat by their first name…once they'd given him permission, of course.

He also knew where he was likely to get a free cup of coffee. I reached for the mug I kept for him under the front counter.

"You're late today," I said, and poured to the brim.

He put in a scant teaspoon of sugar and stirred. "I've been on a call this morning."

There was something in the way he said it, with his eyes on the coffee, not on me. I refilled my own mug, giving him time.

"And I guess that's why I'm here now," he continued. "I guess this is a professional call. Ma'am."

"So tell me what's happened. Officer."

He spooned another dollop of sugar into his coffee. This was how he always did it, a teensy spoonful at the time, until he had a quarter cup of sugar in there. No milk, black as midnight and sweet as a pocket of rock candy.

"I got a call this morning to what I thought was a routine break-in."

"It wasn't?"

"No."

"What made it non-routine?"

"The tarot card stuck on the living room wall."

"Stuck?"

"With a butcher knife."

I winced and shook my head. "It was Death, wasn't it? It's always Death. The Tower is a much more terrifying card, all that lightning, bodies tumbling to the rocks below—"

"It was Death," he said. "And a butcher knife."

Something in the way he said that too. I'd been thinking that this was a courtesy call, that I might get to play divination CSI with the sexy cop. But he was looking at his coffee again. Not good.

I sighed. "You're not here for my professional opinion, are you?"

"No, ma'am. I'm here because the victim seems to think that it might have been you who stuck that card on her wall."

"And who might this victim be?"

"Trixie Daniels."

I stared at him over the rim of my mug. Trixie. I wondered if she knew how lucky she was I took the "harm none" part of the Rede very seriously.

"Now what makes her think that?"

Officer William flipped open his notebook, but I knew it was just for show. He had the details in his head, as always.

"Well. There's the fact that she just moved in with your ex-fiancé."

I blew lightly on my coffee. "So she's living at his place now? Interesting."

Thomas owned a disheveled Victorian on Habersham that kept him on the edge of bankruptcy, since his English professor status barely covered the upkeep, insurance, and taxes. But being a young good-looking academic had its perks, Trixie being the major one. It was such a cliché—the professor and the grad student—but then, Thomas didn't have much imagination sometimes.

I missed that old house. On summer evenings, the moonflower twined and the jessamine bloomed and the air musked up with the smell of the salt marshes coming in from the coast.

"Yes, ma'am," William said. "It happened sometime last night between seven p.m. and one a.m. The thief broke in through the back porch, hidden from the street. The victims came home to discover the front room ransacked and the knife and card stuck into the wall."

"Well, that lets me off the hook," I said. "There's no way I was out on Sunday night. Anybody who knows me knows that."

He tapped his notebook, but his eyes dipped to the pentacle around my neck. "Would that be…ah, religious reasons?"

I smiled. "Season finale of *Game of Thrones*. I wouldn't have missed that for the world."

"Anybody with you to verify that story?"

"No, just Pythagoras here, but he's totally unreliable." I peered into Will's mug. "You're not drinking your coffee."

He took a dutiful sip.

"So why does Trixie think it was me? Surely I'm not the only tarot aficionado that she's pissed off?"

"It's not just the card. There's also the dagger."

"Dagger? You said it was a butcher knife."

"The knife in the wall was a butcher knife, yes, but Ms. Daniels also reported that she'd been robbed of several items, the most valuable of which being a ceremonial dagger." Will consulted his notes for real this time. "Civil War-era, with silver and onyx handle and a serpent-twined eagle on the hilt."

He looked up, and I noticed that his eyes slid toward the glass-fronted display case on the back wall. It looked like a weapons stash right out of *Braveheart*, all blades and hilts and pointy metal, a stark contrast to the rest of the shop, which tended toward oils and incense and bowls of gemstones.

I followed his gaze, then returned it evenly. "And because I sell ceremonial daggers, including some antiques, that's motive? Do you really think I'd be that stupid? To steal something from someone I supposedly have a grudge against and then try to sell it in my own shop?"

He shook his head. "I don't think you're stupid. But I would understand if you had a grudge."

"I don't have a grudge. Thomas made his choice, and I made mine. I didn't even know Trixie collected daggers."

"It was a gift, she said, for her altar."

I sighed again. So Trixie had an altar now. Big surprise. She'd been a lapsed Presbyterian when she'd taken up with Thomas.

"Have you considered this might be someone with something against Pagans and not against Trixie specifically?"

"Of course we have. Unfortunately."

Unfortunately, indeed. I knew it happened. I'd gotten my share of looks over the years, had lost friends. But I'd never been the target of malicious willful criminal conduct, not like this, anyway. Breaking and entering, trashing sacred tools, threats.

It hurt to think about, even if the victim had been Trixie, who, in my opinion…

The door jangled open again. Py hissed, and William put his notebook down fast. It was Trixie. And she looked steamed.

"Ms. Daniels," Will said, stepping right in her path, "what are you doing here?"

Trixie stopped short. She was a lovely girl, with milky skin and black hair chopped in a wild child mop. I noticed that she had a pentacle around her neck—which she hadn't purchased from me—and black nail polish on her bitten-down nails. A black tee-shirt emblazoned with the phrase "Goth Witch" erased any possible misconception that Trixie was in the broom closet.

"They told me you were investigating," she said, looking directly at Will. "I guessed this might be your first stop. I guess I guessed right."

She didn't say a word to me, just shoved a stack of photographs at Will. The top one was a close-up of the dagger. There were other shots, though, including one of a smiling Trixie in black robes, holding said dagger.

She tapped it with her finger. "That's the picture I was telling you about. It took me a while to find it, what with all the mess."

This last was said with a sidelong stab of a glance my way. Py made a throaty growl in the back of his throat. I stroked his back.

"I was sorry to hear about that," I said.

She narrowed her eyes, but didn't acknowledge me. "And," she said, dragging something out of her tote bag, "I found this buried in the front yard, right by the front steps. I'll bet she put it there, some kind of black magic. Thomas said he had no idea what it was or where it had come from, but it's exactly the kind of thing I'd expect from her."

It was a tiny statue, not three inches tall, of a little man in robes. It was plastic, earth-toned, covered in dirt. It hadn't been buried very well if Trixie had spotted it, or maybe a neighbor's dog had marked it for a chew toy. Either way, Will was holding it like it might bite him.

"That," I said, "is a statue of St. Joseph, which people bury upside down on property that they want to sell quickly. I had nothing to do with it, but you might want to talk to the nice Catholic couple Thomas bought the house from."

Trixie looked mean and confused. Will tried not to smile. Pythagoras arched against my cheek and purred.

"You took my dagger because you were jealous," Trixie said. "And then you trashed the place."

"I have my own dagger, thank you. Plus a whole showcase full of extras if I feel the need for more."

"But not one from Thomas."

She was wrong there. The athame on my altar was indeed from Thomas, his first gift to me, our first Yule. I still used it, was accustomed to it, comfortable with it and its history, too much to abandon it. But I saw no reason to tell her that.

Trixie returned her attention to Will. "You can keep those photographs. I have a spare set at home, for the insurance."

"Smart thinking," I said.

She ignored me, just slammed out the door, jangling my crystals as she did. Will watched her go, a little bemused.

"May I see?" I said.

He held out the statue. I shook my head. "No, not Saint Joe. The photographs."

He obliged. I flipped to the close-up of the dagger. It was a fine-looking piece, that was for sure, a nicely chased pattern on the blade with some exquisite work on the hilt. A serpent-twined eagle. Powerful symbolism to somebody.

Will closed his notebook and tucked it into his pocket. "Tell the truth, Callie. You have any idea what's going on here?"

I shook my head. "I'm sorry, I don't. I didn't stick Death to her wall, and I didn't wreck her altar, and I certainly didn't steal her athame."

"Can you spell that?"

I did. He wrote it down.

"It was sacred to her," I continued, "which means I would never touch it, no matter how much I disliked her."

"Do you?"

"What?"

"Dislike her?"

I sighed. "Let's just say I've been doing a lot of release work lately. But it's been successful. So far."

He nodded. "I'm going back to the station to write all this down. I'll call you if something comes up."

"Wait…do you mind if I make a copy of this photograph first? It's a long shot, but somebody might bring it in to sell."

"Sure, not a problem."

I photocopied it quickly and handed it back to him. "Will you let me know if you find out anything?"

"Of course. And if you come up with any brilliant ideas, you let me know, okay?"

Pythagoras nudged my elbow, and I picked him up and tucked him against my chest. "I will. I promise."

• • ● • •

There were few customers that morning, just the woman from down the street picking up her weekly order of herbs, the usual tourist or two. I stayed preoccupied, running my fingers along the photograph.

When the final customer left, I put up the Closed sign and turned the hands of the clock to show that I would be back at two. Then I strolled down to City Market, threading through the flitting sparrows on the ground, following the smell of pepperoni to Vinnie Van Gogo's. Sure enough, I found Thomas at one of the shaded tables, a half-eaten slice of spinach and mushroom pizza in front of him. As usual, he was talking instead of eating, and equally as usual, he was orbited by a ring of students.

He looked like one of them, with his jeans and faded Franz Ferdinand concert tee, his riot of chestnut curls pulled into a ponytail and black wire-rims perched seriously at the end of his nose. Only the wrinkles at the corner of his eyes revealed his thirty-some odd years on this planet, but I knew you had to get really close to see them.

He saw me coming and stood up. The other students eyed me cagily. All but one was female.

"Officer Davis just left," I said.

He took my elbow. I loosed myself from his grasp. The students licked their collective lips.

"Not here," he said.

He threw a twenty on the table and headed for a park bench in Franklin Square, shadowed from the strengthening sun by the oaks and the Haitian monument, its dark bronze boy soldiers marching and drumming, muskets raised. It was a heroic contrast to Thomas, who exuded only sulkiness. He sat in a half-sprawl, his long legs stretched in front of him. He wouldn't look at me.

"I wanted to catch you before…you know," he said.

"Before I got interrogated?"

He started to protest, but I interrupted him. "Never mind. Just tell me how this started."

He told me the story then, that he'd bought the dagger the weekend before, when he was combing flea markets. "It was genuine Civil War-era, the real thing. I saw one just like it last week on the *Antiques Roadshow* marathon, and that one was two thousand dollars, but I got this one for a steal."

"How much?"

"A hundred. She was asking one-fifty, but knocked off fifty just for me. I said thank you, wrote a check, and took it straight home."

I shook my head. Thomas was gorgeous, but sometimes I wondered if there was a brain under all that hair. My antiques dealer friend said people brought in Granny's "genuine antiques" all the time only to discover that Granny was either a not-so-clever patsy or a clever forger.

"You know as well as I do that you aren't getting a genuine Civil War-era dagger for a hundred bucks. It was obviously a replica. You got taken."

"Not really. I looked up typical prices for a replica of that quality, and it was still a bargain."

"Where'd you get it?

"That old guy's shop over on Isle of Hope. You know, the guy with the white mustache who always dresses like Robert E. Lee?"

"The Colonel?"

"Yeah. That's him."

I knew the shop he was referring to, and the man. We'd done business. He had been curmudgeonly but fair, and I'd gotten a nice first-edition Doreen Valiente from him for the shop. There was only one problem.

"Thomas?"

"Yeah?"

"The Colonel died a month ago. His shop is closed."

"Well, it's open now. His granddaughter is on a liquidation spree. Everything at clearance prices. She said she found the dagger in his closet with a bunch of his reenactment things. Bossy as hell, but she was cleaning the place out, and fast."

"Was her name Carolyn?"

He looked surprised. "You know her?"

"I used to, back in high school."

That was putting it mildly. Carolyn Graves used to slip Bible tracts into my locker, along with sweet little notes like, "Please repent, or suffer the fires of damnation!" Then she got too big for her Coastal Empire britches and moved to Atlanta. I guessed she was back taking care of her grandfather's last bits of business and then hightailing it back to the big city as quickly as possible

I got a prickle of suspicion. "You didn't tell her what you wanted it for, did you?"

"No. I don't think so." He considered. "Well, maybe the word "altar" did come up. Why?"

"How did she react?"

"She didn't, not like you're suggesting. This was quick business, no Bible belting."

So maybe Carolyn had changed. Maybe Atlanta had mellowed her and she didn't mind the Colonel's militaria being dedicated to the Goddess and God.

"Did the thief take anything else?"

"Nothing big, if that's what you're asking. No computers, no jewelry. Just some cash I had out and the dagger."

"Trixie said she took the photographs for the insurance."

"Right. So?"

"You never told her it was a replica."

A concentrated pause. Thomas appeared to be assessing the horizon, his eyes slightly narrowed. "There was no reason to tell her then, and there's not one now."

"Even as we speak she is unknowingly preparing to commit insurance fraud. You have to tell her, and now."

He grumbled. "It could have been real. You don't know. And neither does anybody else."

"Sometimes," I said, "I wonder what parallel universe you and I ever existed in."

● ● ● ● ●

I took my time getting back to the shop. The dogwoods and azaleas were on their last hurrahs, but the air was still cool in the green spaces. The bake and broil of summer had yet to start.

I decided not to go back to the shop. Instead, I drove out to Isle of Hope, to the Colonel's store. There was a Closed sign on the door, but I saw movement inside.

I knocked lightly. "Carolyn?"

The door opened a crack. Carolyn still had something of the cheerleader about her, a brightness in the eyes, a flirt in the swing of her red-gold hair. She smiled, puzzled, when she saw me. "Callie?"

I smiled back. "Long time no see."

The place was nothing like I remembered. All the Colonel's haphazard piles had been pushed to one side. The counter was cleared off, the windows thrown open. The air shimmered with dust, making the sunbeams opaque, and the room reeked of pungent air freshener.

Carolyn dusted her hands. "You're lucky you caught me."

"Clearing out?"

"Trying to. Unfortunately, Granddaddy never saw a piece of junk he didn't fall in love with." There was fondness in the curve of her lips. I tried to see if it made it to her eyes, but she moved briskly around the counter, toward the back rooms. "Would you like something to drink? I made some tea."

I shook my head. "No thanks."

I heard her back there, the clink of the ice cubes, the refrigerator opening and closing. She came back, still bright, still cheerful. Her pert capri pants and boatneck top made her look like a page from women's wear catalog. I laid the photograph on the counter, and she came over to examine it.

She tapped it lightly. "I remember this. Granddaddy's knife."

"It's a dagger. You sold it to a friend of mine a few days ago."

"Tall guy, brown hair, ponytail." She waved her hands around her own sleek head. Her eyes dipped to take in the pentacle around my neck, then met mine. "You're still into all that, huh? Like your friend?"

My fingers found the silver pendant. "I'm Wiccan. He's Druid. But it's the dagger I really wanted to talk about."

Her eyes went shrewd. "I told him clearance prices, all sales final."

"You also told him it was a genuine antique."

She cocked her head. "Granddaddy was a genuine antique. That dagger was a fine reproduction, and your friend got it for a good price. Too late to cry foul now."

Behind her was a sepia-toned portrait of the Colonel himself, in full Confederate regalia, his handlebar mustache bristling. I could imagine him leading the charge at Bull Run, the Stars and Bars battering the air behind him. I suddenly realized I would miss him.

Carolyn gestured around her. "You want any of the rest of this stuff? I can make you a good deal."

I looked around the store, at the stuff piled in boxes, the bare floors, the empty shelves. Carolyn, brisk, waiting for my response. She was ready to head back to Atlanta, sweep the rest clean, move on. Maybe that was the way, after all. Empty and let go and move on.

"No thanks," I said. "I have everything I need."

• • ● • •

I stopped at Forsyth Park on my way back. Finding a spot in the leaf-filtered shade near the fountain, I reached into my tote bag and pulled out my old familiar Rider-Waite-Smith. My first tarot deck. I picked up the cards and held them in my hands, listening to the tumble and fall of the water. The air smelled clean despite the humming traffic behind me, and I grounded and centered in that scent, like wet sunshine.

I shuffled the deck lightly and started a quick three-card spread, but stopped after the first card. The Seven of Swords.

I knew it well. The man sneaking an armload of weapons away, his face a mask of deceit and furtive satisfaction.

That did it, as far as I was concerned. But I made one more stop on my way home, just to have something concrete. And then I called the police station and asked for Will.

• • ● • •

Later that afternoon, Will held my quartz orb in one hand and cocked a curious eye into it. "Is this how you figured it out?"

I shook my head. "Not this time."

"What then?"

I shrugged, as if it had been as simple as abracadabra. "As you may have guessed, I have connections in the antique relics department. I took that photograph to one and let him take a gander at that dagger. He said from what he could tell, Thomas really had seen one like it on *Antiques Roadshow*—he suspected it was the genuine article."

"He figured this out from a picture?"

"Not just that. Seems Carolyn had been approaching lots of the dealers around town about buying out the rest of the Colonel's stock. My friend took most of the reenactment things for a flat price."

"Did he know they were real when he bought them?"

"Suspected, yes. Once he got that fact verified, he didn't offer to give the stuff back or anything—he's honest, but he *is* an antiques dealer. He *did*, however, tell her that if she had anything else in that vein, she should be more careful with it. Which made her remember the dagger."

Will nodded. He knew the next part of the story.

So did I. I considered the flow chart Carolyn's mental processes must have taken, how easy she'd decided it would be to just take the dagger back. She had Thomas' address right there on his check. All she had to do was wait until the house was empty, break inside, then trash things up a bit and engage in a little stereotypical anti-Pagan harassment (of which she knew some things).

"Where did you find the dagger?" I said.

"Wrapped up in the trunk of her car. She clammed up real fast when we did and called a hot shot lawyer in Atlanta. For all the good it will do her." He handed the orb back to me and examined the cards on the counter. "Callie, is there anything to all this? For real?"

I considered his question. Coming from anyone else, I would have taken it as a mildly insulting challenge. But Will wanted to know exactly what he was asking. That didn't mean, however, that I had to answer it exactly.

"Why?" I said. "Do you want to get something for yourself?"

"I might." He leaned against the counter. Up close, his eyes were the blue of lapis lazuli. "Would you cut me a deal?"

"I could be persuaded." I leaned on the counter too. "But I have to tell you, Will. Cards and orbs are fine tools, but when it comes to actually solving a problem, witches consider the mundane as well as the magical."

Will nodded. "And greed is about as mundane as it gets."

I started to correct him, started to explain that jealousy was pretty pervasively mundane as well. As was nostalgia, and the tendency to look back, to cling to that which you'd understood, once upon a time. Battle flags and the smell of jessamine and moonflower. All perfectly natural to hold onto, all perfectly mundane.

I leaned closer. "You ever watch the moon come up over the marsh, and it seemed so close you could put your hand to it?"

He examined me curiously, as if he'd been waiting for that question for a long time. "I know a spot in Thunderbolt. Quiet. Secluded."

Always the same and always different, the moon. Ever-changing and ever-constant, so close, so far. The most ordinary of miracles.

I tucked the orb back into its case. "I'll close early. Mondays are always slow anyway."

To see more Poisoned Pen Press titles:

Visit our website: poisonedpenpress.com/
Request a digital catalog: info@poisonedpenpress.com